Mystic Warriors

of the

Yellowstone

Happy Trails!
Elizabeth Laden

Elizabeth Laden

Mystic Warriors of the Yellowstone

My Office Publishing Company
1417 Eton Street
Fayetteville, Arkansas 72703

ISBN: 0-9654107-1-4

Ursus Publications
P.O. Box 709
Ashton, Idaho 83420

This is a work of fiction; none of the characters are based on real people. Any resemblance a character may have to a real person is purely coincidental.

.

Typography and Design:
Jan Cooper   •   My Office
1417 Eton Street
Fayetteville, Arkansas 72703
(501) 575-0135

To John and Ben

Chapter One

After three hours of wine and orgasm-induced sleep, Lynx O'Malley awoke to the obnoxious wail of her newest alarm clock. She cursed the purple plastic sleep buster and flung it across the room. It smashed into a pile of books that were already defying gravity in a sloppy spiral on the edge of her chest of drawers, and crashed with the books onto her oak floor.

She was working too much and not getting up on her own. Out of necessity she bought the alarm, even though she hated them. This one would no doubt end up in the trash, the fate of at least 50 others she'd owned in her lifetime.

"Stupid idea to even think of using one of those things," she muttered.

A bearded head with a halo of long hair fringing an otherwise bald scalp popped out of the sheets.

"What the . . . ?" The head spoke.

"Yo, I forgot you were here," Lynx squawked. "Sorry, Jack. I gotta get up. You just go back to sleep."

Jack grabbed her and pulled her against his morning woody. "Not until I give you some more of this," he whispered.

"Okay, but make it a quickie, please, I have to get to work, Jack."

Jack touched her to see if she was ready, and being a woman who believed it's a crime to waste morning woodies, she was. Respecting her need to go to work, Jack took care of business quickly, but not without giving her a pleasant orgasm.

Lynx watched him fall back asleep. Jack O'Brien . . . in her bed. Stranger things had happened. After all, she and Jack had been friends for years. They'd moved to West Yellowstone, Montana, the same year, gotten married to different people the next year, and six years ago they'd divorced within a few months of one another.

They'd met at the Wild West Hotel, where she worked as the front desk manager and he as the chief of maintenance. Their work was adequate as far as jobs in a tourist town go. It paid survival wages until something more meaningful came up. It gave them a lot of time to talk as they waited for tourists to show up or for something to break down. During coffee breaks and slow periods, they discovered they were the same age and liked the same music and books and hunting and fishing. Still, their many conversations were barely more than small talk.

Jack, Lynx thought, seemed uncomfortable talking with women. There had been sparks of electricity between them now and then in those early days at the hotel, but they'd both turned it off, like married people try to do.

For the past several years, Jack had been working for the city, in charge of making sure the water and sewer systems were functioning properly and the street crew was doing its job. Lynx was a reporter for the *Gallatin Gazette*, a daily newspaper published 90 miles north in Bozeman. Her beat was West Yellowstone and nearby communities close to the west side of Yellowstone National Park, which bordered West Yellowstone. The paper provided her with a computer and modem, so she could file stories from the office in her home in West.

Jack was of her contacts, one of those reliable people who will tell a straight story. He gave her many tips that led to good news pieces and a better understanding of how the people in the city operated on personal and professional levels.

Two days ago, on Saturday afternoon, Lynx stopped by Jack's house on the way home from a run around the perimeter of town. It was late April and her first run of the year. The snow had finally melted in town, and she had been eager to try out her new running shoes. She had just seen a small grizzly bear dragging a swollen plastic garbage bag out of a dumpster a few blocks from Jack's house. She wanted to tell him about the bear and ask him to drive over to the dumpster and close it.

The City Council had passed a law requiring all dumpsters to be bear proof, but some citizens loved seeing bears in their garbage and thought it was a great way to attract tourists to town. They resented the bear-proof ordinance because they were proud of West Yellowstone's reputation as a place where bears could be spotted easily walking up and down the streets. They de-bear proofed their dumpsters by chaining open the lids so the bears could get into them.

Lynx knew Jack supported the bear-proof law's intent to keep bears in the wilderness eating natural food. She knew he would run out immediately and close the dumpster at the very least, and most probably turn in the people who had propped it open.

"Why don't you make yourself ta home while I take care of it and stay for dinner? I was just about to fry a moose burger. One more will be easy," Jack said as he grabbed a greasy red baseball cap off the wall and adjusted it on his head. "You can answer the phone for me while I'm gone. I'm on call."

Lynx loved spontaneous events, like being asked to dinner by someone she thought was pleasant, so she said yes, she would stay.

Jack was not supposed to leave his house until after 11 p.m. when he was on call, unless someone covered for him. Someone from the city had to be within the town dispatcher's office radio range 24 hours a day, every day of the week, to handle emergencies few people in the town ever imagined could happen, like a break down in the sewer system, a shut down of the water supply, problems with the street drainage system, and even an earthquake that could disrupt fire, ambulance, and police communications. Jack had fixed days he was on call, and Saturday night was one of them. This Saturday night commitment had led to his divorce, an event he told Lynx he had not seen coming in even the smallest of ways.

Jack was a black-and-white, no-nonsense, steady sort of man. He stayed on call on Saturday night because all the other city workers were married with children. He was married with a wife and a pack of dogs and saw no reason to have Saturday nights off. His wife, Vicky, did not agree but had never vocalized her dissension. Instead, she simmered like an overheated pressure cooker, spinning the belief that he was purposely working on Saturday nights to avoid taking her out to bars with live bands. The Saturday nights of the summer and winter tourist seasons were the only nights when there was live entertainment in West Yellowstone, and Vicky loved to dance.

She became obsessed with Jack's alleged abandonment of her on Saturday nights. She began to resent him on every level, despising things about him that she once thought were exemplary and charming: his dedication to work, the impeccably neat work room he'd built onto the garage, and the way he drove his truck. She thought he shifted too late.

After years of putting up with him, she left him on Saturday nights and went to the bars alone, all gussied up and hoping to find dance partners. Jack let her go without complaint, wanting her to be happy. Vicky resented him for that. She wanted him to want to be with her. She began to withdraw from him and volunteered to work extra hours at the busy real estate office where she was a secretary. She often took long walks with the dogs along the Madison River north of town, wondering how she could survive much longer with such an unromantic man.

During one Sunday morning walk, the dogs surprised a cow and newborn calf moose lounging in tall willows by the river. The cow freaked and ran towards the dogs, perceiving them as a threat to her calf. Instinctively, Vicky leapt between the dogs and the moose to protect her pets. The moose plowed right through her, knocked her down, and then turned around and stomped her.

Pete Rypple, a townie who knew Vicky and Jack, was fly fishing upstream when he heard Vicky's screams and the dogs' frantic barking, and he crashed through the willows to rescue them. He made sure Vicky didn't have any serious injuries or broken bones, and then carried her to his truck and drove her to the clinic in town.

Vicky was badly bruised and had four broken ribs, the physician's assistant who ran the clinic said, adding that she was lucky to be alive. Moose have stomped people to death.

Pete's rescuing of Vicky was one of those life events that has a far greater impact than on first examination one could ever imagine. To hell with the moose, Vicky thought. Her most vivid memory of the attack was of how it felt to be in Pete's arms. Pete was a handsome man, an ex-football player who still had his muscles and a macho, ready-to-kill look on his face when he thought anyone was messing with him, his friends, or his family. He was also a skilled, sexy dancer and had moved Vicky around the dance floor many times when she escaped to the bars on Saturday night. Vicky had already developed very detailed fantasies of doing more than dancing with Pete. He rescued her not only from the moose, but from the emptiness and longing growing inside her.

The Vicky-Pete story got weirder. Pete was a massage therapist, a good one, and the P.A. had told her that it would be very therapeutic to have her moose-bashed body massaged.

The fact that this handsome, dancing, macho man she was already half in love with just happened to be the man who rescued her, and he just happened to be a massage therapist, and she just happened to need therapy, was Divine Coincidence, or so Vicky believed. She and Pete were Meant to Be.

Pete knew and liked Jack and had often wondered if perhaps Vicky was a bit flaky, leaving her husband to dance with other men every Saturday night. He had no theories about the situation being a divine coincidence that would lead to a divorce and a couple of messed up lives. He thought Vicky was lucky that he had been fishing nearby. He also thought she was lucky to have him around to dance with, because he respected the fact that she was married and would not hit on her like other men did.

Pete drove Vicky home and helped her into the house, where Jack was lounging in front of the television. Jack and Pete helped her settle on the couch, and Pete explained what the P.A. had told Vicky, adding that he would be happy to teach Jack how to therapeutically massage his wife. Jack was genuinely concerned about Vicky and grateful that she was alive. He agreed to bring Vicky to Pete's office the next day.

Naked to the waist, Vicky lay on her stomach on Pete's massage table. She was feeling no pain, imagining that she was alone with him and he was about to make love to her. In reality, he was talking to Jack about what he was about to do to her damaged muscles. He began to touch her, showing Jack how to start out very slowly and gently and add more pressure as the first layer of muscle accepted his touch and relaxed.

Pete's massaging touch ripped through her body like a highly charged lightning bolt, and Vicky nearly passed out with the pleasure of it. The memory of it would never leave her, she resolved, as she somehow got through the rest of the massage and drove home with Jack. She was certain Pete had felt it, too, and knew that the Divine Coincidence machinery was cranking toward the inevitable. She and Pete would be together.

The next evening, Jack massaged her slowly and carefully, remembering everything Pete had taught him, feeling he was doing a great job. He enjoyed touching her and thought about turning her over and making love to her, or not turning her over and making love to her, but he held back his feelings, not wanting to hurt her.

Vicky felt nothing but physical pain when Jack touched her. Her aching muscles were symbols of all she resented about Jack. She felt that she could no longer endure his presence, let alone his touch. She thought of everything he had ever done that had angered her, frustrated her, and forced her to enter the fantasy world she had lived in for so long. They were fantasies she now resolved to make real.

She screamed at him to stop hurting her, and despite the pain that racked her body when she moved, she ran upstairs to their bedroom. "Please," she shouted, "sleep down there tonight. I have to be alone."

Jack let her go. He figured she was doing the right thing since she must be really hurting now that a couple of days had let the soreness set in. He rationalized that she really could use a good night's sleep alone in their bed.

The next morning, Vicky drove her aching body and soul to all the grocery stores and mini marts in town and rounded up a huge pile of boxes. Then she went home and packed nearly all of her personal belongings. She tossed all the plants she had nurtured since the early days of the marriage into the compost pile in the backyard, thinking of herself as one of them. She sat down and blew off years of penned up emotional steam in a 15-page, typewritten, single-spaced dissertation to Jack on her bitterness, loneliness, and sexual frustration. All her misery was his fault. She left it on Jack's desk and bolted.

Jack came home from work that day to a house stripped of plants, paintings, window sill rocks, and all the knickknacks women love to put around a place to make it homey. He didn't notice that anything specific was missing, but he felt the color and texture and personality that had vanished from his home. His stomach knotted up, and he walked over to the desk and looked for the note he sensed would be there.

He read the angry tirade three times and toured the house, observing that she had taken this and that thing he had grown used to seeing, guessing there was more missing than he was aware of. In the living room, he looked through the rows of videos he had neatly arranged in alphabetical order, by title, of movies and documentaries. John Waynes. Orson Welles. Rockies, Rambos, and Lethal Weapons. Lots of classic comedies and musicals from the 1930's and 40's, and National Geographic specials on wildlife. He was surprised to find a dozen tapes he'd never seen before. They were how-to dance tapes for country Western, Latin, Spanish, and ballroom styles of dancing. Where had she gotten them? When had she watched them?

He slid the Latin tape into the VCR. A muscular, dark-haired Latino was dancing with a beautiful, dark-haired woman with enormous hooters and long legs. It was a sexy, slow, sensuous dance, and when the music stopped, they lingered in one another's arms for a second before turning to the camera and smiling at their home audience. Then the man began explaining the dance as his partner demonstrated the steps slowly and methodically.

Jack suddenly saw the romance and sexuality Vicky had longed for that he had not given her. He reviewed her letter and saw that his steadiness had not been an attractant to her at all, but something that had driven her into a fantasy life she must have finally decided to make real. Good luck, he thought.

Jack turned off the VCR and continued his wanderings. He picked up their wedding photo and smiled. They both looked great that day. He was 30 pounds thinner with darker hair all over his head that fell to his shoulders in gentle waves. Vicky used to like to play with it. She was a good 15 pounds heavier in those days, but in the right places. She'd lost too much weight trying to make herself look more attractive, he supposed. He'd never bothered to ask why or tell her he noticed. She had long hair then, like now, only straight and shinier and a bit darker brown. All in all, he thought, analyzing the photo for the first time since she put it on the shelf, Vicky had held up better than he had. It was the beer, he figured, patting his comfortable belly.

He read through the titles on the bookshelves that lined the walls of the study they had shared. There were a lot of spaces on the shelves near her empty desk. A stack of paperback books caught his eye. It appeared that she had gotten them ready to pack and then forgotten them. They were all by a writer named Danielle Steele. He had heard that name somewhere before, maybe on television. All of the covers of the books had paintings of long-haired, bosomy women with dreamy eyes, and the silver and gold lettered titles promised tales of romance, adventure, and intrigue. When had she read these? At night, when he was cruising the town making sure everything was working right, when he stopped for a beer and a game of pool with one of his buddies, on her lunch hour at work? He had no idea. He flipped through the top book in the pile and stopped on a page that looked as if it had been read more than once. Flowery words passionately described sex for the first time between a dark-haired man (like the guy in the videotape?) and a large-breasted 18 year old. Although there was no explicit sexual language, it got the point across. He'd practically raped her, and she'd liked it.

Jack put the book down. He'd read Copperfield, Faulkner, Hemingway, even a little Shakespeare, and he knew this Steele broad was not on their level. Her writing wasn't complete trash, but it was simple. A woman could read it and take off to all kinds of places in her mind without being offended by dirty words and hard- core pornographic descriptions. Jack pictured Vicky lying in bed reading these stupid books and getting horny, then frustrated, and wondered if she masturbated, imagining she was being "taken" by a dark-haired hero. Jack knew that he had never been a Danielle Steele hero and had no desire to be. Jack knew he was Jack, a basic Montana guy. He was embarrassed for Vicky and for himself.

Meanwhile, Vicky was in hot pursuit of her fantasy. She rented a storage space outside of town and moved all her stuff into it. She then went to Pete's and asked if she could stay with him for a while because she had left Jack. Pete said he didn't think that was a good idea at all.

"You mean you don't love me, want me, find yourself attracted to me?" Vicky's eyes were wide open with shock. "I thought you would be happy I left Jack at last."

"Shit, Vicky, I hardly know you, and I like Jack. I don't want to be involved in this one bit." Pete looked at her steadily, hoping the truth would sink in.

"Then why did you dance with me, why did you save me from that moose?"

"I danced with you, actually, because I'm a friend of Jack's and wanted to protect you from the wolves," Pete said, the light of her obsession beginning to dawn. "And I rescued you because you needed rescuing. Dancing with you and rescuing you were the right things to do. That's all there was to either."

To Vicky, Pete's voice was unemotional, practical, and maddening. He sounded like Jack. Vicky felt dizzy. Her world was ending.

"Look, Vicky, you oughta go and think this over. Stay at a girlfriend's for a few days."

Vicky wasn't listening. She turned abruptly and left, got into her truck, and drove out of town with no idea where she was going.

She landed in Billings, Montana, at a battered woman's safe house, where the counselors happily validated her theories that Jack had emotionally trashed her and Pete had led her on when he hit on her in the bars and massaged her. It took her several weeks to settle down, find a job and an apartment, and get in touch with Jack. She wanted a divorce and a chance to make her dreams real.

Jack, who had spent those weeks worrying and wondering about the woman he thought was the love of his life, was relieved to hear she was alive. He didn't ask her to come back. He knew she wouldn't, and part of him was afraid that if she did, they would be miserable.

While he cooked, Jack told Lynx the story of Vicky's leaving because she had asked him to tell her and she had always been surprisingly easy to talk with. He had told people around town that he and Vicky had parted company on good terms when they decided they didn't even know one another any more. It was a classic, acceptable story that a man and woman discovered they were wallowing in emotional voids and must therefore divorce.

The complete story was easy to pour out to Lynx as she followed him around the kitchen, watching him make salad and moose burgers. She didn't lay a guilt trip on him or tell him what moral lessons he should have learned from the experience. She simply hugged him, and said, "Nothing happens without a reason, and it will all work out for you. Let's eat."

Lynx didn't volunteer her story of why she and Lou had divorced. Jack saw that she was a great deal like him, and wouldn't talk about her divorce unless he asked her to. He thought, "I should ask her. I should get her to talk. If I had tried to talk more with Vicky, she would never have left." He served dinner and sat across the table and looked right at Lynx, the question about her divorce at the tip of his tongue.

She looked back and saw it there and said, "Look, I don't want to talk about my divorce now, so don't ask. Let's eat, okay?"

Sweet relief. He knew if he was to ever be with another woman, he would have to learn to communicate with Them, but he just wasn't ready.

They ate silently, and when the silence got uncomfortable, they talked about his dogs. All four were hovering at an imaginary perimeter around the dinner table they had been trained not to cross. Even from that distance they were adept at making humans feel guilty about eating in front of them.

Jack thought Lynx was very pretty in an earthy sort of way, with messy auburn hair and deep blue eyes and great hooters he'd been sneaking peeks at for years. They were both 41 years old, but he thought Lynx looked younger than he did. And here she was, alone with him on a Saturday night, both of them single now. There was no reason why he couldn't kiss her, so he got up to walk over to her. At that moment, the scene in the Danielle Steele book popped into this head, and he picked up his dirty dishes instead and placed them in the sink. Lynx did the same, and her arm brushed against his. Without thinking, he grabbed her shoulders and planted a big wet one on her cheek. She kissed him back, square on his lips, and he felt his knees quiver. She didn't seem to notice.

"Thanks for the great dinner," was all she said.

They washed the dishes and tidied the kitchen together in silence. Jack asked her to stick around while he made coffee, and they spent the next few hours looking through his old photo albums and reminiscing about their early days in West Yellowstone. In those days, the separate crowds they hung out in overlapped only at weddings, funerals, and other special events. Lynx knew many of the people in his photographs and knew all of the places where he had camped, hunted, and fished.

At 11 p.m., he switched off his police scanner and put his radio away in the study, relieved that there had been no emergencies to take him away from being with Lynx.

He stopped in the bathroom to hang a whiz and looked at himself in the mirror. He wasn't bad looking, a little rough-skinned from being outdoors so much, but that was okay for a man. He was horny, and she must be, too, although she didn't seem to act that way. How does a woman act when she's horny, anyway? He had no idea.

Vicky was the third woman he'd ever slept with. The first two were one night stands, and he had blurry memories of slimy kisses, drunken groping, and quick orgasms. He and Vicky had stopped having sex with any regularity a year before she left. She always had a headache or was tired or wanted to stay up late to finish a sewing project. Early on, her excuses hurt him, but he learned to not think about it. It never occurred to him that he could have forced the issue and made her discuss it, that the excuses were a symptom of a deteriorating situation. Before that, they'd screwed a few times a week, always when he initiated it. The fact that Vicky never approached him was something he seldom questioned. When he did confront it, he realized that she may have come on to him in the early years of their marriage, but he had been frightened by her and had put her off. It was probably early conditioning by his mother to think that horny women are bad. Shit. If he could just do it all over again!

He would not find out if Lynx was horny or if she would ever even want him sexually, not that night anyway, because she was standing by his door when he strolled back into the living room, waiting to leave.

He offered to drive her home, but she declined, saying she loved the fresh air and it wasn't too far to walk anyway.

"Aren't you worried about running into the bear?"

"Nah, he ran as soon as he spotted me. He's long gone, Jack."

"By the way," he said, "don't you think it's odd that a grizzly is in town this time of year? They usually start their garbage runs in late summer."

"It is odd," Lynx said. "But haven't you heard about the snowmobile seats? A few days ago, a sow and her two cubs ripped apart all the upholstery on the four machines the park rangers use at the Old Faithful Visitor's Center. They apparently ate all the foam stuffing. Then yesterday, a mechanic at Wade's Snowmobile Tours found six rental machines torn to bits."

"I didn't hear about that."

"They only ate the machines with the fake tiger-skin vinyl. The mechanic found a few piles of bear scat nearby with pieces of the vinyl in it. He called the game warden, who had heard about the Old Faithful incident. They figure it's not the same bears, either. I guess more than one grizzly prefers foam rubber to the winter-killed elk and bison they usually eat this time of year."

"Or maybe they're trying to show us how much they hate snowmachines."

"Yeah, well, that would be fine with me," Lynx laughed. "But you know how people are about snowmobiling around here. It's their bread and butter. Wade's pissed. He wants to recover the cost of the sleds and thinks the park should pay damages because their bears ate his machines. The insurance expired on them almost a month ago, on the last day of the winter season."

"That's bullshit. The sleds are worthless. The tourists beat the hell out of them. Are you gonna write about this?"

"You bet. The headline will be something like, 'Grizzlies discover new food source.' I'm working on it."

He laughed. "Look, Lynx, call me when you get home so I know you made it safely."

"Will do. Now let me outta here. And thanks again for dinner."

Jack closed the door behind her, leaned his back against it and took a deep breath. Her smell lingered in the air, and he liked it.

Lynx ran home quickly to dissipate her sexual energy. If she had stayed five more minutes, she would have dragged Jack to bed. As she settled into the rhythm of running and breathing, her rational mind began to take over. *He is a good friend, and that's it. He doesn't understand women, and he doesn't seem to want to. Forget about it.*

In their separate beds, Jack and Lynx slept restlessly that night, thinking similar thoughts. Wondering what it would have been like, wondering if the other was wondering.

The next evening, Jack showed up at her doorstep with two bottles of wine. "Let's take one up to the Plateau and watch the sunset," he said matter of factly, "and drink the other one here when we get back."

Lynx already had a jacket on and was loading her pockets with .22 rounds.

"Great timing," she told him, "I'm on my way up there now to do some shooting. I like to practice in the last light of the day because it's often the best time to find game in hunting season."

He uncorked the wine and poured them each a plastic glassful. "I don't have any guns with me. Should I go home and get one?"

"Nah, I have a mini arsenal in here," she said, opening a locked closet in her kitchen. She wasn't kidding. There were two lever action .22's, a .270 Winchester bolt action rifle, a .222 Ruger with a 30 round clip, a 30-30 Marlin lever action rifle, two 12-gauge shotguns in cases, a Dixie Hawken .45 black powder rifle, a .38 special and a .357 magnum revolver. There was also a .22 caliber Smith and Wesson Ladysmith double action revolver, the preferred handgun of the early West's prostitutes. Dozens of boxes of ammo were stacked neatly on a shelf. Jack grabbed another .22, and Lynx grabbed a pile of paper plates and a staple gun, explaining that she used the plates for targets after stapling them on the Forest Service snow markers that lined South Plateau Road.

Fifteen minutes later, they were on the top of the Plateau, blasting her targets and laughing like kids with their first BB guns.

"It gives me a real woody to do this," she shouted as she fired off a round into the center of a plate 75 yards away.

"She's crazy," he thought as he fired one exactly to the right of hers. "I like it."

They sat on the ground and watched the sun slip behind the jagged peaks of the Madison Mountains as they finished off the wine. Warm breezes from the obsidian flats below them drifted away, replaced by a stronger, colder wind. She began to shiver, and he took off his denim jacket and wrapped it around her.

"Lynx, I've always wondered what your real name is," Jack confided.

"You don't think it's Lynx?" she teased.

"It's not exactly a normal name. I thought it may be too personal to ask you about, but now I'm trying to learn how to talk to you Women things."

"No kidding! I may not be the best guinea pig you can find for that. Anyway, it's my birth name. Lynx Ann, to be exact. The Ann is to fulfill the Catholic thing about giving your kid a Biblical name."

"So tell me about the lynx."

"I'd have to start with trying to explain my mother. She's a bit weird, has dreams and visions. She's a psychic and gets really out there when she's pregnant. She's had seven kids, and I was the third. She said she dreamed the most when she was pregnant with me and was visited in her dreams by a lynx. The lynx told her I would be sharp-sighted, like she is. You see, Old World people thought the lynx could see so well that it could penetrate stone walls with its vision. They felt that seeing a lynx was good luck and would give a person special eyesight, psychic vision."

"Wow. So she named you after a dream animal. And I thought only Indians did that."

Lynx laughed. "No, but mostly Indians did that, and still do. Actually, you would like my mother."

"Lynx . . . it fits you. You're sort of a wildcat."

She ignored that. "The neat thing about lynxes is how they hunt. They're very tricky."

"How so?"

"The lynx hunts at night. When its prey knows its around, it freezes motionless to avoid being seen. The lynx sneaks up to where she believes the prey to be, then emits this amazingly sharp howl, like this — short, sharp, frightening." Lynx howled.

Jack jumped, startled. "That made me almost soil my pantaloons," he said. "Do it again."

"No. The lynx does it just once. The prey reacts like you just did. It jumps, gives its location away, and the lynx pounces. Like this." She put her hands on both sides of his neck and kissed him on the nose. "Sort of like that, but I left out the kill part." She laughed, and Jack kissed her back.

"That's way cool. You're a lynx woman, wild, sharp-sighted, and a clever hunter of prey."

"I try my best," she winked.

They grew quiet, listening to the sounds of the evening. The sun was gone, and stars popped out of the darkness. West Yellowstone's neon lights began to roll and blink, and they heard a truck start to climb the hill.

"We should grab those plates and boogie," she said, handing him back his jacket. "It wouldn't look good for us to be seen here, drinking wine and blasting targets on Forest Service poles."

"How come you know what I'm thinking? You're one of Them. You aren't supposed to do that," Jack wondered out loud.

"I'm giving you good head. It's an art, cerebral communication between men and women. We've been programmed by the divorce-loving mass media to think it's unattainable. And I love you, man, not mushy in love, just person-to-person love. Now get lost!"

"Okay, okay, I'm outta here, but I'll be back. I like your bed."

"I like you in my bed. See you around," she said as she walked him to the door.

Chapter Two

Lynx had no time to wallow in long afterglows from their great sex. Her day stretched out in front of her, every moment filled with something to do. She had to finish the grizzly bear story by deadline, spend two hours on tomorrow's story, meet her best girlfriend Patsy for lunch, go to the post office and grocery store, do her 65-minute aerobic and weight routine, and cook dinner for Merlin, her 12-year old son. He'd spent the last three days at Lou's house, so would be acting out all kinds of pent-up hostility he had whenever he came from there because he still resented the divorce. She would have to spend time calming him down and helping him with his homework, then take him to a friend's house to play, attend a boring school board meeting, get Merlin to bed after reading him another chapter in *Watership Down*, then read herself. She was still holding true to her New Year's resolution to finish three books a week.

Then, before she could let herself drop off to sleep, she had to spend at least an hour planning the Memorial Day weekend opening of the Museum of Yellowstone Culture, which she managed in the summer. She and Merlin couldn't survive on her 25-30 hour a week reporter job. The five month museum management position was fun and challenging and gave her enough money for extras like downhill ski passes and trips to Arizona and New Mexico, where they could escape for a while from West Yellowstone's six-month-long winter.

No, Lynx was too busy for afterglow. One paragraph more of her grizzly bear story, and it fluttered away.

Jack's afterglow hung around him all day. His work was routine and mechanical, requiring little thought, leaving him plenty of time to think his own thoughts.

He went to lunch at the Triangle, a cafe with great home cooking. It had been run by the same people for several years: Walt, an underpaid town cop Jack had gone to high school with, and his wife, Susan. All the guys who worked for the city, the bank, the real estate offices, and a few other of the town's more established businesses gathered there for lunch.

They always sat at the same counter and nearby round table and were known as the "Boys Club."

The Boys Club was West Yellowstone's most powerful gossip mill, cranking out rumors about anyone they chose to be a victim. The rumors were nearly always based on shaky facts and fantasies about people individual members of the club were resentful of for one reason or another. They also spewed out opinions about politics, sports, and local, state, and national events that would, if written down, barely make a C-minus in a 100 college level political science course.

It was an unwritten but completely understood Boys Club rule that, if your wife or squeeze came to lunch at the Triangle when you were sitting with the Boys, you did not acknowledge one another with more than a nod. You certainly did not talk, unless an extreme emergency, like the imminent death of one of your children, was in progress. If you broke the rule, you were sneeringly dubbed "pussy whipped."

In West Yellowstone's smaller gossip mills, woman-at-home coffee cliques and small groups of men not connected to the power base, the Boys Club was thought of as a cluster of major assholes who had to hang together to pump one another up because in the real world, they would never make the Major Leagues.

Jack hung on the periphery of the Boys Club because he felt his job required him to give them a certain degree of respect. After all, election year after election year, they voted his boss into power. He always answered the gossip grinders' questions about what was going on in the city with as few words as possible, ignored the gossip, and spaced out when the discussion got too political.

As usual, he nodded to the boys who had already gathered at the table and sat down at the counter. George, one of the guys on the street crew, slid onto the stool next to him and nudged him hard on his arm.

"Got laid last night, Jack, didn't you?"

Jack ignored him.

"I saw your car at Lynx's when I cruised town at 6 a.m. That can only mean one thing. I hear she's a great piece of ass."

"Fuck you." Jack used the most acceptable expression for the situation. "Where did you hear that?"

"Don't get off the subject. Did she give you any? Or did your truck somehow break down in her driveway?

"First you tell me where you heard she was a great piece of ass, which she is, but that's none of your business."

"Lynx has been single for a while. She's not a whore by any means, but she has slept with few guys, and I heard one say she was great, but doesn't want to hang around with anybody, just get laid and go about her business. My kinda gal, really, if I ever get a mind to cheat on Julie."

"Small town bullshit," Jack thought, and squirmed on his stool. He looked in the mirror across from the counter as the door opened and Lynx walked in with Patsy, her crazy artist friend.

He watched them sit down and wondered if Lynx was going to tell Patsy about last night. He also wondered how he was going to finish his lunch and walk by Lynx as if nothing was going on between them.

George noticed Jack staring at Lynx in the mirror and poked him. "Look who just sat down, studmeister," he teased.

"Shut up and eat," Jack shot back.

Jack scarfed down his hot turkey sandwich, glancing at Lynx's reflection every few bites. He could hear her voice but not her words. He could tell she and Patsy were talking intensely about something. "Some Woman stuff, no doubt," he thought, "stuff that would scare the shit out of me."

He left the exact amount of the check plus a 15 percent tip on the counter and walked over to Lynx's table.

She looked up at him with a friendly, open face and said hello.

Jack sat down and said hello back.

"What are you ladies doing, goofing off or what?" he asked.

He could feel the curious eyes of the Boys Club, could hear the noise level drop in their corner of the room as some of them stopped talking to try to hear him talk to Lynx. By now the entire town probably knew where his truck was last night.

"We're talking about how busy we are, how we never have any time to play, and have to see each other at lunch or not at all," Lynx said. In her eyes he saw a little of last night's razzle dazzle when they had begun to dance. Just a little. Not enough to be detected by the boys at the table or even by Patsy, he guessed.

He stood up, keeping his back to the Boys. "Well, you gals get back to your talking then. I have to go to work."

He strolled to the door. "That was easy," he thought. "I can do this. And if they know I got laid, what the hell, and if she sleeps around, what the hell? If I'm pussy whipped because I talked with her, far out. I feel good."

"You know, Lynx, Jack, he be a man, a real man, sweet but macho," Patsy said in what she called her Louisiana voice. She'd learned the accent when she spent some time in the South a few years ago. "He's single and has a nice house, although he has too many dogs for my taste. Go for him. He likes you. He even broke the Boys Club rule and sat down at your table. You're being majorly hit on, girl."

"This really is life in a fish bowl, Patsy. By the end of the day, you're going to hear that his truck was parked at my house all night. It was. We had a good time. We don't know where it's going, if anywhere. Period. Don't bug me."

"All right, sister, good for you. You know what he was doing when he sat down with us? He told Them he digs you and They can kiss his ass."

"I know, I know, I know, so now let's drop it and figure out how we can get the hell out of this town next weekend. It's almost summer. We'll be getting even busier than we are now when all the tourons get here."

"I'll go anywhere. What do you have in mind?"

"Nora Spotted Elk and some of her family and Gerry and Bob Little Boy and some of their friends are having a sweat this weekend in the Beartrap Canyon. No booze, no pot, fast a little, sit in the sweat lodge, fish, walk into the hills, sleep in tipis, sing songs around the fire. Get spiritually renewed. Sound good to you?"

"Lynx, I couldn't think of a better way to get ready for summer. I can bring my camera and take pictures to sketch later."

"Yeah you can. Just don't take pictures of anyone without asking them first if it's okay."

• • •

Crunch-slurp-crunch-slurp. The sound of some asshole chewing like a starved pig blasted through Lynx's house. It had to be Lou. Sure enough. When he noisily swallowed whatever he had been devouring, his angry voice jumped out of the speaker on her phone answering machine.

"Goddamn it, Lynx, can't you discipline Merlin? He's got another crazy message on your tape. Call me back. I need to talk to you right away."

Lynx took three deep breaths and reminded herself it was just a voice, Lou was not her husband anymore, thank God, and she did not have to deal with his anger. She wouldn't call him back. "If you want to talk with me, you can change your tone or forget it," she said out loud to the uncaring machine.

The rest of her messages were from people apparently confused about Lynx taking a trip to Japan. It was a mystery to Lynx, too. She played back the outgoing message.

"Hello, you have reached the ex-home of Merlin and Lynx. We have re-located to the Mount Fuji area of Japan to join a Zen Buddhist community. Do not leave a message." It was Merlin's sweet little voice.

"Good delivery. It's pretty convincing, the little bastard," Lynx thought. "I'll kill him."

Merlin was doomed. His father was the most sarcastic person on earth, not to mention a diagnosed psychotic who took three different kinds of drugs every day to help him get through life on a marginally functioning level. The drugs evened out his mood swings somewhat but made him dry mouthed, unreasonable and sexually impotent. Lynx was a close second on the sarcasm scale, but tended more toward playing practical jokes than tearing people apart with words. Merlin could do both. You had to be ready for his tricks and smart ass remarks all the time. But the answering machine was sacred. They would have to talk about it.

Lynx grabbed the hem of her tee-shirt and affectionately dusted off what she called her mean, metallic-gray asshole screener. It was her third machine. She had embraced the new technology as soon as the Japs mass-produced affordable machines, seeing immediately how they could be used to better her life. This new model had a speaker phone and was also a fax machine. It stored 100 phone numbers, could transmit the same fax to up to 20 different places at once, and could record conversations on its mini-cassette tape. This last was an important feature for a reporter who interviews snaky politicians and wildlife managers who like to say they didn't say what they said.

Lynx loved to get up early but hated to get dressed and go out to work. When the museum was running, she had to be there at 7 a.m. to get ready to open at 8 a.m. But from November to early May, she could stay home all morning. Most of the meetings she had to cover were during the lunch hour and in the evening, and she made appointments for personal interviews and photo sessions after lunch whenever possible. In the morning, she lived in her bathrobe as she wrote her stories for that day. She spent a lot of time on the phone checking facts, getting more information, and interviewing regular contacts she did not feel she had to go out and see face to face every time she needed a quote or idea from them. She had interviewed governors, congressmen, senators, artists, actors, and top-level government people like the Secretary of Interior sitting comfortably in one of her five exquisitely broken-in robes, or, when it was hot, a tee-shirt and panties.

Lynx sat in front of her precious machine and leaned toward the speaker to program a new outgoing message. "Hi. This is Lynx and Merlin's house, and the *Gazette*'s West Yellowstone bureau. To send a fax, push the asterisk now. If you wish to speak with someone, state your name, and we'll pick up the phone if we're here. Otherwise, leave a message at the tone, and we'll call ya later."

Safe again. After her divorce, Lynx's house had become a hang out for all kinds of people. Most were single, making their rounds around town on the way to and from work, looking for conversation or music and video movies to borrow. They loved Lynx's kick ass, freshly ground French roast coffee, loved to find out what stories she was writing, and loved to tell her what she should be writing about. In their opinions, there were many conspiracies going in the world, and she should be investigating each and every one of them, uncovering the madness to let people know how truly evil most of the institutions that control their lives are.

Lynx lived on one of the main routes through town, with her back door on an alley. Townies loved to wander the alleys, and they thought that since she had an office at her house, it was sort of a public place. Until she trained them, they would knock once and walk right through the door. Lynx hated being caught in her bathrobe in the middle of concentrating on a story, hated being disturbed when she was working out or napping. After the novelty of having so many visitors wore off, and people started to really bug her, she devised a plan to have more control over her life.

She posted a sign on her door. "Did you call first? Is this a national emergency? Has Jesus Christ come back? If none of the above, no one is home. Love, Lynx."

They got the idea. They called first, and if she didn't want to see them, she didn't pick up the phone. And she wasn't lying, either, to say if she was home, she would pick up the phone, and then not pick it up if she was home. She knew it wasn't a real lie because when she was a young girl at home alone with her mother one day, the phone had rung and her mother told her to answer it and say she wasn't home if her friend Paula was on the other end. Mom had taken the day off from her high stress job as a research scientist at a large drug manufacturing plant that was trying to beat the competition in finding a drug to treat Parkinson's disease, and she was slugging down her second bottle of wine. Paula always gave her a hard time for drinking during the day.

"But it's a lie," Lynx had told her.

"No, it isn't a real lie. I am not home to her." They were Catholic. They had strict codes, commandments and church laws to abide by. To make it through life, all good Catholics had to develop a finely tuned sense of situational ethics.

Lynx had found that situational ethics didn't work except in the area of sex. She tended to view most of life in black and white, like Jack did. If it's right, do it, live by it. If it's wrong, don't do it and don't bend the rules unless the rules are totally unworkable, like the church's marriage laws and the commandments against fornication and adultery. Her first marriage was a Catholic one, and she divorced Kyle after their daughter was born because his sexual preferences were too kinky for her, downright immoral actually. He wanted to watch her have sex with other men. She did it once when she was slightly drunk and stoned on pot. When it was over and she was sober, she felt miserable and knew she could not stay married if he made an issue out of it. Things settled down when she got pregnant and had their daughter, Gwen. Kyle must have thought it was not right to force other men on a pregnant wife or new mother. But when Gwen was a year old, he started pressuring her to have sex with a friend he often brought home from work. One evening, the two men confronted her with what they said were prudish and selfish beliefs. Kyle said he was going to leave the house and not return until she had sex with his friend. That was too much for her. She grabbed Gwen out of her crib and ran. The Catholic Church annulled the marriage the next year.

Lynx loved sex and had spent a long time learning to love it on all levels, from physical to spiritual. From age seven she had been sexually used, abused, raped, and ravaged for eight years by her grandfather, an outstanding member of the Church by way of substantial annual cash contributions to the parish and service as a greeter at Sunday morning Mass.

Lynx had been born with the exceptionally strong spirit of a survivor, and she knew from early on that she would get through whatever her grandfather inflicted on her. She knew she would have to remember it, because when she did try to repress the pain of what he did to her, she would also block out the world around her and get into trouble at school. The nuns did not like to see one of their students locked in a thousand-yard stare all through the day's classes.

So, she trained herself to remember and stay alive and awake. She talked to God a lot about what was happening, and He told her to hang in there, it was happening for a reason, and he would take care of her.

Lynx had never followed the train of thought that says there can't be a God because horrible things happen to people and no God would allow that. She sensed always that terrible things were somehow gifts from God to make you stronger and unique.

Although she survived her grandfather on many levels, she did not always have the self knowledge to see what it was doing to her ability to have positive normal relationships with men. She had problems with intimacy. She loved sex because it was fun to be with someone who wasn't raping you or doing outlandish, scary, kinky things to you. But she wasn't nuts about hanging out with men she had sex with. She felt they were pressuring her and trying to control her.

Her divorce from Lou happened after she had an affair with Sherwood, a fly fishing guide, to fill a void brought on by years of dealing with Lou's drug-induced impotency. The divorce made her realize she needed help. She went into six months of heavy therapy to cope with her problems with intimacy and her promiscuous behavior. She learned that she was transferring the negative feelings she had toward her grandfather to men she did get close to. This made her feel pressured by men when she spent too much time with them.

The therapy led Lynx to give up one night stands with people she barely knew, but it took her a long time to not miss them. She continued to have consistent but infrequent sex with friends. She was a good performer in bed, having learned what men like from granddad, one of the horniest men in the universe. She vowed she would not let the memories of his pathological behavior ruin her pleasure. She did not get drunk and crazy and jump into bed with anyone for a quickie. She made sure she and her partners had hours of great sex and fun. Then she left or he left.

The men she slept with were sometimes involved with a woman who wouldn't or couldn't give them what they wanted, or they were like Lynx, horny but with absolutely no desire for marriage-type intimacy above the naval, or more accurately, nose. Lynx could not honestly feel she was wrong having sex with friends. She loved these men. It had been easy for her to tell Jack she loved him. Love was central to Lynx's universe. It was easier to love people and live in service to them than to focus on conflicts and differences. Marriages, she reasoned after looking at the world around her, are too often not unions between people willing to do the work of cherishing their love and serving one another. The normal differences between men and women are viewed as negative forces each must defeat in the other, rather than celebrate and encourage.

There were a lot of hurting men out there, she found, men whose wives were tightly wound angry beasts refusing to lighten up and have sex. They were angry for all kinds of petty reasons: he didn't bring home enough money, he hunted and fished too much, watched too much television, didn't spend time with the kids, do housework, on and on. Payback was to say no to sex or to give it but just lie there, refuse to give him a blow job, back rub, or anything other than the bare basics.

After two marriages, Lynx had decided it is best to accept the reality of men. Let them be addicted to television. Let them withdraw into their own little worlds and focus on time-consuming hobbies like woodworking and car repair. Let them refuse to do housework, forget about putting toilet lids down. Let them leave sweat-stiffened socks on the floor and throw away toothpaste caps. Let them hoard the two or three remote controls to the AV system on their fat old beer bellies and flip through the channels to their heart's content.

What do men have to overlook? Ugly mood swings every month, listening to moans about cramps, blood stains on the sheets, waiting for the hair and make-up routines to end so they can use the bathroom, waiting for women to come back from hours of withdrawing into wherever it is women withdraw to when they demand to be alone for a while.

In overlooking the strange behaviors that become war zones between men and women, Lynx had gotten very close to many men and learned to play with them, actually celebrate their bizarre behavior as they willingly celebrated hers.

Lynx's theory about the latest craze touted in self-awareness books and on talk shows, of the necessity of separate male and female bonding, was that it was reactive behavior to sexual conflicts. Same sex bonds are formed, she believed, to escape the negative energy of the opposite sex and get some peace and to have someone with whom to do the things you like to do but can't with the opposite sex because of disinterest or physical inability.

Lynx had always been fascinated with the things men like to do, like fly fishing, hunting, backpacking into the wilderness, and winter camping. She was strong enough physically and mentally to do all these things well and to not whine and complain when the trail got tough.

She was very well read and deeply spiritual and aware of what people were thinking and feeling. She could, and often did, challenge people more brilliant than she in thoughtful, mind- expanding conversations.

She was able, then, to give men good head physically and mentally. In exchange, she got good head as well. Lynx had learned that most men would rather be in a duck blind with a woman who could shoot, in the backcountry stalking elk with a woman who would kill one, or fishing on a stream with a female companion who loved the experience with all her heart than to hang out with other men to do these things.

She wanted to know the mysteries in men's hearts, to share the power it takes to stalk game and fish and birds, to share the outdoors she loved so much with them. And she knew that men wanted to share these things with women as long as the women were worthy of the sharing, as long as they weren't whining and complaining and taking them away from their focus. Lynx didn't blame men for wanting to exclude women from their world when they escaped to the wilderness. Most women did not want to walk side by side with men, but wanted to pull them away from the things they loved and make them feel guilty and uncomfortable if they ventured off alone.

A fringe benefit of Lynx's sexuality was that her men friends were more than happy to do all the little things wives could nag their tongues off and never get their men to do. Lynx's wood was always stacked and split, her car tuned, her trash hauled to the dump, and her leaky faucets didn't leak too long. On Valentine's Day and her birthday, she was given enough candy to kill a dozen diabetics and enough flowers to surround a cathedral altar. She even had a drawer full of red, black, and hot pink Victoria's Secret Fashion-of-the Month Club goodies sent to her anonymously. She suspected it was a gift from a wealthy old rancher who lived in nearby Ennis who took her out to dinner now and then.

town. He also tied dry flies and was bringing a supply of mayfly imitations to Ned's store that day. In winter, he ran a ski camp near the Grand Canyon of the Yellowstone. The camp consisted of three eight-sided canvas yurts and a dozen small cabins with wood sides and canvas roofs that slept two people. The community could accommodate up to 50 people for dinner and gatherings. The other two each slept eight people. Yurt and his helpers hauled guests to the camp in vans he had converted into over-snow vehicles. Lynx had spent many wonderful days at the camp, using it as a base to ski all around the Canyon area.

Yurt's real name was Hugo, but he'd been nicknamed Yurt by the first group of winter adventurers he'd brought into the park many years ago. Those people had been fascinated with his multi-sided personality. He invented the snow van, skied superbly, was an avid reader, good photographer, great fisherman, and that was just for starters. In short, he was as multi-sided as a yurt.

Yurt gave her a good lead for a story for the next day's paper. He'd been checking out the fishing possibilities on a stretch of water in the Madison River northwest of town that morning when he ran into a three-legged black bear that Montana Department of Fish, Wildlife, and Parks game wardens had years ago nicknamed Tripod. The bear looked good, he said.

Last fall, Tripod had roamed the streets of West Yellowstone looking for garbage, as he had for many years before that. This time he learned the rules had changed. Bear managers had decided to put to death any bear who consistently wandered in human-inhabited areas. The goal was to eventually have a bear population that subsisted on natural foods and avoided humans. Wardens had trapped Tripod before and moved him to a drainage deep in the mountains west of the river, to territory he was unfamiliar with, hoping he would den there and not return to West in the spring.

Many bear watchers had predicted that he would not make it in a new area because he was so set in his ways. But he had made it, and that was a story Lynx thought was worth writing. Yurt had taken some photos, and they were in the one-hour photo shop. Better yet, they would be developed before the bus run to Bozeman that night, so the paper could run a story with a picture.

Chapter Three

Back at home, Lynx played back her answering machine and was surprised to hear a call from Ursula, a waitress she had not known very long. They were in a woman's book reading club that met every month to discuss a novel or nonfiction work they all decided on together. This month's book had been *Drumming for Sanity*, a book on male consciousness they had heard all the men in America were reading.

Everywhere but West Yellowstone, that is, where the men didn't think they had anything new to learn. None of their mates or men friends had a copy. The book encouraged men to get naked together in the wilderness and beat on homemade drums until they got in touch with their anger and frustration about having to succeed in business, be good fathers, and please women. The reading group had first discussed "Birthing With Bitches," a chapter on drumming away repressed anger about having to be present at the birth of their children to help their partners deal with labor pain and bond with their newborns. Then Lynx and Patsy shared their experience with male drumming.

It had been Lynx and Patsy's suggestion to read the book, which Lynx had reviewed for the *Gazette* after spying with Patsy on a men's drumming group that met under every full moon in the mountains near Bozeman. On the night of their visit, the men were working on the chapter titled "Releasing Your Inner Predator." There were ten men, and not one of them was totally naked, much to Lynx's and Patsy's disappointment. They were all skeletal, like marathon runners, with mousy wire-rimmed glasses and white boxer shorts that glowed in the moonlight. Lynx recognized an environmentalist who edited an animal rights newsletter, a lawyer who specialized in suing companies that discriminated against homosexuals, a bicycle shop owner, and an abstract expressionist painter who taught art history at Montana State University.

They were drumming away resentment about being called pussies, women, and faggots by men in the community who chided them for not hunting. "We can kill, kill, kill if we want to!" the animal righter shouted as he beat his tall, skin-covered wooden drum. "We choose to let animals live, live, live," he went on.

"Real men don't shoot animals," yelled the attorney.

To Lynx's disgust, the artist was into a rap beat. "I'm a man-much man. I think I can. Be prey and predator. And still be your fren'. Kill within. Love without. I ain't no pussy. I got clout."

Lynx was having trouble taking notes in the dark shadow of the bushes they were crouched in, so she turned on her penlight. It was upside-down, however, and the thin stream of light shot out of their hiding place and gave them away. The men threw aside their drums and surrounded them. Lynx calmly explained that she was reviewing the book and wanted her review to include how local men were reacting to it. Patsy added that was going to illustrate it with lovely sketches that would not be detailed enough so anyone would be recognized.

"This is a typical example of how you Women never leave us alone so we become filled with anger and resentment," shouted the bicycle shop owner.

"You could be sued for invasion of privacy," screeched the attorney.

"You could be sued for looking so ugly in boxer shorts," countered Patsy in a voice three tones lower than his.

"You are supposed to be naked. What are you, uptight about your skinny asses?" offered Lynx.

"Get off this mountain, you bitches," the animal righter hollered. "Or I'll kill you!"

"Okay, okay, peace on earth, asshole," Lynx volleyed.

The women left and didn't hear a single drum beat all the way down the mountain.

Their story had given the reading group hysterics and caused a record amount of wine to be drunk, followed by shots of Scotch and bourbon and shared dreams of what they would really do if they could get rid of their husbands, boyfriends, and children.

• • •

Ursula's voice sounded upset, and she said wanted to talk. Lynx still had to do her workout before Merlin came home. She was running late but returned the call anyway because Ursula's tone worried her.

"Lynx, I have to talk to someone. I'm in a real mess and don't know anybody here too well, but I see how well you listen and communicate at book group. Can we get together?"

Lynx laughed, amazed that she appeared to be a good listener at the group. In fact, she usually spaced out half of what they said. It was just that the drumming discussion had been so personal to her. She normally went to the group only because she didn't want people to think she was an intellectual snob.

"Okay, Ursula," she replied. "When do you get off work?"

"I'm warning you. This is weird stuff. Can I come over kind of late? I get off at 10 to 10:30."

"That'll work. My school board meeting will be out then. Come on over, and if I'm out, walk in. I don't lock. Play some music 'til I get here. Oh, and you'll have to wait until I get Merlin to bed before we can start talking."

"No probs. See you later, then. Thanks."

Lynx's workout time was sacred. When she spent it indoors, it centered around one of three 65-minute Firm, Inc. butt-busting, aerobic-weight-training videotapes. Firm users think Jane Fonda workout tapes are for wimps. Firm tapes are fat busters and muscle rippers, if you used the heaviest weights you could handle and pushed yourself hard on the aerobic and floor stretching sections.

Lynx usually gave the workout about 60-70 percent of her energy and did not focus on the weight training with as much concentration as you are supposed to, by isolating each muscle in your mind and visualizing it working at its max. That's because her workout time was also for spiritual renewal. She did deep breathing exercises and Tai Chi for a half hour before the workout to steady her emotions, focus her mind, and relax her physical body. She then opened herself to a seed thought to mull over during the workout, which made it difficult to also concentrate on isolating muscles.

Lynx didn't know anyone else who practiced what she called "seed thought trolling," although she did know some people who focused on someone else's seed thought when they trained, something out of a book of universally known quotes by famous people or the Bible, the Tao te Ching or the Bhagavad-Gita.

Lynx trolled for seed thoughts floating in the collective unconscious that may or may not be manifested in everyday reality. She skipped over thoughts about stories she was working on or dynamics in her relationships and went for the Major Leagues where she knew the Great Spirit and the good people who made it to heaven hung out.

Often the seed thought she hooked and did not release was one that ultimately connected to everyday events but gave her a refreshing and esoteric overview of those events. She used that overview to give her strength, to find balance, and to celebrate the interconnectedness of people, places, and things that makes life exciting.

After years of practicing this, Lynx had gained the reputation of a person to talk to when an overview, a far-reaching perspective, a thoughtful look at things was needed.

Harry Spotted Elk, her closest Indian friend, called her Eagle Woman because of her inner vision, although her Indian name, given to her after a vision quest guided by Harry and his mother, Nora, was Brown Bear Woman. Sometimes she felt she was an eagle, other times a bear, and, of course, a lynx. It depended on which animal's medicine she needed to draw on.

Lynx had had a rather complex life. She wrote news stories on such animal topics as vanishing grizzly bears, threatened trumpeter swans, fading frog populations, and bald eagles disturbed by human sounds. The town she had lived in most of her adult life was about to undergo a major expansion and see a profound increase in development, become more crowded and noisy. Merlin was becoming a nut, her ex-husband was a raving maniac living three blocks away, she was falling into a near intimate relationship with a long-time friend, and a new friend was hurting.

Each of these events gnawed at her as she began her Tai Chi routine with a deep centering breath. Her body moved in rhythm with her breaths, no need to think about executing the movements that had become part of her. Her spirit searched for an overview. It came in a flash, entered her heart first, where it tickled her and made her aware of the offensive movement she was executing at that moment. The feeling crossed the rainbow bridge she visualized connecting her heart to her mind and became words. "When change pulls you downward, race upward to the sky and become the firmament."

It was an eagle thought, and she flew with it.

• • •

Merlin proposed that he would quit messing with the answering machine if Lynx would stop making him do dishes. Lynx said there were no trades. He had to quit, and she had no obligation to do something for him in exchange for behavior he was supposed to practice anyway.

He said he didn't want Lynx to read to him because Ursula was in the house waiting to talk. He said he was embarrassed that his mother was still reading to him at his age and didn't want the outside world to know about it. He wanted to talk about Big Wig, one of *Watership Down*'s star rabbits.

"Is Big Wig bad or good? He kind of scares me, mamma."

"You gotta figure that out yourself, Merlin. You'll see him more clearly as the book goes on. I bet you end up getting over your fear of him and even admiring him. He's a stand up sort of rabbit."

"What's that mean?"

"Stand up rabbits, stand up people, know what they believe in and they live by their beliefs. They're good people to have as friends and allies because they won't let you down when you're in trouble."

"But, mamma, what if your beliefs are screwed up and you are a stand up person, then won't you be really bad?"

"Yes, Merlin, but I'm talking about good stand up people."

"That still doesn't explain Big Wig. If he is bad he will force his evil on the other rabbits."

"You're right, but you will see that Big Wig is good. I don't want to give the story away. Big Wig has a lot of serenity. Truly bad people and rabbits are troubled. You can't fake serenity, and you can't have it if you are evil. The forces of good don't let evil rest."

"How do you get serenity?"

"If you believe in the right stuff and stand up whenever you have to protect your promise to live by those beliefs, you have serenity. The trick is to stand up when you must. You can't store your beliefs on a shelf and take them out when you think it's convenient. If you do, you'll most likely forget they're there when you're faced with a problem. You have to walk your talk, which means live by your beliefs, not just say you have them but go out and do something that doesn't fit with them."

"Do I have good beliefs?"

"The kid can ask questions," Lynx thought. His mind was always working. "What do you think?" she asked.

"I have so many feelings about stuff, and I don't know why," he replied.

"Merlin, you've got to trust yourself. Don't worry so much. You're a kid, for chrissake, an explorer. You're still scouting out the places you want to become an adventurer in. Don't sweat it. Ask yourself what you would do if you were Big Wig. Ask yourself what you would do if you were me and had a kid who messed up your answering machine. But now go to sleep. Think of a beautiful place you've been in, like Black Sands or something. Go there and let sleep overtake you."

Merlin reached out and pulled her by her hair until her face was close enough to kiss.

"Love ya, see ya in the morning, mom."

"I love you, baby. Don't worry, sweet dreams."

Lynx closed Merlin's door and leaned against it. She said a silent prayer that he find peace and fall asleep quickly. Merlin had a lot of symptoms like his dad's, and Lynx didn't know if it was learned behavior or organically caused. She hoped it was learned and had been spending more time with him explaining how he can center himself and become calm and focused on one thing at a time. It seemed to be working. She opened the door carefully and peeked in on him. He was snoring.

Ursula fidgeted with her hair as she sat at Lynx's round maple table and stared intently at the dining area's curved glass brick wall. Lynx turned down the CD she'd been playing, Handel's *Water Music,* and sat down with two cups of French roast coffee laced with B and B.

"What's on your mind?" she asked.

"I think someone is really serious about wanting to kill me," Ursula said, her voice and hands shaking. "I've only lived here a year and a half, and I have no idea how things work around here, but I thought maybe you could help me see things in perspective or at least listen so I can get this off my chest," she went on.

"Who do you think is trying to kill you?"

"This is hard to talk about." She fussed with her long red hair. "It's about Walt. You know him, the guy who owns the Triangle with his wife, Susan. I'll just tell you the story from the beginning. We were both at a three-day Emergency Medical Technician training session up in Missoula several months ago. Jack was there, too, by the way. Did you know they went to high school together?"

Lynx nodded affirmatively.

"Throughout the weekend, we broke up into small study groups to review what we had learned in the large class. Walt, Jack, a woman from Billings, and a man from Bozeman were in my group. We got along very well, and we went out the last night to a bar with live music and dancing. Walt and I danced almost every dance and wound up huddled together at our table talking about all kinds of stuff. He's really interesting, and we hit it off, partied 'til closing, and went back to Jack and Walter's motel room. It must have been really obvious that Walt and I were attracted to one another, and Jack may have been uncomfortable. Anyway, he'd driven up there in his camper truck, and he told us he was gong to sleep in it because he had several guns in it and was worried they would be stolen."

Ursula emptied her cup, and Lynx refilled it with a stiffer shot of B & B.

"We..uh..wound up having sex. Lynx, believe me, I'm not into messing with married men. It just happened. We shouldn't have spent time alone together. But we were so drawn to one another.

"He told me he and Susan were having a terrible time, arguing constantly, not having sex, and were really alienated. He said it was both their faults, they were mismatched from the beginning but stayed together because she got pregnant and he felt he had to marry her, and whenever they seemed to be having more fights than usual, she would get pregnant again. They have four kids.

"Anyway, he went on to tell me that he had an affair with Tami, his best friend Dave's wife. He said Tami had been coming on to him strongly for months, right under Dave's nose, but he was not attracted to her, and he let her know that. Still she kept pressing him and even visited him at home when she knew he was alone.

"He said he and Susan had a horrible fight one night over how to deal with a problem one of the kids was having, and he ran out of the house before he broke something in his rage. He said he never felt so violent or angry in his entire life, even when he was in Viet Nam. He went to talk with Dave about it, but Dave was out of town. Tami offered him a drink. He slammed it down. He said Tami said she understood where he was coming from because she and Dave were fighting all the time, too. Apparently, if he is telling the truth, the two of them drank nearly a fifth of Jack Daniels, and she jumped his bones. He said he forced himself to have sex with her.

"Then, and I find this hard to totally grasp, he kept going back to her, meeting her in another town, screwing her at his house when Susan was out of town and at Dave's house when Dave was gone. He said the entire thing was propelled by anger, that he thought both he and Tami were more turned on by doing something their spouses would detest than by one another."

"That's kind of sick, isn't it?" Lynx asked.

"Yes, that's what he decided, so he broke it off with her. When he told her the affair was over, though, he learned that Tami was not motivated by just anger or revenge. She said she wanted them each to get a divorce and then be together."

Lynx giggled. "I know this isn't really funny, but it does sound like a plot for a made-for-T.V. movie."

"No kidding. Miserable marriage. Bad affair. And then I come along and feel sorry for him.

"It was six in the morning by the time he finished telling me his story. We were supposed to meet the rest of the class for breakfast at 7 a.m. We took a shower together and had a fun breakfast, as fun as you can have when you've been up all night.

"After breakfast, he drove me back to my motel and begged me to stay in town with him for another day. He said being with me was the most wonderful thing he had ever experienced, and he wanted more time together before he went back to his messed up life in West Yellowstone."

"Ursula, let me interrupt a second." Lynx said, "Were you working at the Triangle when this happened?"

"Yeah, and when he hired me, in the interview he had read on my resume that I was an EMT, and he told me how to get my certification transferred to Montana and told me about the seminar."

"Did Susan know you were going to it?"

"Yeah, she had to know, because she does the scheduling and I had to have the weekend off, but I don't think she was concerned. After all, they are married, and I did drive up there alone."

"Had Walt asked you to go with him?"

"No, he went with Jack, and neither of them asked me if I needed a ride. I get the feeling that the original idea was that Jack and Walt were going to party all the way home."

Lynx wondered about that. Jack was not a partier. More than likely, he knew his friend was having trouble and thought it a good idea for them to be alone and talk about it. Missoula was five hours away.

"Anyway, I must have been crazy. I moved here to get away from a guy I broke up with but couldn't get out of my head as long as we lived in the same town. I told Walt I'd stay. I got sucked right into his needy bullshit, I guess. And I wanted to be needed."

Ursula paused and gulped down her drink. Lynx made her another.

"Walt told Jack he was staying another day and riding home with me, but not to tell anyone, and told him to keep away from the Triangle until he got back to town. I don't know what lie he told his wife.

"I know this sounds immoral. It is immoral in many people's eyes, but we had a great day and night. We talked and made love and had a romantic dinner. We laughed a lot. He is so loving. He hadn't been touched in so long, and he received me so openly. We also have a lot in common, a lot of the same interests and goals."

"A lot of the same hormone problems, too, Urs."

"That is part of it, but I've really gotten past that, too. It's much deeper than that now, believe me. Lynx, I really believe he is the man for me and I am the woman for him. I think we have both suffered a long time in the wrong relationships and deserve one another. I know the circumstances are crazy, and I don't know what to say about that."

"I still don't know who is threatening to kill you, Tami or Susan?"

"God, I'm sorry, Lynx. I am taking awhile to get to the point, but all this other stuff comes before, and it's important.

"Since the seminar, we've gotten together two or three times a week at my house and a coupla times in Bozeman. Well, two weeks ago, we were at the Spaghetti Factory in Bozeman having dinner, which I suppose was risky since I guess a lot of West Yellowstone people eat there when they're in town shopping. Anyway, in walked Tami with her mother. She stared at us all during dinner."

"When we got to our motel, Walt was really nervous. He worried that Tami would be vindictive and tell Susan about us. But he came to the conclusion that if Tami did tell, he would be relieved, too. It would all be over. It would force us to act. You see, we were both growing to realize that we're in love and that something had to be done, that he had to get a divorce. We wouldn't live together, but at least we would be free to pursue our relationship and see what would happen.

"Back in West, I started to run into Tami a lot. I know she was and still is following me, hoping to catch me with Walt. I think she learned my routine, when I go to the post office and store, take my walk, and so on.

"Then, three days ago, the restaurant was really slow. Susan went home early to spend time with the kids. She sent the bus person and dishwasher home, too. Walt was cooking, and I was the only waitress. Twenty minutes before closing time, we got hit with a tour bus load of 42 hungry people on the way to Idaho. They were supposed to eat at Big Sky, but their reservations had been messed up. They all wanted full course dinners. Walt called Susan and said he would be later than expected, but we could handle the rush.

"We served them and got them out of there in an hour and a half, and then had to do this huge mess of dishes. We were both very tired and giddy and happy to be alone. It kind of turned me on to have worked so intensely with him. We were both pretty worked up. We started fooling around and were kissing by the sink when Tami burst in on us through the back door."

Lynx knew Tami was moody and temperamental. When Dave married her, many people were concerned. Dave had a temper, too, but he controlled it and was far more intelligent than Tami. Tami was highly manipulative and controlling and had somehow cast a spell on Dave. How else could anyone explain how they were together, although one theory was that Tami was a great accountant and he was horrible at paperwork. Tami ran his business efficiently, and perhaps he had misconstrued her ability and desire to organize and control him as love.

"What did she say?"

"Lynx, the eerie thing is that she didn't say a word. She stared at us, and she clenched her fists, and she looked really, really crazy. Her face was as red as a beet. But she didn't say anything. She turned around and walked very slowly out the door, almost as if she was hoping we'd call her back and talk to her.

"At that point, I told Walt I thought she'd been following me around and that I was going to get another job and would not be back to work at the Triangle. I told him I'd get in touch with him in a few days, but that I needed time alone to sort things out. It'd just gotten too weird for me."

"Did he go along with you?"

"Yes, he did, and see, I take this as a sign that we are serious. We don't want to be underhanded and sneaky. We want peace. I honestly feel that I love him so much that I could go a long time without seeing him, until things settled down and we could be together openly. And I think he feels the same way, Lynx.

"Anyway, the next day I went for an interview at the Hitching Post and landed a night waitress job there that I started tonight. I was home yesterday afternoon relaxing and trying to clear all this stuff out of mind when Tami stopped by. She told me to stay away from Walt or she would have me killed and not to think she didn't have the power and resources to do it. She said she knew I was new in town and didn't know very many people and no one would even miss me. She told me to just go about my business and forget about Walt.

"She was right in my face, an inch away from it. It made me want to hit her, and I've never hit anyone before in my life. It made me sick to my stomach. It makes me sad, too. God, how I'd love to just be with Walt, just the two of us with no past, just a present and a future we both deserve. How can we break out of this? Do you think she's nuts enough to have me killed?"

Lynx saw the stress and sadness in Ursula's face. "I don't know about murder," she said softly, "but I do know that Tami is unstable and your entire situation is stressful. You are right to work at a different place and stay away from Walt for awhile. I'm more worried about Walt than you because she is stalking him, not you. If she thinks you are out of the way, she'll start demanding more from him."

"What do I do? Just forget about him?"

"That would be what I would do, but I'm not you."

"What if I told Dave that Tami has been screwing Walt?"

"They only do that on "The Young and the Restless." You know that's not a good idea."

"Then what?"

"Focus on yourself. You deserve to be happy, and you can't be happy with Walt now. If you are meant to be together, it will happen. Lift yourself out of the murk and have faith. Don't think about controlling the situation."

"I know you're right. I have to stop thinking that my happiness depends on being with him."

"Focus on having faith, Ursula, and stay really busy so you don't have time to get too emotional. Keep your doors locked, screen your calls, and stay away from Tami. Things will blow up between her and Dave on their own. They have to."

Chapter Four

As soon as Ursula left, Lynx stripped off her clothes, wrapped herself in her favorite robe, put Tchaikovsky's "1812 Overture" on the stereo, grabbed her mail, a notebook and pen, and hopped into bed.

She read her daughter's letter three times. Gwen was doing great, loving Minneapolis and her job as a public relations specialist for a chain of "nature" stores that sold bird feeders, wildflower seeds, binoculars and telescopes, wildlife art, and kits for collecting butterflies, rocks, and minerals. She'd just returned from a weekend camping trip to Canada with Rambon, her live-in boyfriend, to a wilderness lake, where they'd cross country skied and ice fished for Northern pike.

Lynx closed her eyes and listened to the powerful violins begin the long build up to the Overture's final explosion. She saw Gwen the day Merlin was born at home in their living room. Gwen was just nine years old then, but so wise and willing to help at the birth, which Lynx had insisted take place at home with just Gwen and Lou.

It was an easy birth. As soon as Lynx went into hard labor, she put herself into a trance and let her body deal with the pain. Her spirit traveled to the South Fork of the Madison River north of town, where a flock of pelicans had gathered to fly to their wintering grounds. They lifted off the river in a spiral that stretched to the southern horizon, and Lynx hooked onto the last pelican and circled the mountains with them. They gave their summering grounds a final look, flew over town, and headed towards Idaho to follow the Snake River south.

Lynx let them go over town and dropped back into her body just as she felt Merlin's desire to let go of her. Poor Lou and Gwen had been sitting for hours, watching her sleep, wondering almost to the point of panic why she was in a trance when she was supposed to be squirming all over the house in labor pains.

After Lynx focused on a few intense pushes, Merlin slipped casually into the world, and immediately looked sharply into their eyes, first into Lynx's, then Gwen's, then Lou's. His look sent shivers up their spines. It was the look of an ancient wise man, a wizard, a sage. This was no ordinary Gerber baby.

"I'm here, and you're the people I will love first and always, but there is something really important for me to do here," the look said.

It was 10:15 in the morning, and the light poured into the southern window over the place where Merlin was born. His skin was covered with a silvery powdery substance that none of them had read about in the numerous books on birth they'd studied. They'd expected a lot of blood, a screaming infant, and an exhausted mother.

Lou and Gwen cut Merlin's umbilical cord, and Lynx pushed out the placenta, which they later buried under an aspen sapling they dug out of the forest. Lou put Merlin on Lynx's chest. He zoned right in on her left breast and began to nurse.

Lynx looked at their newly expanded family, expecting to see a glow of love and peace around them. They had a son and a brother. They had brought him into the world together. No doctors, nurses, no drugs, no hospital. Merlin was a totally planned child, from conception to birth. Lynx had given his formation all of her focus, eating pure food, exercising every day, and making him the center of her spiritual meanderings. She'd taken him to her secret places in the forest and along the rivers and streams, stood naked in the sun, so he could feel its light and warmth, and in the rivers, so he could feel the power of the living water.

Lynx did not see what she expected to see. Gwen was aglow, watching her mother nurse her new brother, relieved that both were healthy. It was Lou who shot an arrow into Lynx's heart at one of the most profound moments of her life. He was watching her and Merlin, and his eyes were dark, unfocused, and crazy.

Lynx probed his mind and heard the voice of a troubled soul say, "I don't want a son."

It wasn't Lou's voice. Its tone was sharp and shrill, with a touch of panic. Pain and shock rippled across Lou's face. He'd heard it, too. He composed himself and walked into the kitchen to open a bottle of wine they'd saved for the occasion.

Lynx knew at that moment that whatever darkness she had seen in Lou would someday destroy their family.

Although she prayed that it would not happen, it did. Lou became clinically depressed. Lynx had heard of women getting post partem depression, but not men. Lou wanted to stay in bed all day. Thoughts raced through his head so he could not sleep or eat. He demanded Lynx's complete attention, something she could not give him because she had to deal with Merlin and Gwen.

Lynx became exhausted. Merlin nursed every three or four hours around the clock. He rarely slept, and when he was awake, he was full of energy. She was sure he was absorbing Lou's negative vibes.

Finally, Lou went to a doctor and got medication that made the intruding thoughts go away, and in two months, the depression lifted. It was replaced by hyper-mania. Lou talked constantly and forced Lynx to listen to him. If she tried to be alone or be quiet, he would get angry and more demanding.

The doctor sent him to a psychiatrist who told him he had bipolar affective disorder with schizophrenia during his manic stage, at the hyper, extroverted pole, and depression when he swung to the opposite pole. The shrink said it was caused by an imbalance of the salt lithium in his central nervous system. He said the imbalance may have been caused by the stress of having a child, by being hit with the reality of having a son and having to become a father. It was complicated by the fact that Lou had had a very combative relationship with his own father, Sam, who had been incredibly handsome, well built, athletic, and successful in business. He had been a World War II bomber pilot in Europe and a community leader in the small New England town he'd settled in after the war. Lou always felt he had to compete with Sam, and he simply could not. Sam was 50 years old when he died of cancer. Perhaps if he had lived, the conflict would have been resolved as Lou eventually figured out what was going on and either found healthy ways to outdo his father, or accepted their differences and shortcomings, and found a way to accept and love himself.

Instead, Lou was threatened by Merlin's existence and dealt with it by trying to have total control over him. He wanted Merlin to love him more than anyone else. He competed for Merlin's attention and for Lynx's attention so she could not spend time with her own son.

"I feed you better than Mommy does," he would say as he shoveled baby cereal into Merlin's face.

"I took Merlin for a walk today," he would tell Lynx when she got home from the news reporter job she had to take when Merlin was three. Lou would not work more than three hours a day because he had to be with Merlin all the time. "And he told me he likes to walk with me more than with you."

If Lynx picked Merlin up and sat him on her lap to read him a story,

Lou would lift him out of her arms and say, "Mommy is a lousy reader. She reads too fast so you can't hear the words. I'll read to you."

Lynx began to withdraw into herself and spend as much time as possible away from the house, living for the four hours a day Lou was away at this part-time janitor job. She took the hotel job, where she met Jack, in addition to reporting, and after a few years, left the hotel to become a fly fishing guide at one of the town's larger tackle shops. By now, Merlin was six years old, Gwen fifteen, and the family was highly dysfunctional. Besides lithium, Lou was taking an anti-depressant, a muscle relaxer, and a mood elevator. He also drank two to three six packs of beer a day. The pills and booze made him sexually impotent, which was fine as far as Lynx was concerned. She was beginning to resent him. In her mind she called him Lucifer the Destroyer. He had undermined their family and made it impossible to have any peace and happiness. She stayed because she had vowed to stay when she married him, and she believed in keeping her word. But she was lonely and tired and constantly fighting depression and despair.

Then she fell in head over heels, fireworks love, with Sherwood, one of the guides at the tackle shop, and after much soul searching, she had a full-fledged affair with him.

Sherwood was in graduate school 2,000 miles away and had taken the West Yellowstone job for the summer to get away from his wife. He had two children and a third on the way. He, too, believed that although their marriage was an empty void because his wife was an alcoholic, he had given her his word and he loved his kids. Lynx and Sherwood talked of getting together every few months until both their kids got older. When he went back home, they called and wrote, but it was too depressing a reminder that each was miserable at home. They decided to give one another up. And maybe someday they would see one another again. In his last letter, Sherwood wrote, "I go outside and chop wood or fool around in the garden and stand up, look West, and shout your name. I will always love you, always miss you."

Lynx felt genuinely lonely for the first time in her life. She still often dreamed of Sherwood when she fell asleep at night.

At the time of the affair, Gwen was in a typical 15-year-old wild stage, coming home late, getting bad grades, talking back when she was asked to help around the house. When Lynx tried to deal with her, to get her to take more responsibility for her actions, to calm down and get her schoolwork done, Lou undermined her. He told Gwen not to listen to Lynx, told her to do whatever she wanted, told her she wasn't grounded when Lynx grounded her for getting a ticket for careless driving and possession of alcohol.

Things grew worse. The school counselor told Lou and Lynx that he had learned that Gwen was drinking heavily after school and on weekends. He asked them to send her to counseling and to a weekend Alcoholics Anonymous workshop in Bozeman for teenagers.

Lou told the counselor to mind his own business and go to hell. The counselor told him to leave the room. He asked Lynx if she thought that Lou and Gwen were having sex.

Lynx froze in terror, all the pain of her own incest crushing her to the bone.

"Look, you have to look at this and stop denying the truth. Your daughter and your husband are alcoholics. He is mentally ill. He is her stepfather. Stepfathers and uncles head the list of child molesters, did you know that? They're drinking together. Boundaries dissolve in situations like this, especially since they are forming a mini enemy community to sabotage any efforts you make to help Gwen get through being a teenager. If nothing has happened between them yet, it could, and what is happening, the drinking and rebellion towards you, is unhealthy because they are doing it as a unit. If sex hasn't happened, be glad, but don't think it won't. You need to get some help. And what about Merlin?"

Merlin was acting out his hatred of the disorder in the house with some pretty scary obsessive behavior that Lou rewarded with compliments and encouragement. Several times a day, he took all his books and toys and lined them up from one end of the house to the other in a special order he had designed in his own mind. Lynx did not think this was cute, but Lou and Gwen actually joked about it.

Merlin would not go to sleep at night without checking his line-up, and sometimes he got up in the middle of the night to make sure everything was still there.

It was obvious to Lynx that he was trying to bring order into his world. Something had to be done, but she knew that Lou would assault her if she brought it up, get Gwen to tell her she was a lousy mother, and get Merlin to think she would make him stop lining up his things. The counselor agreed that Merlin was exhibiting symptoms of a very confused person and suggested that he receive counseling, too.

Lynx left his office and drove to a favorite fishing hole in the Madison River. No trout were rising. She tied a small dry fly to her tippet anyway and cast it upstream into a riffle downstream from a large rock, again and again, far too many times. If a fish was there, it wasn't going to go for the fly. Still she kept casting.

"Ah, but I may as well try and catch the wind," she sang, wondering whose song it was—Dylan, Donovan, Peter Paul and Mary. She couldn't remember.

She couldn't think, feel, breathe. She sat down and made herself calm down. She prayed to the Spirit for help, reminded Him that Gwen and Merlin are beautiful children, begged Him to give them a way out, to give them peace.

A trout rose in the very hole she had worked so fruitlessly, and she cast her fly to it. He took it and ran downstream. A cutthroat, she thought, by the nonchalant feel of his tug.

She let him run a minute, and then began reeling him in. A three pounder, she guessed as she unhooked the fly from his lip and slipped him back into the river.

She saw the trout as a sign. The water had appeared empty and then she prayed. And the fish rose. It could be a sign that things would work out if she kept casting and praying for peace.

Then the shit hit the fan. Lynx came home late one afternoon after an exhausting day of collecting news stories and dealing with fly fishermen who were bitching about not catching fish. Merlin was playing in the yard with some of his friends. Lou and Gwen were in the kitchen drinking beer. They were both drunk and laughing loudly.

"What's going on here?" Lynx asked.

"Oh, Mom, you are really being an asshole now, aren't you?" Gwen shot back.

"She's always an asshole," Lou said. "She can't stand to see us have any fun." He put his arm around Gwen and kissed her on the mouth.

Lynx's heart nearly stopped. She saw the counselor's face, heard his warning words, and her guts felt as if they had been scraped raw.

Had he touched her? Why is he drinking with her? She thought, "God, help me get through this."

Lynx stayed calm and acted as if nothing had been said, as if her daughter and husband were not getting drunk together in the middle of their kitchen, as if he hadn't kissed Gwen hard on the mouth.

She cooked dinner and got Merlin to bed, then waited until Lou took the dog for her evening walk.

Gwen was in her room listening to Prince and drinking black coffee while she read a book.

"Honey, we have to talk."

"Not now, Mom, I'm tired."

"Yes, now, let me just ask you a question or two, please." Lynx turned the music off, and Gwen shot her a resentful look.

"Shoot."

"Do you think it's a good idea that you drink?"

"Lou drinks. He drinks all day."

"Lou is an adult. You are a kid. When a kid drinks this young, chances are that she will have an alcohol problem. You know this Gwen. I'm not making this up. You learned this in health class at school."

"Yeah, but I can quit."

"Do you think it helps the situation any when you drink with Lou?"

"He says it's better I drink with him than with my friends in cars and stuff."

"What do you think? Is it uncomfortable for you at all?"

Gwen grew silent. She would not look at Lynx.

Gwen shuffled the pages of her book. "Kind of. I think sometimes he makes me drink to piss you off. And I like pissing you off. I can't help it. I know it's my age and everything. I really do know I'm wrong to do it."

"Thank God," Lynx thought, "she has a mind and can use it. She has feelings for me."

"Gwen, I don't bite most of the time when you try to piss me off. I know its hormones and testing the waters of adulthood and all that. But this drinking thing is going too far, especially when you drink with Lou. I'm afraid to say anything because he will try to line you up against me. But I have faith that you know I am concerned about you. Please think about it."

"Okay, Mom, I'll tone it down. I know you were very upset today."

"Gwen, I was hurt. And I'm worried about something else. You have to tell me—has Lou ever molested you?"

There, she'd popped the question. Direct, to the point. "Has he molested you. Please tell me," she thought.

Gwen looked away again. "Mom, that's crazy. No. He hasn't." She tugged at her hair.

"Then why don't you look at me when you answer? You're uncomfortable about something."

"Yeah, I guess I am. I think he thinks about it. I think he looks at me like the boys at school who want to get into my pants look at me. And he always tells me how close we are, yet I don't feel that close to him."

"What did you feel when he kissed you on the mouth today?"

"It was gross. And he was using me to piss you off. He was angry because before you came home, Merlin was crying for you."

"Why was Merlin crying?"

"Oh, he just misses you sometimes. I calm him down."

"What did Lou do?"

"Mom, Lou always tells Merlin you work because you don't like us and don't want to be around us. I know it's a lie, that we need the money."

Shock, hurt, and anger welled inside her. How could he do this to them? "Okay, Gwen, give me some time to think about this, and just stop drinking, please. Promise?"

"All right, Mom, I promise you I'll quit drinking with him, but I may have a beer or two with my friends. I don't think I have a problem."

"We'll drop it for now," Lynx said, trying to keep from crying. "Good night, honey."

"Mom, you can't tell Lou about this talk. He'll blow up. He tells me not to tell you anything we talk about. He says he's my real dad because he's been with us for eight years. Mom, it really sucks. Other families aren't like this."

"I know, honey, and something is going to have to change. Don't worry, but if he touches you, tell me immediately."

"Night, Mom."

Lynx waited until Lou was fully into his nightly sleeping pill and beer-and-drug-induced stupor before going downstairs. She sat up all night, thinking and planning how she would put an end to the madness. By first light, she knew. She would get a divorce. Nothing would change unless she took the kids and left. He'd vowed to love and cherish her. Instead he was giving her and the kids emotional and spiritual pain and would neither admit it or heal it. His word was meaningless. He was a sick man, and she twinged with guilt about deserting him. But he couldn't be so sick that he could not somehow, if he wanted, stop the part of his madness that was destroying her and the kids.

Lynx shook off the bad memories of Lou and stared at the blank page of her planning notebook. She started a list of things to do to get ready to open the museum: get in touch with last year's staff and offer to re-hire them, get a temporary person to remove the shutters from the windows, plow away any remaining snow, rake the lawn, wax the floors. She thought about living history presentations and movies that would go with the new exhibit on Yellowstone's bears and other Yellowstone themes. She made a list of people to call for help with that, and she made a note to call all the book dealers the next day and start ordering titles for the bookstore.

She fell asleep thinking of a time she and Sherwood went hot potting in Yellowstone park and made love in the swirling water under the light of a full moon.

Chapter Five

Anton Devier pulled down the black shade that covered the large window in his mobile home's video studio. It made the studio pitch black, except for the small colored lights on the editing deck, analog image processor, VCR's, and four SONY 27-inch color monitors. He filled his brass pipe with a hearty pinch of the seedless Humboldt County grown pot he had picked up in the mail that day and took two deep puffs. He lounged on the queen-sized, video-viewing, sleeping platform he had finished making a few days before and hit the remote control.

For the next three hours, he watched the videotape he had made of an elk hunt near Montana's Paradise Valley, making notes as to what tape he would most likely put in the final edit. It looked good. It would be a major work, he felt, one that would impress Lynx. She would give it a good review in the *Gazette*'s art and entertainment section, show it in the museum theater, sell it in the bookstore, and maybe help him get it distributed all over the Yellowstone area, if not the nation.

Anton loaded his pipe again and took another deep puff. He turned on the desk lamp attached to his kitchen table and opened a thick file that laid there. It was full of carefully cut clippings of Lynx's news articles, going back five years. Also in the file were magazine features she had written on Yellowstone topics, articles reviewing her photography exhibits, reviews of videotapes she had made for public television, brochures on the museum, and clippings from various local papers announcing all the activities Lynx scheduled at the museum's theater and outdoor arena last summer. Lynx was obviously brilliant, creative, and multi-faceted, with a warehouse of wisdom on the Yellowstone area.

Anton had never met Lynx and had no idea what she looked like, how old she was, or if she was married and had kids. All he knew was that he needed her. He'd heard her name at an art opening in a gallery at the top of the mountain the first week he'd moved to Big Sky. The gallery owner had said he was disappointed that Lynx had not come to the opening to review the show by a landscape painter whom he hoped would become more well known. Anton asked why it was so important that Lynx review the show. The owner had explained that she was one of the few people in the media who could write intelligently and fairly about art, so that when a show received her blessing, the artwork inevitably sold well.

He had mentioned that Lynx was also an excellent photographer and videographer, whose own work was always well reviewed, and that she ran West Yellowstone's museum.

For the next six months, Anton collected all the information he could find on her, and he felt as if he knew her quite well. It was time to meet her. He made the viewing/sleeping platform in the middle of his studio for her to sit on when she reviewed his work. And now the opportunity was here. He read the clipping at the top of the pile:

"The Museum of Yellowstone Culture in West Yellowstone will open on Memorial Day weekend for the summer season. The museum staff is looking for videos, films, and dramatic acts with Yellowstone and Indian themes, particularly relating to bears, the topic of this year's special exhibit. Contact Lynx at 646-9998."

He'd left a message on her answering machine that he had a videotape nearly done on elk and that he was a video consultant who could go over the museum's AV equipment to make sure it was in fine working order.

She had returned his call, but he had been in Bozeman buying groceries and a month's supply of Sherman's cigarettes, which he special ordered from a small news and tobacco store.

Anton rewound his answering machine and listened to her pleasant, businesslike voice.

"Hi, Anton, I got your message and would like to meet with you to discuss your video and possibly see if you can help with our equipment. Call me back after 9 p.m. tonight, if it isn't too late."

It was 8:45. In 15 minutes, he would launch the first phase of his plan.

Merlin was in his bedroom playing Nintendo, something he was allowed to do a total of five hours a week. Lynx listened to a John Prine tape that didn't quite drown out the electronic game noise she detested as she packed the things he would need to spend the weekend at Lou's.

"Every time you click a Kodak pic, you steal a little bit of soul," Prine sang. Prine so often sang songs that she related to perfectly. She was always very careful about photographing people, and even animals, because she believed that you could steal a person's soul with the wrong photograph, sometimes with any photo at all.

She gathered the camping and fishing gear for her trip to the Beartrap. She half listened for the phone, wanting to pick it up when this Anton character who had left a message earlier called so he didn't get her canned message again.

She had an odd feeling about him that her normally perceptive mind could not identify. His voice was strong, powerful, resonant, like a coked up DJ on a hip FM station. It was intriguing, but it made her nervous.

The phone rang at 9:00 sharp.

"Hello," she answered.

"Lynx, this is Anton. So nice to hear your real voice after playing phone tag with you."

"Yeah, sure. Hi. So, I guess by your telephone prefix you live in Big Sky?"

"Yes, in the trailer park by Snowdrift Village. I guess I'm around 50 miles from you."

"Lived there long?"

"Just under a year. I took an early retirement from the San Francisco Art Institute, where I was in charge of the video department, to come here and make independent videotapes and get out of the rat race."

"So what exactly is your tape about—elk, I know, but their history, hunting, what?"

"How about I come down and show it to you? I can take a look at your projection equipment, too, if you would like."

She appreciated his enthusiasm, and the equipment did need work. "Let's do it," Lynx said. "How about lunch Monday?"

"Where do I pick you up?"

"You'll find me at the museum. I'll be ordering books for the season. Come in the back door."

"How's noon?"

"Make it an hour later because the restaurants aren't as crowded then."

Anton wanted to keep her on the line and find out more about her. Her voice was sweet, friendly, open, electric. But he knew he'd better stay cool and remain as business-like as possible.

"Okay, then, Lynx, I look forward to meeting you."

Lynx hung up the phone, shivers pulsating up and down her spine like an LSD-induced body rush. There was something about his voice . . .

She put it aside. "Okay, Merlin, shut 'er down and get a move on, time to go to your dad's."

"Come on, Mom, let me finish this game. I'm beating my highest score."

"You have ten minutes. I'll wait for you outside. I'll be on the porch. It's nice and warm outside."

Lynx sat on the top step of her porch, which faced southwest to a view of the snow-covered rocky peaks of the Centennial Mountains, the Great Divide, the spine of the continent, where they formed the Idaho-Montana border. She searched for the mountains near where they would be camping, but it was too dark to pick out individual peaks, so she watched the stars twinkle and listened to a feisty spring breeze rattle the overgrown patch of wild rose bushes at the northern end of the yard. A diehard robin gave its last speech of the day.

She was tired of living in town and had made up her mind to move over to the other side of the Divide, to Henry's Lake in Idaho, just 15 miles away, or at least to buy a small cabin retreat over there. West Yellowstone was getting too noisy and crowded for her. Around 1,000 people now lived in the 400-acre town, compared to barely 700 when she moved there 15 years ago. And there were hundreds of people living in the outlying areas of town near Duck Creek and Hebgen Lake and Lionhead Mountain. Years ago at least half the population left town shortly after Labor Day and did not return until Memorial Day. Now, more and more people stayed to run businesses during the busy snowmobile season.

Lynx was part of a growing faction in town who hated snowmobiles. They were noisy and smelly and out of place in the wilderness. They were, however, the backbone of the town's winter economy, although they made only a handful of people wealthy. She loved any opportunity to write stories that told the world the problems snowmobiles were creating in Yellowstone, hoping that someday the general public who loved the park would call for change. Her editors had loved the snowmachine seat-eating grizzly bear story and held it a day until she could send up photos up of the damaged machines. They would run it on the front page, and it had been picked up by the Associated Press wire service. The paper had received some letters questioning why the park allows snowmobiles if there is any chance at all that their presence would harm a grizzly bear. But Lynx knew that it would take much more than a few concerned people to change the park's winter use policy.

Merlin appeared at the door, his duffel bag draped over his shoulder. "I beat my score, Mom!"

"Great, and probably gave yourself brain and nerve damage in the process. Now let's boogie." Lynx could be nothing but abrupt when it came to electronic games. She believed they were taking over children's minds, messing with their blood sugar levels, giving them early onslaught diabetes, and permanently damaging their neck and arm nerves.

Lou was sitting on his porch playing his guitar to a Bob Dylan tape when they drove up. He kept playing, nodded to Merlin, and handed Lynx a mandolin. "Finish this one with me, Lynx."

The tune was "Every Grain of Sand."

She took his old Gibson mandolin and played and sang harmony. Dylan moved her. She couldn't think of a song he sang that she didn't like. His words were often depressing and bitter and sometimes made no sense at all. Her favorite songs were his uplifting, spiritual ones. His songs reflected a lifetime of changes in his personal life, but always there was a commitment to tell a story and express deep feelings and beliefs.

The happiest memories of her relationship with Lou were of playing and singing together, and it pleased Merlin to see them get along that way. She knew Lou met her with a mandolin in his hand to make Merlin relax about the weekend. He was showing them he was trying, was feeling okay at the moment anyway. She appreciated that.

"Come in and have a beer," he said. "I'm sorry I was so nasty on your answering machine. I was late taking my meds."

"Nah, I have to get home to bed. Patsy is picking me up early."

"All right, then have a good weekend. I'll get the kid off to school Monday morning so you can sleep in, and he'll go to your house after school."

She kissed Merlin good-bye. "You should come in and talk with Dad," he whispered.

Dylan was still playing. She could drink the beer and play a few more tunes. But he would go psycho on her after that, she knew, and probably start an argument about how she was bringing up Merlin. It wasn't worth it.

"No, honey, I have to go. I love you. Behave yourself."

Chapter Six

The Little Boys and Spotted Elks arrived at the Beartrap on Friday and set up the teepee and sweat lodge. One of the teepees belonged to Lynx, and they kept it for her over the winter while they repaired some small tears in the canvas and touched up the paint. It was a Shoshone-Bannock style teepee, decorated with a brown bear painting, Crow Indian symbols for the four directions, and the logo of the Sweetgrass Society, a bundle of sweetgrass surrounded by three circles representing the Creator, His son, and the Great Spirit. It was normally used only for meetings and ceremonies, but Lynx and Patsy would sleep in it.

Lynx's uncle, a Jesuit, had met Nora Spotted Elk in Montana more than 50 years ago and been adopted by the Spotted Elk family. Nora and her family were Crow Indians who had never lived on the reservation, preferring to make their way in life without having to relate to the Bureau of Indian Affairs and the complicated nuances of Crow politics.

When Lynx moved to Montana, she looked Nora up, and they became close friends. Nora was a medicine woman and a council member of the Sweetgrass Society. Sweetgrass is a secret society of medicine people from every Indian tribe in North America and several in Mexico and South America. Its purpose is to pray for the spiritual unity of the Indian people so they can lead the world in its quest for peace and harmony.

Nora, who believed Lynx was gifted with healing and leadership powers, adopted her into the Spotted Elk family and sponsored her membership in the Sweetgrass Society, which allowed non-Indians who are adopted into Indian families.

The council that year had addressed the growing belief in groups all over the planet that the world was reaching the end times, the apocalyptic second coming of Jesus Christ, the destruction of the world. Some Plains Indians predicted that in a few years a pure white buffalo calf would be born, and its father would die shortly afterward signaling that the calf was sacred, a manifestation of the mystical White Buffalo Woman who would unite all people and bring peace to the earth.

Nora and a few others had called the growing obsession with the end of the world "Millennium Madness," an evolving planetary mass hysteria as the year 2,000 grows closer. Was the belief that the world was ending making people not care about taking care of the earth, sort of creating a universal lame duck spirit?

Or could it be used to encourage people to take better care of the planet? Nora believed people create their own reality with their thoughts, so their thoughts should be connected to God. She noted that God has told humankind that only He knows when Jesus will come back and that He is most interested in helping people live good lives, not making them fret about when their lives will end. Nora advised the council to validate the reality that the evil in the world was growing, but to acknowledge that it could be defeated and the earth and its people could be healed.

Nora noted that in recent years more and more white people were listening to Indians speak of the need to love the earth and seek harmony between plants, animals, and people, to keep the air and water clean, and to see the spiritual side of nature. She said the Great Spirit was giving white people Indian medicine because Indians must team up with all people to heal the earth. And she warned against the negativity of many Indians towards white people, whom they called "wanna-be Indians."

Lynx was very quiet and secretive about her relationships with the Indians. She didn't want to be thought of as a wanna-be Indian or have her contacts with Indians used by business people who wanted to buy Indian art and crafts for low prices to re-sell to tourists at great profits. Lynx helped many of her Indian friends sell their art, but only if she could get a high price for it. Patsy was her only West Yellowstone friend who knew the depth of her involvement, and this was the first time she would accompany Lynx to a sweat.

The camp was in a circle of cottonwoods near a creek that flows into the Madison River at the mouth of the Beartrap Canyon, a Bureau of Land Management Primitive Area. A cook fire was burning near the sleeping teepees, and not far from that, Gerry and Bob Little Boy, Crees from northern Montana, were piling wood near the sweat lodge's fire pit. Seventy-six-year-old Nora was hunched over the cook fire, tending a frying pan full of trout and a large pot of coffee.

She reached her arms out to Lynx and gave her a big hug, her strength that of a 30-year old. Her face was crisscrossed with the creases of a person who thinks deeply and smiles often. Harry Spotted Elk, Nora's son, walked into camp with a huge chunk of cottonwood for carving. His wife, Sally Afraid of Bear followed with their twin 18-year olds, Joe and Al.

"So happy you came, Sally said to Lynx and Patsy. "I didn't want to be the only woman here besides Nora."

"Who else is about?" Lynx asked.

"My cousins, Gill and Sol. They were up before dawn and caught this batch of fish for breakfast. Now they're upstream looking for rabbits."

The Afraid of Bears were Shoshones from Idaho. Nora's camps always included Indians from different tribes. In recent years, medicine people had been forced to intermingle more to ensure that their knowledge and ceremonies were preserved and available to all Indians. Medicine wasn't as accepted or utilized on the reservations as it once was, especially the spirit-oriented medicine of the Spotted Elks, Little Boys, and Afraid of Bears.

Many Indians had turned away from the Great Spirit, crushed by the bleak reality of poverty and despair that hung like a dark cloud over most Indian communities, the overdevelopment of the land they were once so connected to, and epidemic level alcohol and drug abuse on reservations near big cities like Billings, Montana, and Pocatello, Idaho. Reservation towns were peppered with Pentecostal churches that reduced the Great Spirit to little more than a dime store prophet, such as those found at the end of 900 numbers. And the reservations were becoming more and more crowded with white anthropologists who thought they knew everything there is to know about Indians and who encouraged Indians to hold onto their so-called culture and not learn anything new to help them live more positively.

Sally invited Lynx and Patsy to her family's teepee where all the bedrolls were neatly rolled up for sitting on. She took her current sewing project out of an ancient deerskin woman's sewing bag. It was a green-white-and-black-beaded, turtle-shaped medicine bag she was making to hold her younger sister's soon-to-be-born baby's placenta.

Sally talked softly as the women admired her work. "Reggie wanted so much to come to this sweat, but she could go into labor anytime. I should really be back there with her, but she insisted I come. She knows I need to get away. Harry's been drinking every day, and he needs to clean out. We argue when he drinks, and he gets so damn negative and hostile. He's really whizzed about the artifacts at the museum in Bozeman. They will not return them to the tribe. He wants to rip them off. I say he should go to the Tribal Council and get an attorney to sue for them. He is tired of playing the game with the university's anthro department and tired of teaching 100-level courses when he wants to do research." Harry was an instructor at Montana State University in Bozeman.

"Yeah, I've noticed that Harry gets hostile when he drinks too much, but at least he knows he needs to stop," Lynx told her as she played with a handful of the tiny glass beads. "He spends time like this and gets it together. Be grateful. He's a good man."

"Shit, I know that. With me and Nora nagging him onto the path he's supposed to be on, he can't stray too far."

"So what's the plan?" Lynx asked. "Looks like if we're eating soon we won't be holding a sweat ceremony today. Am I right?"

Nora stuck her head into the teepee and told them breakfast was ready.

"We're coming, Grandmother," Sally said in Crow, which she was learning from Nora. She turned to Lynx.

"We're going to sweat both days. Nora has a prayer to say before we eat the trout. Then we start our fast. Then we're supposed to get the sweat fire going and stay in the sweat lodge all afternoon and think and pray about certain things she will ask us to focus on. Tonight we can do whatever we want, but I expect we'll all hang out around the campfire. Tomorrow at dawn we go into the sweat lodge again and smoke the medicine grass. Again we will have specific things to focus on, and we could be in there all day or a few hours, depending on how it goes.

an Our Father. And I don't have visions. I'm not very spiritual. If it wasn't for Lynx, I would be a totally shallow person. She's shown me the importance of spirituality, but I'm just beginning to think about doing some of the things she talks about, like praying and fasting and coming here."

"Lynx is a good friend, Patsy. She brought you here because she knows you are in need of God."

"Then shouldn't I be inside, where all the heavy stuff will happen?"

"No, actually you were chosen to be here to learn how to serve and protect the people who will help and strengthen you. If you have been leading a rather shallow life, there's no better way to deepen your awareness of the spiritual than to serve others. Look. The fire is coals, and they are putting the rocks in it. Do you have any more questions before we begin?"

Patsy liked Nora's straight arrow approach. "No, I'm okay. Let's go. And thank you." She hugged Nora.

Harry put on thick leather gloves and carried the rocks to the lodge. The people took their places around the circle. Nora pulled the buffalo hide covering over the entry way and sprinkled the rocks with the blessed water. They hissed and filled the lodge with steam.

Nora lifted her arms and prayed silently as each person got centered and calm. She spoke the opening words.

"Father, we are here to welcome the spring and remind ourselves who we are and where we are going. Each of us you have blessed with strong medicine. We open ourselves to you if you wish to make our medicine stronger. We are here to review our visions, the visions that led us here to this moment."

Nora looked around at her people. "Let's do this now silently. Think of the time of your vision. Review it in great detail as I pray for you to remember it clearly. Renew your resolve to keep the vision the center of your lives so it guides you on your path."

The hot steam began to release the oils in the lodge's willow branch walls and Lynx inhaled the sweet smell as she closed her eyes and returned to the place of her vision.

Nora and Harry had been her guides. It was just a year ago. They camped and fasted together three days at the base of one of the Tobacco Root Mountains not far from Virginia City, Montana, and then at first light of the fourth day, Lynx climbed alone, weak and emotionally emptied from three days without food and only the most necessary talk, to the top of one of the mountains.

There was no trail to follow, so she climbed slowly, stopping often to catch her breath and pray for strength from the Spirit, her only source of strength now that her body was drained of food energy.

There was no doubt in her mind that she would have a vision. The decision to seek one was actually the beginning of the vision, Nora had explained. It had taken Lynx a long time to agree to the vision quest. She felt unworthy of taking time away from Nora, who was always so focused on praying for her community and the wider world. Yet she knew that Nora was her guide and that Harry was there to protect them from any intrusion by people.

Lynx knew that it was time to go a step further on her spiritual journey. In her daily prayer and meditation and Tai Chi, in her weekly Catholic Mass, she had begun to feel there was something she had to learn about and that it would be uncovered only if she went into a retreat mode of some kind. She had shared this restlessness with Nora, who had encouraged her to seek a vision.

"For me you must have this vision, as well," Nora had said, "to confirm my belief that you should become part of us."

"I'm just so uncomfortable with being a part of the Sweetgrass Society. I'm white. I don't know, Nora, I just don't know."

Nora had glared at her. It was the look she gave anyone who said they didn't know. Nora believed that we all know if we open ourselves to the knowledge.

Lynx rephrased her doubts. "Okay, I know I have to be doing something more than I'm doing."

"That's better. Now make the commitment."

And she had. The three preparatory days showed her that it was the right thing to do. She felt on edge, excited yet centered, ready for the Spirit to show her how to proceed on her journey.

Near the top of the mountain she found a grove of pine trees. She made her camp there and built a small fire circle from rocks gathered higher up. She used her Buck knife to chop dead pine branches from the trees for firewood.

She climbed to the top of the mountain and sat facing the wind, which was blowing strongly from the northwest. She became one with the wind, feeling its power, sharing its memories of slowly smoothing down the mountain rocks, touching leaves until they fell from trees, ruffling the fur of animals until they shivered and ran for cover, and breaking the smooth surface of glassy mountain lakes. She felt its coldness, felt how it overpowered the warmth of the setting sun. She smelled the salt it carried from the ocean and the aspen smoke from Nora and Harry's fire.

The setting sun transformed the puffy white clouds on the horizon into flames of yellow, orange, and gold. The rocks that surrounded her reflected their colors in quick hot sparks and then turned cold and colorless. A quartet of ravens coasted below her on the last thermal of the day and disappeared into the valley. She had a great desire to sleep, so climbed down to her camp and crawled into her sleeping bag without starting a fire. She laid on her back and watched the stars come out until she fell asleep.

Lynx awoke to what she first thought was the sound of a snorting pig, opened her eyes, and saw a nearly full moon the color of white satin. She remembered where she was and listened for the snort again. It was getting closer, and it couldn't be a pig. Not in these mountains, miles from ranch land. It was from something very big, something so heavy she could feel its weight shake the ground slightly downhill from her.

She sat up on her elbows and looked toward the sound, forcing herself to breathe deeply and wait. As soon as she moved, the critter stopped walking and snorting. She could feel it seek her out in the moonlight and stare at her, and then she saw its huge dark form. A bear, a very large bear, too large to be a black bear. It started walking toward her again, and Lynx saw the faces of her children on the days they were born and knew that it was not her time to die: Merlin and Gwen still needed her.

The bear came closer, and Lynx took a deep breath and held it. It was carrying something in its mouth, and she strained to see it. The bear halted again, within ten feet of her, and sniffed loudly at the same time it dropped whatever was in its mouth. It took another step toward Lynx, and she saw a glistening, dark beady eye staring at her. It was indeed a grizzly bear, with a silvery gray ring of hairs like a collar around its huge neck.

"I mean you no harm, so please go away now," Lynx told it in a soft, deep voice. The bear stood its ground and continued to stare at her, moving its head from side to side very slowly, so she saw both its eyes several times. It seemed to be telling her something. It seemed to speak to her of its power. It told her that it would not hurt her. She felt its aloneness, knowing it was far from the places where most grizzly bears were seen these days. Perhaps it was there seeking a vision, too.

"Yes, yes," the bear seemed to reply. "I need protectors. For years, the bear has given people power. Now we need your help." The voice was deep and loud in her head.

Lynx talked back, all her fear gone, feelings of profound love and empathy flooding her being. "You have it," she whispered. "I will do all I can to protect you."

The bear stepped toward her, and then turned in a full circle, glanced at her again, made a half circle, and walked away.

Lynx looked in the bear's direction for a long time, saying a silent prayer of thanksgiving, and then remembered it had dropped something on the ground. She crawled out of her sleeping bag to look for it and found it easily. It was a quart size Ziploc bag. She held it in the moonlight and saw that it was full of granola bars. It wasn't from Nora and Harry's camp, she knew. The bear had probably raided a forest service campground down the mountain, some eight miles away. The bars smelled fresh and reminded Lynx of her hunger, so she quickly re-sealed the bag and stashed it in her pack, which she was using as a pillow. She started a fire.

As she stared into the flames of her campfire, Lynx breathed slowly and deeply, letting the reality of the bear's visit overtake her. Any encounter with a grizzly bear could be a fatal experience. If the bear had been hungry or hostile, it may have mauled her and eaten her. Where had it gotten the granola bars? Did it know they were food, and if so, why hadn't it eaten them? Had the bear torn someone else's camp apart or ripped the food from the discarded backpack of a frightened hiker? She imagined the bloody, torn up bodies of people somewhere down the trail. And what was the bear doing here, anyway? Grizzly sightings were very rare in this area.

Lynx thought of what would happen to the bear if the game managers found out it had raided someone's camp. It would be searched out, drugged, and removed to a more remote area of the ecosystem, maybe to deep within Yellowstone Park, some 100 miles away. Did she have a moral obligation to report the bear's visit, especially since it had carried human food so was therefore a "problem bear" that may be too habituated to people? How would she feel if she did not report it and the bear became more bold toward people and someone was hurt or killed?

She dug out the bag and examined it in the firelight. The bear's teeth had made small punctures in it. The granola bars were not individually wrapped, so were probably homemade or purchased at a bakery. Most likely the people the bear raided had reported the incident.

This was a good story for the paper, Lynx realized. But wait a minute, this was happening on her vision quest. Was there a reason for that? Had the bear really spoken to her? Had it understood her reply? Had it really been there?

Lynx clicked off her journalistic thinking and stoked the fire. She stared into the flames and surrendered herself to the Great Spirit. She knew many vision quests ended when a seeker had an experience with an animal and that that animal became the seeker's power animal. Lynx had already accepted that the grizzly bear, bald eagle, lynx, and trumpeter swans were her main power animals. Excepting the lynx, these were the most threatened animals in the Yellowstone ecosystem, the ones she wrote about most often. She already had a lot of bear, swan, and eagle medicine—bear claws and teeth, photos and paintings, swan and eagle feathers—she found on her many trips to the wilderness to watch and photograph animals.

Medicine objects, she had learned, were symbolic reminders of the qualities of the animal that were also helpful qualities for humans to have: the fierceness of a bear protecting her children, the loyalty of trumpeter swans, who mate for life, the far-reaching vision of eagles, the sharp-sightedness of the lynx.

Lynx knew her news stories would help protect them by raising people's awareness of the trouble the animals were in, by educating people as to how human development and behavior are threatening the animals' lives. But any story she told of this night's bear visit would most likely cause the bear to be monitored by bear managers and eventually even killed. Their policy was to let a grizzly get into trouble three times, then put it to death.

Lynx switched off her journalist mind and surrendered to the Spirit again. As she had become the wind as the sun was setting, she became the bear. She followed it on its wanderings around the mountain and heard with its bear ears the distant sound of a truck shifting gears. It was miles away, but she could hear it, and she wondered what it was, knew it was something to be feared and avoided. She smelled the campfires all around her, heard the people snoring and stirring restlessly in their bedrolls. She became aware of all there was to be avoided and feared. It was all human, all a violation of her bear freedom, all demanding that she become what she could never be. She felt pressured and crowded and confused and aware that life would become even more difficult for her unborn children.

Lynx's bear mind touched Lynx's woman mind and saw Merlin and Gwen also crowded and pressured by the lack of freedom to just be that was growing all over the planet as more and more wilderness was eaten up and more and more animals and forests and plants were destroyed. Lynx felt the bear's spirit overcome with weariness and confusion, and she saw the bear's eye look into her and ask her for help. She owed the bear her life. She would tell no one about the bear's visit. It was the Indian way to not share details of a vision, and so not even Nora and Harry would know.

Lynx let the fire die and crawled back to her bed. She saw herself in the bear's mind's eye, knew the bear would never forget her smell and the sound of her voice, and knew the bear could smell her campfire at that very moment. She felt the power the bear still has, the raw physical ability to take the life of any human it desires to kill with one sweep of its giant paw. She felt its power to run swiftly, to bound across talus slopes as if they were groomed lawns, to rip open a bison carcass and devour most of it in a few hours, to lie so quietly in its day bed as to be undetected by a human walking within a few feet of it. She fell asleep seeing her bear visitor's eyes.

Lynx awoke minutes before first light and scrambled to the top of the mountain. She sat in the same spot she had the evening before and prayed for strength and grace to know what she was supposed to do for the bear. She saw the sun coming up behind a pine rimmed ridge across the valley, where she had hunted elk last fall. A trio of magpies flew by and landed somewhere behind her, nagging one another about something. A junco fluttered in front of her and landed a few feet away. A chickadee called, "Chick a dee-dee-dee," and another answered with the same song. The sky turned pink, and the birds talked incessantly as the pink turned to orange and the top of the sun hit the ridge. The rocks took on the sun's colors, and a cluster of flowering stonecrop near her feet turned yellow. The sun flared out from behind the ridge in a blinding gold ball, and all the colors came on. The trees below changed from black to dark green, and the sage covered valley from gray to pale green. A pack of coyotes barked and screamed and yodeled. Lynx listened with her bear ears and heard a mouse squeak and a bird take flight and then land on the ground below her. It was a raven squawking a welcome at the sun.

Lynx began to sing a song that entered her head, a song about freedom and flowing rivers and quiet winds, a song that recalled a time that had ended long ago and could only be found now in the spirit. The freedom song was not a melody played out in the policies of bear mangers and subdivision review offices, in the pages of a newspaper. It was in the human heart when that heart became the heart of the animals and the soul of the wilderness.

The sun was warm now. The flies were coming out, buzzing around Lynx's head. I would be a hot day, and the bear would sleep it away in the cool shade of pine trees on a north facing slope.

Lynx was tired, too. She walked back to camp and fell asleep.

She woke up hours later, when the sun was well along its western journey, and walked slowly around the camp on her hands and knees, looking for signs of the bear. She saw where it had walked into camp and turned in its circle, disturbing the thin layer of pine needles on the black earth. It had left no foot-prints, only tiny marks and scratches and the granola bag.

Lynx packed her things and walked down the mountain, spent, hungry, and suddenly missing Merlin badly.

Nora and Harry were bustling around camp, getting ready for the evening. They both saw Lynx at the same moment and walked toward her, smiling. Nora hugged her and said, "Welcome back. I know you have much to share with us. There's water and soap in my lodge. Go wash up, and we'll get you some food to break your fast. You can bring the thing you hunted, too, and we'll share that."

Nora's ability to know what happened to Lynx and others she served as a medicine woman no longer startled Lynx. Without missing a beat, she said, "Why, Nora, I do have food with me, but I didn't hunt it."

"Of course you did. There are many forms of hunting."

As she washed up, Lynx smelled the elk steaks Harry was turning on sticks over the fire, potatoes and coffee. She let herself be hungry, and it felt good. She was as hungry for the food as she was for the conversation she knew they would have about the essence of her vision. She put on a clean shirt of brain-tanned deerskin, trimmed at the collar and sleeves with stripes of blue and green glass beads, and clean jeans that hung loose on her after nearly five days of fasting. She brushed her hair until it shone and tied it back with a deerskin covered barrette, beaded with a red rose design.

Nora said a prayer of thanksgiving for Lynx's return and for Harry's success-ful hunt and her successful garden that had resulted in the food they were about to eat. They ate in silence, Lynx taking small bites and chewing each one slowly. Her gnawing hunger was satisfied in just a few bites.

Nora poured them each a cup of coffee and lit her medicine pipe, used only after the first meal that breaks a seeker's quest. It was loaded with a mixture of tobacco, sage, and sweetgrass.

Nora took her puff and said quietly, "So I see that you are now Brown Bear Woman. You know what freedom is and the cost when it is lost. You have a new song, taught you by the wind and the sun and the birds. I am proud of you."

Harry was looking at her, his eyes dancing with love and admiration. She returned them both the same look and grinned from ear to ear as she pulled out her granola bars and gave one to each of them. "Yes, that's my new name, and here's what I hunted. Probably the weirdest thing a seeker has brought back to you, and all I can tell you is that I didn't make them myself."

The granola bar was delicious and definitely homemade, with walnuts, rai-sins, tiny chunks of carob, and honey.

• • •

Lynx had been so focused on remembering her vision that she hadn't felt the sweat cover her body and make her shirt stick to her skin. She opened her eyes and looked around. Patsy was placing fresh rocks in the ring. Some people were still in deep meditation, others were watching Patsy.

Lynx smiled at Patsy and closed her eyes and thought of Nora's instruction that they renew their commitment to live their visions.

Ever since she became Brown Bear Woman, she had often traveled in spirit into the bear's mind and had written more often about the spirit of the bear. It showed in her writing, and the editors had at first given her a hard time about it. When she wrote about bears and bear policies, she often threw in a sentence or two about what she imagined to be the bear's point of view. Often she did this by asking bear experts what a bear's point of view would be in a given situation. Their first reaction was to shy away from the question, but most bear experts loved bears profoundly and had looked at life with bear eyes. The really science-oriented people were hesitant to antropomorphisize, but even they gave her good quotes about how it feels to work with bears. She had done similar things in writing about eagles and swans.

And she had started writing about what she called "biopolitics," the fact that humans make decisions ruling animals' lives not just based on scientific data, but to satisfy the demands of politicians. In many cases, political reasons for managing animals were not the same as scientific reasons. Many decisions about bear management were made to satisfy politicians with a large number of loggers or ranchers in their constituency, and the bear lost when its habitat was either destroyed or made unlivable for part of the year.

Lynx had done a lot for Bear Spirit at the museum, too, as well as for the eagle, swan, and other Yellowstone creatures. This year's special exhibit was the "Bears of Yellowstone," with well researched and presented information on the natural history of bears. It addressed the relationships between bears and Indians, bears and trappers, bears and hunters, and bears in myth and legend. There would be movies on bears, and Indians were scheduled to tell bear myths and stories. Some of the talks were designed to help people examine their personal feelings toward bears. Do they fear them, do they want bears to go on living in Yellowstone and other wild places, and do they want to pay the price by allocating land to bears in which to roam and reproduce?

"The most current event to challenge the Bear Spirit is the new development at the south edge of town," thought Lynx. The developer, Randall P. Duncan, also had bear vision, she knew, and when a developer has a spiritual connection to bears, it would of course be manifested from his viewpoint. Randall wanted to build a sanctuary for problem bears that bear managers would otherwise put to death. The local animal righters were furious, accusing Randall of exploiting bears by building what they called a "roadside zoo" so he could bring more tourists to town.

Randall's sanctuary, named Ursus after the Latin word for bear, was hardly to be a roadside zoo, Lynx knew, because she had seen the plans. It would be a state-of-the-art simulated bear habitat. Bears would be rotated from an indoor holding area to the outside viewing facility throughout the day. Visitors would walk through educational exhibits on bears and on how humans should behave in bear habitat before they went outdoors to see the animals. Ursus would also have an IMAX theater that would screen movies on bears and other Yellowstone topics.

Lynx supported Randall's development because she would rather see the bears alive and being used to educate people than dead and cut to pieces by bear researchers. Of course, she did not want to see more development in West Yellowstone, but it was inevitable that that land be developed given the reality that communities all over the West were in a growth period. At least Randall was developing it, not someone else who would fill it with condos and snowmobile businesses. She saw Randall's plans as the lesser of other evils that could be put on the land.

Jack's face flashed into Lynx's head. Would having a relationship with him help her keep her vision? Her immediate answer was no. He was one of those traditional men who would expect a wife to be his partner and never realize he should be her partner as well. Vicky may have been flighty, but she probably left Jack because he ignored her needs while expecting her to fulfill his. He would eventually want Lynx to adapt to his more domesticated lifestyle. If Lynx kept seeing him, she would stop her own growth and he would be hurt.

She realized this had been true in many of her relationships with men. They enjoyed the freedom they had with her, but then they wanted her with them all the time, and she stopped being free and fun when she was pressured. She suddenly remembered the impending meeting with Anton, heard his voice again, and felt that same uncomfortable, puzzling feeling.

Yes, she was fragmented. She had a rich spiritual side that was not being fed in her daily life. She had many friends but few who really knew her. West Yellowstone was a stagnant place, its majority focused on making money off of tourists, not on personal or spiritual growth. People owning and working in the two richest business groups in town were active in churches that Christians called cults, the Mormon Church and the Church of God, the Armstrongians.

Lynx had pondered this often and concluded that the reason why there was so much greed and unrest and gossip in West Yellowstone was that these churches controlled the souls of the majority. The third largest business group wasn't connected to a church, but was owned by people who had run a large concession in Yellowstone Park for years with little or no thought to helping preserve park resources, with most focus given to making as much money as possible off of tourists by selling trashy souvenirs at high prices. All three businesses paid very low wages and provided employee housing at low cost, or sometimes for free, that was crowded and substandard. Even though their religions preached against drug and alcohol abuse, they were responsible for numerous social problems, like alcohol and drug abuse and domestic violence, because the large work force they controlled was in a constant state of despair and depression due to their financial stress. While the business owners vacationed in Hawaii, Southern California, and Mexico with their profits, the wage slaves struggled to eat and pay their bills during West's off-season, two and a half months in the spring, the same period of time in the fall. They collected unemployment if they were eligible, and holed up in their houses, hoping their stash of food would last. If it didn't, they could always charge groceries and gas at the stores of one of their employers, then spend half of the busy season paying off their tabs. They numbed themselves with booze and dope and many took out their frustration on one another. The domestic violence and divorce statistics were high.

Lynx was one of just a handful of West Yellowstone residents who had seen a grizzly bear in the wild, one of the few dozen or so who actually fished, hunted, and hiked in the park or national forest. The park gate was at the edge of town, and the town was surrounded on its three other sides by national forest, yet people were too busy or too broke to enjoy the place. Lynx knew people who made a fortune off of park tourists but had not been in the park for 30 years.

It had always been incomprehensible to Lynx that so many people were out of touch with the place they lived in, even to the point that they ridiculed people like her for being some kind of an ex-hippy nature freak. She was seen by some as a radical environmentalist because she cross-country skied, owned a mountain bike, and spent the night in the backcountry living out of a pack. She would probably be burned at the stake if they knew about her Indian medicine. She said a silent prayer of thanksgiving for her vision and asked for help in continuing her commitment to helping the bear.

Lynx looked around the sweat lodge. Only she, Nora, and the Little Boys were left. They were still praying or thinking intensely. She edged quietly toward the door and went outside. It was late afternoon, and no one was about. She went to her teepee and grabbed a change of clothes and a bottle of biodegradable soap. She walked upstream to a quiet pool and stripped off her sweat soaked shirt, after waving to a fly fisherman upstream who waved back and politely turned away when he saw her begin to undress. The water was painfully cold, so she washed quickly and jumped back onto the bank. Sol came down the trail with a wide grin on his face. He kept his eyes on her face while she dressed.

"Not a bad sweat, was it?" he asked.

"No, some things got clearer, others stayed muddy, but I feel good about it," she replied.

Lynx slept well for a few hours that night after a long chat with Patsy. Patsy had loved being the lodge protector and said she had visualized Lynx talking with a grizzly bear and some of the others with other animal and people spirits. But at 3 a.m., she awoke with sharp pain in her head, throbbing from one temple to the other, and the clear vision of a white man filling her mind's eye. It was Anton, and she felt frightened. She returned to a restless sleep until dawn.

Chapter Seven

That day's sweat was the official greeting of summer by the Sweetgrass Society. Only Nora, Harry, Lynx, and Sol were society members, but everyone was allowed to participate. Joe drew the protector willow. The sweat began with the smoking of sweetgrass mixed with a small amount of mescaline.

The Indians believed that the psychedelic properties of mescaline were sacred, given the plant by the Great Spirit to be used by seekers. In the opening prayers, seekers were asked to surrender to the Spirit-given power of the mescaline and unite their minds and souls with one another, with the Great Spirit who graced them all, with the animals and plants that sustained them physically and spiritually. The entire focus was to be on this unity of spirit which would carry over into their lives and enrich them personally as well as strengthen their communities.

Lynx let the drug flow through her body until it put her in a dream-like state. She flew with eagles, swam and trumpeted with swans, and hunted with grizzlies. She became the wind, the flowing water of the rivers, the songs of the birds. She saw the others on their own journeys and felt their love and strength. She saw all the colors of the rainbow enveloping each person in the lodge and understood how the Spirit uses color to heal minds and bodies and control unhealthy emotions.

After changing the rocks five times, they emerged together and bathed in the same pool Lynx had used the day before. They broke their fast with food and stories of the places they'd been and the Spirit they had touched and shared.

Lynx purchased a dozen cottonwood bark carvings from the Little Boys, ten of faces of Indian warriors and medicine men and two of eagles. She would sell them in the museum's art store. She and Patsy packed their things and began to say their good-byes to each of their fellow seekers. When Lynx came to Nora, her old friend asked her to sit in the medicine lodge for a private talk.

They sat cross-legged so their knees were touching. Nora looked closely into Lynx's eyes, and Lynx saw profound sadness in her.

"Are you okay, Nora?" she asked with concern.

"Child, I am filled with fear for you. I had a vision of you in great danger because of a man who is terribly evil. I saw all your power animals in trouble, too, because of this man. He is a warrior for evil."

"Nora, I don't think I know anyone like that."

"No, you don't, but you will meet him, and you will have to do battle with him. There is not a choice about it. You will need our help."

Lynx felt a shiver of fear pulse through her.

"Lynx, we know that evil is increasing in the world. That's why our medicine must get stronger. We have an obligation to serve the people of good, to help them battle the evil. Perhaps the evil will defeat many, many people. All we can do is help those who are sent us."

"Nora, you're scaring me."

"Fear is a destructive force. You have nothing to fear. Just be loving and kind, except beware of this person. He is totally given over to evil and perhaps cannot be changed."

Nora held Lynx's hands and spoke a prayer of protection in Crow.

Lynx repeated the prayer, faltering at the difficult pronunciation.

"You are a Christian, a Catholic, like most of us," Nora told her. "This faith is very powerful against evil like the type you will soon meet. Keep going to Mass and praying your rosary and start doing one more thing each time you pray."

"What is that?" Lynx got ready to focus on Nora's instructions.

"Whatever you ask for, whatever you pray for, ask it in the name of Jesus Christ. It is the most powerful way to invoke the grace you need for spiritual warfare," Nora said.

"I'll remember that," Lynx promised.

Lynx and Patsy drove back to West Yellowstone in comfortable silence. Lynx had decided to think and pray about Nora's warning later and just relax and enjoy the ride. In no time the yellow and red and blue neon lights of town were on the horizon.

"I could have used some more time out there," Patsy said.

"Me, too," Lynx answered wistfully. "Re-entry is rough. That world and this one are so different. We need the other to survive in this."

Chapter Eight

Anton awoke Monday morning full of anticipation. He showered slowly and took extra time blow drying his long, thick, salt-and-pepper hair. He admired his naked body in his bathroom's full-length mirror. He was naturally muscular and tanned from being outdoors videotaping year round. He flexed his pec muscles, proud that he was 55 years old with pecs like a 26-year-old jock. He slowly massaged his body with Jergen's lotion, which he thought mixed well with his natural man odor and would be very attractive to Lynx, whom he sensed was not impressed by men who wear cologne.

He put on his thick cotton dress pants, gray with huge thigh pockets, and a tight red T-shirt that showed off his muscles. He added a loose-fitting, white cotton work shirt with two deep pockets and slipped into thick wool socks and Birkenstock sandals. He grabbed his AV testing equipment and loaded pot pipe and went outside. He turned around and looked at his mobile home. It was average looking, he thought, and no one would guess it contained a million dollars worth of video production equipment. Inside was more modern equipment than could be found in any Montana television station and ten pounds of quality pot he'd picked up yesterday.

Anton rubbed the weather-washed skulls and spinal columns of the elk, deer, antelope, bighorn sheep, mountain goat, and black bear he had nailed all over the railings of his redwood deck, recalling how he'd used his power to kill all of them. He walked to the wooded area behind the trailer and looked at the gutted bodies of seven pine martens he'd trapped and hung by their necks from the trees. Winter's cold, dry air had preserved the martens' fur and bones, and ravens had plucked away their eyeballs and innards.

He walked farther back into the woods and looked high up into the branches of the tallest Douglas fir tree where he'd hung from their necks a bald eagle and trumpeter swan he'd killed last fall. He spread out his arms and breathed three deep breaths, sucking in the death spirit until it filled his soul with its pure evil. It gave him strength. He projected some of his power into the woods to keep away intruders. It wasn't because he worried about anyone questioning the sanity of surrounding his deck with bones and skulls. It was a mountain custom to nail these things to your home. He'd told the curious he'd been given the animals by friends or found them dead along the side of the road. The animal remains were arranged to envelop the trailer and grounds with evil, and he didn't want any intruders to break his spell.

Anton faced north, where Lynx was, and rubbed the medicine bag he wore around his neck. It was made with the dried skin of a full curl bighorn sheep's scrotum and held a claw from an 11-year-old grizzly bear. His master's power had killed the sheep purposely for the material for the medicine bag, but they had let the bear live after they used their combined power to stun and then de-claw it. Nine others in his group had the remaining claws. Anton visualized his fellow warriors and asked them for strength in his work with Lynx.

Anton's face instantly invaded the minds of the warriors, although all were hundreds of miles away. Their brother needed them, so they stopped what they were doing and focused on him. He felt their power pour into him, and he breathed it into his soul.

Anton walked slowly to his recreational vehicle—a unit with a kitchen, sleeping area, and mini video studio—and climbed in. He would be in West Yellowstone two hours early, in plenty of time to prepare for his meeting with Lynx.

• • •

Lynx woke up tired Monday morning and drank three cups of her killer coffee before sitting down to work. The day's story was about Ursus. She wrote the first sentence and called Randall for the details of when construction would begin, how he planned to get bears, and how much the project would cost. He told her it would be more than over $3 million for the sanctuary alone and gave her some good quotes about how he had come to appreciate bears by studying them in a seminar at the Yellowstone Institute in the park. He said he thought grizzlies were too magnificent to be allowed to go extinct.

Then Lynx called an animal rights group in Maryland and got some quotes opposing the sanctuary. The spokesperson for the group worried that Ursus would encourage the park to dump all its bears in the facility rather than manage them in the wild. He said he was concerned that the facility may not take good care of the bears, although he felt better about that when he learned that it was being constructed by the most reputable zoo architect in the world. She then called a local opponent of the project who said he worried that people would become conditioned to prefer to see animals in captivity and not care if they had wild habitat to live in.

Lynx had just filed the story when Dewey came in. Dewey, 72, widowed, and a full-blooded gypsy, lived in Bozeman and spent three days every other week at Lynx's doing laundry and heavy cleaning and preparing and freezing meals for Lynx and Merlin to microwave when Lynx was too busy to cook. She also baked bread, made Merlin's favorite cookies, and tended him if Lynx had to go anywhere overnight.

Lynx paid Dewey well for these time saving services, and Dewey lived on the income from Lynx and monthly draws from her kumpania, the extended family that supports its elderly members with invested income from real estate holdings. Dewey's grandparents had emigrated to the United States in the 1880's during the Eastern European Diaspora. Their ancestors were from north central India, where gypsies were in a low caste who earned their living by singing and dancing to entertain the upper castes. Their religion, Romania, was monotheistic and centered around the worship of the patriarchal god, Del. They left India for the Middle East in the ninth century to maintain their religious freedom but were persecuted there by Moslems, so they eventually migrated to Europe. In Europe, the Roman Catholic Church persecuted them because many earned their livings by fortune telling and magic, which the Church denounced as black arts.

Dewey could still speak the gypsy language, Romany, and remembered dozens of old songs, dances, and stories related to her by her grandparents. Lynx let Dewey use her computer in the evenings to write these things down.

Lynx's grandmother met Dewey when she was a teenager and had her palm read by Dewey's mother, Rebecca, in New York City. The two women became close friends, an unusual occurrence since Catholics still distrust gypsies and gypsies rarely have friendships outside of their kumpania. But Lynx's grandmother, Mary, was a liberal Irishwoman who had seen her family persecuted by Protestant businessmen who resented Irish immigrants, and she had always opened her heart to other persecuted groups. Several years after meeting Mary, Rebecca and her extended family moved to Montana to trade horses and buy and sell ranch property all over the West. Mary put Lynx in touch with Dewey, and as far as Dewey and her kumpania were concerned, Lynx and Merlin were part of their family, too, by way of Mary and Rebecca's friendship.

Dewey learned to read palms from her mother and taught Lynx palmistry and the use of the crystal ball to invoke God's spirit for healing and prophecy. Gypsy gifts, Lynx found, have been grossly misunderstood by people for centuries. In truth, gypsy spirituality is very similar to that of Christians. They believe that their powers are gifts from God and abhor any use of them for evil purposes.

Lynx hoped to find time during Dewey's visit to ask her if she had any feelings similar to Nora's about an evil presence coming to do battle with her. If Nora was right, she would need all the help she could get.

Lynx and Dewey hugged and sat at the table to share a cup of herbal tea Dewey had brought with her in a thermos. Dewey looked great, dressed as always to accentuate her gypsy heritage. Her long white hair ran down her back in one neat braid secured with a purple velvet ribbon. Her deep brown eyes and high cheekbones were highlighted with huge round silver earrings. She wore a long purple cotton sweater and black tights, a four-inch crystal ball pendant hung from a silver chain between her breasts, and she was barefoot, having kicked off her street shoes at the door.

"Lynx, I'm so happy to be here. I'm greatly concerned about you," Dewey said, taking Lynx's right hand and holding it with both of her hands. Lynx looked at the brilliant red nail polish on her long, well groomed nails and thought it actually looked good with the purple sweater. Lynx was always amazed that Dewey could look so glamorous and have long nails when she worked so hard cleaning and cooking.

Dewey held onto her hand and went on. "I have been getting a vision of you in great danger with a man, my dear, a man who wants to destroy what is very important to you. Could you be having lunch with a new man even today?"

Fear rose in Lynx. She remembered how she had felt this fear even thinking of meeting Anton, and she recalled the strange feeling she had when she heard his voice. "Well, yes, Dewey," she said slowly. "I am meeting someone for lunch, and I have gotten some strange vibes about him, but I don't feel as if I am in danger."

"No, dear, you would not feel it. You see, when someone really evil is stalking you, they put blinders on you so you don't suspect it. I know you are supposed to meet him, and it is inevitable that you will do battle with him."

"Do you see what he looks like, Dewey? That would help."

"No, and this is a problem. I can usually see the face. His power is strong, and he has the ability to block anyone who is trying to read him."

Lynx suddenly felt very tired. A voice from somewhere else screamed in her head, a man's voice, "Don't listen to these old women. You are fine." She said a silent Hail Mary.

"But enough of that," Dewey said, releasing her hand. "You have protection, dear, in the form of your faith and your friendships and my love. Let's get this list of things for me to do done. I want to get a few hours in on the computer tonight."

"Here, Dewey, I have the list all made out. If you could go shopping first, that would help. We're out of milk, and Merlin has a habit of chugging down a quart as soon as he comes home from school."

Dewey ran through the list and left for the store.

• • •

The phone rang. It was Mullein White Horse, a Nez Perce firefighter who worked at the regional fire center in Boise, Idaho, and was an amateur photographer. He and Lynx met at a photographer's convention last summer and later spent three days photographing grizzly bears in the park with a team of bear researchers. They hadn't been alone during that time because each of them were assigned hikes with a different group of researchers. When the trip was over, they'd gone to dinner with the group in Gardiner, Montana, a small town just outside the park's northwest gate. After dinner, they talked briefly alone when they danced at one of the local bars that had a live country Western band. They'd learned they both loved to hunt so decided to hunt together sometime. Last fall, they went on a deer hunt near Ennis, Montana, with six other people who were friends of Mullein's.

They'd been the first people up on the first day of the hunt and decided to work a willow and aspen filled coulee cut by a small spring fed stream. The plan was that Lynx would walk up the bottom of the coulee and flush the deer up toward Mullein. She put the sneak on a buck whose antlers she had seen sticking out of the willows until she was just 50 yards from him. He stood up slowly, and she shot him straight in the heart with her 30/30. The sound of her rifle sent another buck up the hill, right into Mullein's sights. It was the easiest hunt either of them had experienced. They drank a couple of beers and admired their deer—hers a 4 by 4, his a 5 by 5. They hung the animals on the camp's meat racks, cleaned up, grabbed their shotguns, and went up the hill behind camp in search of a nap followed by a hunt for sharp-tailed grouse.

Halfway up the hill, they stopped to rest and drink a beer. Lynx sat downhill from Mullein, and he scooted close to her so she could rest her head on his knees. He rubbed her neck, and they chatted about their easy hunt. He asked her the usual question about how she got her name, and she told him her story and told him she wanted to know how he got his name, which was almost as weird as hers.

"I'm named after a weed," he told her.

"Do you mean the mullein plant?" She turned around and faced him, her legs crossed. "I know that plant. I thought your name was spelled M-u-l-l-e-n. The plant is m-u-l-l-e-i-n, right?"

"Right. Smart girl."

"Oh, I wrote about it once. It's actually a lot more than a weed. The Indians used it to make yellow dye for clothing and drank its tea to ease respiratory distress. Sometimes they smudged sweat lodges with it, and they even ate the new leaves at the bottom of the stalk. They taste pretty good. So why are you named after it?"

"It saved my mother's life. She was sick with pneumonia just before she was to marry my father. Her grandmother treated her with mullein tea and put her in a steam tent of mullein vapors, and she lived. Soon after that, she married my father and got pregnant with me."

"That's a neat story. Women do strange things when they're pregnant. How about 'White Horse?' Where is that from?"

"My ancestors were some of the best appaloosa breeders and traders in the Nez Perce nation. My great great grandfather's prize breeding mare gave birth to a pure white stallion, probably an albino. He rode that horse in many battles and neither he nor the horse was ever wounded. They said the horse was sacred."

"You have an interesting family history, from just the little you've told me. Where are your parents now, Mullein?"

Mullein looked away. "That's something I don't want to get into now. They're alive, though, and well." Mullein didn't want to tell her he was adopted, although the fact didn't bother him. He had said enough to this woman for now. She was the first woman he'd ever talked this much with, and it frightened him.

A rifle blasted a half mile away. Grateful for a chance to change the subject, Mullein told her it sounded as if someone else had scored on the hunt.

Lynx smiled at him and turned around, leaning against his knees again. Mullein suddenly felt an urge to kiss this woman he could talk with so easily, who had also accepted his telling her he didn't want to talk about his parents. He turned her head around until he could reach her for a kiss and dove his tongue into her mouth. She kissed him back.

They were both horny from the hunt and the hard work of dealing with their animals. Only a person who has hunted and killed and skinned out a wild animal can understand the mental and physical high it brings. A successful hunt is the strongest aphrodisiac in nature. Lynx and Mullein had one another's clothes skinned off in milliseconds. He turned her so her head was facing downhill and entered her powerfully, all at once, like any self respecting hunter woman would like it. She opened her legs to let him in as far as he could go, and he took his powerful arms and held them around her shoulders so she would not slide downhill as he continued to probe her deeply. Then he let go of her shoulders and moved in her until she slid downhill, her back scraping against the grass and dirt and rocks. She held him inside her and took him with her. They moved sideways and tumbled together until they hit a flat spot. They felt no pain, just the ecstasy of reaching a mutual climax after the build-up of the hunt. Their squeals echoed off the hills, and someone who heard them fired a rifle three times into the air.

Still naked, they grabbed their clothes and carried them to a grove of trees farther up the hill, where they napped until the sun began to set. They each shot a grouse on the way back to camp, where they were met with amused grins.

After that, Mullein and Lynx lived in their different worlds and assumed they would never meet again until another hunting season. Now, the memory of that hunt could be heard in the melodies of their voices as they talked with one another.

"Lynx, I think you may have a big story to write. Just wait 'til I tell you. And I also wanted to hear your voice. I've thought so much about you since our hunting trip, but I've let time slip away without calling you. I'd like to see you again."

"It's great to hear you Mullein. I've thought about calling you, too, but you're so far away, and I guess we're both pretty busy. Anyway, what's up?"

"We flew in a fire prediction team of fire experts from all over the country last week. We brought them together because of the drought all over the West, and a special group of them addressed the Yellowstone situation. They're really concerned there are going to be major wildfires there this summer, and they're talking about revising the park's fire policy. Could be a good story."

Lynx could hear the excitement in his voice and her reporter instinct knew she better really listen. "How so, revise the policy?"

"The current policy is to allow all naturally ignited fires to burn."

"Right, because most of the trees in the park are lodgepole pine, a species that can't reproduce without fire."

"That sounds like us. You light my fire."

"Bad joke. But true."

"Sorry. Anyway, under normal conditions, wildfires caused by lightning will burn themselves out. They'll hit a ridge, a river, or a stand of healthy, moisture-filled trees."

"And we don't have normal conditions?"

"No, sweetie. Have you not noticed we are in a drought period? There is no moisture in the soil, no moisture in the debris, in the deadfall, pine needles, twigs, anything on the forest floor. No rain is expected in any significant amounts all summer, and high winds are predicted. These are all the conditions for wildfires that could wipe out thousands of acres of trees. Not just in the park, either, also in the national forests that surround it, although the national forest areas managed for timber aren't nearly as loaded with debris."

"If the fire prediction team has found that the forests are so dry, aren't they going to recommend that the woods be closed to campers and wood-cutters?"

"That will happen, I'm sure," Mullein said. "Usually it happens to some extent in late August anyway, because the forest dries out nearly every year even under normal conditions. Some sections are closed, and others are heavily patrolled to make sure people are careful with fires and chainsaws. This year, dry means dry like it hasn't in a long time."

"The national forest fire policy is different from the park's, right?"

"Bingo, baby. They put fires out because they want to preserve the trees for timber."

"So I bet the fire prediction team is divided about policy?"

"You're on the money, honey. Your cute little journalistic nose smells that rat, for sure. The park people believe in letting wildfires burn, and the national forest people want them put out. The team is saying the entire park could burn down."

"How do the park people react to that?"

"They point to other times in history when the forests out here did burn down, other periods of drought, and say its merely nature taking its course, cleaning out the dead trees and letting new ones sprout up. It's natural regulation, and park policy supports natural regulation."

"Well, it hasn't always been into natural regulation, Mullein. Rangers have shot pelicans they thought were killing too many fish and coyotes and wolves they thought were killing elk and bison, and even elk and bison when they thought there were too many animals on the winter ranges."

"Right, but in recent years there has been more scientific management of park resources, and the natural regulation policy pretty much rules now."

"Mullein, that makes sense in the best of all primitive worlds, but how about the buildings, motels, gift stores, and all that in the park, not to mention the tourists?"

"That's the rest of the story, baby. If the fires come as they predict, it will be a management nightmare to keep people and buildings from being hurt. And to keep West Yellowstone, Cooke City, and Gardiner from burning down."

"And the park won't look so great after the fires have passed over, will it?"

"Not unless you get turned on by the sight of acres and acres of charcoal. The average American tourist won't want to burn too many brain cells to understand the ecology of wildfires and will not believe they benefit the ecosystem in the long run. The charred trees won't make good photos."

"What will happen to the wildlife?"

"Oh, we're going to lose some animals. Normally they can run ahead of a fire. But if it's as big as they say, some will be trapped. The worst will be later. Forage will be burned up, so animals won't have enough food to eat before winter and will die of starvation next spring."

"That's part of natural regulation, too, I suppose," she said. "Mullein, this really sounds interesting. Were there any reporters at this meeting?"

"No, hon. It was closed. They didn't want to leak this to the press until they have made a decision on whether to fight the fires or not."

"And I bet the park is concerned about tourism."

"You got it. They think that if the word gets out the park may burn down, people will skip Yellowstone this summer."

"And what do the national forest people think about leaking the story?"

"That's why I'm talking to you. The national forest people figure it will take at least 50 million dollars to control the fires and every available firefighter now trained plus hundreds more, maybe even the Marines and Army. Emergency funds will be needed, and we know how tight the economy is already. And by the way, they think there will be fires all over Montana, Idaho, Wyoming, New Mexico, and a few other places like California, as I recall."

"So they want to prepare the public and let the politicians know they will have to demand release of emergency funds?"

"Sure, plus they want to show how they maintain healthy forests by putting fires out and saving trees for the timber industry. Anyway, I thought that the best place to generate a leak would be right there in Yellowstone, not through a California or New York paper. You could give this story good head. You have a lot more knowledge of the area than a city journalist would, and you would be kind and present both sides."

"Thanks. I agree that it would be nice to have it come from here. So who do you know on the fire prediction team that would talk to me?"

"Call Fred Vallejo. He's a fire behavior expert at the U.S. Forest Service, Washington D.C. Put in years as a firefighter, studied every aspect of fire, weather, the whole thing."

"Does he know I'll be calling him?"

"Yes, and he knows how cute you look naked with your head pointing downhill."

"Thanks a lot."

"Lynx, I'm kidding. I don't kiss and tell, and that time we had together is a really precious memory to me."

"Me, too." Lynx looked at her watch. She had to get over to the museum and meet Anton for lunch, and she hadn't showered yet. "Tell him I'll call him this afternoon, around 2:30, and to call my machine and leave a message as to a better time if that won't work. And thanks for the tip, Mullein. You're great."

"My pleasure. It's gonna be a long, hot summer, baby."

"Will you be assigned to the fires here if this all materializes?"

"Yeah, most likely in charge of ground crews somewhere in the back country. Hope I can come in and see you on my days off."

"Oh, yeah, we'll be in touch."

"Send me a copy of your story, then, and take care of yourself, babes.

"You, too. Thanks again."

Chapter Nine

Lynx listened to her answering machine as she dried off from her shower. Jack called late last night, was going to Bozeman today, would call her tonight. The *Gazette* wanted to know what stories she had planned for the week. A book house wanted her to order 200 copies of a new Western novel to sell in the museum's bookstore. Patsy wanted her to call back when she had the time. The last message was puzzling.

"Lynx, this is Walt at the Triangle. Need to talk with you. Want to stop by tonight after we close at 10:30-ish. If this is not okay, call me back. Otherwise, I'll see you then."

His voice was tense and hurried. "Must be about the mess he's in with his wife, Tami, and Ursula," Lynx thought. "Lord," she prayed, "don't let me get in the middle of this. Show me how to be a good friend without making this a bigger mess than it is."

• • •

Anton strolled into the Trading Post on West Yellowstone's main street because he had been attracted to the rocks, crystals, and Pueblo Indian pottery artfully arranged in the store's windows.

Jedidiah, the shop owner, was Anton's age and looked like a mountain man with long hair, a bushy beard, and a fringed buckskin shirt. He liked to size up his customers and guess if they had money to spend and even what they would most likely spend it on. He watched Anton walk around his shop and decided this new customer probably had money and was a bit on the eccentric side.

But there was something about this man Jedidiah just didn't like. He couldn't bring himself to talk to him, so he nodded and didn't say hello when Anton caught his eye. Maybe Bettie, his sales clerk, would connect to him. He found her in the back room unpacking a new shipment of fossils.

"There's a customer out there I think you may be better off dealing with than I would be, Bettie," he whispered. "For some reason he gives me the creeps."

A man. "Far out," Bettie thought. She'd been trolling for a man for the last two years, after finally deciding that she was over a 22-year relationship with an asshole who beat the shit out of her whenever he got drunk. She'd been working out at the gym every night after work, eating a fat-free diet whenever possible, and visualizing her evolving beautiful self living contentedly with a new man. She figured if she hung in there long enough and worked at a busy place like Jedidiah's, she would meet Mr. Right. She wanted it to happen before her 45th birthday, the day she figured she would become an official middle-aged woman. Time was running out, since her birthday was two months away.

She fluffed up her short, curly blonde hair, added another layer of cherry red lipstick to the three already on her mouth, and walked out to the shop. Anton's back was to her, and he was still wearing the loose shirt over the T-shirt, but she could see he was well muscled, and she adored his hair at first sight, so thick and wavy and sexy.

Something awoke between her legs. She didn't recall that the husband who beat her made her react that way, too, when she first met him. And she had no idea that Jedidiah was madly in love with her and had hired her because he was hoping they would become more than co-workers.

Anton smiled broadly at her. "I like the art in your shop," he told her, his eyes looking directly into her. "How much is this?" He pointed to a turquoise Zuni Indian bear fetish in a glass case. The stone was flawless. The bear had inlaid onyx eyes and mother-of-pearl teeth and claws. Polished arrowhead shaped chunks of coral, buffalo horn, and lapis were tied with sinew to its back. Anton wanted it for his medicine bag.

Bettie unlocked the case and handed Anton the bear, feeling a surge of electricity that almost made her faint when she touched his hand briefly.

"This was made by a real craftsman," she noted, her voice shaking a little. "It's priced at $1,200."

"Wow."

She explained how old it was, how pure the stone was, how it was a Zuni spiritual talisman. He listened intently.

"How about I give you $900 cash?"

"That's quite a discount. Let me ask Jedidiah if he would take that amount. He owns the shop."

Any other time, Jedidiah would have okayed the deal. He paid $500 for the fetish and it was the beginning of the season, when cash flow was still a slight problem. But he loved this piece, and one of the reasons he put so high a price on it was to keep it around. He didn't want Anton to have it and was not happy that Bettie seemed to like this guy.

"No deal," he told Bettie firmly. "He won't find a piece like that in this town. The Sante Fe Indian art shops have work like it marked at $1,500 to two grand."

Anton was within hearing distance. He nodded to Bettie that he heard. "Okay, then, here's a credit card. I'll take it at your price. I have to have it."

It was a power struggle. He was aware that Jedidiah didn't like him and didn't want him to have the fetish, but he also knew that Jedidiah would not refuse to make money in order to stick to a principal.

Jedidiah glared at Anton. "Okay, Bettie, wrap it up for him," he ordered before he turned abruptly and walked to the back of the shop.

Jedidiah's attitude puzzled Bettie. He usually stuck around and chatted to customers who spent this kind of money. Many times his friendliness resulted in another sale.

Anton pretended not to notice Jedidiah's irritation with him. "Hey, do you happen to know a gal named Lynx?" he asked Bettie, his voice full of charm. "She runs the museum and writes for the *Gazette*."

Jedidiah, a long time friend of Lynx, opened his ears, walked a few steps back toward Anton and Bettie, and pretended to polish some silver earrings.

"Ya, she's a good friend of both of us," Bettie said.

"Is she single?"

"Why do you want to know that?" Bettie asked him.

"No special reason. I'm meeting her for lunch to discuss business."

Jedidiah stepped closer and interrupted. "If it's business you have with her, what difference does it make if she's married or not?"

"Well, well," Anton said, anger showing in his voice. "Are we so touchy because we're interested in her?"

"That's none of your business," Jedidiah shot back.

"Oh come on, guys, lighten up," Bettie bubbled. She looked at Anton. "Lynx has been single for awhile. She dates a few guys. She's very pretty and outgoing and very busy all the time. You'll have fun with her at lunch."

Anton smiled at Bettie.

"And if she doesn't seem interested in you, give me a call," Bettie said, handing him her business card. "I'm always looking for someone to have dinner with, or whatever."

Anton was well aware that Bettie was flirting with him. He took her card and grinned at her. "Thanks, I'll keep that in mind. Like I said, it's strictly business I have with Lynx. I may call you anyway to see if you have more of these fetishes later in the summer."

As soon as Anton was out the door, Jedidiah grabbed his jacket and told Bettie, "That guy really pissed me off. He's an arrogant son of a bitch. I don't know what possessed you to flirt with him."

"Oh come on, Jedidiah. You're in some kind of a mood. He's really charming and good looking. I wish I was meeting him for lunch."

Jedidiah glared at her. "I'm going out for coffee," he grumbled. "Women."

"Come back in a better mood," she countered, giggling. "And bring me a double espresso."

• • •

Anton and Lynx sat at a table for two at the Triangle that overlooked West Yellowstone's busy Canyon Street. Lynx checked her appointment book for a time to watch his video. It couldn't be today because of her interview with the fire expert. It looked like a pretty overloaded schedule, with most of this week penciled in. Anton watched her carefully. She was busy, but she was not frantic and hurried. She appeared to be happy, even bouncy, but also centered and calm. And she was very beautiful. A true mountain girl, he thought, deep blue eyes, glowing auburn hair, and a great body with a tan from being outdoors doing things, not lying around on a lounge chair like some bimbo. He put her age at 35, but she said she was 42.

When they'd talked about his video and his offer to help work on the museum's equipment, she had listened to him carefully and seemed truly interested in him, his work, and his ideas. And she had a girlish innocence about her he was very attracted to. She was obviously a well educated woman of the world, yet she had an open, loving look: life had not burned her out. Something kept her sweet. Yet when he probed her mind to see what it was, she stopped him. She had some kind of awareness when she was being probed, which meant she could probe, too. And whatever the sweetness was, she protected it and would not easily let anyone in.

"Okay, Anton, I got it," she said happily. "How about Wednesday at 7 p.m.? Merlin is going to a pizza and video party at a friend's house, and I have no meetings scheduled then. Can you manage driving down here at night?"

"That'll work, Lynx," Anton replied. "I am not as busy as you, for sure. If we run late because your equipment needs a lot of work, I can sleep in the R.V. Could I park it at the museum?"

"Sure." Lynx looked into his eyes. He was incredibly handsome. Great hair, great body, and brilliant. They'd talked for over an hour and shared many of the same thoughts about media and Yellowstone issues. He had some kind of a spiritual base, she saw, but she couldn't pin it down. He had looked into her mind (she had felt that, just as she looked into his). It was rare to meet someone who could do that, and she had put up her shield, as he had his. But he was hiding something, not simply protecting his serenity. It was something dark, maybe a past hurt.

Lynx sensed he wanted something from her, something more than help with his video and work at the museum. She couldn't tell if he was the man Nora and Dewey had warned her about. He seemed sincere and harmless. She was most puzzled by her complete lack of sexual attraction to him. That was all right because she only wanted to deal with him on a business level, but she naturally wondered why such a hunk didn't turn her crank. He was confusing her, so she let it go. Now he was asking her something, so she leaned toward him and listened.

"Lynx, I can't help notice that you have nothing down in your book for Sunday," he said, pointing to a day of blank hours. "Why don't you come up to my studio then and see a few hours of my work?"

Lynx never scheduled anything on Sunday. Either she was camping, hunting, fishing on a weekend trip, or spending the day alone or with Merlin. And she never missed Mass when she was in town.

"I don't work on Sunday," she answered.

"But this wouldn't be work."

"Oh yes it would, no insult intended."

There's time, Anton thought. She's being cautious. "Okay then, we'll plan on Wednesday.

"Great. Well, I better get going. I have an interview in a few minutes for a story I'm working on."

"What's the story?"

"Sorry, Anton, I can't tell you that. Read the paper tomorrow."

"Sounds interesting, so secretive and all."

"No, it's not like that. I just have a personal policy to not talk about stories I'm working on. It spreads out my focus."

They split the check, and he walked her out of the restaurant.

"I'm going straight home," she told him. "I just live down the street. So I'll see you soon."

"I'll walk you to your door," he replied. He was looking straight into her, looking for a way around her shield.

"Nah, it's out of your way, and I'm in a hurry," she said steadily despite the electric shiver that ran across her shoulders when she looked at him. Why was he so intense? What did he want? "See ya," was all she said, after which she turned abruptly and walked toward her house, feeling his eyes on her.

• • •

Dewey was hard at work on her memoirs and Lynx on reading her notes from her interview when Walt showed up. Dewey told Lynx she would stay out of the way while they talked. Walt fidgeted in the same seat at Lynx's dining room table that Ursula had sat in the week before and rolled the nearly full beer can he brought with him between his hands.

"I know you know the whole story of what's going on between me, Ursula, my wife, and Tami. That's why I'm here," he told Lynx.

"Yeah, but that puts me in the middle. I'd rather not get involved. It's a small town, and your soap opera story is kind of scary. I thought you and Urs were not going to see one another until you get your life together."

"We aren't."

"Then how do you know we talked?"

"She told me. After you two talked, she got in touch with me and told me she had made up her mind to not see me."

"So why don't you leave it at that?"

"Because I love her, and I'm going to do something that's going to hurt her deeply."

"Like not get a divorce?" Lynx looked at Walt's nervous hands, and they were making her irritated. She took a deep breath. "Sorry, Walt. I'll let you talk. It's just that this whole thing makes me uncomfortable."

"I can see that. Me, too." He walked over to the kitchen, crushed his beer can, and threw it in Lynx's recycling bin.

"I know you are one person who can keep a secret, and that's why I'm here. I need your help, and I need your utmost confidentiality."

"Okay, you got it," Lynx said, softening as she saw that he meant business and was really hurting inside.

"Lynx, I've messed up my relationships with women, but I'm still human. I have dreams. I want to fulfill those dreams," he said intensely.

"And," he went on, "those dreams actually don't involve women at all. In fact, I think I'm one of those people who gets involved in little messes so I won't pursue my dreams. It's a self esteem thing, a lack of confidence. It's like if I mess up in one area, I can blame that mess on why I don't do what I really want to do. Now, for once in my life, I want to do what's important to me and this woman thing is keeping me from doing that. Or could, if I let it."

"What would that dream be?

"To be an undercover narcotics agent."

"A narc?"

"No, Lynx, not a narc in the sense you're thinking. I don't care about the little guys who deal a bit of pot now and then. Half the work force in West Yellowstone smokes pot. I know that. And a lot of the shop owners in their 30's and 40's are into weekend cocaine use. I want to bust the big guys, the ones who bring heroin and coke into this country and are responsible for all the inner city kids getting strung out and into guns and gangs."

"Why?"

"For the intrigue, the rush, the danger. And I'm good at it. I've worked undercover before. I can't tell you about that, of course. I've had a lot of specialized training in intelligence, weaponry, stuff like that. Remember when I was supposed to have gone on a desert sheep hunting trip with Dave last year?"

"Yeah, you didn't get a sheep but he did."

"That's because I didn't go with him. I went back East to a training school run by, er . . . TDP, The Drug Police. Dave covered for me."

"Never heard of TDP. What is it? Did Dave know about what you were doing?"

"No. He knew I was doing something very important to me, something no one here could know about, not even my family. He's a good friend. That's another reason why fucking his wife has been a killer. It would hurt him so much. Forget I ever mentioned TDP by name. I shouldn't have."

Lynx stood up and paced slowly around the room, trying to absorb what he was saying.

"So relate all this to the here and now, please," she urged him.

"I've been recruited to be part of a special undercover operation."

"Where?"

"South America. Can't be any more specific than that."

"And?"

"And I'm going. I'm going to disappear. And not look back, not to my wife, kids, Ursula, not to this town and the restaurant. This mission could take at least two years, and I'm not allowed to tell anyone about it. I have to disappear in such a way that I will be presumed dead, and I have to take an oath to never return here if I do make it."

"I don't get something," Lynx said, trying to let it all sink in. "Why would they want an unstable person like you who can't even get his personal life together to be part of an undercover operation?"

"Lynx, I'm exactly what they want. I've nothing to lose. They know I want out of this situation, and they know I have the skills to be of service to them, including the coldness in my personality that allows me to do things like desert my family to follow their cause. TDP is full of people like me."

"TDP doesn't care that you would walk out on your wife and kids, coldly and without ever looking back?"

"No, Lynx, they don't. It happens all the time. She'll get over it. She and I don't get along anyway. She'll get the restaurant, and she can openly fuck her little boyfriend."

"I didn't know she had a boyfriend."

"Yeah, she's been screwing the morning cook for months."

"You mean Lonnie? He's a kid."

"I guess she likes them young and frisky."

"So how come you're telling me this? Won't it put me in danger with TDP?"

"They'll never have to know. I'm telling you because I love Ursula."

"You love her but you will leave her. I think we define love differently, Walt."

"Right. That's my cold side. But I've got these twinges of conscience because she's been hurt before. I don't want to make her a victim again."

Walt stared at Lynx and she stared back. "He is one cold son of a bitch," she thought.

"Look, everyone here knows I have a temper. I need to channel that anger into my work, not hang around in dysfunctional relationships. I'd have no trouble shooting someone in cold blood if I had to. I proved that in Nam. This is the kind of mind they need."

"But you have strong feelings for Ursula."

"Yes, but I'm realistic enough to know that sooner or later I would get angry at her, too, for preventing me from achieving what I really want, and we would fight. It would be a repeat of me and Susan."

"So what do you want me to do?"

"Be there for Ursula. She's going to have a really hard time. But you can't tell her I'm with TDP. Just tell her I'm really a mean asshole and she's better off without me."

"Give me a minute, Walt. You're overwhelming me with all this stuff. Just let me think a minute here and don't talk to me."

Lynx sat quietly, breathed deeply, and closed her eyes. She wished he'd never come here and told her this. She could keep a secret, but she did not want to have to deal with a grieving Ursula. Walt was right to call himself an asshole. He should never have gotten involved with Ursula. He used her. Now he would be gone, and she would have to go on living. Lynx realized it would be pretty easy to tell Ursula Walt was a bad choice. She looked at him. He was squirming in his chair, waiting for an answer.

"Look, Lynx, I reckon you've smoked pot now and then, but I know you're a highly moral person in most areas. You'll be helping me take part in a major sting operation that could significantly slow down the drug traffic to this country, hopefully for a long time."

Lynx laughed. "Walter, that doesn't wash with me. You can't bust everyone. Drugs are a permanent social problem, a reality world wide. They ought to legalize them. I don't like what they're doing to kids any more than you do, but I'm realistic enough to know you could bust the number one drug trafficker in South America, and the drugs would still keep coming. If they were legalized, they would be controlled, taxed, and eventually the dealers would be put out of business."

"Okay, then can I appeal to my yearning to be free to do what I want to do?"

"That's fine. And I know that sometimes when a person decides to be free, others can be hurt. Frankly, I'll have no difficulty telling Ursula you're a prick. You are. You make me feel angry. You should have never gotten involved with her, and now you're abandoning her and leaving me to pick up the pieces."

"I never said I wasn't a prick. Maybe I'm telling you all this for myself and not just so you'll help Ursula, though."

"Come forth with an explanation."

"I needed to know that one person out there knows I disappeared for a good reason and that I'm not dead or with another broad . . . er, woman."

"Okay, Walt, so when are you bolting? How are you going to pull this off?"

"TDP will take care of that. I really don't know what they have planned. And if something ever happened and you ever tell anyone about this conversation, I'll deny it. TDP will deny it." Walt's look was ugly, threatening. "What woman would ever find him attractive?" Lynx thought.

"Walt, go now. I've heard enough. I hope you can live with yourself. But I hope you wake up some day and really feel badly for leaving your kids, at least."

"Susan never lets me have my way with the kids. We disagree on everything, fight all the time. They'll be better off without the fighting. When they're old, if I survive this, I'll find them and let them know the truth."

"It's just not anything I'd ever understand."

"You're sweet. I'm rotten to the core, honey. I can't change." Walt stood up, rubbed Lynx's head, and walked out of her house without waiting for her to comment.

Walt's visit had drained Lynx, but she pushed herself to read and work on museum planning. She'd promised to meet Jack for breakfast at 6:30 a.m., and she tried to cheer herself up with the thought of seeing him. But she realized more than ever he was not the right guy for her and that it would not be right or possible to keep things casual with him. He should be free to look for a more permanent relationship.

Dewey came in and said good night, promising to get up early, make Merlin breakfast, and get him off to school.

Lynx decided she was too distracted to do anything, and she didn't want to think about anything. She put Mozart's horn concertos on the CD player and let his glorious music lull her to sleep.

Chapter Ten

Jack laid awake most of the night and thought of Lynx and Walt. He'd seen Walt come out of her house when he'd driven down her alley earlier. He hadn't been checking on her. He'd drunk four beers at Frank's Yellowstone Bar, and he always drove the alleys when he'd been drinking, not that the cops would stop him and give him a DUI. He was a town employee, and they liked him. He just didn't want to flaunt it.

He knew Walt was sleeping around on Susan, first with Tami, whom he thought was a stupid bitch, and now with Ursula, whom he thought was pretty and sweet. Was he after Lynx, too? He tried to push the thought aside. By now Walt must have heard about him and Lynx, and he wouldn't step in on that, or would he? He didn't seem to have had a problem sleeping with Dave's wife. Most likely he was seeing Lynx on a news matter, and she would tell him about it at breakfast. But why had she said she would meet him at the Triangle for breakfast rather than invite him to her house or agree to come to his? He wanted to be alone with her.

Just thinking of Lynx gave him a woody. He reached under the covers and felt himself grow harder.

But then he remembered the bizarre encounter he'd had on his way back to town from Bozeman that afternoon, and his woody shriveled up in a second.

Jack had stopped at the Specimen Creek pullout on U.S. 191 some 25 miles north of West Yellowstone and in Yellowstone Park, to hang a whiz and stretch his legs. He pulled in next to a mobile travel unit, thinking it was parked there while its occupants took a hike up the trail. Instead, he'd seen a man sitting on a portable lawn chair near the unit's side door. After he whizzed, he walked over and said hello, expecting to see an old timer, the kind of person who usually travel around in RV's. But this guy wasn't that old, and he had long hair. He'd thought perhaps he was one of those retired yuppies who'd made a bundle in the stock market.

The man heard his hello and turned slowly to look at him. His eyes were the color of fresh blood, and the look on his face was one of pure hatred. Jack had seen that look only once before in his life, in Viet Nam, when a gook not older than ten was running toward him with a knife in his hand. He'd blown the kid's head off without hesitating. No kid with eyes like that should live.

In a split second, the stranger's eyes changed from red to blue and the hatred was replaced with a friendly, phony smile. They chatted for a few minutes about the weather, and he learned that the man's name was Anton and that he had been visiting West Yellowstone and lived in Big Sky.

And Jack had instantly known without being told that Anton had met Lynx in West. As he talked with Anton, he could see them together eating lunch somewhere, as if a little movie was running through his mind. The thought frightened him. He asked Anton if by chance he knew a woman in West named Lynx, and Anton had said yes, he'd just met her. He gave no details about the meeting, and Jack hadn't asked for any. He was troubled by the fact that he knew something without having experienced it in concrete reality. Was that ESP or something like it, or was he going nuts? It made him almost sick to his stomach. He forced himself to relax and fall asleep, but he tossed and turned all night long until his sheets were a mangled mess.

• • •

Anton's elk hunting video, "A Yellowstone Country Close-up—Elk Hunting in Paradise," began with the skinning of a 6 by 6 bull elk killed somewhere in the mountains bordering Montana's Paradise Valley. Sitting next to Anton in the museum's darkened theater, Lynx held back her desire to vomit as she watched the hunters skin and gut the animal.

Although she skinned nearly every animal she killed without becoming even slightly nauseous, these hunters were sickening in the way they handled the animal. They were actually excited about tearing the animal's innards out of its body and throwing them on the ground after fondling them and even taking bites out of the liver. They argued over who would keep the elk's massive balls, and tongue, and ivory teeth, which they yanked out of its mouth with a pair of pliers. Anton had edited the tape so that the hunters faces were not visible, and the animal and its butchered body were seen in extreme close-up. Lynx could almost smell the blood and was utterly repulsed by the hunter's conversation, so gross and disrespectful to the animal they had sacrificed.

When the debauchery was over, Anton let the viewer see the hunters as he interviewed them about their experience. Lynx was shocked to find that she knew them. They were Jake, Scotch, and Moe, members of a loose-knit clique of around a dozen self-styled mountain men who lived in the Gallatin Canyon near Big Sky and called themselves the "bo-hunks." Every one of them had been busted at one time or another for hunting and trapping out of season, for wasting game meat, and killing the wrong sex or age group in season. Each year they hauled thousands of dollars worth of elk antlers and ivory teeth out of Yellowstone Park, where it is illegal to remove them, and sold them to a dealer in Ennis, who then sold them to craftspeople and antler collectors. The shed antlers from living elk were made into jewelry, lamp stands, belt buckles, cribbage boards, cabinet handles, and even buttons. When the bos really wanted to make money, they didn't pick shed antlers off the ground. They shot the elk out of season and immediately sawed off the fresh antlers, which they sold to a dealer in Livingston, Montana, who shipped them to a Chinese pharmacy in San Francisco where they were ground into powder and used as an aphrodisiac.

The bo-hunks were a scourge to all ethical hunters because anti-hunting animal righters pointed to people like them as examples of why hunting should be made illegal. Besides being poachers, they were lousy shots and even poorer trackers. When they failed to deliver a fatal shot, they rarely bothered to track the animal down and finish it off. Hunting season for the bos was party time, and the booze and pot were plentiful whenever they hunted. Their motto was, "First we smoke," and when they were toked up, they forgot about the rules of gun safety, if they ever knew them. Scotch had lost four toes a few years ago when Moe shot him in the foot with a 12-gauge shotgun during duck season. In the bars, where they spent nearly every afternoon and evening, they boasted of being so proficient at hunting, fishing, fur trapping, and antler and ivory tooth gathering that they did not have to work at regular jobs to sustain themselves and, therefore, never had to pay taxes. In truth, a few were TFB's (trust fund brats who lived off their wealthy parents), and the rest were pot and cocaine dealers who faithfully catered to the druggies in Bozeman, Big Sky, West Yellowstone, and Ennis.

Lynx was astounded that the bos didn't even clean up their act for Anton's benefit and were pointing loaded guns at one another and hanging out in a camp with garbage and animal guts strewn about.

When the gutting scene was over, the tape flashed back to the kill. Scotch shot an elk at 150 yards that was standing on a steep hill across a narrow ravine. He hit it in the rear left leg and then in the heart, and the elk tumbled down the hill. Then followed a discussion of whether or not to climb down into the ravine and get the animal. "Too much work—it would bum our high," Moe said. But Scotch worried that the game warden was around, so they decided to play by the rules and find the bull.

Lynx thought it was an absolute miracle that they were able to track down the elk several hours later. In fact, she wondered if they really had killed the elk on that hunt. She asked Anton to rewind the tape and, sure enough, Anton had slipped up. Scotch was wearing a different red plaid shirt in the first part of the tape.

"Anton, I think there's some tricky editing going on here, and these are two different hunts. That guy is wearing a different shirt, or did he change it?"

"Very observant, Lynx," Anton replied. "They are two different hunts. The elk kill was last year, and the elk they wasted was this year. I told them to wear the exact same clothes, but he lost that shirt and substituted one like it. I doubt if the average person would notice that. But come on and watch the rest. It's almost over."

Anton fast forwarded the tape to the end. The bos were sitting around a campfire roasting chunks of fresh meat and talking about past hunts and planning future ones as they passed around a fifth of Yukon Jack and a couple of fat joints. The final shot was of a full moon over the jagged peaks of the mountain range they were camping in.

Anton flipped on the lights and turned to Lynx. "What do you think? Would you show it here at the museum?"

"He can't be serious," Lynx thought, and replied, "No way, Anton. I know these guys. They're the biggest bunch of poachers around, they handle guns like retarded four year olds, and they get stoned and drunk on camera. They're lousy excuses for real hunters."

"Lynx, these guys are true native Montana country folk, a rare breed, a part of the culture."

"Not on your life. They're from California, New York, and Minnesota, so how can they be 'native'? And Big Sky is a resort, not the country."

"No one who watches this video will know that."

"So you're into deception, like when you edited two separate hunts into one hunting trip?"

"That's my right as an artist."

"Then you have to make sure the viewer knows you've produced a work of fiction, and you make this appear to be a documentary. That's unethical. It would be like if I made up quotes, characters, and situations in a news story but tried to pass it off as real."

"Lynx, what is real, anyway?"

"Real is the true story, as close to the truth as you can tell it. I hope you can do better adjusting the projector and sound equipment than you did producing a so-called elk hunting video."

"I'm really sorry you don't like this. I thought you were an artist."

"If to be an artist is to lie and show people poor examples of dealing with wildlife, then I'm not an artist in your book, and that's fine." Lynx tried to stay calm, but Anton was pissing her off.

Anton smirked at her, thrilled that he had found the first button he could push. "What's wrong with making people think? You can teach by proper example, and you can teach by showing the wrong way to do something."

"I fail to see how you presented this information as the wrong way to hunt. You nearly glorify these guys."

"No, they glorify themselves. I just let them make themselves out to be the idiots they are."

"You're very subtle."

"Okay, Lynx, I see we aren't going to agree on this, so why don't I look at your equipment, then we'll go from there. Maybe sometime you can show me what you think is a 'good' hunting video."

"I'd love to do that. In fact, there's going to be a wildlife video festival in Kalispell next weekend. The Wildlife Watch Collective is sponsoring it, and all the best videos of last year on hunting, wildlife, and so on will be screened."

"Is one of your pieces going to be shown?"

"Yes, as a matter of fact, two will be. One's on trumpeter swans, the other on bison."

"Why don't we go together?"

"Because I've made plans already to take my son there. We have motel reservations and plan to take a drive up to Glacier National Park on Sunday morning before they screen the last few tapes."

"Well, then, I will see you there anyway, and I'd love to take you both to dinner."

Lynx softened. He was trying to be charming, trying to see her viewpoint. "Okay," she said, "you have a date. How about dinner Saturday night after the 5 p.m. screening, which is of my tape."

"Great." Anton grinned at her, and she thought again how handsome he was.

"Well, I'm outta here. Do you think you can get the equipment up to speed tonight?"

"Yes, it needs only minor adjustments. I'll leave the bill on the counter in the bookstore. Call me if you have any questions."

Lynx walked home slowly, shaking her head whenever a scene from Anton's tape ran through her mind. He was the weirdest person she'd ever encountered. She remembered her breakfast chat with Jack, in which she told him she wouldn't be seeing him anymore on an intimate level and had upset him so much. Still, he told her he wanted to continue their friendship, and she'd been happy about that, as she really did care a great deal for him. And he told her about his strange meeting with Anton at Specimen Creek. She told Jack she had hired Anton to tune up her AV equipment and would be watching a video with him, and he scowled at her and said, "Watch out for that guy."

And she wondered about Jedidiah and Bettie, both of whom told her they'd met Anton but had different reactions to him. Bettie thought he was the most charming and good looking male specimen she had seen in a long time, yet Jedidiah thought Anton was a pompous, self-centered asshole who probably beat women up. Whatever he was, Lynx had the feeling he would be an important part of her life, and she hoped it would be a positive experience.

Chapter Eleven

Dave pulled his rubber raft onto the banks of the Henry's Fork Outlet, sat on the sandy ground, leaned his back against the raft, and closed his eyes. He listened to the raucous screams of a pair of sandhill cranes warning one another that an intruder was nearby and heard a flock of geese honk overhead. He stood up and took the three-pound cutthroat he'd just caught and stuck on a metal stringer out of the water. He'd snagged it on closed water, but he didn't care. He kept at most three fish every season, and he hadn't wanted to wait until the fishing season opened to have a trout dinner. He wanted to be alone, and soon the place would be overrun with tourists. Now there was nothing there but him and his thoughts, which were so heavy his chest pounded and he gasped for breath.

West Yellowstone was some 20 miles away, but at that moment, it could have been halfway round the world. Dave belonged on the banks of a river filled with fish, under skies where wild birds flew, near mountains where elk and deer and bear roamed and could be hunted. He'd worked all his life to build a successful business he could sell when he was around 50 years old for a price that would ensure he be comfortable for the rest of his life. He didn't want to put time in on a career that wouldn't give him enough money to retire on until he was too old to enjoy what he worked for.

He was five, maybe seven years from his goal when he met Tami, and it seemed at the time that he could share both his present and his future peace with her, maybe even make it happen sooner because she was not afraid to work and was very clever and resourceful with money. She helped him with his excavation, snow plowing, and concrete businesses, landing some major contracts that substantially increased his annual earnings. She invested money he had stashed in low interest savings accounts before they'd met, and it now earned two and three times what it had been getting.

When they were first married, Tami enjoyed spending weekends with him fishing and hunting. But two years ago or so, she began to complain that she was tired of running around the wilderness stalking animals and on the rivers and lakes getting sunburned in his raft and motor boat. She wanted them to work every weekend for several weeks at a time, and then take week to ten-day vacations at glamorous resorts advertised in the numerous chick magazines she read. She told him it would cost them less money to spend a week in a condo in Hawaii than to fish and hunt every weekend.

Dave knew his outdoor hobbies weren't cheap. He bought the best equipment and had costly non-resident licenses for both of them to fish and hunt in four states, in addition to their resident Montana licenses. He also paid big money for private hunts for trophy deer and sheep and high rod fees to fish on private waters. But he felt he earned his pleasures, and custom made fly rods and rare guns were a good investment. Hell, he could sell half his guns and fishing gear and live off the income for three years.

But he had given in to Tami and agreed to go on one resort vacation. He hated it—lying around with hundreds of other people on a hot beach, eating complicated full course dinners in fancy restaurants where smoking was not allowed, shopping for souvenirs to prove you had been there and make other people jealous of you, dancing in bars where one drink cost five bucks and had half the booze you would expect it to have. He especially detested dancing and shopping, but had done both to please her. She did work hard for him, and it wasn't really fair that they always did just what he wanted. But he felt ripped off and betrayed, too, because in the beginning, she had acted so happy to be with him. She was a good fisherman and a decent shot, and although she made him clean the fish and skin the animals she killed, he didn't care. He used to think it was kind of cute that she was a bit squeamish about handling dead animals.

Although her good management of the business had resulted in extra income, she was now spending the extra and more. He had peeked at the books the other day and seen that. She was spending a fortune remodeling the house, buying brand new appliances, even though the old ones were fine, just not high tech enough for her. And she was buying clothes he could not see that she needed, getting her hair done three times a week, and constantly running to the beauty salon to have her fake fingernails repaired. She was spending almost a grand a year on keeping those phony plastic things long and painted, and he hated them.

Although Tami was starting to look like the cover girl of a <u>Cosmopolitan</u> magazine, assisted by $30 underwire bras she bought at a fancy lingerie shop, she turned him on less and less. He dressed in jeans and old shirts and work boots most of the time and felt he looked like a fool standing next to her. Lately she had begun to nag him about his clothes and bring home new outfits for him to wear. Dockers slacks and pink, purple, and lime-green shirts. Fag shirts. Colored socks and slimy leather shoes. He took her out to dinner at the fancy Mountain Inn dressed in one of her fag shirts, and later got teased to high heaven by some Boys Club members who were there. After that, he refused to let her dress him and began to think that maybe it was she who looked foolish next to him.

Even worse than the clothes and trips was the communications kick she was on, sparked by her daily doses of television talk shows and by her constant reading of the latest how-to books and articles in chick magazines. Her favorite themes to read about, other than how to make herself more glamorous, were how to have "real" communication with your spouse and how to assert herself as a woman to raise her self esteem and make him feel like an inadequate, impotent shithead. She went to the office at 7 a.m. every day so she could end her work day at 3 p.m. and make it home in time to watch Sally Jesse Raphael and Oprah Winfrey. She called these women her gurus.

Sally and Oprah and the books and articles had her convinced he was the source of all her unhappiness and feelings of emptiness, and she made sure she let him know about it constantly. She had even tried to convince him that he was a lousy lover because a woman on Oprah had said a normal woman should have an orgasm after her clitoris was stimulated for 33 seconds. Sure, he'd told her, by a high voltage dildo. Is that what she wanted?

Trouble was, she was beginning to have a really shitty attitude about any argument he gave her about the changes she was demanding he make. She was trying to control him and his money, and he resented it. If he even raised his voice at her when they argued, she accused him of threatening her and reminded him that one out of every four males is an abusive son of a bitch dedicated to physically overpowering women. And lately, he figured she was having an affair. She had three or four unexplainable absences a week. He asked her about them for awhile, but she'd given him such vague, lame excuses that he felt ashamed of her lying and had stopped asking her.

Dave was no expert in psychology, especially when it came to women, but he was beginning to sense that she wanted him to hound her about where she was, wanted a confrontation, wanted him to know she was fucking someone else, and then get angry at her and possessive of her. In fact, he almost hoped she was. He was sick of touching her skinny, tight aerobic-exercised body and kissing her makeup plastered face, and she seldom touched him anymore because of her phony nails. He fucked her when he was so horny he couldn't stand it anymore, not horny for her, just needing to get laid. The only thing that irked him when he thought of her fucking someone else was that it would finally become an item of gossip around town, and he would be embarrassed. But maybe not. A few of his friends had commented about the way Tami was looking these days and alluded to the fact that they didn't find her all that attractive.

Dave thought about his marriage vows to Tami. He'd meant them, said them to the Tami he thought she was and would grow to be. Should he try to patch it up with her, force her to change back into the sweet thing he once thought she was? Or was she just deep down an evil bitch who was taking him for a ride and always had been? If she was going through some sort of mid-life crisis, he could be understanding. But if she was finally becoming some high class bitch with a fancy home and fancy clothes she had always dreamed of being, she could go to hell.

Dave felt himself getting more and more angry, and he opened a beer to calm himself down. He looked around at the willows, the gently moving river, at the trout he just cleaned, and felt better. Forget about her for a while and enjoy the moment, he told himself. He started a small fire with some dead willow branches and melted some butter in his ancient iron frying pan. He rotated the fish until it was cooked and ate it with some potato chips and another beer, thinking it tasted better than any dinner Tami had ever made him eat in those five star restaurants she was so fond of dragging him to.

But he couldn't get her out of his mind. He thought of her latest scheme, to take him to a ritzy resort in Palm Springs where they would learn to golf from some pros who charged $200 bucks an hour for lessons. She'd ordered new clubs for them both, and golf outfits, and God knows what else. When he told her that morning the vacation was no dice, he was going back to fishing and hunting every weekend, she stormed out of the room and told him to go to hell, she would go alone. He yelled back, "Go, and take your boyfriend with you."

She strutted back into the room and stared at him, triumph in her eyes. "What did you say? I have a boyfriend now?"

"No, forget it, sorry I yelled. I just hate your resort vacations, and I work too hard to suffer through them. I'm not going anymore, and you can go alone or take a friend or whatever. It's fine with me."

"Do you really mean that, Dave?"

"Yes."

"So I'm to take it you would rather be alone than with me?"

"No, that's not it exactly." Dave was confused and felt manipulated.

"Then what?" Her shiny red claws were planted on her bony hips, and she glared at him. She looked like Snow White's wicked stepmother. His dick shriveled up.

"It means this." He looked straight at her and willed himself to over-power her. "It means I work my ass off to make us money that you have too much fun spending. I have a right to spend my leisure time in peace and quiet, and if you don't want to share it with me, that is your choice. Go ahead to California, but when you get back, we're going to have a serious discussion about who spends what money on what leisure activities, clothes, makeup, stuff for the house, the whole shittin' shibang."

"Well, aren't you the controlling male," she sniveled.

"No, we have a partnership. You are becoming the controlling person in this relationship, and I don't like it."

Her glare cracked the makeup around her eyes and mouth. She looked disgusting.

"I suppose you'll give me no credit for the fact that I work my ass for you, too, and I deserve a break, and deserve to do what I want some of the time."

"I thought you had worked that ass off in aerobics, which costs me $100 a month. Look, quit being a bitch. I told you I appreciate your hard work."

"Funny, Dave. Fuck you. Have it your way and go to hell," she shouted at him before pounding out of the room, slamming the back door, and peeling out of the driveway in her new Bronco with the custom interior and paint job.

He actually hadn't given a shit where she had taken off to. He'd gotten his gear and headed to Island Park to fish and get away from any thought of her.

But it wasn't that easy. He had to find a way to calm things down around the house or cash in the chips.

As he was leaving town for Island Park, he passed Walt, who was driving into town to go to work at his restaurant. Walt had hailed him to stop, and they chatted a few minutes. He wondered then if Walt was bang-ing Tami. Not likely. Walt was not into broads that looked like wanna-be Las Vegas call girls, but then you never really know what even your best friend likes in the bedroom, do you?

But Walt had asked him to go black bear hunting with him that week-end, and he had accepted. Let the bitch go to California with her gigolo.

He would be delighted to pay for it, and maybe she would get her brains fucked out and leave him alone. He and Walt would have a better time in the woods anyway.

A few feet from the bank, a fish rose to snatch an emerging mayfly. Dave shouted at the fish, "You bitch, you bitch, go away," aimed his .38 special at the center of the rise, and shot until the barrel was empty.

Somewhat more relaxed, he paddled back to his pickup and drove to the Sundowner, a bar that was the last business in Idaho before the Continental Divide and the climb down into Montana. He needed a few more beers and a good talk with the locals before he would be calm enough to go home.

Olive, an older woman with red hair and huge hooters whom everyone thought was sweetness personified, was bartending. The place was filled with happy locals, a few retired couples who had just arrived for the summer, and three construction crews who had just stopped work for the day. The talk was of the impending opening day of fishing on Henry's Lake, just a few miles down the road from the bar, of the enormous summer homes the crews were building for Californians who would use them three weeks every summer, and of the story Lynx had in the paper about the high probability of fires in Yellowstone that summer. Dave had done the excavation and foundation work on all three homes and settled into a friendly chat about the progress the construction crews were making.

In a lull in the conversation, Olive leaned across the bar and told Dave Tami had been in the bar a few hours ago.

"She said she was heading down to Salt Lake to hop on a plane and go to California on a golf vacation, and I asked her if you were going along," Olive whispered.

"What did she tell you?" Dave tried to keep his voice casual and low, but his heart was pounding with anger, and he sounded shaky. The goddamn bitch. She bolted a day early and didn't even wait to say good-bye to his face.

Olive, who never forgot what any of her customers drank when they were upset and needed a shot, poured him a jigger of Jack Daniels.

"Shoot this with your beer, Dave," she said softly. "I can see you're a bit upset."

He gulped it down, and she poured him another.

"She said she needed to get away alone, that you guys were having problems."

"Yeah, we are, but I didn't know we were supposed to make a public issue of it," Dave replied, letting the whiskey and Olive's concern numb his anger.

"Look, Dave, I've been around the block a few times, and it seems to me that Tami is in some kind of a mid-life crisis, the way she's dressing these days."

"You've seen her before today? Didn't you just get back up here for the season?" Olive lived in Billings to be near her grandchildren during the winter and spent the summer in a small house trailer on the lake. Dave hadn't seen her since last fall, when he and Tami were elk hunting in Island Park.

"I've been back two weeks. I came early this year to do some work on my trailer. Tami came in with Walt the first shift I worked. Didn't she tell you?"

"With Walt?" The anger came back, and he chugged the second shot. "Give me another one of these Jacks, Olive. This is bullshit. I didn't know that. Now why do you suppose she didn't let me know?"

The entire bar was listening, but Dave didn't care. These were his friends, people he'd known long before he'd met the evil bitch. Probably some of them had seen her with Walt, too.

"If it makes you feel any better, they were arguing, sitting right over there at the end of the bar and going at it like cats and dogs," Rick, the foreman of one of the crews, told Dave.

"Yeah?" was all Dave could say.

"You try not to listen, but you can hear everything everyone says at this bar. You can't help but wonder why anyone would try to talk about anything too personal here if they didn't want it broadcast all over the valley," Rig, a dry wall man, chirped in.

"Well, since you all know so much, who wants to tell me what the fucking bitch is up to with my best friend?" Dave looked around the bar and raised his beer can. "Drinks around, Olive," he added.

Rick waited until everyone was served and they toasted Dave. Olive collected a quarter from the stack of change Dave had piled near his drink and put it in a cookie jar. The bar collected a quarter every time anyone used the F-word. In the summer, it took around two months to build up enough change to finance a pig roast with all the trimmings, free to all locals.

Dave watched her take his change and shouted, "You got it, she's a fucking bitch," as her threw Olive another quarter.

"Fuck her," added Woody, a Mexican logger who lived in a trailer behind the bar and was the official pig roaster. He grinned and gave Olive another quarter. The old retired couples were laughing and handed Olive quarters even though they personally didn't think it proper to say damn, let alone fuck.

"So come forth, somebody, clue me in," Dave said.

"Okay, okay, they were breaking it off," Rick said. "He was telling her he didn't want to see her again, and she was having a fit and telling him she would tell his wife he has a new girlfriend, someone named Ursula."

"Yeah, and when this Ursula was mentioned, Walt got pretty rowdy and told Tami to keep her out of it," Rig added.

"At which time, Tami called Ursula the C-word, the word we gentleman would never pronounce in front of a lady," said Marko, a go-fer on Rick's crew who had a master's degree in early English literature, "and Tami sweetly added that she would shoot Ursula's head off."

"Who's Ursula?" asked Olive.

Dave tried to remember. "It has to be the redhead who waitressed for Walt for awhile. She quit and went to another place."

"So Walt was doing your wife and one of his waitresses?" Rick laughed. "I didn't think he was so randy. Isn't he still married to Susan?"

"Yeah, he's married," Dave said. "But they don't get along, and he's cheated on his women ever since I can remember. We went to high school together, me and Walt and Jack. Jack and I have always told him to quit the cheat thing, but he seems to like it. Who would have thought he would do it to me, though? Never did before."

"You sound as if you really don't give a fuck," Marko noted. Olive grimaced and collected another quarter.

"Not really, not any more. She just bought herself a one-way ticket to Divorce City," Dave said. "Give us another round. We're celebrating my upcoming freedom from the most evil rat bitch from hell a person could ever know. And let's shake for the music. I'm in a partying mood."

Olive took the dice cup off a shelf behind the bar, and she and Dave rolled. He lost. He gave one of the retired couples a dollar, and they played Hank Williams and Patsy Cline songs.

"Next time, give it to me, and I'll play rock and roll," Rig said.

"What are you going to do about Walt?" asked Rick.

"Funny thing, he stopped me on my way out of town today and asked me to go bear hunting with him this weekend," Dave replied.

"That means he won't be banging Tami in California," Rig added.

"No, they really did break it off that day here," Olive said. "They left in separate cars at separate times. She left first, and he stuck around for a couple more drinks but didn't say a word about her."

"Dave, why don't we just get drunk and forget about it?" Rig said.

"Shit happens, man. You can come home with me. I got an extra bed in my trailer at the construction site, and we only have to drive a mile. You'll get a DUI if you drive back to West. You can go fishing tomorrow and sort it out then."

Dave was starting to feel fuzzy, and the idea of thinking about as little as possible appealed to him immensely. "You got it," he slurred, as he knocked his can against Rig's. "Party on."

• • •

Dave was still foggy after his three-day drunk in Island Park, but he was trying to work off his hangover by catching up on the long work list Tami had so sweetly left him. He had four foundations to dig for new homes near Hebgen Lake, a half-mile-long dirt driveway to grade for some rich Californians who would soon be up for the summer, and all kinds of petty chores. A third of his mind was on his work, a third on Tami, and a third on Walt.

He had decided to confront Walt about Tami when they were on their way up north to hunt. He was sure Walt had an explanation, and if it was a fact that they had been sleeping together, so be it. He was going to dump the bitch anyway and would warn Walt to stick with Susan because Tami just wasn't worth it. He tried to imagine them sleeping together. Did she more or less just lie there like she did with him? Maybe they turned each other on, but he couldn't imagine that because Walt and he were too much alike. Walt had told him time and again that he could not understand what he had seen in the bitch anyway.

At least he was powering through his job list and would be through with all the work by Thursday afternoon. The bitch would be coming home then. He didn't want to see her until after he talked with Walt. He decided to get done as early as possible on Thursday, pack for the hunting trip, and go up to Bozeman for the night. He could catch a movie there, and Walt could drive up and meet him on Friday.

At the end of the day, Dave called Walt. He was surprised that he felt anger and distrust the second he heard Walt's voice on the end of the line. "Must be natural to resent someone who's fucking your wife, even if she's a stupid bitch," he thought as he took a deep breath and told Walt his new plan.

"Shit, I have no problem with that," Walt said cheerfully. "Where in Bozeman do you want to meet?"

"Probably the truck stop, but I'll call you. I'm not sure which end of town I'll be staying in yet."

"Call me when you know and I'll be right up. I'll be at the restaurant."

As soon as Walt and Dave hung up their phones, Ben VanDiver, a TDP agent in charge of recruitment, clicked off his listening device and smiled. It wouldn't be long now before he could get out of this podunk town and back to where the action was.

He walked to the nearest pay phone and called Walt.

Chapter Twelve

Walt left Susan in charge of the Triangle because he had a meeting with Ben VanDiver, a TDP heavy whose exact position in the organization he did not know. He told Susan he would be fishing alone in the Madison River below Hebgen Lake, but he headed south of town instead to meet Ben on a dirt road that skirted the Madison's south fork. He was a half hour early for their meeting, but Ben's rig was already there. Walt left his truck slowly without banging his door and walked toward the river, where he found Ben fishing with a spinning rig in an off-limits area.

Walt sneaked up behind him, certain Ben was unaware he was there. He skipped a hello. "You know, boss, this is not the place to be caught fishing."

"Like I give a shit?" Ben replied gruffly, not moving a muscle or looking in Walt's direction. His line was in some calm water, and he was staring at a large red and white bobber.

"And you're using worms to boot. You're an asshole."

"Yah, so let's skip the small talk. You're going out this weekend."

"So soon? Last time we talked, it was going to be next month."

"Like we'd give you that much advance notice? Do you have a problem with this weekend?" Ben turned and glared at Walt, waiting for an answer.

Walt glared back and kept silent.

"Because if you do, you're not going anywhere. That was part of the deal. I'm antsy enough about you as it is. We've been watching you, Walt. Listening to you. You've got some problems with broads, and we don't like it."

Walt wasn't surprised he was being watched. Still, he resented Ben's tone of voice. He let it go, figuring it was all part of the testing process they put you through to see if you can maintain your cool.

"Yeah, I'm in deep shit with my wife and a couple of other broads, but that will all be behind me once I get out of here, and I'm ready to leave this minute if I have to."

"You had better be. We have to make your leaving appear to be a permanent disappearance. I'm most worried you'll contact one of these broads and blow the whole thing. We're watching them, too, and listening to them, so don't even think of trying anything. As far as they're concerned, sometime within the next week you're a dead man they'll be mourning for in one form or another."

"How?"

"That's for us to know and you to find out." Ben looked back at his bobber. It wasn't moving. "Shit, my worm is probably off the hook." He reeled his line in and added a fresh wiggly earthworm to the small piece of slime that remained from the last one.

"You have to jerk the thing around so the fish know it's there," Walt told him.

Ben turned around and faced Walt directly. He was four inches taller and outweighed Walt by at least 50 pounds. "Look, you little piece of shit, I know how to fish, so shut up. Just be ready. Now get the fuck out of here."

Walt didn't bother to reply. He knew he wasn't supposed to, so he turned and went back to his truck and pulled out his 16-gauge double barreled shotgun, loaded it, and shot in Ben's general direction.

"That should make the motherfucker jump," he thought. He climbed in the truck and drove back toward the road to town. As he was turning onto the highway, Jock Draw, the local game warden, was pulling onto the dirt road. They rolled down their windows to say hello.

"There's some son of a bitch fishing down there, with worms no less, just three miles down the road," Walt told him.

"The asshole," Jock replied. "I'll get him."

Walt drove slowly toward town, wondering how he was going to die, and when.

Chapter Thirteen

Lynx dragged herself and her pounding headache out of bed, wondering why she was still exhausted and headachy after a solid eight hours of sleep. For some reason, she felt no joy about the upcoming three-day weekend away from West Yellowstone with Merlin, no anticipation about watching the screening of her trumpeter swan video before hundreds of wildlife videographers and filmmakers. As she ground her coffee beans, she suddenly remembered a dream she had last night, and as she brought it into more detail to her active memory, her head pounded even harder.

She'd been in a dark living room, overfilled with Victorian-style mahogany furniture. Large long windows were draped with scarlet velvet curtains that let no light in. She was sitting at a round table with two men who placed a large book in front of her. The words in the book were handwritten in blood, in old-fashioned style script. The men didn't tell her the ink was blood. She had known, even though it was nearly black.

The pages of the book were yellowed at the edges and smelled musty. As she read the script, she began to cry and turned away, saying she didn't want to read any further. One of the men was Anton. He stood up and walked behind her and took her head in his hands, forcing her to look at the words. She closed her eyes, and he told her that wouldn't work, she would receive the information anyway. As hard as she tried, however, she couldn't recall what that information was. What a strange dream, she mused as she finished making her coffee and walked across the house to wake Merlin up.

He was already up and dressed and stuffing Nintendo games in his duffel bag.

"I don't think so, Merlin," she told him, taking a game out of his hand. "No Nintendo. You'll be too busy watching screenings and meeting other kids to have time for that."

"Oh, Mom," he whined. "What if there aren't any other kids there I like?"

"Then you can go to the motel and swim. Take those game cartridges out of your bag! Look, they're wrinkling up your clothes anyway. Now let's get going. I'm taking you to the Triangle for breakfast so we don't mess up the kitchen."

The Triangle's waitress had called in sick that morning, so Walt took Lynx and Merlin's breakfast order. Lynx watched him intently, going over their last conversation in her mind and wondering if he would really go through with leaving the Triangle, West Yellowstone, and his troubled relationships with women. He looked tired and stressed out and she tried to picture him befriending and then busting her stereotyped visions of cigar smoking drug dealers in three-piece silk suits.

Susan walked in with a grouchy look on her face and stormed back to the kitchen without acknowledging Lynx, Merlin, or Walt.

"She's going to be in a fine mood all day, or at least until we get a new waitress, Walt said, looking at Merlin. "Women."

"Women," Merlin dutifully volleyed.

"Call Patsy," Lynx said. Her sister Anne is staying with her this summer and is looking for a job. She has plenty of waitressing experience."

"What's the number?"

Lynx gave Walt the number, and he walked toward the phone just as it began to ring.

It was Dave, calling from Bozeman. He asked Walt to meet him at 2 p.m. at the truck stop, and Walt agreed.

"Shit, I hope this Anne woman can work. I have to meet Dave this afternoon," Walt told Lynx. "What was that number you just gave me?"

Lynx repeated it. Strange, she thought, that Walt and Dave would be hanging out. But her head ached too much to think. She picked at her breakfast, praying the aspirin she took for it would kick in, while Merlin gulped his food down like it was his last meal on earth.

Chapter Fourteen

As Walt drove to Bozeman, he popped a best of the 50's tape in his cassette player for background sound because music helped him think better. He guessed he would be taken out sometime during his hunting trip with Dave. He figured TDP would follow them and wait until they were well separated, and then pick him up, making Dave think he was lost. His conscience ached slightly at the thought of Dave frantically searching for him. It bothered him, for some reason, more deeply than thinking of how Susan and the kids and Ursula, and even Tami, would go through the days following the official pronouncement that he would no longer be searched for.

Dave had been his main hunting partner for many years, through wives and girlfriends and children and superficial friends. When Dave learns he's lost, he will feel personally responsible and that will hurt. He wondered how many taxpayers' dollars would be spent on the search, once Dave realized he couldn't find him alone, wondered if TDP would tell the local authorities what was really going on so they would conduct only an illusory search. No, that wouldn't happen, he reasoned TDP wouldn't care how much taxpayers money was spent on anything.

Walt mentally ran through the list of things he would be able to take with him. The clothes he was wearing and his .357 caliber Magnum Ruger Security Six, an untraceable gun he'd gotten from Dave in a trade. He had a savings account book he planned to use as I.D. to open a post office box in Bozeman, and would then mail the book to the box. He would pay the box rent three years ahead. He had withdrawn half of his and Susan's savings from the bank last month, and had put the money in a savings account in an out-of-state bank under the name and social security number he'd gotten from a dead man he'd dealt with several years ago when he worked for the county sheriff. The man had no relatives or close friends, came to Big Sky from back East, and hung himself in a rented cabin. In one year with TDP, he would make more than the Triangle could hope to make in five years. So, he really didn't have to take the money, but felt he deserved something for his years of hard work building the Triangle into a successful restaurant. Anything could happen once he was in TDP's system, and he needed some security, even if it was a lousy $15,000 bucks. Susan would have the business, the house, the vehicles, and her hot blooded boyfriend. He'd told her he had invested the money with a financial manager in Billings, and so when she realized he wouldn't be coming home, she would probably try to find it, but he doubted she would talk to any police authority looking for the missing money's connection to his disappearance. As for TDP, fuck them. They didn't seem to know about the money, so they weren't watching him as closely as they tried to make him believe they were.

Yeah, there was a lot of ragged shit surrounding his impending disappearance, a lot of feelings would be hurt, but what the hell? They would all get over it and he would be a free man. He would not look back. "Lavender blue, dilly dilly," he sang along with his tape. Time to stop worrying and get on with the program.

Lynx pulled off the highway into a rest area and leaned out of her car and vomited. Her headache had increased tenfold since that morning, and she couldn't figure it out. Merlin was worrying about her. She could see the concerned and anxious look on his face, and told him she may be getting a flu. Somehow she didn't think so, however. She wasn't feverish or achy—it was just that her head was exploding. She couldn't shake the thought that it had something to do with the dream, because whenever it pounded particularly hard, she saw the bloody handwriting stuck in her face.

"Look, Merlin, Mommy has got to put the seat back and rest for a minute, until this headache goes away a little. Is that okay?"

"Are you gonna be all right, Mamma?" Merlin only called her "mamma" when he was worrying about something and wanted her to reassure him.

"Yeah," I just need to rest and do some deep breathing."

"Okay, I'll get my book out and read while you rest."

Lynx drove slowly to a parking spot under some trees and closed her eyes. She thought of Nora and Dewey's warnings, and wondered if she was dealing with some kind of an evil force. Bullshit. Or was it? She began to breathe deeply and say Hail Mary's, a prayer she had learned practically before she could walk, a prayer that had never failed to calm her down, put her to sleep, let her overcome fear and worry. Catholic magic. It worked. She fell into a deep sleep.

Twenty minutes later, Merlin stuck his head in her face and said, "Mamma, you'd better wake up now. It's getting hot in the car."

She woke up and saw his two huge blue eyes, and realized gratefully that her headache was gone. "Thanks, Merlin. This is one time I'm happy you woke me up. I feel like a new woman. Let's boogie, shall we?"

Merlin grinned from ear to ear. He had been worrying, imagining having to figure out how to drive Lynx to the hospital, and had made up his mind to watch how she drives so he could figure out how to take the wheel if she ever got really sick. He had even said two Hail Marys, even though he felt he had grown out of saying prayers he didn't make up himself.

"Can we listen to music, Mamma?"

Lynx didn't feel like hearing his rock and roll at the moment, but he needed to stop worrying and have a good time, so she said he could put a tape in the player. Surprisingly, he played Handel's "The Water Music."

"I know you meditate to this, Mamma, it may keep your headache from coming back."

"She kissed him. He could be so sweet, the little shit.

Chapter Fifteen

Anton stood in the window of his third-story hotel room and watched Lynx and Merlin pull up and get out of the car.

She was wearing a tailored white blouse and dark jeans, her hair pulled back in a pony tail. She looked very beautiful and rested. Good, he thought. She didn't bring their programming session with her into her consciousness as the memory of a bad dream. If she had, he was sure she would look tired and disjointed. This meant that she'd slept deeply. Perfect.

The desk clerk handed Lynx two messages, the first from Anton: "Hi. Call me as soon as you get settled, and we'll make a date for dinner tonight. I've already scouted out a restaurant I think you and Merlin would like. Anton, Room 316."

The second was from someone she had never heard of. "Lynx, my name is Daren Bush from the CNS Foundation's Washington, D.C. office. We've previewed your video—it's excellent, and we would like to talk with you about it. Can we get together sometime this evening? D.B. Room 322."

Lynx knew of the CNS Foundation. It gave away what they called "genius grants" to people they felt were creative, upbeat, and making a difference with a variety of contemporary problems, including wildlife and wilderness issues. Their teams searched communities all over the country for people to give money to, and CNS did not accept grant applications. They either wanted to see if she would be interested in being funded to do a video or writing project, or they wanted to talk to her about someone else they were soliciting whom she knew. She called Daren Bush first.

Anton left his room and walked down the hallway to get some ice for his bourbon. He saw that there was someone else at the ice machine, a familiar shape, a tall, well-built man with a full head of unruly, bristly white hair. Could it be...? Daren Bush turned around and gave Anton a surprised look.

"Anton? What are you doing here? Last time I saw you, you were in San Francisco at the Art and Culture Institute. Was that three years go?"

Anton looked steadily at Daren, letting the hate he felt for him show in his gaze. "Yes. It was in California. You were trying to steal two of my students away from me."

"Trying? I believe we did. Loretta Yarndo and Elizabeth Carter, as I recall. We gave them a grant to produce a video on homeless women and children."

"Despite the fact that they were in the process of doing an important work for me."

"Are you seriously angry about that? You know that receiving a grant from us would help them more in their careers and creative lives than grinding out something in your video lab. And look at the national and international awards they received because of the work they produced for us. Surely you can't resent that."

"Oh no, why would I resent the interruption of my own project, which I considered to be far more important than yours?" Anton was swollen with sarcasm.

"What was it exactly anyway? They never explained it to us, but I had the feeling it was not so socially conscious as their efforts to raise public awareness of the plight of homeless women and children. They didn't appear to have any regrets about leaving you."

"They never told you what they did for me because it was none of your business and still isn't."

"Where are Loretta and Elizabeth now, anyway?"

"Why? Do you need to use them again?" Anton stressed the word "use."

"Anton, you know our awards are one time only, no exceptions. They could have gone back and worked for you after their year with us was up. Apparently they didn't?"

"Am I interested in working with people who are disloyal to me?" Anton asked, his voice low yet powerfully focused. It flashed through Daren's mind that he was dealing with a paranoid psychopath. That was too bad, since Anton was also the best video editor in the nation and one of the inventors of the image processor. CNS had considered giving him funding in the past, but Anton was not interested in doing projects of social importance.

"Look, Anton, we have no hard feelings toward you. In fact, we admire your technical expertise."

Anton smiled at Daren and willed himself to appear forgiving, knowing he wouldn't get anywhere if he continued to show hostility. "Yeah, it's water under the bridge," he said amiably. I'm a bit irritable from long ride. What are you doing here anyway?"

"We're hoping to meet with Lynx O'Malley, a journalist, and one of the videographers on the program. We like her work, especially her videos on trumpeter swans and bison, the commentaries she's been writing on the grizzly bear, and the bear education she's doing at the West Yellowstone museum. Do you know her?"

The wheels were cranking full speed in Anton's head. What luck! CNS was scouting Lynx!

He smiled at Daren again. "Yes, I know her. I'm here for the weekend with her."

"A man-woman thing you mean?" Daren asked, surprised.

"No, I'm here to see her video. We're in separate rooms. She pulled into the parking lot a few minutes ago, in fact. I left her a note about dinner tonight, so I best be getting back to my room. She'll be calling soon."

"Yeah, I left her a note too—see you around," Daren said as he walked away. As he approached his room, he heard his phone ringing. Anton was behind him, and he heard it, too. Anger welled up in him again. It was Lynx, he knew, calling Daren before calling him. That showed where her priorities must be. He went into his room, poured himself a stiff drink, chugged it, and walked back to Darren's room. The walls were thin enough so he could hear Daren talking. He was right—he was making an appointment to meet Lynx at 9 p.m. in the arboretum.

As Daren walked over to answer his phone, he made a mental note to call the main office in Atlanta and ask the person in charge of follow-up to find out what Loretta and Elizabeth were up to these days. If they were looking for funding for a new project, CNS couldn't help directly but could ask another foundation to help them.

He told Lynx about his encounter with Anton, hoping to find out how she felt about him. If she had a lot of respect for Anton, it would clearly affect his recommendation that she be given a grant. It could mean that she was unstable.

"I don't know Anton too well," she told him. "I saw one of his pieces on elk hunting, and I had a problem with the ethics of it, although its production values were superior. I invited him up here to see how we make wildlife videos here in the West."

Daren was relieved to see she had a head on her shoulders. "We can talk more about his video later. See you tonight. I look forward to meeting you."

"Likewise."

piece of mail? These Montana pukes were inefficient and uncooperative just like the FBI back East and everywhere else in America. Arrogant asshole. The phone rang.

"Is this the Hitching Post Motel?" a sweet little thing asked.

"No, bitch, it's a goddamn pay phone."

Unruffled, the sweet voice said, "Well, do you know the Hitching Post's number? I have to cancel our reservation—our car is broken down in Idaho."

"Ain't that a goddamn shame. Go look it up your ass and get the hell off this phone," Ben yelled.

"Well you don't have to be so rude to a per . . . "

Ben slammed the phone onto its hook and lit another cigarette.

The phone rang again. It was the agent. "Walt has mailed himself a savings account from a Wyoming bank. It's got 15 grand in it. We checked the name and SS number, and that's why it took so long to get back to you. These assholes out here have Stone Age technology. The name and number belong to a deceased man from Virginia."

"A lousy 15 grand and he would risk that for his cover," Ben growled.

"I doubt the IRS would figure it out. The dead man had no living family. He was a suicide. And the FBI has no idea who we were checking on. They were reasonably cooperative, if slow."

"Okay, okay. Then keep close to him, and we'll still go hunting with him."

"We're on it boss," said the voice on the other end of the line, the voice of a trained, highly programmed killer who would shoot his own mother without a flinch.

Ben got into his car and drove south out of town. He used his car phone to call another agent who was tailing Lynx named Pithy Rice. He figured there was no way Walt had told his wife or either of the bitches he'd been fucking on the side that he was a TDP agent and would be splitting town, but he may have told Lynx.

She was a news reporter, and his check on her had found she was a good one—the kind you can trust with a secret, but also the kind that can sniff out a good story with her nose plugged and her eyes closed. He knew Susan, Tami, and Ursula had been seen at her house. Lynx had been observed frequently at the Triangle. Could be small town stuff, everyone knowing everyone else, whatever. But she was leaving town the same day Walt had and traveling in the same direction, supposedly to a wildlife media convention. And that's what the agent confirmed. She was with her son and had checked into the hotel where the convention was. She'd left hours ahead of Walt and not even stopped to pee in Bozeman. "Do you want me to have a talk with her?"

Ben thought. He was working on instinct alone. They'd tapped her phone after they'd seen Walt there and watched her house. Walt had not called her and had never gone back. That made him think Walt had told her something in confidence. It was most likely related to his problems with women, but Ben couldn't risk letting it go completely.

"Yeah, talk to her," he ordered. "She's a seasoned reporter, so she won't give anything away. But scare the living shit out of her if you even think she knows anything, and even if you don't think she knows."

"Who do I tell her I'm with?"

"Show her your CIA credentials like we did with the FBI in Bozeman. You know the routine."

• • •

Lynx was just getting out of the shower when someone knocked on her door. Merlin got up on his tiptoes and looked through the one-way peephole.

"It's a big guy in a suit, Mom."

That wouldn't be Anton or Darren, Lynx reasoned. They'd both been dressed in casual clothes.

"Tell him your mom will be right there," she said, pullling on a bath robe.

Pithy flashed his badge and asked Lynx to take a little walk down the hall with him and leave the kid in the room.

"I'll be right back—it's okay," she told Merlin.

In the ice room, Pithy tried not to look at Lynx's boobs, which were sticking sweetly out of her robe, and spoke to her in his most authoritarian tone of voice as he held out his badge again and gave her time to read it.

"I'll get straight to the point. You can talk now, or I'll haul you into questioning in Bozeman on Monday." Lynx was looking at him with wide eyes, registering no emotion whatsoever. "We know you had a conversation with Walt Yander not that long ago at your house. What was it about?"

"It was strictly personal business between me and Walt," Lynx answered coolly.

"Somehow I don't believe you."

"That's your problem. I don't have to talk to you, and you know goddamn well I don't have to go anywhere with you for questioning. So I'm going to turn around and go back to my room. I'm here to enjoy myself."

"Look, little lady, you can get smart with me but that will get you nowhere fast. I hope for your sake it was personal." He searched her eyes for fear. They were stone cold.

"I hope you aren't threatening me," Lynx said softly.

"Let's just say that if it was more than a personal conversation and you talk to anyone about it or write about it, you'd better not ever again in your life walk down a dark alley alone or send your kid out to play by himself."

Obviously, Lynx thought, these assholes aren't really CIA and they probably would hurt her or Merlin if she told anyone about Walt. She figured they were with TDP, whatever that really was.

"Look, a lot of people visit me at my house since it's also my news office. They talk about all kinds of stuff. I don't even remember what Walt talked about, probably some story he thought I should write that I have no interest in. I forget that stuff. I have enough important shit to remember," Lynx told him, looking straight into his eyes. "Sorry you wasted a trip up here. Now leave me alone. I have a dinner date to get ready for."

Pithy watched her butt as she walked back to her room. He knew she was lying, but he knew she wouldn't talk, either. She was a stand-up bitch. He phoned Ben with this observation and headed back to Bozeman.

As she dressed, Lynx cursed Walt for involving her in his bullshit and ran over in her mind what she would do if the TDP didn't leave her alone. She thought of calling her attorney, but reasoned that if they were tailing her and using phony CIA credentials, they would probably be watching her for awhile, maybe even tapping her phone. Best thing to do would be to forget about it and go on with her life. She had nothing to worry about.

She put her encounter with Pithy at the back of her mind and told Merlin he was an insurance salesman. Merlin was too interested in a PBS special on turtles, his favorite animal, to even listen. Just in case there was trouble, however, she made sure a round was loaded in the chamber of her Colt .32 and that the pistol was tucked in her purse.

Chapter Sixteen

The two women sitting at the corner table of the Leaf and Bean in Bozeman were so magnetic that all eyes in the crowded coffee house were on them.

Dewey and Nora hadn't expected the place to be so packed at 9:30 in the morning, just after the first round of coffee drinkers had come in for their wake-up buzz and not quite before the pick-me-up period. Individually, with their exotic cheekbones, faces softly lined by lives of love and service, long white hair, and golden auras seen by even those who don't believe in auras, Dewey and Nora drew glances wherever they went. Together they were knockouts.

The two sages were meeting to discuss how they could help Lynx. Although each had warned Lynx that she was soon to be under spiritual attack, both knew she needed more than warnings. She needed their help. They also believed that God predestines spiritual warfare in the lives of those who are trying to live in service. So rather than try to think of how to prevent Lynx's upcoming crisis, they were thinking of ways to help her along. She had lessons to learn, and so would they as they assisted her.

Jack walked into the Leaf and Bean and ordered five two-pound bags of different flavored coffee beans before he spotted Dewey and Nora. He was on his monthly errand run to Bozeman, where he purchased all the supplies he couldn't buy in West, did his banking, and visited his brother and sister. He was surprised to see Dewey and Nora together, although he knew both were friends of Lynx, having seen them with Lynx now and then in town. He was especially surprised to see them because he had dreamed of Lynx all night last night. They were dark, terrible dreams of her being in deep trouble and calling for help as Anton, looking like a scaly beast with the same blood-red eyes he'd seen at Specimen Creek, tore at her throat with long, sharp teeth and screamed at her.

He finished his purchase and strolled over to Dewey and Nora's table. He introduced himself as a close friend of Lynx who had seen them with her in West and asked if he could join them. He sensed that it was not a simple coincidence that all three were there at the same time, and as he had done after his encounter with Anton, he squirmed at the thought that something exists outside of concrete reality.

Dewey and Nora had never met Jack before, but each knew immediately that he was indeed a friend of Lynx's and that they could trust him. They invited him to sit down. Jack looked out across the room at all the staring people, who were even more curious about Dewey and Nora now that he was with them, dressed in his well worn work jeans, red plaid shirt, and work boots. He rubbed his thick, curly beard and stared back. Suddenly, everyone seemed most interested in what was in the bottom of their coffee cups.

"We're meeting here because we're concerned about Lynx," Nora told him.

Jack felt relieved and frightened at the same time. Maybe the nightmares didn't mean he was going crazy.

"We've been thinking for a long time now that Lynx is going to have a difficult time, and we are looking at ways to help her," Dewey told him.

When Jack looked into Lynx's eyes while he was making love to her, he thought he'd seen the deepest, most soulful eyes in the universe. Looking into Dewey and Nora's eyes, he saw the same depth and a great deal more of something else. Was it wisdom? He didn't know for sure.

"Last night," he told them, I had terrible nightmares. Lynx was being attacked by a monster, a real monster, in my opinion. It was that Anton guy she is somehow involved with."

Dewey and Nora shared their growing concerns about Anton.

"That tears it," Jack said angrily. "I'm going to pay him a visit and tell him to stay away from her."

"No," Nora said, "You can't do that. Anton is working for a very powerful, very evil group. We don't know which one yet. Physical and verbal threats won't make matters better."

"What, then?" Jack thought of holding Lynx, of smelling her, of shooting guns with her and watching the sun go down behind the mountains. His feelings for her were much more than sexual. She was his friend. She was the first woman he'd ever really connected to and had helped him restore confidence he lost after his wife left him.

Dewey and Nora saw what he was feeling and smiled at one another.

"We have to pray for her," Nora said.

Jack let that sink in. He wasn't a pray-er.

"We are working this out right now," explained Dewey. "We are going to pray for Lynx every three hours around the clock."

"You can join us from wherever you are. Just stop and ask God to send her grace. When you feel God's presence, He will draw you into deeper conversation and awareness, and you may think of more things to say to Him or even ways to help Lynx on the physical plane," Nora told him.

Jack explained that he was not into praying.

"Take it on faith that this would be a help and give it a try. Obviously you didn't walk in here when we were here for no reason. When three people link up in prayer, it is very powerful, even if one of the angles in the triangle is a beginner," Nora smiled.

"Oh, and remember this—Lynx will be fine. She is just one of those special people who loves so deeply that evil forces are attracted to her as well as those who need love. The evil in the world is getting stronger and stronger, but we already know that good will win. We are here to help that happen. In the time between the times we stop and pray, we put the battle out of our minds and just enjoy living. That is very important to do, or you could become very depressed," Dewey told Jack.

"I'll try. It ain't exactly what I do when I have a problem, but what the heck," Jack said. "What hours do we pray?"

"Every three hours beginning this day at noon," Nora answered. She didn't tell him that many of these hours are also the times when Christians all over the world pray from the "The Liturgy of the Hours," and she certainly did not mention that the forces of evil, under such names as Light Trust, Triangles, Inc., the New Group of World Servers, and the Love and Light Foundation, unite with great focus at these same hours to invoke the forces of evil which they serve.

Dewey leaned close to Jack and touched his arm. "Let me tell you about something that happens to us when we make a commitment to pray. A kind of spiritual numbness overtakes us at the appointed hours. We forget to look at the clock, we forget to pray. We then feel we are failing and it's all useless. Don't let this bother you. The evil forces we are combating do this to us at the beginning of their prayer hours, which are the same as ours, to keep us from praying. We must do it back by beginning our prayer with a strong affirmation."

"What does that mean?"

"The strongest one I know of is 'In the name of the Father, and the Son, and the Holy Spirit,'" Nora said. "Say it with authority. It means that you are praying in the light of the Trinity, the union of God the creator, his presence on earth in the physical form of Jesus Christ, and the wisdom and counsel he sends us through the Holy Spirit. It is very powerful."

"I've heard that affirmation, as you call it, all my life and never saw it is a powerful thing."

"Ah, yes, we are so mechanical in our prayer life. But believe me, the Evil ones are not. They are most focused. We have to be, too. If you read a prayer or say one you memorized, never forget that the words have power and say them with all your heart."

"You know I really love that lady," Jack confided. "I thought we could get something going together, but she won't go for it. She told me that down the line it wouldn't work out because she thinks I need a more conventional woman."

Nora laughed. "Lynx isn't conventional by any means. I think she was being fair to you. You see, you're attracted to her uniqueness and even frightened by it. But it may not be what you need in a wife."

Jack took off his hat and rubbed his scalp. "I don't know what I need in a wife. I thought my first wife was the gal for me, but she left me. She was living in a different world from me, and I didn't see it. It was a shocker, and then I got together with Lynx and felt things I never experienced with Vicky. Good things. I don't want to let go of that, but Lynx wants me to keep looking. She says I will find the right gal. At least she gave me confidence that I am someone a woman would be attracted to."

"And she may have opened up your mind to new experiences that are good for you besides being with a woman, huh?" Dewey asked.

Jack thought a moment. "Yes, and those are what frighten me. ESP sort of stuff. It's scary."

"Right," Nora said, laughing again. "I can assure you that you will not be harmed by what you call ESP. It's simply developing your spiritual intuition, learning to hear the words of the Holy Spirit, and it is going to be good for you." She looked at the wall clock. "Well, it's getting late, and we have to go."

Jack took their check and put the money on the table. "Let me walk you ladies out of here," he said.

They said good-bye, and Jack watched them walk down the street together until they were out of sight, wondering what he'd gotten himself into now.

He finished his errands in a daze, mulling over the morning's conversation. At noon, he walked into Holy Rosary Church on Bozeman's Main Street and sat in one of the back pews. A dozen older women were kneeling in different pews closer to the altar, moving rosary beads through their fingers or reading prayer books. He thought about asking one of them for help and wondered what they were praying about. He looked at the large crucifix over the altar and wondered who Jesus really was and why he let himself be crucified if he was God.

He felt more confused than ever. Why couldn't life be simple? He remembered that Nora had said the forces of evil were increasing around the world and had a sudden awareness that God was calling him to prayer. He asked God to protect Lynx and himself and all the people who were being attacked.

Later, Jack went to the attic of his sister's house, where many of his childhood things were stored, and found the Bible his grandmother had given him when he'd been confirmed. He would take it home and read it. Maybe it was time he found out more about God.

Chapter Seventeen

Dave sat in a window booth overlooking the truck stop's parking lot and sipped his fourth cup of bitter coffee. His head pounded with a hangover, and he had trouble remembering what happened last night.

He'd gone to the Molly Brown after watching a lousy action movie in his motel room since nothing decent was showing in the theaters around town. There he'd met two guys who were drinking themselves through some pretty sticky divorces. Their soon-to-be ex-wives were trying to get half of what they'd worked for all their lives. One was an electrical contractor, the other a building contractor. The guys were so distracted and depressed by their impending divorces that they said they hadn't worked in weeks without making mistakes and found no enjoyment in what they were doing. They had each finally gone to shrinks who gave them Prozac for their depression. They were ignoring their doctors' warnings about not mixing Prozac with booze. The combination helped them get through the night, they told Dave, when they had too much time on their hands.

Dave was not into drugs, but he'd taken a handful of Prozac when they offered it to him, and had popped one before he went to sleep and another when he woke up. They seemed to deaden his emotions. He pulled another out of his shirt pocket and wiped the fuzz off of it before washing it down with his last sip of coffee.

Soon life began to move along in slow motion. He was not as worked up over Tami as he had been last night, but he still felt a bit on edge when he thought of Walt. How could Walt have done this to him? His new drinking buddies had made him see the light. A best friend simply does not fuck your wife, they told him. It's inexcusable. Dave knew he had to take a stand. There'd be no hunting trip. How could he trust Walt again? It would always be there. "Shit," Dave suddenly wondered, "what if I really loved her? My heart would be broken along with my pride."

Walt walked in, and Dave watched him look around the room until they made eye contact. The rising tide of hate toward Walt overwhelmed him, and he felt like flinging his coffee cup at Walt's head. Walt sat down, and Dave stood up abruptly.

"You're late," he said, "I'm coffee-ed out. Grab a go cup and meet me in my camper. It's out there." He pointed to his rig.

"Man, you look like shit. Sit down a minute, will you?" Walt told him.

"Yeah, well I have reason to look like shit, and I don't want to be in this place anymore," Dave countered as he walked toward the door.

Walt knew at that moment that Dave had heard about him and Tami. Great, he thought, so much for the hunting trip. He'll probably shoot me. He ordered a coffee and cinnamon roll and went to the camper.

Dave was sitting on one of the beds, holding a double-barreled shotgun. "I should shoot you right now and get it over with. I know you've been banging Tami," he told Walt, his voice very low and shaky.

"I'll be straight with you, Dave," Walt answered, trying not to look at the gun. He smelled last night's booze on Dave's breath and noted how unsteady his hands were. "It's true, man. But you have to hear the whole story."

"Nah, don't bother me with that. You'll say she jumped your bones—you'll have all kinds of excuses. They may be good ones, but the bottom line is that no matter how it came down, you did it and I can no longer trust you."

"It was the worst mistake of my life, and I'm sorry," Walt said softly.

Dave set the shotgun down on the floor in front of his feet. "I ain't gonna shoot you, man. You ain't worth it." His voice shook.

Walt looked at Dave without responding. He was on something, not just hungover, something that was making him short-fused and irrational. Sometimes if you play to that kind of temperament, they snap out of it, he remembered from his police training. He reached under his arm and pulled the .357 out of its holster.

"Dave," he said steadily, "remember this? We traded it. Take it back and shoot me with it. A lot of people know I have it. They'll think I committed suicide. You'll get away with it and put me out of my misery as well."

Dave scooted the shotgun under the bed, took the .357, and pointed it at Walt. The coffee and Prozac and trace of booze in his system were making his head spin and his hands shake.

"You would love such an easy way out, wouldn't you? Maybe I'd like to kill you slowly, watch your business run down when the entire town knows you fucked my wife and one of your waitresses, watch Susan finally dump your ass."

"You don't have to worry about any of that," Walt countered. "I'm out of here. I've been planning a way out for a long time. I don't intend to ever return to West Yellowstone."

"What do you mean?"

"I mean I went to buy a loaf of bread and never came back. I mean I'm past tense. Gone. Out of here. It was to be our last hunting trip together. Wouldn't you run if you were in the mess I'm in?"

Dave glared at Walt. What a coward, he thought. He put his finger on the trigger, thinking of how it would scare the shit out of Walt and make him beg for mercy.

Instinctively, Walt jumped up to grab the gun. It went off. Walt felt the round hit his head, but there was no pain. The gun was on the floor near his left foot. He picked it up and looked at Dave, who was stumbling toward the door.

"Get the fuck out of this camper and take your goddamn gun with you, asshole," Dave shouted.

Walt felt blood run down his neck and held his head as he nearly fell out of the camper at Dave's push. He looked around the parking lot and saw a TDP agent standing by a van he'd seen in West Yellowstone. For once, he was glad they were following him. The agent nodded to him and pointed to the highway, giving him a sign that he would be picked up there. His head was pounding now—from the wound or the stress he could not tell—and he hurriedly walked in the direction he was pointed in. He didn't see a vehicle that looked like it was ready to pick him up, so he kept walking. When he was around a curve in the road that hid him from the view of the truck stop and the parking lot, he saw the van. Its back door opened and a hand beckoned him in.

He jumped inside and was in a helicopter within 20 minutes, on the way to the plane that would take him to South America.

• • •

When he heard the report of Walt's removal from Bozeman, Ben went ballistic. Surely someone had heard the gunshot, surely someone had seen Walt dazed and walking down the road, maybe even get into the van.

He was furious that he would have to stay behind in Bozeman and clean things up. He checked into a dumpy motel, called Pithy and told him where he was, and thought the situation over as he paced the room and chain-smoked. He would have to go on the belief that no one saw Walt get into the van. That would leave witnesses who saw Walt and Dave in the cafe, blood stains in the camper, a possibility of someone hearing a gun shot, and the possibility of someone having spotted a man with a head wound to work with—a lot messier than the getting-lost-in-the-wilderness plan. He would have to stick around and see how the local police handled it when Susan reported Walt's disappearance and go from there.

Chapter Eighteen

"Cut my pizza for me, please, Mom," Merlin asked Lynx. He had hated knives ever since he had cut himself trying to chop up an earthworm in their backyard when he was four.

Lynx picked up the knife, and Anton put his hand over hers. "I'll do it for you," he said gently. A pleasant electric shiver rippled through her, sparked by his touch and his voice. He seemed to be a different man than she felt he was before. He was charming and sweet, and it felt real this time.

She wondered if she had misjudged him, as she had in the past misjudged people, especially men. Maybe it was just that they had a difference of opinion about media. Maybe in her deep unconscious she was deeply attracted to him but resisting the idea. Perhaps her old fear of intimacy had resurfaced. She let herself feel the pleasurable electric tingling. It was okay. Perhaps his being there at the same time CNS was going to offer her a grant was a positive thing. She would need a technical assistant if she were to do video, and Anton was good. It was the content of his stuff that bothered her, but perhaps it was a failing that she judged him completely because of that difference.

Anton could see Lynx softening and refining her view of him. The programming was working, and it made him feel powerful because she was not a particularly yielding person. If he could succeed with her, what else could he do?

He kept their conversation light and avoided talking about her upcoming meeting with CNS, his video, or her AV equipment at the museum.

He noticed that she became brighter and more beautiful as their dinner progressed and she relaxed and let herself enjoy their conversation. By the time he walked her to her motel room door, she was positively radiant, and Merlin was bouncy and at ease as well. He touched her arm and thanked her for the pleasant time, and she returned his touch. He felt electricity flowing out of her, and it gave him an instant erection. That surprised him. He hadn't had sex in many years, preferring to redirect his sexual energy to his higher goals. That her touch could make him respond sexually without thinking stunned him and shook his confidence in his own power.

• • •

The coyote stretched his body out to its full length and crouched down until he looked almost like a weasel, his eyes fixed on the trumpeter swan downwind of him. She was sitting peacefully on her nest and watching her mate, whose tail feathers were sticking out of the calm water as he fed on plants growing in the river bottom.

He skulked over dry ground through the tall grasses that surrounded the swan's nest. He had looked at this nest the previous four wet springs, when it was surrounded by water and mud. The swans had always detected him when he approached it because they heard him slosh through the mud. This year's dry spring had left many traditional nesting places unprotected, but many swans and geese and ducks hadn't adjusted to the drought. Creatures of habit and instinct, they returned to remodel and repair their old nests rather than seek out new and safer areas in which they would have to build from scratch.

The coyote froze when he was three feet from the nest, still undetected by either swan. He leapt into the air, opened his mouth wide, and pounced on her neck, biting it nearly in half. Every nerve in her lovely white body twitched violently as the life went out of her. The unusual movement startled the cob, who had just lifted his head out of the water and was swallowing a slippery chunk of snail-covered weeds.

He let out a huge trumpet, ending in short, jerky grunts as he nearly choked on the weeds, and swam toward her with all his power. The coyote had by then grabbed hold of her broken neck and was running with her through the tall grass, across the road, and up the hill into the lodgepole forest. In seconds he was out of view. Some of her feathers clung to the grass that had broken under his feet, rustling like laundry hung out to dry in the wind.

Her mate looked at the nest holding the four eggs they had been taking turns sitting on, threw back his head, and screamed. Trumpeter swans mate for life. When they fly, their call sounds like a trumpet celebrating the beauty and freedom of the wilderness. But when they lose a mate, they scream. The sound is dissonant, mournful, and unforgettable.

Lynx had captured that sound, along with the entire death scene, on videotape the previous spring. She had been working on a piece about the effects of Yellowstone's drought on nesting birds, something she had observed but could not find any scientist who studied birds to confirm. They'd all told her that birds adapt to drought, but she had seen with her own eyes that swans, great blue herons, and even bald eagles were returning to nest in areas that were once safe because they were wet and muddy, but had dried up and exposed the nests to predators. She thought that if she documented this on video, bird managers, especially those who spent more time in their offices doing paperwork than they did in the field, may listen.

Taping the swan death had been difficult. Lynx had been watching the swan couple longer than the coyote had and had named them Olga and Olaf. They were some of the most photographed animals in Yellowstone because they nested so close to the road.

Their nest was near the Seven Mile Bridge over the Madison River, halfway between West Yellowstone and Madison Junction, and they were a prolific couple. Lynx had seen them produce some 35 cygnets in those many years. She had not expected to see the coyote the day she was taping. She was trying to document the dry areas around the nest and the distance Oleg was feeding from the nest because there was no water close by, and she had glanced away from the camera for a second and seen the coyote out of the corner of her eye.

When she saw he was going to succeed at his hunt, she thought of stopping him by shouting or throwing a rock at him, but she knew that would be wrong. Nature was taking its course, and a journalist chronicling that reality had no business messing with it. She was not responsible for Olga's death in that context. But the part of her that felt she was a friend to the swan ached.

The script to Lynx's video told the story of her painful decision to let the scene before her unfold naturally, despite her personal friendship with the swans, and the story of the wildlife managers' apparent lack of interest in the drought's effects on swans and other birds. Nora Spotted Elk narrated the story in her soft, deep Indian voice. The effect was tremendous, evidenced by the moment of complete silence followed by loud and long applause from the audience at the end of the screening.

The next screening was a film on grizzly bears in Yellowstone's Lamar Valley made by one of the best wildlife filmmakers in America. His work was exceptional in every way, showing he spent hours in the field waiting for the best shots. He scored his work with beautiful music but made no commentary on the declining grizzly bear population. Lynx noticed that although his film had been made during the previous two years, three of the bears he'd photographed had been killed in park "management actions" for seeking human food sources. However, this fact was not relayed in the film.

Lynx's bison video was screened after a half hour break in which Lynx didn't get a chance to talk with Anton or Daren because she was cornered by a representative of a video production company that wanted to mass produce her swan piece. She politely told the man she would think about his offer to pay her a flat rate for the video and a royalty each time one sold.

Lynx fidgeted in her chair as the bison video began, nervous that it would be too controversial, especially among the many National Park Service and National Forest Service people who were at the conference. "Oh, well," she thought. "They may not like it, but it's the truth as I see it."

The video documented the fact that in recent years, Yellowstone's bison had begun to wander out of the park in larger numbers, usually beginning their migration in late fall. Not being able to read maps, road signs, and property markers, the bison roamed onto ranch land north and west of the park, where domestic cattle grazed. Yellowstone's bison carry a disease called brucellosis. Brucellosis also invades livestock herds and causes cows to abort their calves. Usually after one miscarriage, the cow is immune to the disease, but cattlemen don't want brucellosis in their herds. Besides causing the loss of cattle, brucellosis can be transmitted to humans, as Bang's disease. The disease is not fatal, but it makes humans quite sick with intestinal problems and could cause already sick people a great deal of grief.

Years ago the livestock industry made it a requirement that only brucellosis-free animals could be exported to other states and nations. Each state's livestock board worked at ensuring that its state had brucellosis-free status. Since bison carry the brucella organism, the livestock boards went into a panic when the bison left the park and turned up on ranch land. They demanded that the bison be shot immediately or somehow returned to the park.

The Montana Department of Fish, Wildlife and Parks responded to the livestock industry's demand by initiating a hunt. Hunters applied for permits to shoot the wayward buffaloes and went on the hunts with game wardens. The bison had never been hunted before, and in the park, they grazed peacefully near roads while tourists snapped their pictures. Since the bison were so fearless, the bison hunt did not have the character of any other large mammal hunt. The hunters were able to approach the animals closely to shoot them. Rarely did the animals run too far when they noticed the hunters, even after one of them was shot.

The hunt was controversial for many reasons. Most of the hunters picked out the largest bull to shoot because they wanted to mount its head and have a large hide to hang in their dens. If the hunt was what it was supposed to be, a control action for brucellosis, only bison cows should have been shot. The brucella organism is hottest in the afterbirth of a bison calf, and hot only for two or three days. A domestic cow would have to lick the bison's afterbirth to catch the disease, in theory. In reality, however, Lynx's investigation had found that there had never been a documented case of any wild bison giving a domestic cow brucellosis.

When the national media learned about the bison hunt, reporters were sent to Montana from all over the country. The vast majority of them were from large cities where hunting was neither a favorite sport or a tradition as it is in Montana. The media was shocked when they saw the hunters walk right up to the bison, a national symbol of the West and Yellowstone Park's logo, and shoot them in cold blood. They gave this more play than the fact that the brucellosis concern was probably bogus, especially when most of the animals being shot were bulls.

The media also ignored the age-long political power battle between the National Park Service, National Forest Service, whose land some of the bison were hanging out on, and the livestock industry. They also didn't show the hunting of any wild animal in a good light, since most of them were anti-hunting and slanting their stories against hunting, to the delight of animal rights groups.

As more and more bison were killed, even hunters began to denounce the hunt because it was giving hunting bad publicity.

Lynx's video covered all these controversies in interviews with bison biologists, livestock board veterinarians, ranchers, hunters, visitors to Yellowstone, and officials from all the public agencies involved. One of the most important messages she tried to convey came from bison biologists who said that allowing snowmobiling in Yellowstone was a mistake if the public didn't want wildlife to leave Yellowstone's boundaries. The biologists said that the bison left in greater numbers when they had an easy way out over the snow on groomed snowmobile trails. They also said that if the bison couldn't leave and find forage in other places, many would remain in the park and die. Winter-killed bison were an important spring food source for grizzly bears emerging from their dens, they argued.

Making the video had been time consuming but easy for Lynx. The interviews had gone well and didn't require a lot of fancy camera work. The bison hunt she taped was classic. Six hunters picked off an equal number of bulls in less than two hours, accompanied by an entourage of game wardens, friends to help them skin out the animals, and other reporters. Lynx cut several shots of bison she taped in the park the previous summer into the video. They were exquisite shots of newborn calves, yearlings at play, and bulls and cows grazing in meadows near the Firehole River. Her bison video received the same strong applause as the swan piece had, and she was surrounded with people who wanted a copy and wanted to congratulate her on telling the entire bison story.

Anton's reaction was different. Over coffee after all the pieces had been screened, he told her he'd expected more from her.

"More of what, exactly?" she asked, trying not to get angry. Perhaps he would have something useful to say.

"Your tapes are like your news stories. They are factual and accurate, but they don't show the true personalities of the people you're presenting."

"How so?"

"Take that animal activist you interviewed, the guy from Maryland. He's a faggot. He hates hunting because that's part of his homosexual gestalt. You could have played that up. And take the big fat hunter who came all the way from Minnesota to kill a bison. He was a slob."

"I don't know if you're right about either person. And even if you are, so what? What does that have to do with the essence of the story? All animal activists aren't gay, and all hunters aren't slobs."

"But the ones you taped are." Anton's voice was strangely soft, paternal almost, Lynx noticed, as if he were trying to tell her something obvious.

"Okay, Anton, going along with your train of thought," she replied, using her most maternal voice, "what should I have done?"

"Off the top of my head, I suggest something like this." He was serious now. Lynx felt like shooting him. "For example, with the hunter, you could have cut in a few extreme close-ups of his big belly hanging over his pants."

Lynx laughed. "That would be cruel."

Anton ignored her. "As for the fag, you could have done some close-ups of those cute little red sneakers he was wearing and his city clothes, or pressured him more to express his beliefs."

"You're crazy," Lynx told him. "Anyway, he wears sneakers because he won't wear leather shoes or anything made out of animal products. He doesn't even eat eggs or cheese. I don't even think he's a fag. I think his physical appearance is delicate and gentle because he doesn't eat meat. And zeroing in on him would have meant that the story wouldn't have been as balanced as I wanted it to be."

Anton could see that, at that point in time, Lynx could not be argued with. At least, he thought, she believed strongly in what she was doing. "Okay, Lynx," he told her. "We look at things differently. Maybe I should make a bison video of my own."

"There you go," Lynx told him, glad he wasn't going to keep arguing with her. "Now I've got to get some sleep so I'm rested for the drive home tomorrow. Thanks for coming, and I hope you're here next year with your work."

Anton stood up. "That's a promise. I'll call you later this week, and we can get together. Have a safe trip home." He hid his disappointment that she didn't want to spend time with him that night. He knew, however, that if he showed her a certain amount of respect she would be more responsive to him later

. . .

Lynx took her first cup of Monday morning coffee back to bed and sipped it slowly, relishing the memories of the weekend. CNS had offered her a half million dollars to produce 26 six-minute television segments on the Yellowstone Ecosystem. They would be part of a weekly show on wilderness areas all over the world. She would also produce three hour-long specials on Yellowstone.

She would be given total freedom as to the subject matter she chose. She could focus on pretty animal pieces or politically hot controversies. Technical freedom was limitless, too, and the reason why the award was so large. She could purchase any type of equipment she chose and edit the sound and the pictures any way she liked.

She decided on her drive home to sell both videos to the production company, which would give her enough money to live on until the grant money started coming in. Anton had been a pain in the ass, but she'd learned over the weekend that she could tolerate their differences. If he would agree to give her total control of the content of her work, she would definitely ask him to help her produce her pieces for CNS.

Merlin had been perfectly behaved and had met three kids he related to beautifully, all children of other media people. It was very important to Lynx that her son have as much exposure as possible to people other than West Yellowstone-ites. She didn't want him to have too narrow a view of the world.

And last night, Jack had stopped by. They'd had a wonderful talk. He'd asked her many questions about the weekend and seemed genuinely interested in what she was doing. Lynx thought of the dark look that passed over his face whenever she talked about Anton, but figured he may be a touch jealous. That had made her a little horny for some strange reason, she recalled, and she had hugged Jack when he got up to leave. He hugged her back and then kissed her, and it was only because she had a rule about sleeping with men when Merlin was there that she didn't change her mind about not having sex with him and take him to bed. They had made a shooting and picnic date for tonight, when Merlin would be staying with Lou.

Lynx had also decided while driving home from Kalispell that she would find an assistant manager for the museum and split her salary with that person, so she would only have to work there 15-20 hours a week. She had all summer to prepare her project proposal for the CNS Foundation, as shooting would not begin until December. Still, working on it would take around ten hours a week, she figured, and she would surely be running full steam for the *Gazette* if it turned out the Yellowstone fires erupted as predicted.

She was running through a list of people to offer the assistant job to when the phone rang. It was Myrna, her city editor at the *Gazette*.

After small talk about their weekends, Myrna told Lynx that the morning's police report included a missing person report on Walt. "Since he's a prominent member of the West Yellowstone community, we want you to write a piece for today, just a little background on him and his family. Talk to the law, see what they think might have happened."

Lynx thought quickly. She couldn't write about Walt's disappearance. Not after he'd told her about it and she had been visited by a CIA agent, or whatever that man was. She told Myrna she didn't want to do the story because she knew Walt and several of his close friends well.

"Lynx, you know everyone in West Yellowstone. Foul play isn't suspected. It's a straight story. His wife reported him missing Saturday morning, and they officially listed him as missing this morning."

"Look, Myrna, you've always told me I have a nose for a story. Trust me on this one. It won't be a simple lost-in-the-woods, expected-to-return deal. I just have a gut feeling it's bigger than that, and I don't want to cover it."

There was a long pause. "Just a gut feeling? Or do you know something?"

"Just a gut feeling. Besides, I wanted to work on my feature on Island Park for this Sunday's paper. I still have a lot of people to interview and photos to take."

"That's right. You have three features due by Wednesday on Island Park, an artist interview, and something on education. Are you on it?"

"If you leave me alone and let me work, I'm on it."

"Okay, okay, just get your features in by 10 a.m. Wednesday."

"Thanks, Myrna."

"Oh, and by the way, congratulations on your success at the conference. We're proud of you and are running a story on it. It seems a lot of people reacted well to your complete bison coverage and were touched by the swan piece."

"Thanks, but you know the best thing that happened to me over the weekend was that CNS offered me a grant."

"Wow! That's a story, too."

"Yeah, it will be. They'll announce it and send you a release, and I'll be leaving the *Gazette* when I start my project sometime late in the fall."

"The boss will love to hear that."

"Well, don't tell him yet. It will still be a few weeks before my contract with CNS is signed, and I know my timetable. Don't panic him now."

Lynx called the local Job Service office and asked the job counselor to make appointments for her to see the people on her list and anyone else with the qualifications to be her assistant manager, loaded her camera equipment and notebooks in her car, and took off to Island Park.

Before she headed back to West, she stopped at the *Villager*, Island Park's local weekly paper, and took out a classified ad looking for a small cabin to rent or buy near Henry's Lake. She was surprised to see Dave walking into the *Villager* office just as she was leaving.

"What's up, Dave? Did you hear Walt is missing? The *Gazette* called me this morning and wanted me to write about it. And what are you doing down here, anyway?"

A flicker of pain shot across Dave's face. He composed himself and smiled at Lynx.

"Listen, Ms. Reporter—one question at a time. Nothing's up—I'm putting an ad in the paper for my business. No, I didn't hear Walt is missing, and I now have a condo down here. I'm spending the night."

"I didn't know you had a place here," Lynx replied, wondering if she should tell him she had heard Walt arrange to meet him in Bozeman Friday. No, she had to stay out of the story. "That's what I'm doing," she went on, "trying to get a place here so I can get away from West sometimes."

"I just leased the condo this morning for the same reason. I need a getaway. Tami and I are getting a divorce."

"That doesn't surprise me too much, Dave," she replied, her voice sympathetic. "But I'm sorry. It's still hard, even if it is the best thing."

• • •

Only one person wanted to apply for the museum job. West Yellowstone employees were more interested in making big money on tips in the summer than having jobs where they had to think and have a great deal of responsibility. It was one of the people on Lynx's list, Sylvan Miller, an older man who loved to read books. Retired from a railroad executive position, he worked primarily to fill time. "He would be perfect," Lynx thought. They got along well, and he'd purchased so many books at the museum's store over the years that he wouldn't need much book sales training. He could also start the next day. Lynx hurried home and changed into her grubbies for her date with Jack.

This time, they took their guns to the top of Two Top Mountain, shot cans and cardboard man targets, cooked steak on his portable charcoal grill, and watched the stars for a few hours. When they returned to town to have coffee at Jack's house, a message on his phone told him to call the police department immediately, which he did.

When he hung up the phone, he told Lynx, "They arrested Dave a few hours ago and charged him with the murder of Walt. They want to question me, I suppose because I know them both. I can't believe it."

Nor could Lynx. Her stomach was in knots. How could this be? "Where did they find Walt's body?" she asked.

"They haven't. They've searched a lot of places, too. But they found blood and human tissue in Dave's camper and a gun on his inventory list is missing, same caliber as a round that put a bullet hole in the camper."

Lynx thought quickly. So Walt didn't make it after all. What a bad deal.

"Jack," she said, "I was going to head home now, but is it okay if I wait until you get back from the Cop Shop? I'd like to know what's going on."

"So you can write about it?"

"No, I took myself off this story when the editor asked me to write about Walt's disappearance. I'd just like to know what's going on."

"Sure—stick around." Jack kissed Lynx on the cheek as he headed for the door and remembered suddenly how many such automatic kisses he'd given Vicky when he'd left for work. He turned around, put his arms around Lynx, and kissed her hard. "Practice," he thought.

Chapter Nineteen

Lynx stared at the knotty pine ceiling in her cabin's master bedroom. It would not stop turning around. She'd barely made the 16-mile trip to her new Island Park cabin nestled in aspen trees with a great view of Henry's Lake. She'd bought it for a steal from an old couple who wanted to move to Arizona as soon as possible. The deal wouldn't close for a few months, but they'd agreed to let her live there until the sale was final so it wouldn't be empty when they were away.

Her head ached intensely, with sharp, stabbing pains behind her eyes that made tears flow down her face. She was nauseous and, whenever she laid down, extremely dizzy. Maybe she had an ear infection, she thought. But do ear infections give you recurring nightmares? And don't antibiotics and decongestants knock them out of you pretty quickly? She'd started taking both, leftovers she'd kept in her medicine cabinet from past illnesses. But the headaches and dreams hadn't gone away, and the dizziness was more intense than ever. She'd been living for this weekend, when Merlin would be with Lou and she could spend time alone in Island Park.

Lynx reviewed the last three weeks of her life. It seemed as if months had gone by.

Dave was out on bail, charged with murdering Walt. He insisted he was innocent. Walt had not been found, but Dave apparently was the last person to see Walt, and the police believed he had a motive. Walt was screwing his wife, and a gun was missing from his inventory. Investigators found that Dave's camper had been recently cleaned and new carpet installed. And Dave had changed his story when interviewed by the police about Walt's disappearance, first saying he'd never seen him in Bozeman, then admitting he had and that they had fought. He said Walt had left the camper wounded but not fatally so. Dave told the police Walt had said he intended to leave West Yellowstone without telling anyone so he could start a new life. He'd reminded the police that Walt had walked out on his first wife without notice, too.

Lynx wished she could believe Dave did it. Then her conscience would not haunt her so. But she felt that Dave had been set up and was in a turmoil about whether or not to risk telling the police that TDP was involved. She felt she had to take seriously the threat to her and Merlin's life from the asshole who visited her in Kalispell. She prayed Walt's body would be found or he would be located somehow.

It was most curious to Lynx that not a single story of the murder charge was ever picked up by the AP wire service. The editors at the *Gazette* had assured her they'd wired all the stories on the incident to the state AP office. "You would think," she reasoned, "that a murder without a body would be news in every paper across the country." Nor, she discovered, were any photos of Walt or missing persons reports being sent around the country. Surely it would make sense to continue looking for Walt, dead or alive, over a wider area than his home turf. Somehow someone was holding the stories so they wouldn't be picked up by out-of-state papers.

She suspected that local authorities may have been told to not look for a living Walt, to put on a show of searching for his body in the West Yellowstone area, where Dave could have used his excavation equipment to bury it, only to make it look as if they really believed Dave killed Walt. "Still," she wondered, "how could this be pulled off? Didn't someone, on the local level at least, have any integrity? How could they put an innocent man in jail?"

She thought of driving over to Dave's condo. Like herself, he was spending a lot of time in Island Park. He was tired of being followed everywhere by police who thought he had Walt's body hidden somewhere and would try to recover it and hide it permanently. It was most puzzling to Lynx that the police did not object to Dave's staying in Island Park since it was in another state. They had to know he spent as much time there as possible, since they were following him. And Dave had been seen in all the bars in Island Park, too, usually just drinking coffee, but sometimes staying late when a band was playing. Lynx was told by the *Gazette* reporter covering the story that conditions of Dave's release on bail included that he not go to bars or leave the state.

The county had so far spent thousands of dollars digging up nearly all of Dave's excavation sites, even ripping apart some concrete foundations he'd laid most recently, looking for Walt. Lynx and many locals she talked with about the case thought this was ridiculous. Given the fact that everyone knew

Dave had excavation equipment, wouldn't he avoid using it to bury a body, especially in an obvious place?

Investigators had sent blood and tissue samples they'd found carefully combing through the cleaned-up camper to a lab back East. "Still," Lynx wondered, "even if the blood matched Walt's blood type, and the tissue had the same DNA composition as Walt's, how would that prove that Walt was dead?"

Lynx wondered if her headaches and nightmares were connected to her worries about Dave, but doubted they were. For one, the headaches had started after she met Anton. Anton, however, was no longer in the nightmares, although they were still filled with dark-hooded men trying to force her to read the same bloody writing. Although she had no memory of what the writing was about, she "knew" she had read over half the book, because they told her so in her last dream.

Although Jack, Nora, and Dewey had all warned her about Anton and she had told them he made her feel uncomfortable, she now felt that he was one of the brightest spots in her life. She was enjoying her company with him tremendously. Or was she really? There were moments when deep down inside herself she felt afraid of him, felt that the brightness she felt around him was somehow not real. But these misgivings were always brief flashes, and she continued to blame them on her own inability to form intimate relationships. Perhaps the place in her inner psyche that may never trust men was trying to sabotage her relationship with Anton.

Lynx was beginning to notice that she was gradually becoming genuinely guilty about her sexual behavior. She was becoming aware that perhaps she should worry about how easy it was for her to have sex and on faith be more moral about her behavior, even if she in reality did not seem to have a problem with it. She had shared this thought with Anton, and he told her that she was doing the right thing. He wasn't a Christian, he told her, and had even said he did not believe in God, but still believed that relationships should be monogamous because two people should attempt to become one, to share the same soul.

Anton had told her she shouldn't have agreed to even stay friends with Jack after she broke off their sexual relationship. He told her Jack would always believe he had an "in" with her if she remained friendly towards him. She went along with Anton by not responding, although she disagreed with him and did not want to a make an issue of it. She and Jack enjoyed their time together as friends, shooting and hanging out in the outdoors. What harm would it do to continue that?

Lynx laid on her side and looked out the double-glass doors that led to a small deck. The cabin had a wonderful view of the lake and the Centennial Mountains. Just watching the water was calming. She planned to not leave the cabin all weekend for any reason, except to run down to the Little Church in the Pines at Mack's Inn for Sunday vigil mass. She would just rest and work leisurely on her CNS project proposal. She hung blankets around the deck's railing so she could not be seen by passing vehicles and people, took off all her clothes, and fell asleep in the sun.

• • •

Anton locked his doors and pulled down the black shades on all the windows in his mobile home. Not one beam of sunlight penetrated his dark haven. He laid down on his bed and thought of Lynx, and immediately got an erection. He was used to this by now. Whenever he was near her, whenever he thought of her, he became aroused sexually like he had never been before.

He was beginning to realize that this immediate and powerful sexual arousal would become a powerful tool in his quest for Lynx's soul. It was a direct result of her own weakness in sexual matters, he believed. She was innocent about sex, although until lately she'd rarely hesitated, as far as he could tell, to give herself to any man who wanted her, providing she believed that man was a friend.

Anton had, through psychokinetic probing and simply observing her, discovered that her greatest weakness was in the area of sexuality. Through psychokinetic programming and seemingly lighthearted conversations, he was re-forming her views, encouraging her to operate on what, in language she would relate to, he called a more moral plane. Being some kind of a Christian, she'd bought that lock, stock, and barrel. He'd played into her guilt, and she'd risen to his lure. He'd even quoted the many passages in her Christian Bible, which he knew by heart, that encouraged monogamous and soulful unions between men and women.

It had been laughably easy to program her to break it off with Jack. And she didn't have a clue how much she aroused him. Apparently, she had not opened her sexual channels to him. That would be the focus of his weekend in the darkness. He would call on all his powers to actualize this, and she was unknowingly making this easy for him, retreating to Island Park to be alone. He'd made sure the Masters would stop programming her so she would have no headaches or nightmares, just a quiet, serene time focusing on the CNS project. She would soon be totally open to him. The next time they were together, it would be highly electric, he was sure.

• • •

On his way back from a morning of successful trout fishing on Henry's Lake, Dave drove by Lynx's cabin and saw that she was home, and he guessed, sunbathing on the upstairs deck, since blankets were hung all around it.

God, he would love to talk with her and tell her his entire story. He knew she would believe him. He pulled over to the side of the road and thought. He needed to talk with someone before he went totally mad. He'd gone off the Prozac and stopped drinking. Nearly everyone in West Yellowstone believed he'd killed Walt, even some of his long time friends. Luckily, his attorney did not.

Dave genuinely believed that Walt would learn of his arrest and come back, or at least call, to get him off the hook. But what if Walt had left the country? Only local newspapers were carrying the story, and since not one authority believed Walt was missing, there were no missing person reports out that Walt would even run into. Dave had to believe that if this went to trial, he would win. And his attorney seemed confident of this because there was no body.

Dave was deeply crushed by Tami's behavior surrounding this incident. She was telling everyone, including the police, that he was a violent man and had probably killed Walt. How could she say these things about him? He had given her so much, put up with so much, and had rarely raised his voice to her, no matter how difficult their life had been. Certainly, he had never hit her. If anyone was weird and violent, it was she. He had to talk with someone. He turned his rig around, pulled into Lynx's driveway, walked around to the front of the cabin, and called her name.

Lynx had just wakened up to turn over and was still a bit drowsy, but she distinctly heard a man call her. She grabbed a towel and looked over the edge of the deck.

"Dave?"

"Yeah, can we talk a bit?"

"Sure, come on in the back door. I'll be right down." As she quickly pulled on some clothes, she noticed gratefully that her headache had disappeared completely. She walked downstairs and found Dave sitting on the edge of her couch, looking like a whipped dog.

"God, Dave, you look terrible, which I can understand, but relax! How have you been?"

He heard the caring and concern in her voice, and for the first time since Walt's disappearance, he felt hopeful.

"You know I didn't kill Walt, don't you?" He looked into her eyes.

"No, I don't think you did." She wished she could have said she absolutely knew he didn't do it. She couldn't even imagine what he must be going through.

"I don't understand what's going on, Lynx. Where is Walt? Why doesn't he show up and get me out of this mess? They're so sure I did it that they follow me all over the place as if they expect me to lead them to Walt's body."

"Did they follow you here?" Lynx was worried. She didn't want to be questioned by anyone who may be curious about her being with Dave.

"No. I slipped out of West the back way, on the old railroad road, and no one saw me."

"Good. I think if you're going to visit me, I'd like it to be a secret." Let me fix you some coffee.

"What does your lawyer say about all this?" Lynx asked him as she walked to the kitchen area.

Walt followed her and sat at the counter. "Best case, he tells me, is Walt will show up and I'll get off. Worst case, Walt doesn't show and I go on trial."

"Yeah, but how about the absence of a body?"

"Apparently the D.A. is fascinated with the idea of a murder case where there isn't a body but a lot of so-called circumstantial evidence. Making a murder charge stick would bring him fame and glory, and he needs it. Ever since he got that DUI, he's had problems with popularity, and he wants to get re-elected."

"Hmm. Circumstantial evidence. Like what?"

"Like blood, tissue. They're running tests on it. And it doesn't look good that I cleaned the camper and put a new rug down. And, of course, I made an idiot of myself by denying I ever saw Walt and then admitting I did. I was panicked. And I know he isn't dead."

"Why did you clean the camper?"

"Why, to hide evidence, of course," Dave laughed. Lynx raised her eyebrows.

"I did it because I didn't want blood in the trailer. Patched the bullet hole, too. What the fuck? If I was going to hide evidence, I would've gotten rid of the goddamn thing. Told 'em I sold it. Gave 'em a phony bill of sale. Shit, if I wanted Walt dead, I would have waited until we went hunting and faked an accident. That would be really simple."

"Why don't you think they buy the story that you struggled and the gun went off and Walt bolted?"

"Lynx, I don't know. I admitted I lied at first. Maybe that's why. But I have the feeling there's something going on that I don't know about. I have no idea what it is. It just seems so strange that they're so severely out to convict me. Shit, half the people in West Yellowstone I believed were my friends think I did it. It's miserable over there—jobs canceled, dirty looks, being shunned. It's driving me nuts."

"Surely some people think you're innocent."

"Yeah, but it's strange. Not as many as I thought. Tami isn't helping things. She's telling everyone I'm a violent, crazy man who was insanely jealous of Walt."

"Who would go along with that?"

"Lynx, I can't understand it. Part of me was glad I had an excuse to divorce her. We weren't getting along. Sure, I went a little nuts when I found out it was Walt, my best friend. A male pride and ego thing. But I would've forgiven him."

"All you can do is hang in there and wait it out. If Walt doesn't get word to the police that he's alive, you have to get off. It just can't happen any other way. Don't think it will. Stay positive."

"Well, thanks, Lynx, I'm glad you are on my side," Dave told her. "You know, all the years I spent in West Yellowstone, I saw the gossip mill grind, and I stayed out of it. I heard people pass around all kinds of rumors that I knew were bullshit, and I kept silent. And it's ironic that the Boys Club was so much a part of that crap, since they hang out at Walt's place. Now I'm a victim. It's more fun for people to think I did it than to stand up for me. It hurts."

"I know how you must feel," Lynx told him, touching his hand. "I've watched the gossips in West. They haven't enough to do in the off season, so they hang out in the coffee shops and get a sinister kind of power in hacking apart their neighbors. It's sick."

"Funny how I thought because I ran a business there and had been there so long, I was somehow 'in' and they wouldn't do this to me." Dave put his hat back on and got up to leave. "Say, why don't you come over to my condo tonight? I'll make you dinner. Kind of a payback for listening to me."

"No, thanks. I'm here to be alone all weekend and get some thinking done, some relaxation in, catch some rays." Lynx didn't add that she wanted to keep her distance from Dave as much as possible. "Hang in there, bud," she told him as she walked him to the door.

Chapter Twenty

Every so often the law enforcement departments in large communities all over America make a grand show of burning or otherwise destroying mounds of pot and other drugs confiscated in drug raids. It satisfies the public's curiosity about what the cops do with all that stuff they bust people for. Any discriminating person who follows these stories and then takes the time to tally how many drugs are confiscated in busts against how many are destroyed may reach the conclusion that only a small percentage of the drugs are actually destroyed. One may then wonder where the rest of the stuff is stashed.

Or if one were really clever and knew how to access computer files, one could find the answer in the bowels of the TDP. TDP doesn't exist, as far as the federal government is concerned, but it is a highly sophisticated organization, and it has computers. It's a phantom organization funded by the sale of the confiscated drugs that somehow disappear regularly from the police departments of America's major cities and by the carefully laundered donations of other phantom and underground organizations that want drugs wiped out of America. These organizations believe the world was better off when organized crime was in charge of such socially acceptable pastimes as gambling, high-class prostitution rings, shady real estate deals, controlling the brands of beer sold in bars, and fixing horse races and fights.

The fact that TDP financed some of its operations by recycling the confiscated drugs back to suppliers didn't bother the organizations that donated money to TDP. They would rather have TDP selling the dope to suppliers they were assured would sell the stuff to dealers that supplied the middle and upper classes, college students, and the military, than to the scumbag dealers and pimps who were taking over the streets.

TDP's biggest customer was the man whom Anton called his Master, DK. No one knew what his initials stood for. The drugs he bought never reached the street, were never smoked or used by the average American drug consumer or abuser. The best of the best went straight to the people he controlled, and the junk went in the incinerator. DK never made a dime directly from the drugs. His profit came from the work of the people he controlled, whom he called his "adepts." The adepts had IQ's of over 150. DK's careful programming led them to believe they could reach their innermost power source, one connected with the greatest power of the universe, through the careful daily, prayerful use of cocaine and marijuana, augmented occasionally with speed and sleeping pills. The adepts believed that only people with higher intelligence should use drugs because only they had the mental capacity to tap into the power that drugs could amplify.

DK funded TDP's operation in South America. His goal was not to shut down the drug dealers. It was to own them so he could control them.

Anton was one of DK's most treasured adepts. He was the first assigned to a relatively primitive area of America, one untouched by urban civilization—Yellowstone National Park. Wilderness all around, unspoiled, pristine land. Millions of people visiting it every year, totally open to nature, yearning to be refreshed and renewed before returning to their robotic jobs in the cities and towns. Anton's project was to see that these people were not refreshed and renewed with love of nature and the God they so foolishly believed created it. It was to see that they returned more dedicated than ever to fulfilling the Plan of the Masters. Anton was partnering with a woman who could be a valuable resource in this objective. And how amusing that in the very town where Lynx O'Malley lived was a TDP recruit that she knew. DK loved the little twists and turns of fate that even he could not control.

If Lynx were implicated in Walt's disappearance, her focus would not be on bonding with Anton. He had to stop that. He'd called a meeting of TDP's directors and let them know that Lynx had to be kept alive, but that they had to absolutely guarantee that she wouldn't talk to the police. If they messed up, their funding would be cut off. He had enough drugs stockpiled to supply his adepts for five years, easily, and he could get along without TDP. By the time his storage was used up, he could have another operation going, one with new blood.

TDP got the picture. They sent one of their best agents to West Yellowstone with one of DK's most highly functional mind programmers. They were there to show Lynx what they would do if she didn't go along with them. DK was sure they would succeed. If not, he would have to give up Anton's experiment and move him somewhere else until the time was right for Yellowstone again. But he was unwilling to pull Anton out now, because all of his charting had shown him that Yellowstone was ripe to become an open channel in which to program a manifestation of the Plan.

DK had spent hours reaching into the minds of those in Yellowstone who may have foiled his plan. He didn't know yet whom the minds belonged to or how they were connected, but he did know that somehow Lynx had protection. That protection was in the form of what humans so stupidly called love. Some people knew Lynx was under attack and were praying for her. But their prayers were not focused yet because they didn't know for certain what form the attack was taking, had no knowledge of DK's plan. He could have Lynx's life taken within 30 minutes of a phone call. But if he did this he wouldn't learn who these people were and what power they did have. To put it simply, he wouldn't have any fun. Would his hesitation result in any failure in his plan? He thought not. His power was too great; he was certain of that.

• • •

Lynx sat in the fifth pew from the front of the Little Church in the Pines and prayed the words of the Mass with all her heart.

Just one evening and day of relaxation and aloneness had made her feel refreshed and renewed, and she thanked God for that. She'd done some good work on her CNS project, taken a nice long bath, and had decided to visit Dave's lawyer, Frank Goodman, and tell him everything she knew. Surely he could get in touch with TDP and they could work out a deal to get Dave off. Surely she'd panicked about the threat to her and Merlin. How could they get away with it? She and Frank would leave a trail behind them so if anything did happen to her, all hell would break loose.

When she received Holy Communion, a feeling of peace washed over her. She knew she'd made the right decision.

Chapter Twenty One

When Lynx walked out of church, still glorying in the feeling of peace she had received at communion, she was startled by the touch of another person's hands on her arm. It was Ursula.

"Hi, Lynx," she said, a thin, forced smile on her lips.

"Urs! Whatcha doin' here?"

"I went to Mass, too, but I sat in the back. I wondered if you'd seen me."

"No, I didn't. But why did you drive down here from West? There's a Mass there."

"I figured you would be here. I saw Merlin at the city park, and he'd said you'd come down to spend the weekend in your new cabin."

"Yeah, I needed to get out of there and be by myself for awhile. "

"I know, and I won't bother you long. I just want to know what you know about Walt."

"I think Walt bolted and left Dave in a very bad way. I know Walt isn't right for you, and I hope you forget about him," Lynx said carefully as she walked toward her car.

"If he bolted, he could have just left me a note. I can't believe he's gone. I can't believe he's dead, though, either. I just don't feel it."

"I don't think he's dead, either, but I do think he isn't the right man for you and that you really have to go on with your life. If he's alive, I assure you you'll never see him again, and even if you did, how could you trust him? Come on, follow me to the Sundowner, and we'll have a drink and talk about this if you want."

"Are you sure? I know I'm bothering you."

"No, you're not bothering me. Let's go."

The Sundowner was packed, but they found an empty booth in the corner by a window and watched a group of carefree people dance to country tunes on the jukebox. They watched a rental car with Utah plates pull into the parking lot and two casually dressed men get out.

Lynx looked them over carefully and knew they were not just tourists out for a good time. They were extremely centered and focused on important business, and she knew it was connected to her and Ursula when she saw them look just a few seconds too long at her car, parked not far from theirs. She felt sick to her stomach, but put it aside and focused on Ursula.

"Okay, Urs, it's like this. Get over Walt, period. I'll talk to you about that. That's the only place I can see you going. If you want to go on and on about where he is and why he did it, find someone else to talk to. If this sounds harsh, it is. But it's the right thing."

Ursula stared into her drink and started to cry softly. "I know you're right. I guess I don't really know what love is. I hate the thought that I have to go back to searching for that."

"Don't. Just live. Living is loving if you do it right. You need to grow, like all of us. Just forget about Walt. Practice it. Love will come. And it won't take as long as you think."

"You know, the police asked me if I ever heard Walt say he was threatened by Dave or anything like that. I told them we'd never talked about Dave, and that was true. And they asked me if I was sleeping with Walt and I said no. You know that was a lie."

"They were just fishing around," Lynx told her. She saw the two men order drinks at the crowded bar and look around the room for a place to sit. Again she had a funny feeling.

"Ursula, those men are watching us," she said.

Ursula looked in their direction. "They certainly don't look like your basic tourists, do they?" She fiddled with her hair nervously. "Are they going to ask us about Walt?"

"I don't know. Let's just go over to my place. It's too crowded here anyway. We'll see if they follow us."

"Nah, I really just wanted to get a quick dose of reality and support from you. I'm okay. You're right about Walt. I'm heading back to West. We'll see if they follow you or me. We're probably just paranoid." Ursula took one small sip of her drink, put the nearly full glass down on the table, and stood up. "I'll walk you out."

"Okay, but if they do follow you, call this number when you get home. It's my next door neighbor's. I know he's home. He said I could use his phone until mine is installed."

Lynx turned as she walked toward the door and noticed that the men had sat down and were both looking in their direction.

The two women hugged and got in their separate cars. Lynx headed south, toward the road to her cabin, Ursula north to West Yellowstone.

When Lynx turned onto the road to her home, she pulled over, stopped, and looked back. Somehow what she saw didn't surprise her. The Utah car was heading toward West Yellowstone. The thought entered her that she would never see Ursula again. She put it aside. Squirrely feelings she had come to Island Park to escape were coming back, and she didn't want them. She thought back to the peace she'd felt at church and tried to force it to return. Maybe she was creating scenarios that weren't real. She would go home and wait for Ursula to call.

• • •

Within five miles of her drive back to West Yellowstone, Ursula realized that she was being followed by the men she'd seen at the bar. Perhaps, she thought, the local police had flown in experts from the FBI to investigate Walt's disappearance. She tried not to tense up and stayed well under the speed limit. Surely she wasn't a murder suspect. She was at work when Walt had supposedly been murdered. Perhaps they believe Walt had disappeared and wanted to see if she was going to meet him. Or maybe they wanted to stake out her house or tap her phone.

Ursula thought back to the times she'd been with Walt, trying to focus on the bigger picture. They had been wonderful times, but she had always sensed that Walt was holding something back from her. She had put her suspicions aside, wanting only to experience him as her lover and friend. She had been stupid.

Lynx was right. She had to forget about Walt. She would not cooperate with these men, even if they were in some kind of law enforcement. If it became public that she was having an affair with Walt, who knows what would happen? She would have to stick around and answer questions, maybe even be subpoenaed to Dave's trial. She would leave town and not look back.

Ursula pulled onto a dirt road two miles from West Yellowstone and drove to Black Sands, a spring that was one of the sources of the South Fork of the Madison River. It was a favorite meditation spot for locals, she'd learned from Lynx. The rented car followed her. She parked and walked down to the water, and the car parked a few feet from her vehicle but no one got out of it. She ignored the intruders and focused on how she could get out of town.

She had decided when she ran from her last relationship that she would be a waitress in a resort town long enough to save enough money to go back to college and finish her degree in elementary school teaching. She picked West Yellowstone because it bordered Yellowstone Park, a place she always dreamed of seeing. Her second choice had been Mohab, Utah, because she loved to mountain bike and the country near Mohab was a mountain biker's paradise. Her third choice had been Lake Havasu City, Arizona, because she was also interested in being in the desert. She decided to try Mohab first, and if she couldn't find a job there, she would move on to Arizona, although it wasn't exactly peak tourist season there until the fall and winter. Or she could live in Mohab until fall, then move on to Arizona.

A plan. She felt better. She would pack tonight and be in Mohab by late tomorrow evening if she didn't stop anywhere to spend the night. First she had to deal with the men in the car, and they couldn't know she was leaving. She got up and walked over to them.

The driver rolled down his window and nodded at her.

"Why are you following me?" she asked, trying to sound casual and unworried.

"I think you know," he answered slowly.

"It must be about Walt."

"You got it, sister, so why don't we go to your house and talk about it?"

"No, I'd rather straighten it out here and now."

"We'd rather go to your house," he shot back.

She could see his partner staring at her, watching her. Shivers of fear ran down her spine.

"I don't even know who you people are—are you cops, or what?"

Ursula thought quickly back to books, news articles, television shows, movies, trying to remember what her rights were. She could refuse to talk to anyone, could demand to see identification, could say they would have to get in touch with her lawyer. And all that would complicate things, would force her to have to stay in West Yellowstone. She had to run. The need to be gone was growing by the second, spurred on by the beginning of a serious tension headache.

He didn't answer her question, and she didn't press it.

"Okay, come along then," she sighed. "We'll talk, but you'll find I have nothing to tell you."

Ursula had no time to call Lynx. The men had tailed her closely and were right behind her when she unlocked her door. They sat side by side on her couch, listened intently to her story of the affair with Walt, and knew she was telling the truth. They could see she was a weak, broken woman in search of love and blinded by Walt's need and charm. They were sure she knew absolutely nothing about Walt's involvement with TDP after they had probed her mind when she was sitting by the spring. They knew she was planning to leave town, not because she hoped to find Walt, or be found by Walt, but because she wanted to put it all behind her.

They told her they were special investigators called in on cases where no body had been found but where there may be enough evidence from blood and body tissues to prove that a murder had been committed. She believed them and had even been convinced that Walt must indeed have been murdered by Dave. Now she was pleading with them to keep her out of it, saying she wanted to avoid any embarrassment of having to admit publicly that she and Walt had been screwing.

As far as they could tell, and they were highly trained, Ursula was an innocent pawn, and she should be allowed to go on with her life. They were sure Lynx suspected that Walt had disappeared, sure she knew about TDP, and now sure that Lynx had mentioned none of this to Ursula. For some reason DK wanted Lynx around for another purpose. If it was up to them, they would arrange an accident for Lynx to remove her permanently from this life, but they had orders to follow. They thanked Ursula for her cooperation and assured her she would not see them again. And they warned her not to discuss their encounter with anyone.

As soon as they left, Ursula locked her door and began packing, her head and spine throbbing with pain she had never experienced before. She thought of calling Lynx, but decided to take the men's advice and forget they'd ever talked. Surely they had no intention of going back to Idaho and finding Lynx.

Ursula was a simple woman, a victim of men who had used her. She had let herself be a victim without developing any mental strength to defend herself. When DK's goons had probed her mind, they had easily seen that she was planning to run, and that she was using all her strength and survival instinct to resist telling them her plan.

Few people can survive such a probe, and Ursula's resistance was low because of her stress about Walt and her lack of mental discipline. She took three aspirin, but that didn't ease the intense headache pain that was growing by the minute. She kept packing and cleaning, trying to ignore the pain. It increased. She finished at 3 a.m. and slept fitfully for three hours, with horrible nightmares of the men who had interrogated her. She awakened with a worse headache, loaded her car with her few worldly belongings, wrote Lynx a note, drove to Lynx's house, slipped it under her door, and left West Yellowstone without looking back.

The headache grew worse as Ursula drove, and she had no idea how to handle it. As if to escape it, she drove as fast as she dared, concentrating with all her strength on staying on the road.

Hundreds of miles away, DK became aware that his agents had damaged Ursula, fried her brain cells with their psychokinetic probing. He felt her pain, knew she was somewhere in Utah, and laughed. She was just one of a multitude of totally weak, unknowing minds he had to work with. He could send her healing bolts, could save her, but why waste his power?

Ursula made it to Salt Lake City, but she knew she would never make it to Mohab that day. Her headache was too intense, and the mental pictures of the interrogators were becoming so vivid that sometimes she could barely see the highway.

She checked into a cheap motel in a small town south of the city, washed down four aspirin with a can of ginger ale, and tried to force herself to sleep. But the faces were still in her mind, and now they twisted into ugly demons that were beating her as they laughed at her. Explosions went off in her head, lightning bolts of yellow and red and orange light, and an artery burst in her brain. DK felt the life leave her and chuckled. Another one down, and so easily.

Late the next day, an hour after the motel's checkout time, a maid unlocked Ursula's door, saw the dead woman's lifeless eyes, and screamed.

At the very moment Ursula's soul left her body, Lynx was sitting on her West Yellowstone porch, reading the note she had just found when she returned to town.

"Lynx, I'm going to Mohab to find a job. My apartment is clean, and I paid a $400 deposit. Could you go to my landlord and get it back? Tell him I had a family emergency and had to leave quickly, and mail it to General Delivery, Mohab, Utah. Don't tell anyone where I am. I want to forget about West Yellowstone forever. Thank you for your friendship. Love, Ursula."

Lynx tried to visualize Ursula's face framed by her flowing red hair, tried to remember how she looked when they'd hugged and gotten into their cars. Lynx had always been highly skilled at remembering details, at conjuring up sharp images of people she was thinking about. But Ursula's face did not come clearly into her mind, so she strained to see it and saw instead something that took her breath away until she found herself choking and nauseous. It was a face that could only be described as demonic, evil, inhuman. Her head began to ache, and she went inside her house, sat at her dining room table, and cried softly as she ripped Ursula's note into tiny pieces.

Chapter Twenty Two

Lynx sat on the deck of Frank Goodman's summer cabin north of West Yellowstone and sipped an ice tea he'd made for her. The cabin was on a hill overlooking Hebgen Lake. Not a boat was on the water. It was too hot for good fishing, and the fires in Yellowstone and the national forests were scaring people away from the area. Frank had finished a trial in Bozeman that morning and was inside changing out of his court clothes and showering.

He came outside with a drink and a legal pad in his hand and sat across from Lynx, his back to the view, looking all business despite the shorts he was wearing that showed off his muscular legs. He was a marathon runner and cross country ski racer, and he loved to fish and hunt. He could have been a prominent criminal attorney in a big city, but like so many talented people who live in the Rocky Mountains, he only wanted to make enough money to support his outdoor pleasures.

Lynx smiled as she watched him towel off his wet, curly dark hair. She was sure she hadn't been followed to his cabin. She'd made the appointment to see him from a pay phone, but she doubted TDP was monitoring her any longer anyway. She'd taken the long way there, going south to Island Park and then taking the road along Henry's Lake, over the pass back into Montana, past Earthquake Lake to Hebgen Lake. It was 50 miles out of the way, since Frank's cabin was 14 miles from West on the direct route, but the drive through pretty country had helped her relax and gather her thoughts. Still, she nervously watched the road for vehicles that may have been waiting near the cabin to see if she would stop by.

Lynx told Frank everything Walt had told her about going to work for TDP, about TDP's visit to her in Missoula, and about everything she knew about Tami and Susan and Dave and even Ursula: the affairs, the unhappiness, all of it.

He leaned forward and listened to her intently, making occasional notes, never interrupting her. She couldn't tell if he believed her or not. His face was expressionless. When she was finished, he told her he'd never heard of The Drug Police. Her heart sunk. She hadn't expected that. She'd never heard of TDP either, but assumed a criminal lawyer with lots of contacts with the outside world would have.

"Not that I don't believe you, or doubt TDP is a viable organization," he told her gently, seeing her concern. "Did they or Walt tell you where they are based?"

Lynx thought carefully. "No. The only clue is that Walt said he went back East somewhere for training. Maybe you could check his credit cards for an airplane ticket, motel, etcetera."

"Maybe, but if its a highly secret deal, they would have paid cash or used other names or some such thing."

"Would they have made themselves known to any local law enforcement, the FBI maybe, or the county sheriff?"

"I'll check, but I doubt it. And you have to realize that if I go around telling people there's this group called TDP Walt is working for, and they never heard of it, it could work against the case, make it look as if we're desperate. They would say we were making it up to divert them, plant doubts. I must have concrete proof TDP exists and Walt worked for them. Then they would have to admit to it and reveal where Walt is. If they are involved with international drug traffic, one man falsely accused of murder wouldn't be enough to risk uncovering their work."

Lynx watched a strong gust of wind ripple across the lake, making waves that rolled to the shoreline. She felt hopeless.

"I have no idea how to go with this. And of course I'm worried about Merlin—about myself, too. What would happen if TDP knew I was trying to get information on them? You should have seen that man who talked to me."

"Lynx, I have to think about this. Of course I'll do all I can to find out whatever can be found out. I'll need some help from someone else, because it may be that TDP would watch me to see if I know anything."

"Who will help you investigate this?"

"I'm not sure yet. It's not anything you should have to worry about," Frank said kindly.

"You have no idea how much better I feel now that I've told you this. It's been killing me," she told him.

"You know, Lynx, this could all be taken care of at the trial anyway. Meaning that I don't see how any jury would decide that Dave killed Walt, beyond a shadow of a doubt. There's no body, and we have witnesses that will say that Walt talked of leaving and starting a new life. We have others who will say they talked with Dave about Tami, and Dave planned to divorce her, so the motive that he supposedly killed Walt for screwing Tami doesn't hold water."

"Won't the prosecution still insist that was the motive?"

"Sure, but there's no proof. Tami will not admit that. I sure as hell won't try to prove it."

They were silent for awhile, watching a chickadee munch on the peanut butter in Frank's bird feeder.

"Birds have it made, don't they?" Lynx thought out loud. "They're so free. I sometimes feel the weight of the universe is on me."

"Everything will work out. All we can do is keep trying," Frank told her, reaching over and touching her knee. He turned the conversation to small talk about the fires, museum, West Yellowstone politics, and running, until she got up to leave.

· · ·

DK snatched the newly arrived fax from his secretary Goldie's hands, ordered her to wait a few minutes there in his office, and speed read the 12 names and addresses of the jury for Dave's trial. He reached into a file in his desk and pulled out a list of names of some of his superior adepts.

"Copy this jury list and get it to each of these people," he told her. "They are waiting for it, and they already have my instructions."

"Will do," she said briskly. She didn't know what it was about, didn't want to know. DK owned her, heart, soul, and body, and she loved him entirely with what he had told her was the highest form of love a woman could have for a man. She was his slave. Whatever it took to help him, she would do without question. It beat being a third rate downtown whore, the only life she'd known before DK found her, bought her from her pimp, and began her training.

DK had instructed the adepts on his list to program the jury members to convict Dave. He knew they would succeed. It didn't matter to his Plan that Dave spend the rest of his life in jail, or go free. It was a purely joyful exercise for him to see if his adepts could pull it off, to see if he was correct in believing they could. And Frank Goodman's search for TDP was most amusing. DK and his adepts had blocked him at every attempt, and Goodman had given up, clinging only to his self-pride that he would convince the jury Dave was innocent. Stupidity: the stuff DK preyed on.

A side effect of the entire matter was that the number of programmed people in the Yellowstone area would go up, and that could only help him and Anton in the long run. The more confused and misdirected people in that area were, the better. He pulled out Lynx's file and studied her picture. Celtic. Catholic. Open and honest. Operates with strict moral values. Those values had led her to Frank Goodman, a person like herself in many ways, only Jewish. Wholesome people, pawns in his game.

Chapter Twenty Three

Nora Spotted Elk stood motionless in the back of the theater of West Yellowstone's Museum of Yellowstone Culture and took three deep, centering breaths as she looked intently at the backs of the people she was about to speak to. There were no empty seats. Lynx was in front talking to a group of children sitting on the floor, leaning against their mothers in the front row.

Nora's heart went out to Lynx, and Lynx felt her love, looked up, and smiled at her. Nora grinned back and nodded that she was ready.

Nora thought of Lynx as the daughter she had never had. Nora loved her five sons unreservedly, but a woman's love for a daughter was not the same as it was for a son. You taught different things to boys than to girls, spent time with them differently, touched them differently, made them strong in different ways. Except for Harry, her other sons had little interest in her medicine. The other women in her family were too focused on keeping their men sober and working. They had little time or energy for spiritual matters. Nora felt more strongly than ever that God had sent her Lynx to be a vehicle to help teach white people the ways Indians knew would heal the earth and help all people battle the deep evil that was growing on the planet, its purpose to keep people away from God.

Anton slipped into the room and stood in the back. Nora shot him a look and said a quick prayer asking for protection for herself, Lynx, and everyone else from his evil. "If only Lynx could see more clearly what he is doing," she thought, but he was using all his power to numb her perception.

Lynx began to speak. "Welcome to the Museum of Yellowstone Culture. As you know, this week we're celebrating the people who were here before white people came to our continent, the Native Americans, the Indians. On our schedule you'll see we have beadwork and quill work classes on the portico, films about Indian history, and lectures explaining the artifacts in the exhibits. But most important, I feel, is that you hear Indians tell their own stories, and so I introduce to you Nora Spotted Elk, a Crow medicine woman who lives here in Montana.

"I know a lot of us are very confused about the fires that seem to be destroying Yellowstone Park. Hiking trails are closed down, roads are closed, and the smoke is choking us. We worry the fires will burn down the buildings in the park and even here in West Yellowstone. Nora is going to tell us the story of fire as the Indians have always viewed it, and I hope this makes your visit to Yellowstone more meaningful and even more spiritual by giving you a deeper view of fire."

Lynx nodded to Nora, and she walked to the front of the theater and smiled at the open faces that told her they were ready to listen. She nodded to Merlin, who was sitting in the third row, all ears for Nora's story. Nora wore her 30-year old ceremonial brain-tanned elk skin dress, decorated with elk teeth and beadwork, beaded leggings, and beaded dress moccasins.

"The Indian knows different things about Fire than the white people do," Nora began. "To the Indian, Fire is a gift from the Great Spirit given at a time when we needed it for our very survival.

"When the People, and by People I mean ancient Indians, the ancestors of the Crow and other tribes, first walked on the Earth, the world was warm, and the game and plants were plentiful and tasty. There was no need to cook. Cooking did not exist as we know it now. Sometimes we ate the meat from the animals we killed and the plants we gathered when it was warm and fresh and what you would call raw. Other times we laid it out in the sun to dry and ate it much later. There was no need to wear much clothing then, either, and we kept ourselves warm when the sun went down by wearing the skins of the animals. We built shelters with these skins or out of the trees and plants surrounding us or we slept in caves.

"As more and more people were born, we had to walk further and further to find enough animals to feed everyone. The animals moved away from us as we pursued them into lands that were colder and harsher. Not as many children were born when the people had to struggle against the cold, and many of the families who lived in the cold country grew smaller.

"The ancestors called a great council of their family and many other families to discuss the shortage of game and the difficulties many people had in keeping warm and finding proper shelter against the cold. They sent Great Bear Woman, a very powerful medicine woman, to the top of a mountain in what you now call the Gravelly Range, here in Montana. Does anyone know where I mean?"

Several hands shot up. The Gravellys are popular camping and hunting grounds, and a talc mine there employs many people from Ennis and the Madison Valley.

"Great Bear Woman spent ten days on that mountain and had many visions. She saw into the future, even into present times. She saw many people living in the valley below and moving over the earth in what she told her people were strange structures with four round turning stones, what we now know are cars and trucks. She saw many different kinds of living shelters, and even airplanes, which she said were noisy birds without faces. She even saw people skiing down snow-covered slopes on what she told the People were long flat sticks. Great Bear Woman saw the mountain we now call Lone Mountain, the one in Big Sky where the ski resort is. The People's name for this mountain is 'Hill that Points to the Heavens.'"

Again several people nodded.

"In her vision, she was able to see the valley on the other side of the mountain, the Gallatin Valley. Again she saw it as we see it today, with many people and houses and businesses.

"The Great Spirit told Great Bear Woman that he would give the People a gift that would solve their problem with the cold, but that when the gift was given, Hill that Points to the Heavens would be desecrated and the People must never go there again."

Nora saw question marks on the faces of many of the children.

"Desecrated is a big word, isn't it? It means that a place once sacred, once very special, becomes destroyed, evil, and unlivable for the People and animals.

"You see, sometimes the Great Spirit gives us gifts that we have a great need for, and for a long time, the gift is good, but then having it and misusing it leads to something not so good.

"The Great Spirit told Great Bear Woman to instruct some of the People's strongest and bravest hunters and warriors to go to the top of Hill that Points to the Heavens and wait for the gift. He promised that the people of Great Bear Woman's time would live long and well with the gift and would not see the time when the gift resulted in the desecration of Hill that Points to the Heavens. But he also told Great Bear Woman to never forget that this would come to pass.

"When Great Bear Woman returned to the People, they listened closely to all she said, and many had trouble believing her vision. Some did not want to risk sending the strongest and bravest men to the top of Hill that Points to the Heavens. But those who were the strongest and bravest knew in their hearts that Great Bear Woman spoke the truth, and they argued in the council for the blessing to go and for the supplies they needed.

"After three days of prayer and discussion, the men were sent. They awoke three hours before the sun was to rise, but the full moon gave them light to see. As they were leaving, Great Bear Woman gave them a medicine bag she had made for them to carry the gift back in. It was made of thick elk skin and lined with small pebbles and moss she had gathered in a thick pine forest. She poked holes in the sides of the bag with a sharp stone, and used powdered red and brown rocks to draw an outstretched eagle on both sides for decoration. Remember Great Bear Woman did not know what the gift would be, but the Great Spirit had led her to making the medicine pouch, and she had not questioned His instructions. It looked very much like this one I made to show you."

Nora reached into the pocket of her dress, pulled out the medicine pouch, and passed it around the room.

"See if you can guess what the gift would be," she said. "But don't say it out loud and spoil my story." Nora watched Merlin turn the pouch over in his hands and saw by the way his face lit up that he had guessed what it would carry. He looked up at her and she nodded.

When the pouch was halfway around the theater, Nora began speaking again.

"When they began their journey to the top of Hill that Points to the Heavens, the weather was warm and the sky was clear and full of stars. They walked all day, stopping now and then to eat the wild berries that were plentiful that time of year. Soon after the sun was highest in the sky, at the time we now call noon, great clouds began to rise from behind the surrounding mountains, and the wind began to move strongly and loudly.

"The men weren't afraid. They knew the Great Spirit was sending them a storm. They kept walking and began to climb Hill that Points to the Heavens. They were strong, as I have said, and they did not grow tired. The storm gave them energy and purpose. They reached the very top of Hill that Points to the Heavens a few hours before the sun would slip behind the mountains. They sat in a circle near a group of old pine trees and sang songs to the Great Spirit. The songs thanked the Spirit for their safe trip and told the Spirit they were ready for the gift. The storm grew stronger, and the men huddled closer together and sang louder so their voices could be heard over the wind.

"Suddenly, a great crack of lightning shot from the darkest storm cloud, followed by a loud thunder clap. The men sang even louder, and the lightning came down again. This time it struck the tallest tree near them, and the tree began to burn. The wind blew the fire to the trees nearby, and soon all were burning. As suddenly as it came, the storm went away. The men said later the clouds vanished in a single moment, but the air around them was very cold. They were drawn to the stand of burning trees, where the heat was intense and made them very warm. As they walked toward the fire, a young deer hobbled out to them, its hide smoking and flaming, and died at their feet. A large tree fell on the dead deer and the little animal began to burn. The smell of its flesh was pleasant and made the men feel hungry.

"The Great Spirit put it into the men's hearts that the burned meat was good and could be eaten. The Great Spirit put into their hearts that they could gather the fire and use it to keep themselves warm. But how, they wondered? In the past, some of them had seen lightning start fires in the grass on the plains and in the trees on distant mountains and had seen the rain put the fires out. They had never walked too near the charred grass or trees of a fire. They thought it was Bad Medicine. Now it was clear to them that the Great Spirit wanted them to have the fire.

"The men approached the burning trees and watched them closely. They saw how sparks fell from one tree to another and started a new fire. They played with the fire, taking burning branches and carrying them to trees that were not yet burning to make them burn. Before long, they knew how to make new fire with existing fire.

"Great Bear Woman's son, Running Elk, had the same gift of good medicine as his mother and was the kind of person who would be a great scientist in the present time. He was thoughtful and inventive. He played intensely with the fire and discovered that just a small coal could start a large branch on fire if the branch was dry and dead and if he made wind with his mouth, if he blew on the coal. He realized then that the medicine pouch was to carry a coal back to the People and that coal could be used to make new fires with wood that lies on the ground of the forest. He shared his idea with the others, and showed them how to do it. They asked the Great Spirit to help them find the most sacred coal of the great fire He had given them, and they were led to a coal that was the burning knot of the center an old, old tree. This they placed in the medicine pouch, and this they gave to Running Elk to keep. They then used long sticks to push the rest of the burning trees into a great pile that burned all night and kept them warm.

"Running Elk found the young deer and butchered it. He gave the cooked meat to the others, and they enjoyed its taste so well that they knew it was a very special gift from the Great Spirit.

"At first light, Running Elk looked in the medicine pouch and saw that the coal was still alive. He and the others cut the rest of the fawn into small pieces to bring back to the people.

"Can you imagine the people's surprise and joy when the men made the first fire and they all gathered round it and felt its warmth? Stop a minute and picture that."

Nora paused as the theater full of people grew very quiet.

"Fire is something we take for granted, but to that group of people, it was the most sacred thing they had ever encountered, a gift directly from the Great Spirit, a gift they knew would bring health and happiness to them, a gift that would mean they would survive and prosper. Those people at the first campfire were most blessed. Next time you gather around a campfire that was started in a few moments with a match or a lighter, and maybe some gasoline, think of how that first fire was made and thank the Great Spirit.

"As the sun rose and fell and the moon changed shape in the sky month after month, the people became more knowledgeable about fire. They learned that when they used it to cook meat, the meat lasted much longer, far into the winter. Running Elk figured out a great secret. He figured that if a burning coal is laid on a dry piece of wood and a new fire is started, perhaps a fire would start if you rubbed two pieces of wood together without the coal and blew on them, pretending you were the wind. After many tries, he learned to do this and then realized that the harder the wood you used, the more likely it would be to start a fire. From there he figured out how to use sharp, hard rocks to create fire by making a spark and directing it to soft and dry wood shavings.

"Whenever he figured out something new about fire, Running Elk believed that the Great Spirit was putting the idea in his mind. He believed that because he always felt a special feeling that led him to try something new. We would call it today a burst of energy or intuition or a showering of grace. In those long ago days when wisdom was not something you discovered in library books, most people believed wisdom came for the Great Spirit. It still does, and that includes the wisdom in many books.

"Running Elk was so in tune with the Great Spirit's desire that the People know all about fire that his name was changed to Fire Medicine, and he became one of the Peoples' most loved and respected medicine men.

"One day, many years after the People had been given the first fire, Fire Medicine was playing with a large twist of tobacco he had gotten in a trade from people from very far away. He took a piece of the tobacco, threw it on his small cooking fire, and inhaled the smoke. It made him dizzy. He thought the dizziness was a good spirit that had entered him, and he began to pray. He felt great peace and strength.

"He thought about this in his usual careful way, and he made a small bowl in which he placed a tiny coal and a piece of tobacco. He called a meeting of the strongest and bravest men and women of his People, and they passed the bowl around the circle as each person breathed in the tobacco smoke. Eventually the People made pipes to draw the smoke into their bodies, and learned they could light the tobacco with a small coal on the end of a stick and did not have to place it on top of a coal. Smoking then was a sacred act when the People wanted to come together in peace. Fire Medicine's power grew very strong after he was given the tobacco. His direct descendants are still alive today in a secret society that promotes peace throughout the world when Indians come together with other people to learn about the earth's gifts and powers. It is called the Sweetgrass Society because then the Indian name for tobacco was sweet grass. It is not the same as the sweet grass that grows on the prairies."

Nora paused and watched the people react to her story. She could feel their minds working, thinking back to the time when fire and cooking and smoking were given to the People, looking to the present and thinking how much in the world had changed.

"In your studies of history you will learn that after the People had fire, their lives changed, slowly and gradually, because the fire made them warm, allowed their food to last, and allowed the People to prosper. Now we think nothing of it. But look what has happened. Look at Big Sky, at Hill that Points to the Heavens. To many, it is a place to play and have fun. But to the Indian, it is no longer sacred because it is not wild and free and not much game lives there anymore. The sacred tobacco plant is giving people cancer because it is not smoked to bring peace but to calm our nerves. It is not pure, but filled with additives. It is addictive. The gifts of the Great Spirit were misused in many, many ways."

Nora's voice was calm and strong. No one moved.

"Let's think about the great fires in the park. Many of you think they're bad. Let's accept them as gifts from the Great Spirit, see them as the Great Spirit working. Then we can see the bigger picture. The Spirit is cleansing the park of old trees that make it more difficult for the wild animals to live, opening up the forests so new growth can begin, new plants can grow to feed the animals. That's why the Spirit has sent us great winds to fan the fires and has withheld water from us in the form of rain that would slow the fires down. When the fires threaten to burn down our buildings and homes, we should stand up to them and defend ourselves, but also see that it may be part of a greater plan that we have some losses. We must thank the Great Spirit not only for obvious gifts that make our lives easier, but also for things that make us suffer. These are what we call learning experiences.

"When the fires have passed, there will be a time of great healing in the lands that were burned. Watch it. The Earth wants you to know she can heal itself. Yellowstone is teaching you. Thank you."

As the people clapped to show their appreciation of her story, Nora surrounded herself with her Go Away Spirit, something she did after she told a story of great power. She did not want to talk to anyone at these times, preferring to quietly go away alone and let the story's power sink in. Often people wanted to talk with her and ask her questions, but she knew all the questions had been answered in the story, and it was best for people to digest it alone.

The Go Away Spirit stunned everyone long enough to let her walk away. On this occasion, it gave her time to leave the museum as Lynx thanked everyone again for coming and reminded them that in four hours, there would be a painting workshop and anyone who wanted to could work on putting the fire story into images on a mural set up a outside the museum's teepee. And Lynx told the people that Nora would relate the fire story again that evening, and they were welcome to come back and hear it again.

Anton followed Nora and found her sitting on a rock near the back of the museum, looking toward the rolling pine-covered hills south of West Yellowstone. Beyond them, in Yellowstone Park, were giant nuclear bomb-shaped plumes of thick smoke, the North Fork Fire, out of control and on its way to Old Faithful. Anton squatted on the ground beside her, told her how much he'd enjoyed her fire story, and asked her if he could tape her when she told it again that evening.

Nora was pleased that Anton had found her and at last she could talk with him face to face when Lynx wasn't around. She looked into his eyes and all her fears that he was an instrument of pure evil were justified. She could imagine how Lynx had not seen it. He covered it well with good looks, a pleasant yet powerful voice, and good listening techniques. Somehow he knew Lynx's weak points and had zeroed in on them to completely blind her to his real self. As well as she knew Lynx, Nora was not able to figure out just what it was about her that Anton saw. Nora perceived Lynx as an extremely discerning person. It must be a man-woman thing, she thought, something that she could not easily see because she was looking at Lynx through her own old woman-eyes. Or it could simply be that Lynx saw evil but dismissed it because she did not want to face the fact that it is real.

"Why would you want to tape my story?" she asked him. "Isn't it enough to simply hear it yourself in the moment?"

Anton felt Nora's probing look and knew he was dealing with a major player it wouldn't be easy to manipulate.

"For myself, sure. That story, because you told it so well, so passionately, from the bottom of your heart, will stay with me forever. But my media, videotape, would allow millions of people to hear it that would otherwise miss it because they could not be in your presence."

"My feeling is that if they are meant to hear the story from me, they will."

"And your 'meant to hear' doesn't include experiencing it on videotape?" Anton asked, keeping his voice friendly.

"My presence, as you call it, does not transmit on videotape."

"Can you be sure of that?"

"Oh, yes. My presence is real, in real time. Videotape is light and sound imagery."

"Sounds like you've thought about this before."

"Yes, I have. You aren't the first person who tried to film me or take pictures of me."

"So you are going by the old Indian belief that photos take your soul?"

"Old beliefs, new beliefs. Some beliefs are eternal, unchangeable, as correct now as they were when they were manifested. Take the ten commandments for example."

Ah, the commandments, Anton thought. He was most aware that she was looking inside him, was trying to trap him.

"You needn't respond to that," Nora told him. "There is no discussion. I'm set in my belief about not wanting my image on videotape, although I have used my voice to narrate a video for Lynx." She didn't bother to add that she knew his videotapes may appear to be a celebration of Yellowstone, but in fact were being used to make people turn away from any understanding of the beauty of Creation and, therefore, the Creator himself. Anton and the people he was working with had Yellowstone under siege more than any wildfire ever could. "Let's move on to another topic, one I choose."

"Fine, Nora, I'm ready to do that and to accept your feelings about being taped."

"It is more than feelings, Anton," Nora countered. "And you know that, so stop."

"Okay, so what is your topic of choice?" Anton noticed that Nora was as headstrong as Lynx.

"Oh, I think you know that it's Lynx." Nora turned to face him and watched the slight change in his face. He was uncomfortable, she saw, but he hid it quickly.

"What about Lynx?"

"What are you doing with her?"

"You know, Nora. I'm helping her design a media project having to do with Yellowstone that will be funded by the CNS grant. I will provide her with technical assistance."

"How do you define your relationship with her? Are you falling in love with her? I think you are."

"Is this conversation between the two of us only?" Anton asked.

"Yes. Lynx will never know about it."

"Then I can tell you, yes, I am falling in love with her. But I don't think she is aware of that, and I don't think she is feeling or thinking anything towards me but business."

"I think you are right about that," Nora answered, and knew that she had made a mistake.

"You wouldn't like that, Nora, would you, if Lynx and I did fall in love?"

No use steering now, Nora thought. "No, I wouldn't. I sense something destructive about you and sense that you're hiding your true self and true purposes from me and Lynx. Somehow Lynx doesn't see that, although she has been warned."

"Perhaps that's because you and whoever else has warned her about me are dead wrong." Anton stared at her, waiting for an answer.

"No, I'm too old, too wise about such things to be wrong. If you hurt Lynx, you will pay deeply. That's the point I must make with you. Now, go away and leave me in peace." Nora turned back to view the forest and became a still and speechless rock.

Anton watched her for a few seconds and left.

Chapter Twenty Four

When the theater emptied, Lynx gave Merlin a roll of quarters for video games, money for pizza, a reminder to meet her back at the museum for the mural painting workshop, and a big kiss and hug.

She was exhausted, and she unlocked her mountain bike and pedaled home slowly for her afternoon rest. Sylvan was doing a great job keeping the museum running smoothly, and business had dropped because of the fires, but she felt she had to spend as much time as she could in the museum during Native American Week because it was something very important to her.

She was surviving only because she forced herself to take a two-hour nap every afternoon after her workout, no matter what. The fires were so widespread now that the *Gazette* had assigned different fires to different reporters. Hers was the North Fork Fire, and she had to write a story about it every morning, along with at least one other feature on fire ecology or a human interest piece on firefighters or how residents of communities near the park were managing with the drop in tourists. And she was still working on the project proposal for CNS, something Anton was helping her with and being wonderfully un-argumentative about.

Anton. Was she falling in love with him? She just didn't know. Nora and Dewey and even Jack had given up warning her about him. Lynx knew they were praying about it and hoping she would have as little to do with him as possible. But Lynx needed him for her CNS project and believed the project was worthwhile, a viable educational tool to show people the beauty of Yellowstone as well as the threats to that beauty. Her idealistic mind believed that if people really knew that the park was threatened, they would work to preserve it.

Anton was a powerful person, and one of the most unusual people she had ever met. Lynx observed that he made everyone nervous because he was so different. She knew that Nora and Dewey had the gift of prophecy and had foreseen her meeting with Anton, but she dismissed their warnings because she figured they simply hadn't known how offbeat Anton is.

She parked her bike in the garage and went inside the house, which Dewey had cleaned that morning. A vase of fresh wildflowers Dewey must have picked on a walk in the national forest was on the kitchen counter with a note.

"Lynx, I hope everything looks good. See you in two weeks. It came to me when I was dusting this morning that you should read a passage in the New Testament, Paul's letter to the Romans, Chapter 8, verses 18-25. Maybe it would be a good thing to read before you meditate today. I believe there's something in it for you. Much love, Dewey."

Lynx knew some of Paul by heart, but couldn't recall those exact verses. She walked around the house, pulling the curtains, checking to make sure her answering machine was turned down, and then changed into her workout clothes before grabbing her Bible from her bedside table.

In her New American Bible the verses were titled "Destiny of Glory." She read them carefully.

"I consider that the sufferings of this present time are as nothing compared with the glory to be revealed to us. For creation awaits with eager expectation the revelation of the children of God; for creation was made subject to futility, not of its own accord but because of the one who subjected it, in hope that creation itself would be set free from slavery to corruption and share in the glorious freedom of the children of God. We know that all creation is groaning in labor pains even until now; and not only that, but we ourselves, who have the firstfruits of the Spirit, we also groan within ourselves as we wait for adoption, the redemption of our bodies. For in hope we were saved. Now hope that sees for itself is not hope. For who hopes for what one sees? But if we hope for what we do not see, we wait with endurance."

There was a great mystery in Paul's words, Lynx felt, and she underlined them and memorized them. There was something there that applied to her present moment, something Paul knew the people should know in his time and as long as there were people waiting for the return of Christ, something Dewey knew she must think about. And so she thought, and prayed, and breathed, and kept thinking during her workout and a long, hot shower afterward. She napped with Paul's words underlined and open on her bed.

Anton opened Lynx's door with a credit card and slipped quietly into her house, knowing she was sleeping. He slid out of his sandals, tiptoed to her bedroom door, and listened to her breathing. She was down, and he entered her mind and pushed her down even farther. Her breathing deepened and slowed down.

He opened her door, stood over her body, and saw the underlined verses from Paul. He needed to read only the first verse before knowing exactly what she was focusing on.

Knowing her as he did, Anton could see that she would relate those verses to herself, her relationships, the fires in Yellowstone, and to the project she was preparing for CNS. She was such a Christian, such a Catholic, so innocent, so easily programmable. He turned and walked into her living room, sat on the couch and looked into her room.

He wondered how she had decided to read those particular verses which contained a great mystery so veiled that few people really understand them. The Bible was full of such passages, and luckily for Anton's side, most people who read the Bible these days are fundamentalists who skip over complex ideas they can't inter-apply easily to everyday reality. Theologians understand, but who reads theology except other theologians? The spiritual numbness of the average churchgoer watered Anton's playing field.

Anton thought back to his earlier encounter with Nora. Nora's warning that he stay away from Lynx made him smirk. Nora could never protect Lynx from him. It was a certainty that he would take control of Lynx and get exactly what he wanted from her. If all the protection Lynx had was a few Bible readings, he had it made. His attraction to Lynx was real, and he had never counted on that. He sometimes felt like a little boy around her, wanting to play and laugh and enjoy what was there. But of course that would happen—he was human. He recognized those feelings as human but unacceptable and would not act on them. Still, sometimes it was extremely difficult. There was just something about her that made him feel something he had never felt before, something that could be called love, he guessed. But she was there to be used, and he would keep that goal above everything else.

Lynx stirred and he watched her wake up slowly and suddenly notice that he was there.

"Hi," she said. "How did you get in?"

"Through your door."

"I locked it."

"No, Lynx, it was unlocked," he lied. "I thought you never locked."

"Yes, but I have been lately because I have been sleeping so soundly during my naps. I've been worrying that people would come in here and rip off my computer. I'm sure I locked it today."

"Well, apparently you're wrong," Anton lied again.

"I guess so. Do you want some coffee? I could use a cup. I'm kind of fuzzy."

"Let me make it for you, then, while you get the CNS file we have to look at."

"Okay. You'll be surprised how far along I am with my project proposal . . . our project, I should say. But we only have a little time now to talk about it. I have to pick up Merlin at the Geyser's video game room and get back to the museum."

They settled down at the dining room table to read Lynx's first draft of the project proposal. They sat close together so they could read together, and Anton smelled her freshly washed hair and the lotion she must have rubbed into her skin. He was overcome with attraction to her. Without thinking, he put his arm around her and drew her to himself. He felt her become startled and pull away, but he pulled her harder and kissed her face. She grabbed his hand to push him away, and he held onto it and placed it over his erection, remembering that he once did that to a girl when he was in high school.

"Are you crazy?" she told him, pulling back, trying to think, feeling herself wanting him and not wanting to.

"I feel great attraction to you," he said, his voice sounding formal and making her laugh. "Why are you laughing at that?"

"Perhaps I feel something similar toward you, but I'm not going to let this go any further. So bugger off," she told him, still laughing.

Her laughter outraged him, but he forced himself to not show it. "Then I apologize. You run along to the museum, and I'll finish reading this and leave you notes. How's that?"

"That's fine," she said, getting up quickly and nearly running out the door.

Sitting on the lawn in front of the Geyser, Merlin watched his mother walk toward him. He was glad to see her because he was getting bored just sitting while all his friends were inside, playing video games. He had gone to the bank and exchanged the roll of quarters Lynx had given him to play games with for a ten dollar bill he would stash in his toy bank at home. That would bring him up to $200, mostly saved by not spending money on games.

Merlin's goal was to save $1800, the figure a travel agent he called had given him for a trip for two to Disneyland in California. He planned to take Lynx there in the fall. By then the fires would be over and she would need a rest. It bothered him to see his mother work so hard, especially when she had a headache. And he wanted to take her alone someplace, away from Anton, whom he hated. He was sure Anton had designs on his mom, maybe even wanted to marry her, and he could not let that happen. He had hinted around to Lynx that he didn't like the guy, but always Lynx had told him not to worry about it, that they were just in business together for a short time.

But he knew better. His mom seemed to be liking Anton more and more each time they were together, even had the same look on her face that she had sometimes when he'd seen her with Jack, and, long ago, with his dad. Merlin thought of his dad and winced. He was glad they were divorced and he didn't have to be around him so much. Lou gave him the creeps. Merlin was always scared his dad would go off in an angry tirade or pull a crying fit and try to make Merlin feel sorry for him.

Why couldn't he have parents that were cool? A dad who went to work every day and brought home the bacon, a mom who didn't have to work day and night, who could stay home and be there for him. Gwen was lucky she was grown up and living in a big town.

"Hi, kid! How did you do? Spend all your money?" Lynx asked him as she reached down and pulled him to his feet. She didn't let him answer. As usual, she was in a hurry.

"We gotta get going over to the museum. Are you ready to paint something? Did you like Nora's story? Did you get enough to eat?"

Merlin didn't answer any of her questions. She didn't seem to notice.

"How does your head feel, Mom?" he said instead.

"Fine, honey—why?" Lynx heard the concern in his voice and realized she was hurrying and had not even waited for him to answer her questions. Anton had really flustered her. She stopped and squatted down on the sidewalk to be at his level.

"I do want you to tell me everything, Merlin," she said, taking a deep breath. "Did you do well with the video games; did you eat; do you want to paint now?"

"Yes to everything," Merlin answered, squirming a little about not being straight about the video games. He so wanted to surprise her.

"Look, kid, I love you, and I'm sorry I'm so occupied with work and stuff. It'll slow down when these fires go out and the museum closes, you know. But don't worry about me. I feel great. I'm a little tired, but that's normal."

They started walking again. Lynx looked down at her son and wished with all her heart that she had more time for him. She cursed Lou for being such an asshole, but that didn't make it better. She watched Merlin walk across the museum's lawn to the place where dozens of children were already gathered to paint, and saw him turn back and give her a brave wave and a smile. How much was he putting on to not upset her, how much was real? Was he still worrying about her and Anton? She wasn't sure about any of it. She checked to see that the painting workshop started on time, then went to the museum's office to catch up on paperwork, trying not to think about Anton's move on her.

Patsy and Pete were waiting for her there. They were a sweet couple, Lynx thought as she watched them sit close together. Pete's massage business was going well, and Patsy was getting more and more creative with her artwork. Their lifestyles fit well together, and Lynx was sure they would end up married. The only problem they seemed to be having was finding time to spend together.

Pete and Patsy were there to ask Lynx to allow Patsy to exhibit some of her work in the museum's contemporary art gallery. Patsy pulled out a portfolio of her photographs and sketches and explained her latest project.

The images were of the trailer park in Big Sky where Anton lived. Locals called it Dog Bark Trailer Park because all of the people who lived there had at least one pet dog. The dogs ran around in a friendly pack that barked at whomever came into the trailer park, resident or visitor. The trailer park's residents all worked at one of the businesses in Big Sky, and like all resort town employees, their wages were too low for them to afford to buy homes.

Not long ago, the Big Sky Corporation had told Dog Bark residents that it had sold the property the park sits on to a developer, and soon after that, the developer had given everyone an eviction notice. The land, he explained, would be sold off in six-acre lots to luxury home builders. There was a shortage of such lots in Big Sky, and land was at a premium price. He would lose money allowing the trailer park to stay there. The fact that Dog Bark residents were the backbone of Big Sky's work force and the mobile home park land would be sold to people who would build expensive second homes they would live in a few weeks every year was not important to him. Developers are not the most socially conscious members of society, Lynx had found.

Lynx had written the story of Dog Bark's demise for the *Gazette*, upsetting many of Big Sky's business people because she'd made them sound greedy, they'd told her editor. Lynx had quoted people who were angry that the Big Sky community seemed to have little regard for providing affordable housing for its underpaid workers. Anton had seen the eviction notice in a better light—something that forced him to move his trailer to West Yellowstone, where he could be closer to Lynx.

Patsy had read Lynx's story and driven up to Dog Bark Trailer Park to photograph the place before and after it was torn down. Her artistic eye had seen Dog Bark as a place where people had made real homes for themselves, despite their lack of money and the run down old mobile homes most of them had to live in. Nearly everyone in Dog Bark hunted and displayed the antlers from the deer and elk they killed on the outside of their trailers. Some used the antlers to hang their fishing gear on or even the long electric extension cords they used to plug in their cars in the winter. Nearly everyone had a well-tended patch of flowers or vegetables, and several people had rather elaborate dog houses. Mountain bikes and downhill and cross country skis leaned against the sides of the trailers, a testimony to the fact that the residents enjoyed the outdoors on their days off. Patsy had also photographed and sketched the trailer park's residents puttering around in their gardens, talking with one another, barbecuing, and sharing a huge campfire together while playing guitars and singing songs. Her photos of the trailers when the people lived in them sharply contrasted with her photos of the trailer sites when the trailers had been removed, either to a junkyard or another trailer park far away from Big Sky. The abandoned sites held things that people had left behind: old tools, the steps that had led to their doors, decks they had sat on hot summer days, as well as the hook-ups for electricity, water and sewer.

Patsy wanted Lynx to write a story to go along with her photos for the exhibit, titled "Dog Bark Trailer Park—the Destruction of Community." Lynx agreed to help and to display the exhibit in the museum's gallery for one week. She urged her friends to stick around the museum and listen to Nora's story on the desecration of Big Sky, telling them that the Indians had prophesied many of the things that were coming to pass there now. She asked Patsy if any of the photos were of Anton's trailer.

Patsy and Pete gave her a long look before Pete answered, "We intend to go to Nora's talk. But first—we haven't shown those to you yet, and that's another thing we want to talk with you about. Check these out."

Patsy handed Lynx an envelope full of photos of the dead animals Anton had hanging in the trees near his trailer and the skulls and bones he had strewn around his deck.

"This just isn't the same kind of thing that you see in the other pictures," Pete told her. "There's something really sick about this, like he's into some kind of ritual animal slayings and has these things arranged for some sinister purpose. I think the guy is nuts."

A chill ran down Lynx's spine when she looked at the photos. "You know," she told Patsy and Pete, "I never went up there to see him, although he kept inviting me. And now he's moving down here, to the empty lot next to my house actually. He's having utilities installed this week, and a company from Bozeman will haul the trailer there next weekend. I wonder what he would say if I saw this stuff. It's definitely weird. Maybe you should include these in the exhibit."

"No, I wouldn't do that," Patsy replied. "It doesn't fit with the rest of the stuff. He doesn't work in Big Sky, and the people there don't associate with him."

"How do you know that?"

"I talked with everyone who lives there, and they all said they stay away from him, said he never comes out during the day, keeps his windows covered with black cloth, barely nods to people when he does go out."

"Don't they know his trailer is actually a video studio?"

"I don't think they do. And they are uncomfortable about all the dead animals. They didn't let their kids go near Anton's place."

"Wow," Lynx said.

"I'm concerned about his moving here and so close to you, Lynx," Pete said.

Lynx looked thoughtful, shivering as she remembered Anton grabbing her. "Look, I know Anton is strange. A lot of creative people are, you know," she said. "I'm sure he has an explanation for the dead animals and stuff. He is very good at what he does with video. He works hard and is very bright."

"Check it out," Pete told her. "You go up there before he moves and stand in those trees with the dead animals, and I'm sure that you'll feel really strange vibes. Bad vibes. Confront him and make sure you are dealing with a full deck before you let him move down here."

"Well, I will do that, but I can't keep him from moving his trailer. It has to be moved, and he is a free man. He can go wherever he wants. And I need him for my CNS Project."

"You mean you can't find anyone else who knows video?"

"Who? You guys both know there isn't an abundance of talented media people around West Yellowstone. The really knowledgeable people prefer to live in the cities, where the jobs are. Anton is talented, and besides, he has all the editing equipment I'll need, and I value that. Otherwise, I'd have to spend a fortune using the equipment at Montana Sate University in Bozeman or at a T.V. station in Bozeman or Idaho Falls, and that would mean a lot of travel and expense."

"I thought your grant covers equipment costs," Pete noted.

"Yes, it does, but if I can use Anton's equipment instead of buying new stuff, I'll have more money for other expenses, like travel and salaries for other helpers."

"Then maybe you shouldn't do a video project," Pete countered.

Lynx looked at her friends and thought a moment. "You guys are really worried about Anton, aren't you? How could he hurt me, even if he is as weird as you say? All of us are a bit eccentric. And I actually like Anton. We enjoy one another's company."

"Yes we're all a bit eccentric, for West Yellowstone standards, anyway," Patsy replied. "But we aren't evil. We don't give off evil vibes, don't hang dead critters by the necks in our shrubbery." She looked hard at Lynx. "Oh, no, Lynx, you aren't having sex with him are you?"

"Hell, no. I admit I thought about it, but I won't do it. In fact, he sort of attacked me earlier today, and I resisted him. You should be proud of me," Lynx said.

"Just be careful, Lynx," Pete told her. "And if you need us for anything, let us know."

They stood up to leave, and Patsy tossed the photos on Lynx's desk. "Keep these, and think about what we said. That's all we want because we love you."

Lynx examined Patsy's photos of Anton's animals and wondered what he was about, what exactly he was doing in Big Sky, would be doing with her. It was so puzzling.

The phone rang and snapped her out of her thoughts. It was the *Gazette*. They had two stories for her to work on. They'd received a report that a Jane Doe stored in a Salt Lake City morgue had been identified as Ursula Pedroni, a young woman who had worked in West Yellowstone. Died of a stroke. Did Lynx know her? Could she write something about what Ursula did in West? And they'd just received a report from the Fire Command Center that tomorrow would be a red flag day in Yellowstone, with high winds and temperatures predicted on top of the unusually low humidity. She was to skip covering a meeting with West Yellowstone officials and residents and Yellowstone Park Superintendent Bob Barbee; they would get a report of the meeting from the AP wire service. Instead, she was to go to Norris Junction, where the North Fork Fire was expected to make a serious run under those red flag conditions.

"Get in the park early," her editor told her. "We expect they'll close the roads sometime tomorrow, and we want you in there taking pictures and getting reactions from firefighters and tourists."

Lynx had to put thoughts of Ursula and Anton on hold, find Sylvan and make sure he would cover the day for her, find Nora and tell her she wouldn't be around, and make sure Merlin was ready to spend the weekend at Lou's. She looked out her office window at the giant plumes of smoke from the North Fork Fire, not ten miles away. The air in West Yellowstone was greasy with smoke. No one had expected the fires to have lasted so long, not even Mullein White Horse, who had been so busy with his fire crews that he hadn't been to visit her yet. It was August 19th, and the fires had been burning since May 24th.

What could she say about Ursula? She was a waitress, had read a lot of books, was a sweet gal, and was on her way to Mohab to work for the winter. She appeared to have been extremely healthy. How could she have had a stroke? Had she not been able to handle Walt's leaving? Lynx didn't think so. Sure, Ursula was hurt, but she was a strong person. She would have gotten over it. A stroke just didn't make sense.

Life was feeling too complicated. Lynx decided to get the day's business out of the way fast and go fishing. Fishing always gave her a new perspective. Tomorrow would be an intense day, and she needed to relax.

She was on Cougar Creek an hour before sundown, in the middle of a dense caddis fly hatch which some nice sized brown trout were attacking vigorously. The creek ran through dense clumps of tall willows, so she let out some line in front of her to roll cast. She watched the fish feed for ten minutes and picked out the biggest trout she saw. She cast an elk hair caddis to him, and he rose to it but turned away suddenly and went back to a holding position. She cast again. He rose again, and this time took the fly but spit it out before she could set the hook.

"You no like my fly?" she asked him. "Come on, take it."

She cast again, and this time he angrily smashed out of the water and gulped the fly before it hit the surface. Lynx slammed her rod back hard. The trout dove and pulled the fly downstream. She gave him some slack. He stopped moving for a second, and she tightened the line. He dove and swam again. She kept her line tight and followed him downstream for 20 yards and then reeled him in quickly. He was not happy about that at all, but she had him solidly hooked, and he could do nothing about it. She pulled him to a quiet, shallow spot in the creek, grabbed hold of the line a few inches above his mouth, laid her rod on the bank, and reached into the water to unhook him. She held him steady for a few seconds, pointed him upstream, and let him go. He bolted right toward the spot where she'd caught him. He was an 18 incher, she figured, a good size for Cougar Creek.

The hatch was thinning out now, and the sun was getting ready to set. Lynx sat on the bank and thought that fly fishing is as good as life gets. She'd forgotten every worry, concern, and undone item on her lists of things to do as soon as she'd hit the creek and seen the rising trout.

"Thanks, guy," she told the trout. "Live a good life and get bigger. Catch ya later."

As she was putting away her gear, she heard a truck engine start up. It was pretty close—maybe 100 yards downstream, hidden by the willows. Something told her to walk in its direction and check it out. She moved deftly and quietly through the brush and came to an opening to a parking area.

A totally bald man she didn't recognize was putting a large burlap bag and a shovel and pick ax in the back of a brown pick-up. The truck had Gallatin County plates, and the driver wore a black cowboy hat. She hadn't seen either man around West, but they could be from Bozeman or Big Sky. Lynx ducked back and crouched in the willows until they drove away and she could no longer hear the sound of the engine. They'd left in the opposite direction from her parked car, so she doubted they'd known she was around. She walked to the spot where they'd parked and saw several small patches of white powdery material on the ground. They made a trail which she followed into the willows, to an open area, to a place where the earth had been disturbed. Some of the white stuff was mixed with the soil, and she leaned over and smelled that it was lye. It appeared that they had dug a hole some six feet long, three feet wide.

Had they buried a body? Or were they getting a spot ready to bring a body back to? Those would be obvious guesses, but then why had they left so much evidence, a virtual trail to the spot, close to a parking area that many people use when they fished, when fishing on Cougar was good. Lynx had been surprised that no one was around, figuring it was because people didn't want to be out when the air was so smoky.

Lynx thought about reporting her find to the police, who were still checking out all kinds of tips people were phoning in about where they thought Walt's body was, even though it would be pretty decayed if found now.

No, she decided, she'd let someone else find the damn thing. It was probably bogus anyway. Lynx and quite a few other people around town had begun to suspect that the tips were all bullshit, that there were people out there that wanted to promote the idea that Walt was dead and were doing so by suggesting places he was buried in. Maybe these guys were trying to make it look like this was a potential burial spot, setting it up so it would be found before an actual body was dumped there.

Some figured Susan had something to do with the bullshit tips, or Tami, who wanted Dave to get the maximum sentence. Others thought it was Dave's enemies, or even the prosecuting attorney, who wanted the public to believe there was a body. And now that Dave was about to be sentenced, more tips were coming in again—more than when Walt first disappeared. The West Yellowstone police had even received a letter that was supposedly written by Walt, stating he was alive and had deserted his family, and they should leave Dave alone. But they claimed that a hand-writing expert who analyzed the letter said it was not written by Walt. Lynx walked back to her car, grabbed her hunting knife out of the trunk, cut a leafy branch off a willow bush, and walked back to the disturbed soil. She then walked backwards to her car, brushing away her tracks. She'd seen that trick long ago on a Lassie episode.

As she drove back to town, Lynx thought about Dave's trial. How could the jury have convicted him? Frank had put on a powerful defense. A nationally acclaimed DNA expert had testified that he would never con-vict a person based on his own testimony that the body tissue found in Dave's trailer that his lab had analyzed did match Walt's family's DNA type. It still didn't prove a murder had been committed, and in fact the jury was careful to state that they didn't find Dave guilty because they felt the DNA expert's testimony was valid. They simply didn't believe Dave, al-though many people who watched the trial had been convinced that he had lied when first questioned about Walt's disappearance only to protect Walt, not himself. And after the trial, Frank had talked with three jurors who had told him they were uncomfortable about the verdict, one stating she had awakened one morning a few days after the verdict was delivered feeling downright confused that she had gone along with the others in voting that Dave was guilty.

None of it made sense. And Frank had never found TDP, although he was working on doing so more than ever now, hoping to learn something before the appeal. All Lynx could believe was that justice would prevail and Dave would get out.

As she got closer to home, Lynx noticed fire crews wrapping the elec-tric wires going into West Yellowstone with fireproof material, to protect them when the fire made its expected run on town. Now that the fires were so widespread, Lynx was surprised more than ever that Yellowstone Park had decided to let the fires take their course.

Park officials were now saying they never believed the fires would have consumed thousands of acres of trees and grass, never imagined how windy, hot, and dry the weather would be.

But Lynx knew their official statements were untrue, knew that park fire experts had been given enough data about the predicted drought, winds, and lightning strikes to have decided long ago to suspend its let-it-burn policy and stomp on any wildfires. When the park finally admitted the fires were not going to burn themselves out, the largest fire fighting effort ever made in U.S. history was launched, but the fires were still out of control.

Lynx had a feeling tomorrow would be a nightmare. She did not look forward to going into the park and breathing the thick smoke all day. And she had grown more than disgusted with the news media that had come from all over the country to cover the fires. They scurried around gathering half truths about fire behavior, firefighting strategies, and fire ecology and made it sound as if the park was being destroyed for all eternity.

They filed photo after photo of flaming forests and enormous plumes of smoke without explaining that most of their fire photos were actually of backburns started by firefighters to consume dead trees and deadfall under controlled situations before the actual wildfire hit it. They did not tell the entire story of some of those backburns, either, that winds had pushed out of control until they actually met the wildfires or made runs in unpredicted directions. It wasn't all the reporters' faults, either. A lot of it had to do with the editors who cut everything but the most dramatic news out of their stories.

Secretly, a lot of the *Gazette* reporters were calling the paper McGazette, after McNewspaper, their nickname for *U.S.A. Today*. Now that newspapers were competing more and more with television and other electronic media, the *Gazette*'s editors had decided to model their paper after McNewspaper, cutting stories short and using a lot of color and graphics and columns of quick news briefs to make the reader feel he was watching a T.V. news show.

Lynx and the other reporters had tried repeatedly to file in-depth pieces on fire behavior, on the unusual circumstances that were making Yellowstone's fires so widespread, on the political battles between firefighters who had wanted to stomp the fires when they were much smaller and the let-it-burn people, but the editors cut most of the meat and left the most sensational. Lynx was grateful that the CNS grant had come along when it did because she had lost faith in the *Gazette*'s commitment to quality writing and information. She didn't want to work there anymore.

Chapter Twenty Five

On Saturday, Lynx stood a few yards from Yellowstone's Grand Loop Road near Norris Junction and watched a bull bison limp slowly and painfully toward her from a stand of burning lodgepole pines. A Fire Information Officer working the North Fork Fire told her winds were gusting to 70 mph, and firefighters were asking tourists to leave the park. He said she could stick around that area for just a few minutes, and must then head to Norris Junction, where the fire crews were. He warned her to wear the hard hat she'd been issued by the Fire Command Center, along with a complete outfit of fireproof clothing.

The bison was burned and bleeding. Pieces of blackened flesh dangled from his legs, exposing his bones. Lynx put her camera on motor drive and took pictures as he walked toward her, climbed onto the road, and sat down in the middle of it. Burned trees fell onto the road, and thick smoke cut visibility to just a few yards. The bison stared at Lynx, and she was so close to him that she could see the pain in his eyes and the life leaving him. She wished she had a rifle with her to end his pain.

A van full of tourists heading to Mammoth Hot Springs broke through the smoke and stopped. The tourists took photos of the bison through the windows. When the vehicle started moving again, the bison stood up and walked across the road to a meadow that as yet was untouched by the fire. He staggered 20 yards into the tall, dry grass and sat down again. Another gust of wind came up and hundreds of flaming coals and tree branches flew through the air and landed in the meadow, exploding into tiny fires the instant they hit the ground.

Lynx heard the main fire roar like a jet plane, and the air grew heavier with smoke. A park ranger came by and told Lynx to get in her car and head up to the Norris Ranger Station, where firefighters were working to save buildings and the nearby campground by drenching the area with water. She did so, knowing the bison didn't have a chance of survival.

Whenever flying conditions were okay, the helicopters lifted buckets of water from park rivers and streams and dumped them on the fires to slow them down. Planes did the same thing with fire retardant. Now the winds were so high and erratic that all helicopters and planes were grounded. That left a few pumper trucks to dowse the buildings and put out any spot fires.

Lynx parked in the lot at the Norris Geyser Basin and walked over to the historic log museum that overlooks the thermal feature-filled Porcelain Basin. She photographed a pair of firefighters who were hosing down the museum's shake roof, to keep it as wet as possible so blowing embers would not set it on fire. The fire roared closer, pushed by hurricane force winds, and it seemed as if everything would ignite: buildings, people, every living thing in the area.

Lynx said a quick Hail Mary and thought of Merlin. She suddenly wondered what she was doing there anyway. Was a story worth her life? As the fire approached the museum, flames leapt 200 feet high from the tops of the trees just 150 yards away. Trees exploded and Lynx walked toward her car to be as close as possible to it if she needed to run. She pulled a bandanna over her mouth and nose to filter the smoke. With one hand she held on to the fire shelter the Command Center had issued her—an aluminum tent or "brown-and-serve bag" that she would pull over herself if the fire overtook her. With the other hand she snapped photos of the firefighters at work. Miraculously, no one needed to deploy their brown-and-serve bags. The fire halted at the edge of the geyser basin.

When firefighters told her the crisis was over at Norris and the fire was moving on to other areas, she drove slowly back to West Yellowstone, stopping now and then to photograph spot fires and a red-tailed hawk sitting on top of a burnt tree stump. Wearily, she walked into the Command Center, now housed in the International Fly Fishing Center in West Yellowstone, where dozens of firefighting personnel were on telephones and computers trying to track the fires and give information about them to the media.

They named the day "Black Saturday." By evening, fires in the entire Yellowstone area had consumed an additional 165,000 acres of trees, increasing by more than half the acres all the summer's fires had burned to date in that single day. Although dozens of firefighters had to run from fires they simply could not battle, no one had been injured.

Lynx was grateful for that. She was not a reporter who liked writing about death. She talked to a few fire information officers to get exact facts about the Norris area's burned acreage, number of firefighters, and wind and weather conditions, and headed home to change out of her smelly clothes and get something to eat before writing and filing her story. She made a quick stop first at the bus station to send her film to Bozeman. Four rolls of film, and maybe one photo would be used—probably the one of the bison, she thought, unless some other photographer on another fire had something more dramatic.

After she was showered and changed, Lynx decided she was too tired to cook and would go out to eat. She walked to the her favorite dinner restaurant, the Totem, and sat at a small table in the back. A few smoke jumpers who worked out of the West Yellowstone Airport were sitting at the bar and asked her to join them for a drink.

They told her they had just started a two-day furlough and were more than happy to get away from the fires for awhile. Lynx knew she should get her reporter's notebook out of her handbag and interview them, but thought, "What's the use? They'll cut most of the story anyway." No matter how many adjective and power verbs you used, no story would ever come close to explaining exactly how awesome the fires were and how it felt to be in the middle of them.

The editors thought the public was most interested in the number of acres burned every day, in how many animals were killed, and in whether or not buildings burned down. The overall picture of nature renewing Yellowstone by weeding out millions of dead trees was lost.

The firefighters were angry and told Lynx they were fed up and disgusted with Yellowstone's management of the fires. Although they agreed that wildfires were important to Yellowstone's ecology, they said that the let-it-burn policy should have been suspended early on in the summer when it became obvious that it wouldn't rain, that the moisture content of living trees was extremely low, and that there would be major winds throughout the area. And the North Fork Fire, they pointed out, was human-caused so should have been stomped on the day it began.

Amateur woodcutters had started the fire on the Targhee National Forest near Island Park, close to the border of Yellowstone. When the fire passed into the park, officials could have had it put out because the let-it-burn policy covers only wildfires, but park fire managers didn't want to send bulldozers into the area to create a fire line the fire wouldn't cross. Bob Barbee, the park's superintendent, had said that scars from bulldozers are not repaired as quickly by nature as are fire scars. Barbee had also been insisting all along that firefighters had no way to predict just how hot, windy, and dry weather conditions would be. Lynx told the firefighters she knew that was not true, since Mullein White Horse and other fire experts had been predicting such conditions for months and had warned Barbee about it.

Why had Barbee, whom the angry public had nicknamed "Barbee-que," not paid attention to the fire experts? The firefighters told Lynx their theories: he wanted to make a name for himself by putting Yellowstone in the limelight all over the world, and fire stories were in newspapers, magazines and television broadcasts all over the planet; he wanted to attract more tourists to the park to view the aftermath, more researchers to look at wildfire behavior and ecology; he was stupid, plain and simple. Another theory was that in recent years Yellowstone's budget had been cut drastically and park roads were in a state of disrepair. Park personnel had been cut in all departments, and it was showing in litter on the roadways, messy restrooms, and empty entrance stations, since there was no money to pay rangers to sit in them and collect entrance fees. Perhaps, the firefighters suggested, if Yellowstone were showcased through the fires, the American public would pressure Congress into giving the park the funding it needed.

Lynx leaned toward the theory that Barbee was listening to the scientists. She knew he wasn't stupid, and she knew he was interested in ecology more than in pleasing people. She figured he was willing to take the heat about the enormity of the fires in exchange for the bigger picture, that it was time for nature to take care of business. Fires of this magnitude had burned through the region several hundred years ago, and fire historians said they had been beneficial to the ecosystem.

The conversation moved on to more practical matters, again sparking in Lynx an interest in writing about what she was hearing. Fire management was as out of control as the fires, they told her. The logistics center at the West Yellowstone Airport was plagued with theft. Fire Command had rented trucks and four-wheel drive vehicles from rental services all over Montana, Idaho, and Wyoming, to transport firefighters and supplies into the park. Several trucks had been stolen and thousands of dollars worth of firefighting clothing and equipment were missing. No one would ever know how much money was wasted on all this stuff. And what happened if money ran out before the fires were out?

Lynx decided to take notes on some of what she heard and check into it later. By now, the smoke jumpers were on their fifth and sixth drinks, and she couldn't think of them as reliable sources. She sat back down at her table and ate slowly, thinking about how she would write up the Norris fire when she returned home. She felt awful from breathing smoke all day, and the food tasted like wood smoke, no matter how thoroughly she chewed it.

Chapter Twenty Six

Dave sat with his head between his legs in his cell at the Law and Justice Center in Bozeman, waiting for the guard to escort him to the visitors' area. He'd just heard the latest Yellowstone fire report on his radio and was thinking bitterly that he would love to be in West Yellowstone now. Surely the firefighting crews would have some use for his excavating equipment. He wondered if his house would be safe if the fires came close to town, wondered if anyone would bother to protect it.

His life had become a nightmare, but he had resigned himself to the fact that he was in jail and lived one hour at a time with the hope that Walt would return. If not, he felt confident that his appeal would succeed. He still couldn't believe the jury had convicted him, that 12 people honestly believed beyond a shadow of a doubt that he'd killed Walt. There was no evidence, no body. The jury had decided he'd killed Walt because of what the press called the "Tami triangle."

It was crazy. Dave knew he had come off as a weak, dishonest person during part of the trial, when he had to admit that he'd lied at first about ever seeing Walt and later had to tell the truth, that they had met and quarreled and a gun had been drawn. But he had only tried to protect Walt.

Dave still hoped Walt would hear about his arrest and let people know he was alive. But perhaps Walt left the country and would never find out. The police still hadn't attempted to search for a living Walt, although they were still digging all over the county for a body. And who the hell was phoning in all those tips about where they believed Walt's body to be buried or stashed or burned up? Dave thought of the most recent, a grave-sized hole laced with lye near Cougar Creek. The rumor had flown around West Yellowstone that Dave had told a couple of his Bozeman friends to move Walt's body there from where he'd first stashed it in a rented storage unit. The police had staked out the alleged grave and caught a local burying a poached elk in it.

Now all he could hope for was the minimum sentence and a successful appeal and, perhaps, freedom during the appeal period. His attorney warned him that he would probably not be released during the appeal process because Tami would continue to paint a picture of him as a violent man who would kill her if he was let out.

"Thank God for Maria," he smiled. He'd met her at a laundromat in Island Park two weeks after his arrest and arraignment and release on bail. She was busy folding dozens of sheets, laundry for the resort she worked in, and she'd asked him to help her. It had actually been fun, once he'd gotten the hang of it and learned how to snap the sheets without pulling them out of her hands and dropping them on the floor. She'd been so grateful to him that she offered to take him out to dinner for his kindness, and he accepted. As they ate, he told her about his predicament, and she'd said she vaguely recalled reading about it in the local papers. She listened to his story and made no judgments about it for three weeks. During that time, they never spoke of it. They played golf together, fished, ate out in restaurants, and made love at her house or his condo. It seemed that each of them needed to have fun more than anything else.

Perhaps they were in love, Dave thought, but how could he know, how could he tell, with all this hanging over him? And she was still healing from a financially and emotionally devastating divorce nearly two years ago. They were both lonely, and they enjoyed one another's company. She was nothing like Tami. She worked hard and didn't spend her money on frivolous things like fancy clothes and exotic vacations. He thought of her as his guardian angel, sent to him at the lowest point of his life. She gave him strength, believed in him. She was strong herself as well. It wasn't as if she needed him as a service project or anything like that, and he appreciated her for that. He saw Maria's arrival in his life as a sign that eventually things would work out. If they did, he would think about love. But if they didn't, and he didn't even want to imagine that, it would not be good for her to be in love with someone in prison.

"Your visitor is here. Let's get going," the guard told him as he opened his cell. Dave got along well with the jail staff, several of whom told him they believed he was getting a bum deal. They gave him updates on the Bozeman grapevine. It seemed that a large number of police, attorneys, and community leaders had been shocked that the jury had found him guilty. Many people thought that if Walt hadn't been an ex-cop, things would have gone differently. There were even whispers that Walt was undercover somewhere as a narc.

Dave saw Maria waiting for him behind the glass barrier and remembered her advice. Don't let your mind take you all over the place with this. Have faith. Read, watch television, think of anything but the case and what may or may not happen. He gave her a long look as she smiled up at him. She certainly was different from Tami in every way, an Italian with nice curves, naturally wavy, dark hair, and normal, well groomed but unpainted fingernails. She was fun to make love with. In the last few years he'd hurried through sex with Tami to get it over with a quickly as possible. But Maria was fun to touch, and she genuinely enjoyed herself. God, he wished she could reach through the glass and touch him now.

They chatted briefly about his upcoming sentence hearing. Maria had called his friends and people he'd done business with for years and asked them to write letters testifying to his good character. Several had agreed to do so, and that was great news.

Their conversation moved to a discussion of fishing. Maria had fished nearly every day since her last visit, so she would have stories to tell him. She told him she'd caught a huge rainbow trout on the Henry's Fork with a grasshopper imitation from his fly box, and he watched her eyes sparkle as she described how she landed it and took a picture of it before she released it. She flashed him the photo. It made him feel better. He told her the locations of a few of his favorite fishing holes on the Madison until their time was up. The next time he would see her would be in court, at the sentencing.

Chapter Twenty Seven

Vicky finished her third reading of Henry David Thoreau's "Civil Dis-obedience," in an antique, leather-bound anthology Martin Parsons, her new boyfriend, had given her. She looked across the living room of her apartment and smiled at Martin, who was slumped over his journal writing about their recent trip to Mexico City, where they'd attended an international conference on endangered species.

She was reminded of Jack, whom she'd often watched working at his desk, catching up on the statistics he had to keep for the City of West Yellowstone. She'd resented Jack so often then, resented all the time he gave to his job and so many other activities that excluded her. It wasn't his fault; she could see that now. She'd been unhappy about herself, and rather than do anything concrete for herself, she'd created a fantasy-filled world, and then resented the fact that it was nothing like her real life.

How things had changed! She'd met Martin at an Earth First! gathering in one of the Billing's city parks. She was sitting on a bench, minding her own business and relaxing at the end of a week of work, when he'd sat down next to her and given her a flyer about the plight of the grizzly bear in the Yellowstone Ecosystem. Her immediate reaction was to tell him to go away, she knew all about grizzly bears, having lived in West Yellowstone for many years. And she wasn't interested in radicals with a cause, or was she? She'd suddenly realized that the remark about radicals would be something Jack would say. Jack didn't like politics, but in a way, she did. It was one of those things she was discovering about herself. So she took the flyer without voicing her cynicism, and asked Martin to tell her what it said because she didn't feel like reading at the moment.

As she listened to him, she took note of his baggy, second-hand-store clothes, long black hair tied in the back with a thick rubber band that probably once held broccoli together, and his incredibly thoughtful, sincere eyes. Earth First!, he told her, had been getting a bum rap lately because some of its members were extremely radical and had spiked trees in Oregon to protest logging there. Some loggers had been injured when their chain saws hit the spikes. Other people claiming to be Earth First!ers had burned up piles of logs waiting to be shipped to Japan, and still others had vandalized construction equipment at a huge shopping mall under construction back East, close to a forest of rare black bark pine trees. But this local Earth First! group was "mellow," he assured her, and interested in educating the public about the decline of grizzly bears in the park.

Vicky told Martin that, although she wasn't a political activist, she had been thinking often lately about becoming more involved in politics because it kind of interested her, and she actually thought some of Earth First!s more radical approaches were "interesting." Martin said he was still trying to find the best methods to protest what he called "eco-rape."

He then asked her if she'd read any books by Edward Abbey, and she'd had to say, no, she'd never heard of him. Did she read at all, he wanted to know. Sure, she'd told him, listing the names of the romance novelists she read the most. A smirk crossed his face, and she realized that at that moment, he was debating whether or not she was stupid. For some reason, he concluded she was worth talking with anyway, and he'd asked her to walk across the park to a small cafe that served fresh ground coffee.

She agreed to go with him, and he waved good-bye to his group, which was finished with their meeting and hanging out on the grass.

"What were you meeting about?" Vicky asked him as she perused the group of long-haired, baggy-clothed hippy types and thought they looked comfortable, if unkempt.

"We're getting ready to do some guerrilla theater in Yellowstone," he answered.

She looked at him, eyebrows raised.

"We're going to try to let the tourists know about the destruction of grizzly bear habitat in a park that is supposed to manage the threatened grizzly bear first, then the people who visit," he explained.

"How?"

"Actually, we don't tell people who aren't committed Earth First!ers exactly what we will be doing, or when, when we go on a protest. If word gets around we're coming, the rangers find out about it and try to meet us at the park entrances and keep us from going in."

"How can they do that?"

"We pass out flyers without a permit. We don't think its constitutional to have to get a permit to express our opinion."

"Don't they do that so every person with a cause doesn't descend on the park with flyers that will end up being thrown on the ground?"

"Oh, sure, they have some good reasons to discourage such things, but we believe the real reason is censorship. Yellowstone Park doesn't like to be criticized. Did you read Alston Chase's *Playing God in Yellowstone*?"

"No, but that's one book I have heard of and seen in the stores in West Yellowstone, and I know people who have read it. To tell you the truth, Martin, I've been a mental slouch most of my life and when I read, it's romance novels. I guess I'm kind of embarrassed about it."

Martin looked at her out of the corner of his eye. There was something about her he liked, and he realized she wasn't stupid, just living a life without a commitment to improve her mind. Not everyone could be as political as he and his friends.

Over coffee, he offered to give her a list of books to read on eco-concerns, if she was interested, starting with Playing God, which he told her reads like a mystery novel and uncovers all kinds of interesting facts about how the park has mismanaged wildlife and other resources.

"You know, Earth First! isn't a typical organization," he told her. "We don't have officers, for example, or by-laws, or any rules, really. We just get together with people of like mind and try to do things to educate people in a creative way about the destruction of our planet."

"Yeah, but aren't you all anti-hunters and vegetarians? I can't go along with that. I really have thought about hunting and its role in keeping wild-life populations down. I was married to a hunter and hunted with him sometimes. I think anti-hunters are out of touch with reality."

"A lot of us are vegheads," Martin replied. "But not all of us are, and I personally agree with you. I've hunted since I was a boy, and I try to eat only wild meat. I don't like to eat domestically raised livestock because livestock graze on and ruin wildlife habitat. I call cows 'land maggots.'"

"I've seen antelope, elk, and deer feeding right next to cows, over in the Madison Valley, for example," Vicky told him. "Cows aren't as bad as you people say they are. It's more the way the grazing is mismanaged. I've been following the stories on grazing issues in the local paper."

"Yeah, and the fact the cows are grazing where the bison once roamed hasn't been noted in those stories yet, has it? Also the cows trample the vegetation around streams, rivers, and lakes, and their waste pollutes the water."

"And wild animals do not?"

"Not like cows do, because they spread out more, and they don't hang out passively around water sources. Look at the problems they have over in Henry's Lake near West Yellowstone, where the ranchers let the cows graze on the lake shore and along the banks of the tributaries. The abundant animal waste in the lake has provided nutrients that have caused the aquatic plants to prosper. The lake has a terrible weed problem."

Vicky let him make his points. It was obvious he knew a lot more than she did, and that was all right with her. She was enjoying the conversation and holding her own when she could. It felt good to be challenged this way.

"Vicky, why don't you come down to Yellowstone with us? You may have fun, may learn something."

"I work ten hours a day, Monday through Thursday, as a secretary."

"Cool. A lot of us work, too, and we're not leaving town until Friday, around 3 o'clock. Be back Sunday night."

And so it began, and now she was with Martin most of the time and reading as many of his books as she had time to read. She'd stopped thinking about Pete in West Yellowstone, something she'd been addicted to doing and now felt totally ridiculous about. She was actually learning to read, too, which is why she read everything three times. Martin had given her *How to Read A Book*, by Martimer J. Adler and Charles Van Doren, written nearly 50 years earlier. It was fascinating, explaining that reading is an art form and that it's important to read books that are difficult and challenging to exercise your mind. She rubbed the cover of the Thoreau anthology and felt pleased that she actually understood most of what he wrote, with only occasional help from Martin.

Her daydream wandered to their first weekend together in Yellowstone. The guerrilla theater, it turned out, was fun. Five Earth First!ers had dressed in grizzly bear costumes and walked growling on their hands and knees into a restaurant at Grant Village, a development on grizzly bear habitat near Yellowstone Lake. They ordered cutthroat trout and wild berry pie and explained to the other guests in loud, gravely voices that trout and berries were once plentiful there, before Grant Village (which they called Grant Pillage) was built. Outside the restaurant, Vicky, Martin, and five other Earth First!ers passed out flyers explaining that there were several proposals to build visitor services in bear habitat, and that the bear was a threatened species in the lower 48 states because people have for years infringed on its habitat.

Some people took the flyers and read them or stuffed them in their pockets. Others walked them over to the nearest trash can and tossed them out, and others stayed around and talked with the group. In about 45 minutes, three park rangers pulled up in their cars and asked them if they had a permit to distribute the flyers. When they said no, the rangers ordered them to leave. Martin explained that Earth First! believed it had a constitutional right to distribute flyers without a permit. A huge crowd formed to hear this most interesting argument as the Earth First!ers continued passing out flyers and the rangers called for reinforcement.

Vicky had a lively conversation with an older tourist from California who was concerned about the decline of grizzly bear populations, and she explained that this was her first protest and she didn't know a lot about the problem, but would get Martin. She looked around for Martin and saw Lynx at the same moment Lynx had looked over and seen her. Lynx and Martin were talking intensely, with Lynx taking notes. She waved at Vicky.

Vicky waved back and gestured for them to come over. She introduced the tourist to Martin and then looked sheepishly at Lynx.

"I bet you're surprised to see me here."

"You bet I am. How are you?"

"I'm fine, Lynx, and you? How did you come to be here? Are you covering the fires?"

"I'm doing well, writing about the fires every day. Martin called me this morning to let me know Earth First! would be here. It's nice to have a story to cover here that isn't fire-related. I'm getting sick of the fires."

"You know Martin?" Vicky was surprised.

"Besides being an eco-activist, Martin is a damned good wildlife biologist. Used to work for the national forest but is independent now. He's really quite brilliant. He lets me know just before Earth First! does something, and I try to show up and write a balanced story. This is also a good photo opportunity, with the people dressed like bears and all. The editors like good photos and sometimes they actually allow some content in a story that goes with the picture if it's about bears and I insist."

"Actually, Lynx, I'm here with Martin, kind of a first date. Not to change the subject, but I ran into some guys from West at a bar in Billings, and they said you were dating Jack. True?"

"Dating isn't exactly the right word. We were kind of involved for awhile, but now we're just friends."

"When I heard it, I wasn't surprised. He used to talk about you often, say you were smart and stuff. How's he doing?"

"Fine. Just his usual. Job, fish, hunt, shoot."

Vicky laughed. "Old steady, predictable Jack. He's a good guy. I know I hurt him, but I needed to get away and grow."

"And are you growing, Vicky?" Lynx asked, still recovering from the shock of seeing her and amazed at how transformed she looked. She seemed happy, and it was strange to see her in old jeans and a T-shirt, straight hair pulled back, no make-up.

"I'm having fun. I like Martin, and I'm not sure about this Earth First! thing, but the people are sweet and mellow and thoughtful, and it feels good to be here. Tell Jack I said hello. He'll probably be amazed that I was here."

They turned to listen to Martin argue with a ranger, who was still trying to convince him to cooperate and leave.

"We've got a serious fire situation in this park now, you know that. We can't spend time dealing with people like you."

"I know the fires are serious, but grizzly bears are, too," Martin volleyed.

"I'm giving you all tickets for passing out information and gathering in a group without a permit. You'll have to either pay a fine or show up at court in Mammoth. If you keep passing out flyers, I'm going to have to arrest someone."

Lynx snapped a picture of the two of them talking, and the ranger winced.

Martin called to Wyld Grizzly, a young woman from Red Lodge who was in charge of the flyers.

"Wyld, how many flyers are left?"

She waved a handful at him. "Just these 50."

"Run over to the Hamilton Store and get rid of them, quick," he told her. "There's a lot of people over there."

"Okay," Martin told the ranger. "We're outta here. We've reached some people, I hope."

"You hope. Personally, I hope so, too. I don't like what management does any more than you do. I just think you have to work in the system to change things."

"And I obviously don't. I tried it."

"I know you did. Just get a permit next time."

"I don't think so."

The ranger looked tired. The bears walked up and surrounded him. He pushed himself past their circle and walked to his car, nodding to the other rangers that it was okay to leave.

Lynx went to her car to drive back to West and file her story. The Earth First!ers stuck around another four hours, talking to tourists who wanted to take pictures of the bear people but had no interest in boycotting the businesses in the area because they displaced bear habitat. A newspaper from

Utah and three television stations covering the fires interviewed them, but the media, like the tourists, were more interested in the bear costumes and the general idea that Earth First!ers are unconventional than in grizzly bear issues.

• • •

After the park trip, Vicky saw Martin every weekend and a couple times during the week. She began to feel sexually attracted to him, although physically he didn't fit her fantasy that Male Perfection means tall, dark, handsome, buffed, and utterly romantic. He was tall and thin and strong, and not romantic at all that she had seen, in the sense she thought of as romantic. He didn't open doors for her or show her any special treatment because she was a woman. As Vicky got to know other Earth First!ers, she noticed that most of the women were feminists and didn't want special treatment from men.

Martin's apartment was fairly clean, but it was cluttered with piles of books, C.D.'s, notebooks, and the computer he used to create Earth First! flyers. He was a great cook, and they ate together often. When he ate at her place, he did the dishes; at his place, she did them. He believed that men and women should share household tasks, a belief Jack would have found laughable: she did all the cooking and cleaning. She laughed, remembering that when they were first married he'd asked her why the toilet was turning yellow.

On the Thursday two weeks after they'd met, Martin greeted her at the door of her office, holding a bouquet of wildflowers.

"We met two weeks ago today, do you know that?" he said as he handed her the flowers. And to celebrate I'm making you dinner tonight at my place. Okay with you?"

"Two weeks?" Vicky hadn't kept track. "That's nice—thanks," she said, taking the flowers pensively, impressed that he had brought them. I'd love to have dinner with you. I gotta go home first and take a shower and change, though."

"You can do that at my house. I got clothes to fit you, only you'll have to roll up the pants."

Vicky felt frightened for a second. It seemed a bit too intimate to shower at his house and wear his clothes, but why not? "Okay, you're on," she smiled.

He bought live Maine lobster, fresh corn, good wine. The lobster was in the sink.

"Is this an eco-aware dinner? Lobster?" she asked.

"You know, I don't know or care. I like it, it's romantic. I want to be romantic with you. Is that okay?" Martin looked like a little boy. Vicky could see that he was slightly afraid, too.

"Hey, I have no problem with romantic," she answered. "I've been wondering lately if you feel that way toward me."

"Oh, yes, yes," Martin said, hugging her close. "I just didn't want to step into your space if you didn't want me to." He kissed her.

Her response to his kiss was immediate. She surprised herself. Martin was suddenly no longer a male friend she hung out with. As he kept kissing her, and she kissed him back, she felt the power of his masculinity and his attraction to her. He was breathing like a grizzly bear, and she liked it.

Soon they were in his bed naked and forcing themselves to go slowly because they were both about to go nuts. With every touch, barriers created by the respectful friendship they'd maintained broke down, and they began to experience one another's souls: that's the only way Vicky could put it. They came at the same time, his orgasm hers and hers his. It was the most intense feeling she'd ever had. Martin didn't roll over and grunt good night, like Jack used to. He held her in his arms for a long time, stroking her hair and saying nothing at all. Then he jumped up, pulled her out of bed, hugged her, and took her hand. He pulled her into the bathroom, and they showered together until the hot water ran out.

She loved the way he looked naked. He had just the right amount of hair on his chest and arms and was much more muscled than she'd imagined. He was hung like a bear, too, she noticed.

He gave her a shirt, and he pulled on a pair of shorts. They cooked dinner together, and fed one another lobster, and drank all the wine, and talked. The way they talked had changed, she noticed. It was more open, personal, close.

"Let's put some music on and go to bed," Martin told her. "I don't want you to go home. This is just too much fun."

He loaded the C.D. player with two Hank Williams discs, a total of 40 hits.

"You like this?"

"Oh, yes, I love Hank. He's the best in country, I think."

"Good, because I really like him." Martin began to sing along. He had a great, deep voice. He could yodel. It turned her on.

In bed, Martin Hanked her. No words can describe what it was like to be touched and licked and sucked to 40 Hank hits, to have so many orgasms she'd lost count, topped off by the last one, when he exploded inside her and blew the top of her head off. They fell asleep in one another's arms and didn't wake up until long after the sun was up.

Things had only gotten better between them, Vicky thought, watching him still writing in his notebook. Making love, Hanking, being together, reading, listening to him sing and play guitar, which he did incredibly well.

She'd learned that when they'd met, Martin was waiting for a grant from a non-profit wildlife research foundation to map grizzly bear habitat in the Yellowstone area. Not long after they'd made love the first time, he was awarded the grant money. Again they celebrated with lobster, wine, lovemaking, Hanking. In the morning, he asked her to quit her job and help him with his research. "The grant funds a secretary to enter my data in the computer, get my reports ready, help in the field, and so on."

Vicky hesitated. She wondered what would happen if they spent all their time together.

"I know you're wondering about being together all the time."

She was getting used to his knowing what she was thinking. "Yes, I am."

"What could we lose? We love each other. We spend a lot of hours together now without any problems. If it gets difficult, we can always do something else. I really want to try it. And to entice you even more, the first task on the agenda is to go to Mexico City to a conference on endangered species. I have to give a paper there on Yellowstone grizzlies."

"Mexico City?"

"Yeah, its a huge place, not too wonderful, but we can take time to get out of the city and explore the little communities and countryside. You may like it."

"Give me a few days to think about it."

"No problem."

By the end of the day, she'd said yes, given her notice to her company, and they'd gone to Mexico City.

• • •

"Vicky, what are you thinking about?" Martin asked her, I've been watching you for the last ten minutes, and you're in another world, I think." His notebook was shut, and he was holding his head in his hands, grinning at her.

"Just all the stuff that's happened to me, to us. It's been great," she told him.

"Are you happy?"

"Oh, yes, and you?"

"Absolutely. I'm going to cook dinner now, okay? You just sit there and dream--are you liking Thoreau?"

"Immensely. It's very empowering, his essay "Civil Disobedience." It makes you think you can have some charge over your life."

Vicky listened to herself chat with Martin about Thoreau and she felt proud. She had never known she was capable of understanding and thinking the things Martin had led her to. And she felt her own mind expanding. She wasn't just following him around like a puppy dog.

They grew silent again as he chopped veggies for a stir fry, and Vicky went back to her daydreams.

She thought of the strange encounter she'd had in Mexico City. She was sure she'd seen Walt from West Yellowstone. She'd seen him walk out of a hotel across the street from where she and Martin were staying and had followed him. She'd always had a knack of identifying people by their walk, and she was rarely wrong. She was positive it was Walt from his walk, which was a fairly noticeable duck-type gait that Vicky had seen many times before. It wore down a person's shoes on the outside, and this Mexico City man had shoes that were worn down the same way she'd observed Walt's to have been worn in the past. His hair was long, and he had a beard and different glasses, and he appeared to have gained some weight. She'd jogged through the crowded streets until she caught up with him and yelled, "Walt! Hi--it's me, Vicky, from Montana. I thought you were dead."

He didn't turn toward her voice. She took three fast steps and grabbed his arm. He turned around, looked right into her eyes, glanced away quickly, and pulled his arm away, muttering something in Spanish.

Could Walt have a Mexican look-alike? If so, it was the most amazing thing Vicky had ever seen. This man had Walt's eyes. She even felt he spoke Spanish with a slight English accent but couldn't be sure because he hadn't said enough.

He walked away from her quickly and turned around the next corner, and she didn't follow him. She was probably wrong. Walt had to be dead or they never would have convicted Dave of his murder. Still, she'd thought perhaps she should say something to the West Yellowstone police when she returned to Montana.

Later, Martin told her she was having hallucinations. "When you're in a very strange place, and this place is weird, your mind wants to recognize something familiar. This guy had the same body type as Walt, so it's logical his shoes would be worn out the same way Walt's would be. Your mind's playing tricks on you."

No matter how hard she tried, Vicky could not get the idea out of her mind that she'd seen Walt. When she phoned the West Yellowstone Police Department and told an officer about it, he said he would look into it. From his condescending tone of voice, she doubted he ever would.

Chapter Twenty Eight

Walt fidgeted restlessly on the edge of the king-sized bed in one of Mexico City's most luxurious hotels. His suite was spacious and comfortable, but in the weeks he'd been there, it had become a prison. He was allowed to go out once a day during the week to Spanish class, always in a chauffeured car provided by TDP that took him both ways. That day, he'd left class 15 minutes early to walk the five miles back to the hotel. He simply couldn't stand the inactivity any longer, nor being baby-sat by TDP when he should be in South America.

He had suspicions as to why his trip to South America had been aborted. He didn't buy TDP's story that at the last minute they wanted him to go to language school. He was already quite fluent in Spanish. He could have picked up the local dialect in the area his mission was to have been quite quickly. No, it had something to do with Dave, or perhaps Lynx had talked and told people he was going undercover, so TDP had decided to hold him in Mexico for awhile. Ben had insisted neither theory was the case, stubbornly sticking to the language story. Still, in the off chance that Dave had been in trouble, perhaps because someone had heard the gun go off and sent police to his trailer, Walt had mailed a letter to an old friend in Island Park, Paul Leary. He'd told Paul that if Dave was in any trouble, he should write a note to the authorities and sign his name to it, stating that he was alive and had left West Yellowstone to start a new life.

Walt had gone through a lot of trouble getting the note to Paul, bribing one of TDP's drivers to send it to someone in Washington State to mail to Paul so it would not have a Mexican postmark. He had no idea if the letter ever reached Paul, but he was pretty certain TDP's driver had mailed it and would keep his mouth shut. He'd told him the letter was to a pregnant girl friend he'd left behind and had qualms about, but that the letter did not identify where he was. Now he was certain mailing it had been the right thing to do. Vicky had said she thought he was dead. Not missing, dead.

Now what would happen if Vicky went back to Montana and talked about seeing him? He had to believe she didn't think it was really he after he'd responded to her in Spanish, but he couldn't be sure. Shit, he'd done fine ignoring her until she grabbed his arm and he made eye contact with her. That's all it would take, a split second of recognition.

There was nothing to do but tell Ben. If Vicky did talk, Ben would wonder why he hadn't said anything. Things were botched up enough as it was. He had to pay his dues and tow the line so he could get out of this godforsaken place. He had no idea where Ben was, probably hundreds of miles away on the mission he was supposed to be on. He dialed the local TDP connection and said he had to talk with Ben as soon as possible. Ten minutes later, TDP phoned back and said Ben would call him later that night.

Walt stood up and paced around the room, glancing at himself in the wall mirror behind the bedroom's Jacuzzi. He thought he looked terrible. He hated his long hair and geeky-looking glasses, although he didn't mind that his body was bigger from all the weight training he did to pass the time. TDP had put a SolarFlex weight training machine in his suite. He tugged on his thick beard and wished he could shave. It was too hot for a beard. He looked closely in the mirror again. How could Vicky have recognized him, he really did look different, and what was she doing here anyway?

He stripped off his street clothes, put on a pair of gym shorts, and began working out. It was the only thing he could do to calm down and pass the time.

Ben called three hours later. Walt was sitting in the Jacuzzi letting his muscles recover from the hard workout he'd put them through.

"Ben, what the fuck am I still doing here?" Walt hadn't meant to ask the question and had resolved to be polite, but he couldn't help himself. As soon as he heard Ben's voice, he was overcome with anger that he was trapped in Mexico City.

"Fuck you. Don't tell me that's why you called."

"Can you at least tell me when the hell I'll be out of here? I'm going nuts."

"Look, there are problems. That's all I can say. As soon as things are straightened out, you're on your way."

"Can't you be more specific?"

"No. Now, what do you want?"

Walt told him the story of seeing Vicky.

"Are you absolutely positive it was her? Do you know where she's staying? And by the way, what the hell were you doing outside on the streets anyway?"

"Yes, no, and I had to get out and walk. It's killing me to be cooped up."

Ben was disgusted. This was the last straw. Walt could have been a good agent, but his removal had been so botched up, he couldn't risk working with him anymore. If Vicky talked, it was highly possible that an all out search for Walt would ensue. After all, a man was in jail for murdering him, not that TDP gave a shit about the morality of that. Walt was getting expensive and expendable. Now they would have to monitor Vicky and somehow get a feeling for whether or not she believed she'd seen Walt.

"What's Vicky's last name, and where does she live?" Ben asked, trying to sound nonchalant.

Walt immediately registered Ben's apparent change of attitude. "It used to be O'Brien," he said evenly, beginning to make a mental list of things he must do to escape, "but she's divorced. She lives in Billings. Moved there from West Yellowstone."

"We'll figure something out," Ben told him. Most likely she'll think she saw a Mexican who looks like you. Don't go out again. Don't worry about it."

"Okay. Just do something to get me out of here."

"We're working on it." Ben hung up, lit a cigar, and called one of the snipers on his special list. He gave him Walt's location and 48 hours to take care of business.

Walt knew from the tone of Ben's voice that his gig was up with TDP. "What the hell," he decided. He'd made a mistake thinking he would ever succeed with the bastards. He would sneak out of Mexico and go back to Montana. If Dave was in trouble, he would get him off. He would find some way to do it before TDP offed him. He was ready to die. Shit, if that wasn't true, he wouldn't have taken the job to begin with. But at least he could do something decent before he went. It wasn't going to come down the way he'd imagined it, but that's life. A royal screw job, through and through.

Time to concentrate on getting away with minimal funds, no passport, no vehicle, no nothing. His first task would be to get out of the hotel, past the guards TDP had posted in the room next door and outside somewhere.

Chapter Twenty Nine

THE GREAT INVOCATION

From the point of light within the mind of god
Let light stream forth into the minds of men
Let light return to earth.
From the point of love within the heart of god
Let love stream forth into the hearts of men
Let christ return to earth.
From the center where the will of god is known
Let purpose guide the little wills of men
The purpose which the masters know and serve
From the center where the will of god is known
Let love and light and power restore the plan on earth
And seal the door where evil dwells.

Dewey and Nora were at Lynx's Island Park place, each on their third cup of herbal tea, studying the words to the Great Invocation. Harry had stolen a stack of business-card-size cards engraved with the "prayer" from Anton's mobile home.

The women knew something about "The Great Invocation." They knew it was the central prayer of several New Age movement groups and that these groups were campaigning to make it the universal prayer of what they call the One World religion. Dewey even recalled seeing it in a full-page ad in the *Reader's Digest* several years ago, the words printed over a blossoming lotus flower, with an invitation to those who wanted more copies to write to some New Age organization in New York City.

It had been easy for Harry to break into Anton's trailer. Many people had seen him with Lynx over the years, so no one questioned why he was standing on Anton's steps, since Anton's trailer was parked in

Lynx's backyard. He was skilled enough at opening locks that it had taken him less than a minute to get into the place.

Years ago, Harry took a correspondence course in locksmithing, one of his many attempts to find lucrative employment to support his family while he was finishing up his degree in anthropology, and he still had a fine set of lock picking tools. Nora and Dewey sent Harry to Anton's when they were sure Anton was on his regular trip to Bozeman. They wanted him to look for some evidence they could give Lynx that Anton was not a good person, and they wanted to know specifically what he was doing. They'd stretched the truth a bit to Lynx about their being at her cabin, telling her they just wanted to get away and relax. Lynx had been delighted to let them stay there. Little pleased her more than to think the two most important women in her life were good friends.

Harry returned from Anton's with The Great Invocation, noting Anton had piles of them in his storage room. He also brought back six video-tapes, all produced by Anton, noting Anton had at least a dozen copies of each one. He took Polaroids of the contents of an old wooden trunk also in the storage room: a black-hooded robe, candles, an cross on which Jesus Christ hung upside-down, a hand-woven, round rug some 10 feet in diameter with a pentagram and numerous geometric symbols woven into it, and a large, round pendant with a gold chain with the same design etched into it that was on the rug.

He also took photos of the books in the trunk: *Book of Necromancy, Book of Satan, Protocols of the Order of Zion,* and three well worn, hand-written volumes, leather bound, in a language Nora and Dewey didn't recognize. Harry photographed several pages of each of these books. The ink was the color of dried blood, and some of the pages were decorated with the same geometric figures that were on the rug and pendant. He told Nora and Dewey that the storage area was crammed with books, videotapes, cassette tapes, piles of files, automatic weapons, an assortment of rifles and handguns, and piles of ammunition. He'd also found several gallon-sized jars with peanut butter labels on them and what appeared to be peanut butter in them, but when he looked closely at them, he'd seen that the peanut butter "just didn't look right." He'd opened the jars and seen that they were lined with fine sandpaper and filled with strong, skunk smelling pot. The sandpaper looked like peanut butter.

Most interesting of all, Harry thought, was a file in Anton's spare bedroom marked "Lynx." He said just seeing it made his spine tingle and his brain ache. He read its contents and tried to memorize what was there before pulling some of the items out of the file and photographing them.

The file, he told the women, had numerous articles Lynx had written, articles written about Lynx, and pages and pages of notes on her behavior as Anton had observed it, but the pages said nothing about why he kept the records. It was just plain spooky.

Dewey and Nora knew about the books in Anton's trunk. They were important volumes to Satan worshipers. They suspected the handwritten books were volumes they had heard about but never seen, dealing with the true beginnings and purposes of freemasonry and witchcraft. Perhaps, they thought, The Great Invocation had some connection to the ancient volumes.

Nora and Dewey had long ago figured out that the New Age movement was basically evil, and not new at all. It went back to the beginning of the world when Lucifer defied God. Although astrology and healing with crystals and meditation and channeling spirits that spoke about such things as how to eat well and how to program your own reality seemed innocent enough, many of these things were controlled by Satanists. Nora and Dewey believed that most New Agers were innocent and believed they were living a pure, holistic lifestyle. They would have no idea that their energies were being mined by the real Satanists of the world, the people who promoted a New World Order that falsely spoke of healing the planet but was truly meant to get as many people as possible to not believe in the one true God.

Somehow, Anton was part of this inner group. He was probably one of the psychopaths that the real leaders, the Masters as they call themselves, are convinced are powerful and essential to the unfolding of the Plan. The Plan, they believe, is quite simple and revealed completely in the Bible. It is that Satan will control the world until Jesus returns. On an elementary level, most people believe that the world belongs to Satan and heaven is the realm of God. But they mix up the world and worldliness. They figure that anything that breaks the Ten Commandments is a personal manifestation of worldliness, and they need only believe they are forgiven and must keep on trying, Jesus has mercy on them and they are saved. What they don't see is that the Masters work constantly to control the world so that they can recruit as many innocent people as possible into working for them and eventually selling their souls to them. Most Satanists, and certainly all the Masters, take no stock whatsoever in the Bible or Christian beliefs of any kind. They believe in Satan as strongly as Christians believe in Jesus. They therefore don't believe that Satan has been defeated.

Satan was created as an Angel of Light. He would not manifest himself as an evil, ugly serpent, a Devil all twisted and repulsive. He comes as an Angel of Light, with promises that people will be happy and peaceful if they develop what he calls their "inner selves." That's what the New Age movement promotes, and its followers are basically convinced they are happy and in control of their lives.

The point is, Dewey and Nora agreed, that it was never God's promise that his people be happy and in control of their lives. It was that they have a relationship with Him, and sometimes they won't be happy. They suffer, and rather than attempt to be in control, they have to give themselves to God. New Agers promote the idea that a healthy person is in control. Satan wants people who are in control, so they are no longer in relationship with God, are no longer receptive of God's grace and, therefore, of salvation.

The Great Invocation is to the New Agers what the Our Father is to Christians, Nora and Dewey figured, as they read it and re-read it. Only, Dewey noted, on the surface it seems to be a very spiritual, God-oriented prayer.

"But it doesn't say what the Our Father says, not at all. Substitute 'Satan' in this so-called prayer with 'god,'" she said. "And 'evil' for 'light,' and vice versa, and you have its real meaning." She crossed out words and wrote new ones over it:

THE GREAT INVOCATION
From the point of evil within the mind of Satan
Let evil stream forth into the minds of men
Let evil return to earth.
From the point of love within the heart of Satan
Let love stream forth into the hearts of men
Let christ return to earth.
From the center where the will of Satan is known
Let purpose guide the little wills of men
The purpose which the masters know and serve
From the center where the will of Satan is known
Let love and light and power restore the plan on earth.
And seal the door where light dwells.

"Remember," Dewey said, "the Satanists have many ceremonies and signs that are direct reversals of the Christian's. Take their Black Mass, inverted crucifixes and crosses, for instance. And look at the word 'invocation.' It's the opposite of prayer. In prayer, we ask God, we talk with him, we listen to him. Invocation implies the belief that one make demands on a higher power."

"Sure," Nora said, "and it reflects the belief that we can bring power down upon us, not that God gives us grace, at times when we ask for it and at times when He sees fit to give it."

"Most upsetting is the word 'christ,'" Dewey noted. "Most folks think christ and Jesus are the same. Christ is just a word for 'anointed one.' Jesus is Jesus the Christ, shortened to Jesus Christ. The christ here is Satan, anointed by God, in a sense, when he was cast down, to rule the world. This invocation is a well veiled request for evil to be showered upon us."

"Enough talk of this for the moment," Nora said. "What do you want to do about the videotapes? Lynx has a VCR here; should we watch them?"

Dewey looked thoughtful. "I don't know. I sense that we should get some help. Anton can't be working alone on this. We shouldn't be. But who? A priest, maybe. What do you think, Harry?"

Harry had been sitting at the counter bar in Lynx's kitchen, thinking and listening and trying to control his anger. He cared deeply about Lynx and didn't want to see her hurt. He hadn't told Nora and Dewey how he had felt when he was at Anton's. He wasn't sure he could describe it accurately, and he didn't want to worry them even more. He had the eerie feeling that Anton knew he was there and was actually trying to get into his mind to see who he was and what he was doing. He'd had a headache like nothing he'd ever experienced before, an intermittent sharp, nearly disabling pain behind his eyes. Somehow, he knew he should fight it by thinking of anything other than where he was and what he was doing, so he had visualized himself hunting in his favorite mountains and was still doing this whenever the pain came and the anger welled inside him. Harry was also extremely concerned about the weapons, but again, he felt the pain whenever he thought about them, so he was trying to imagine how he could think about all this without feeling pain. He'd been watching Dewey and Nora to see if they were feeling uncomfortable physically, but they seemed okay. Perhaps he should tell them about the headaches. No, they would worry. What had they just asked him?

"Sorry, I was listening to most of what you said, but I didn't hear that question," he told them.

"God, Harry, you look awful, are you feeling okay?" Dewey asked.

"Yes, I'm just trying to put this all together. I'm concerned about Lynx and all of us."

"We are, too, which is why we asked you if we should get help, and if we should watch the videos," Nora said.

"No, I won't let you watch those videotapes or listen to the cassettes," Harry said firmly. "Let me think a minute."

The room grew very quiet. Through the sliding glass doors that opened onto Lynx's front deck, they watched the sun setting over the Centennial Mountains, painting the sky with pastel colors. A bald eagle screamed somewhere over the cabin, and they waited to see if it would fly into their view. It swooped onto the dead limb of an aspen tree a few yards from the cabin and settled down to watch the sunset.

"Ah, the eagle," Nora said. "God has given it the gift of seeing a long way. We need that gift now, I'd say." She began to pray silently.

"I know someone who may help us," Harry said. "He's a media expert at MSU and an Indian. He asked me for help when he produced a videotape on Chief Joseph's flight through Yellowstone Park."

"I remember him, Arthur Red Fox, isn't it?" Nora asked. "You had him over for dinner."

"That's him. He's a totally spiritual man. This stuff wouldn't freak him out," Harry said. "I'll take him the photos and everything first thing in the morning." He thought a moment. He was very uncomfortable being around the stuff. "Actually, I think I'll leave now. I don't want this stuff around you women. I'll get to Bozeman late, sleep in my pick-up, and catch Arthur early, before he goes to work at the university." Harry's head was pounding now, and he was struggling to keep the pain at bay and think of anything but the tapes.

Nora felt his pain. "Your head is aching, I know," she told him. "This is very evil stuff. I think you'd better pray to keep the pain from coming in. Anton has a lot of power, but the power we have through prayer is greater. It's been promised. Don't forget that."

Dewey began to bustle around the kitchen, making Harry sandwiches and coffee for his trip. She'd almost argued that he spend the night and leave in the morning, when he would be less tired, but something told her it was best to get the tapes as far away as possible as soon as possible.

"Let's decide how to proceed with Lynx," Dewey said. "I think we should tell her nothing until we know what's on the tapes, and then we should take her away somewhere and explain everything we know to her. She would be in more danger if she didn't know everything we can find out, and we have to get her away to tell her so she has no distractions."

"I like your idea," Nora said. "She's very busy now with the fires and all, and I don't think she's planning to really work with Anton until things settle down. I understand she hasn't even finished her CNS proposal."

"That's fine with me," Harry said. He was loading Lynx's 30-30 and even cranked a round into the chamber. He checked his own handgun to see if it was loaded before putting it in the pocket of his jacket. "Now I'm going. You two be careful. This is loaded and you know how to use it, Mom. If that creep comes here, shoot him. I didn't like seeing all those guns and ammo in his trailer." He put the rifle by the door. "And lock all the doors when I leave."

"I think we're protected, Harry, by our prayers," Nora replied. "But of course we'll lock up. I think we'll watch one of Lynx's John Wayne videos and just enjoy ourselves for the evening. Our minds need rest. You be careful." She hugged her son, and she and Dewey stood in the doorway and watched him drive down the road.

Chapter Thirty

Anton's trip to Bozeman had been a debacle, a string of petty annoyances that had him agitated and nearly out of control emotionally.

The tobacco store hadn't received his special order of Sherman's cigarettes, and he'd had to wait five hours for the late afternoon UPS shipment, which he was assured they were on. But they weren't, so he'd had to buy Camel straights. They were stale and foul tasting. He was given a similar story at the electronics store. They hadn't gotten around to repairing one of his VCR's because they were still waiting for parts. And the videotape supplier hadn't received his special order of high quality tapes.

Bozeman. The Bozone. What a joke. Nothing ever came in on time, and no one cared. They liked being what they called "laid back." He called it stupid, incompetent, and worthless. How he hated dealing with these people. Half the people he talked with that day were stoned on cheap weed, he noted, and since they started out with the IQ of a dead person, being stoned only made them more moronic.

Anton detested killing time. He walked around the old section of the county cemetery at the edge of town, smoking pot and examining all the gravestones. He admired some of the artistic engravings of cowboys and wildlife that had survived the weather for decades, but laughed in disgust at the spiritual inscriptions that announced that the dead were resting in peace with the angels.

He went to the Museum of the Rockies and watched all the slide shows and videotapes of Montana history, noting with disgust how amateur they were. These people had no awareness of how to edit, how to correct color and light to get the most information across. And he couldn't stand how much space was given to the Indians. Indians. It was so difficult for him to go along with Lynx's celebration of a culture that should have been eradicated long ago. They were a useless, stupid people, and the modern movement to renew the Indian's ancient spiritual connection to the earth was bothersome to his work.

He'd been distracted all day by the feeling that someone was in his trailer. He was certain of it. He'd tried to enter the place and see who was there, but couldn't get in. That made him reason that it had to be one of his own kind. DK and ten members of his hierarchy were due in West Yellowstone in three days for a ceremony, and maybe they were early. But still a restless, uncertain feeling returned to him that someone was checking him out from the other side. He'd know for sure when he got back. No one could penetrate his space without his knowing it, and he knew exactly what was there and would find out immediately if anything had been touched or stolen.

When his errands were over, Anton headed back to West Yellowstone. He decided to take a little side trip up a long dirt road off U.S. 191 that ended at a meadow at the edge of a trail to mountains in the Gallatin National Forest. He parked at the trail head and watched a herd of mule deer graze in the meadow. He was overwhelmed with the desire to kill one, to rip out its liver and eat it.

How he detested hunting seasons! A man ought to be able to kill an animal anytime he needed to. He listened for the sounds of other vehicles or people and heard only the slight breeze rattling the dried grass. Nobody wanted to come into the mountains because they were all scared of fire, and the forest service had officially closed all the backcountry trails accessed by dirt roads. He grabbed his old Winchester Model 94 deer rifle from the back of his van, sighted it on the heart of biggest doe in the herd, and shot. She dropped. The other deer bolted into the trees. He pulled his knife out of its sheath and walked down the hill to cut out her liver. It tasted magnificently warm and strong, and it made him feel more in control. He wiped the blood off his mouth and climbed in the van to drive back to West Yellowstone.

A line of vehicles heading to Bozeman caused Anton to wait several seconds at the stop sign at the end of the dirt road before he could head south to West. As it approached, the last vehicle in the row looked familiar, and he stared at it, trying to place it. "Oh, yes," he thought, "that belongs to Nora's son, Harry."

Harry was filled with fear the instant he saw Anton's van waiting at the stop sign. Instinctively he grabbed the .38 Special out of his pocket and set it on his lap. He took a deep breath, passed Anton, slowed down a bit, emptied his mind of all thoughts, and waved. Anton waved back and sat at the intersection until Harry's truck was no longer in sight. He tried to probe Harry's mind and found it a complete blank. Was Harry simply relaxed and driving leisurely down the road? Or did he know something, and know that he had to keep that knowledge hidden? Anger churned inside him. Harry's mind had reflected too much blankness—he must know how to prevent being probed. He'd know for certain when he got back to West, but he was pretty sure now that Harry had been the one who invaded his studio. He threw his transmission into drive and peeled out onto the highway.

Chapter Thirty One

Lynx stood with her camera at the top of a hill that overlooks the Madison River, at the end of what locals call Boredom Boulevard, a one-mile long trail from the east edge of West Yellowstone. She screwed her longest lens onto her camera and snapped photos of firefighters on the other side of the river who were setting a backburn they hoped would defend West Yellowstone from the approaching North Fork Fire.

To start the backburn, the firefighters piled dead brush along the riverbank, which they ignited with propane torches. The piles flared up and merged, consuming more dried brush and grass before the main fire, which was a quarter mile away, could reach it. It was hoped that this would slow the main fire down and prevent it from crossing the river and making a run on West Yellowstone.

Earlier and closer to town, fire lines had been made with explosives and bulldozers to stop or slow down the fire if it did cross the river. In town, firefighters had passed out an evacuation plan just in case the worst scenario came to pass. Fifty-five fire trucks were parked throughout the town to stomp on spot fires and spray down buildings, and most residents had their garden hoses ready to wet down their own roofs and vehicles. In the past two days, many people had stockpiled groceries, drinking water, electric heaters to use if their propane had to be turned off, and batteries to run their flashlights. Some had packed all their valuables in their cars and trucks. Others left town to visit relatives in Idaho and Utah and even farther away because they were getting sick from breathing so much smoke.

Lynx had interviewed people all around town before coming down to the river. People were basically confused and disgusted, she learned. They didn't know if they could trust Fire Command when it stated that it was sure it could defend West Yellowstone against the fire. The fires, most people said, seemed to have minds of their own and behavior more unpredictable than a grizzly bear.

Lynx heard footsteps behind her and turned from her camera to see Yurt, her fishing guide buddy, whom she hadn't seen since he'd told her about Tripod being trapped. He told her he'd walked down to the river to take pictures for his family in California, who called him every day to see if he was still alive. Guiding was very slow since tourism had all but come to a halt, he said.

"The Mormons," he told Lynx, "don't think the firefighters can defend West Yellowstone, so they're hauling irrigation equipment in to surround the town with sprinklers. That may be a good story."

"How did you hear about that?"

"I heard it at the Bear Cafe. The owner, Lyle, is a Mormon, and it was his idea. He called his brother, Forest, who owns an irrigation equipment company in Utah. Lyle and Forest have called farmers all over Utah and Idaho, and they're on their way here with the equipment from their farms and lots of people to help."

"What does Fire Command say?"

"I haven't talked to any of them, but knowing firefighters, they resent it. They think they have control of the situation."

"Lyle is one of the people who hasn't thought that for weeks now. He thinks they should have had all the fires out by now."

"The only way to stop the fires now is to have lots of rain and snow very soon, Lynx. Get your Indian friends to do a rain dance or something."

Lynx laughed. "I would give anything to see this end. But you know I really don't think we've anything to worry about in town. There are plenty of fire trucks and plenty of water." She took her last photo and started packing up her equipment.

"I'll walk you home," Yurt offered, hiking her camera bag onto his shoulder.

"Great. I appreciate the help. I'm getting a stiff neck from carrying all this equipment every day."

"Actually, Lynx, I was half hoping you would be down by the river working on a story. I need to talk with you. I left a message on your tape, so ignore it."

"Talk about what, Yurt?" Lynx stopped walking and looked at her friend, thinking that she didn't really know him too well, but she had always liked him. Their friendship didn't have a lot of story in it. They fished together a few times each year, usually during the salmon fly hatch on the lower Madison, and they talked about the stories she was working on, especially those that he had turned her on to.

She met Yurt the day she'd killed a bull elk high on a ridge in the mountains north of Hebgen Lake. She'd been hunting alone, not expecting to see any game, doing it more for the hike and the view from the top of Snowline Ridge. But she'd practically stumbled on the elk, which was downwind of her, and she had an unobstructed shot at him from less than 100 yards, so she'd taken it. Clean kill, heart shot. She tagged the animal, stashed her rifle nearby, and jogged back down the mountain to her truck. Then she drove back to town and called Roger and Nancy, a couple who hunted and had told her they would help her pack out any animals she killed, if she returned the favor.

Luckily they were home and available to help her. Yurt was visiting them, and he asked to come along as well. Later that season, when her elk was butchered and stored in her freezer, the four hunters enjoyed an elk steak feast Lynx and Nancy cooked, and she'd given Yurt its antlers. He liked to make antler belt buckles and tie tacks to sell to his fishing and hunting clients.

She'd guessed in all the years she'd known him that he had female problems and didn't seem to know how to eliminate them. He'd had numerous women, nearly always short, skinny blondes who started out looking happy hanging on his huge, muscular arms, but began to frown and look restless when hunting season started, and were long gone by Christmas, never to be seen again.

"Where do I begin?" Yurt asked her, squirming and readjusting her camera bag nervously.

Lynx smiled at him, expecting him to tell her about the latest blonde she'd seen him with.

"You gotta know I'm not nuts, right? I mean you know me sort of well, and you've never thought I was nuts or weird or psycho?"

Lynx nodded a negative.

Yurt looked around, located a dead tree that would seat two people, and motioned that they should sit down.

"This won't take but a minute," he explained. "But maybe we better have a sit down when I tell you."

Lynx was getting rather curious.

"I read a lot of fantasy books, as you know."

"Yeah, go on."

"Well, when you read these books, it doesn't take long to see that many of them have the same theme. There's a quest for something of great symbolic or real value. A lot of magical powers are used, both good and evil, and crystals, and wizards and beasts in enchanted forests, and on an on."

Lynx nodded.

"And sometimes the wizards and heroes with magic powers use tones, chants, and songs to invoke those magic powers, right?"

"I guess so," Lynx answered, wondering where he was going with this. "I have read such books, but I'm not a fantasy fan. I think Tolkien is so superior to any of the more contemporary stuff I've read that I just re-read his trilogy when I want to read a fantasy. And I don't have a lot of time to read bestsellers we aren't stocking at the museum. Go on. Just shoot it out."

"Okay." Yurt took a deep breath. "I actually saw a scene from one of those fantasy books. People in long, hooded robes, crystals, chants, songs, sounds that made the hair on my neck stand up—a feeling that I was in the presence of evil more intense than any passage I've read of that nature in any book, Tolkien included."

Lynx thought of her headache dreams and shivered. "Saw in a dream, you mean."

"No, saw for real."

"Where, when, how, why, what, who?"

Yurt didn't smile at her barrage of questions. "In the Centennial Valley, back in the sand dunes near the Red Rock Lakes, yesterday at sundown, with my eyes and then my spotting scope. I was scouting antelope. What? Now that's the killer. Who? A close second."

Yurt held his head in his hands and rested his elbows on his knees. "Whenever I think about this, my head aches, a dull ache between my eyes, with intermittent sharp pains behind the eyes. It's got me very tense."

Lynx stiffened, remembering her own headaches and suddenly wishing she was anywhere but there, talking to Yurt. "Tell me more," she said softly, rubbing the back of his head.

"I climbed one of the dunes near the road to get an overview of the ranch land and spot the antelope. I turned and looked north and saw another higher dune. I wanted to see what was on the other side of it, so I climbed down the first dune, and then up the higher one. When I got to the top of the second dune, I started walking along the top of it.

"I kept below the ridge line, though," Yurt went on. "You never know who's around that country with a rifle looking to bag something before the season opens, and I didn't want to be mistaken for a deer or antelope. After I'd walked 80, maybe 100 yards that way, I began to see human tracks going up the dune, a passle of them. I reckoned that whoever made the tracks had parked on the same road I'd parked on, but approached the dune by climbing a dune I'd driven past that wasn't as high as the first dune I'd climbed. Are you with me?"

Lynx was listening intently, her eyes closed so she could picture where he was, since she was pretty familiar with the country he was describing. "Yes—I see where you were. Go on."

"I was pretty curious because there were so many tracks, and I hadn't seen any vehicles parked on the road when I went by. It made me feel slightly jumpy, too."

"Sure, mysterious tracks, no vehicle. I can relate to that."

"Good. I hope you can relate to all of this. I hope you believe me, and I hope you have an explanation." Yurt rubbed his head. "I followed the tracks down the other side of the dune, which is covered with willows and sagebrushes, and into a stand of aspen trees and up a hill, and then I heard the sounds coming from the other side of the hill. Men humming. Harmony but not harmony. A lot of different tones, high, low, middle. I'm not a musician, but I listen to a lot of different kinds of music and have never heard anything like it."

Suddenly Lynx remembered one of her nightmares. The hooded men were as usual trying to force her to read the words written in blood. She had looked at them, and as usual couldn't have read them if she'd wanted to, because they were not in English or any other language she'd ever seen. But she'd sensed what they were about. It was about tones, something about being given your tone, your own power tone to use in your "work."

Lynx had done what she'd always done when she'd been forced to look at the book and sensed what it was saying. She'd forced herself to wake up and dismiss any memory of what she'd sensed. But now the memory of the tone power came back, and she knew that if she really thought about it, she would be able to recall everything they'd put before her. She looked at Yurt. He'd sat up and was staring at her.

"Lynx, you know what I'm talking about, don't you?"

"Oh, Yurt, I don't know, I just don't know. Go on, keep talking."

"I became very frightened, and I regretted that I'd walked on their trail, thinking they would see my tracks when they returned, if they returned that way. I thought of bolting, but something inside me had to know what was there. I walked backward in my tracks and then left the trail and used my jacket to brush away my new tracks back towards the woods. I paralleled what I guessed was their trail, staying 20 yards from it. By then the sun was down, and the light was fading. The humming, or whatever you call it, seemed louder, and not just because I was getting closer. I saw a clearing up ahead, and I crouched down and moved slowly until I was as close to it as possible, and I hid behind some juniper bushes. I was about 20 yards from them."

"Them?"

"There were 12 men. I'm guessing they were all men, because I didn't hear any woman's voice, but they were wearing hooded robes, and their hoods were pulled around their heads so it was difficult to see their faces, and some of them had their backs to me. They were sitting in a circle around a fire pit, and the pit was loaded with firewood." Yurt paused and took a deep breath.

"Ten of them were wearing black robes, one wore a white robe and another a purple robe. They guy with the white robe was sitting to the right of the purple guy. It seemed as if they were all staring at the pile of firewood."

"You mean it wasn't burning?" Lynx asked.

"No," not right then.

"It's very strange, Yurt. What else did you see?"

"Lynx, I started feeling afraid when I was at the top of the ridge and first saw the tracks. I had a feeling I was going to see something strange or weird, and the feeling got more and more intense. I kept wanting to turn back, but something made me keep going. I think I know what it was, too."

"What do you mean, Yurt?"

"I think I was supposed to see that so I could tell you. Or do you already know? Are you part of this?"

"No, I'm not part of it, not at all. Tell me what else you saw."

"The white-robed person's hum could suddenly be heard distinctly over the others, where at first they blended together. His hum grew louder and higher in tone, and he leaned forward slightly and stared directly at the firewood. Then, are you ready for this?"

Lynx nodded.

"The wood burst into flames. It behaved like wood does when it's been soaked in gasoline and you throw a match on it. But no one had thrown a match. I'm sure of that. Somehow, he'd done it with his tone and his mind, maybe drawing on the others' power to help. I know it, but I don't believe it.

"When the fire ignited, it lit up the whole area. I got a good look at the face of the man in white. It was that guy in the trailer by your house. Anton's his name, right?"

Lynx nodded and shivered.

"When the fire ignited, they stopped humming, and they stood up, one by one, starting with your buddy."

"Look—he's not my buddy. He's my business partner," Lynx interjected.

"And they started chanting, but not in English. It may have been German. It was kind of harsh-sounding. I listened to them for a few minutes, but then I left. I figured that whatever they were doing, they were doing in secret, and I wouldn't be able to figure it out, and I wasn't going to walk in on them, so I'd better leave. Besides, I was starting to feel really lousy. I had a splitting headache, and I felt sick to my stomach."

Lynx cringed. Headaches when Anton was around were beginning to be too common to be coincidental. "Did you go straight back to your truck then?" she asked.

"Yeah, and I hooked onto the path they'd taken as soon as I could rather than stay in the trees. I figured that if they did see a foreign footprint, maybe they would worry, and for some reason, I think they're evil and should worry."

"Yurt, I've been warned and warned about Anton by friends and acquaintances. But something happens when I spend time with him. I begin to feel that he is a really special, wonderful, good person. I've even felt sexually attracted to him, and I wonder if the people who are warning me about him are just jealous or something."

"Lynx, you've got to be kidding. Maybe he's putting a spell on you." Yurt smiled at her.

"Yurt, I think he may have. I find myself thinking and feeling things about him that I later know are totally off base. They don't fit the other thoughts and feelings I have about him, and they don't fit the warnings I'm getting. It's like he's doing something to make me like him and feel attracted to him. And I get headaches a lot, especially when I think about him."

"Exactly what business are you in with him, anyway?"

"Oh, Yurt, that's what's so sad about all this. One of my dreams is coming true, and here I am having to deal with this craziness."

"Lynx, make some sense, please," Yurt put his arm around her.

"I have a grant to produce television specials on Yellowstone. It means a lot to me because I can get away from the *Gazette*, which is becoming more and more boring, and do something really creative."

"But what does Anton have to do with it?"

"I've asked him to do all the technical work, some of the camera work, editing, sound, and so on."

"Can't you find someone else?"

"Sure, Yurt, I suppose I could if I advertised, but you know how limited the talent for that kind of thing is around here. Now I'm wondering why Anton is so interested in helping me anyway. What is he doing? Why is he so bizarre?"

They were silent, thinking, trying to put the pieces together.

"Lynx, if he is into this secret ceremonial deal, maybe it's meant to involve you somehow. Maybe we should find out what he's up to."

"Or maybe I should just tell him our deal is off."

"You could do that. But what if he and his buddies are into something really big, really major, and you could expose them?"

"Yurt, you're talking to the journalist in me. I'm thinking the same thing. They may be using me because I have something they don't have."

"Like a vast knowledge of the Yellowstone area, a grant to produce television shows on Yellowstone that will reach millions of people."

Lynx stood up. "Let's start back to town, Yurt. I've got stuff to do."

They walked and thought. "You know, Yurt," Lynx said, "Anton met me before I was awarded the grant."

"Yes, but he could have decided to connect with you and worry about how he would use you later. I'm thinking more about whether or not you are in danger. Face it. Ordinary people don't meet in remote areas of the Centennials to engage in strange rituals. We don't know who those people are or what they're up to, but they aren't playing around."

"That's for sure. They seem to have developed a way to control what other people are thinking. I know that's what's been happening to me. Actually, Yurt, a lot of strange things are happening in this so-called sleepy mountain community. Why they are happening is a mystery, but life around here has become rather peculiar."

"One thing is clear to me, though, Lynx."

"That's good news, because it's getting muddier and muddier from my side," Lynx smiled.

"We have to find out more about that ritual. It has to be part of some kind of a cult."

"How can we find out about it?"

"That I don't know for sure. But I do have a friend in Bozeman who's been studying occult philosophies, working on a thesis on the New Age movement for his senior project. I'm going hunting with him next week, and I'll pick his brains. Meanwhile, stay cool, and if Anton tries anything that frightens you, get ahold of me or Jack or one of your friends. Don't think you haven't people around this town you can call on for help."

They reached their vehicles. Yurt opened Lynx's car door, looked inside and laughed. "Wow, things could be living in there. That's scary."

"Hey, knock it off," she countered, watching him examine the mess in her car. The floor was knee-deep in Styrofoam cups, deli sandwich wrappers, and film cases. "Who's got time to clean a car?" she laughed. "And not all that stuff is mine. All my media buddies hitching rides into the park have contributed."

"This, too?" Yurt reached in and picked a fat marijuana roach out of the ashtray.

"Oh, great. I never saw that. I bet it's Anton's. He smokes pot all the time, lights 'em up wherever he is. I tell him to quit, but he says he knows how to use drugs to better himself. He must have left this in here last week when I let him use the car to run errands and his van was in the shop. Here—you take it."

"Nah, just toss it. I quit smoking out last winter. Costs too much, and it makes a person's mind kind of fuzzy. I can't believe Anton would think it has the opposite effect. That might explain why he's out there past Pluto, in my opinion. Anyway, I'll come over and clean your car for you. This is really bad," he said, pointing at the mess.

"No need to, " Lynx told him. "I'll get to it." She slid into her seat and threw some of the junk in the back so she could reach the pedals. A firefighter pulled up and asked them to move their vehicles right away so he could park his truck in their spot. He said his was the last truck to take a position for the night in case the fire raided town.

First thing the next morning, Lynx filed her story about the backburn and planned defense of West Yellowstone, then hurried over to the edge of town to photograph and interview the Mormon irrigators.

They told her they had many friends and relatives in West Yellowstone who depended on tourist trade from the park, so it only made sense to come up and help them protect their businesses. By midmorning, they had irrigation pipe laid along the east and south borders of town that were shooting out water pumped from the Madison River through a mile-long pipe they'd laid after blasting a hole in the river with dynamite to make a deep hole for the pump. Lynx made exact note of where "Mormon hole" was, reasoning that the big brown trout that run out of Hebgen Lake in late fall may find and use it.

Lynx hustled from the Mormons to the bus station to send her film to Bozeman, then back home to her computer to write the story. Ash rained on the town and the air was dirtier than L.A. at rush hour. A United Parcel Service delivery man was just pulling in to Lynx's driveway, bringing her first batch of video equipment purchased with the CNS grant money. Even though her final proposal hadn't yet been submitted, CNS had allowed her to start ordering equipment. She planned to videotape the fire's expected run on Old Faithful for a future story on the fires, so had made sure the *Gazette* would send another reporter to cover Old Faithful so she could concentrate on videotaping and not have to worry about writing a story, too.

As she signed for the packages, she glanced across her backyard to Anton's trailer. His van was there, but Lynx hadn't seen him for two days, since just before he'd left for a trip to Bozeman. He must be hard at work on some project or another, she thought, and she had no desire to disturb him. She was busy enough as it was.

As soon as her story was finished, she planned to check on things at the museum and then take Merlin out to the Island Park cabin for a relaxing evening. They would take a hike along the lake shore and practice using the new video camera. She looked over at Anton's trailer again and noticed that the curtain on his studio window, which faced her house, was parted slightly. Was he watching her or simply checking out the UPS truck? She shivered. The UPS driver was asking her about the fires, and she hadn't heard his question because she was feeling very strange vibes from Anton. She dismissed them and looked at the driver, who was staring at her, waiting for her answer.

"Sorry—what did you say?" she asked, trying to smile at him.

"I just asked you if you think the fire will hit town, or do you think they have the fire lines set up well enough to stop it? Are you okay, Lynx? You seem a little spacey."

"Yeah, I'm spaced out all right. Trying to do too much, like we all do in the summer. And the smoke is getting to me. But I'm not worried about town. I think the Mormons are panicking, and so are the people who are moving their stuff out of their houses. There are plenty of firefighters around. All they have to do is stomp on the cinders that blow around until the fires burns itself out at the lines."

"What's the deal on that guy who lives over there?" he asked, nodding towards Anton's. The curtain suddenly went back to its normal position. "Look—he was watching us. Is he your boyfriend?"

"Is that the rumor?" Lynx laughed. "No, he and I are doing a video project together. That trailer is his home-studio. He moved it here because they shut down the mobile home park he was living in at Big Sky, and it's more convenient to have him close by."

"If you ask me, he's some kind of a nut, the way he dresses and the way he looks at people. He gives me the creeps."

"Oh, he's an eccentric all right, but he's very intelligent and good at what he does." Lynx wasn't about to tell him Anton was the most puzzling person she'd ever met, and she was sick of hearing how negative everyone felt toward him.

• • •

Inside his trailer, Anton's parabolic microphone pointed at Lynx's house. With its earphones, he could hear everything they said. So the UPS man thought he was nuts. Big deal. Most important was that he'd delivered the video cameras, and they could begin their work. Lynx had defended him. Good. That meant he'd won her over.

So what if Harry had checked him out? That Indian son of a bitch had stolen six videotapes and had probably gone through his stuff. Anton couldn't be sure if he had, but he knew the tapes were missing because he kept an exact count. Still, he couldn't tell what else Harry had looked at. He was either very careful and knew he had to block any thoughts about what he'd seen so Anton couldn't learn what he knew, or he'd simply stolen the tapes and run.

Anton turned off the microphone and sat down at his work table. He opened a jar of rubber bands and emptied them out on the table. At the bottom of the jar was a vial holding an eight ball of pure cocaine. He took out a large crystalline piece and used a razor blade to chop it into a fine powder, which he then divided into six lines he snorted into both nostrils. In a few seconds, he felt less sleepy and ready to get back to work. He hadn't slept since the night before he went to Bozeman. He'd been riled beyond belief at the thought that someone had invaded his space, actually picked his lock and entered his private domain. And although he'd tried with all his power to enter Harry's mind, he couldn't discover exactly what Harry had done there or what he was doing with the tapes.

Chapter Thirty Two

Walt figured the best thing he could do would be to follow his normal evening routine, to show TDP he had no idea he was about to be removed while he figured out how to get away.

He ordered a snack and the evening paper from room service and ate while his Jacuzzi filled with water. He slipped into the tub and scanned the paper. An ad in the travel section caught his eye because it was illustrated with a photograph of an unusual looking statue of a long-haired, armored warrior with wings.

The ad copy advertised a daily bus tour to the Shrine of San Miguel del Milagro in Tlaxcala, located in the mountains outside the city. The ad was from a prayer group based at the Metropolitan Cathedral of St. Francis and said that in 1631, St. Michael the Archangel appeared in Tlaxcala to a peasant named Diego Lazaro. Apparently St. Michael, who was the winged warrior in the picture, touched his staff to a spring and infused the water with miraculous powers.

Diego, the ad said, took the water to the local bishop, who gave it to all the sick people in a nearby hospital, and all were cured after drinking it. The Catholic Church later pronounced the apparition and the miracle of the water "worthy of belief," meaning that the church believed them to be divine manifestations. The water still had curative powers, according to the advertisement.

"Good," Walt thought, "maybe if I go there, it can cure me of my current situation." That gave him an idea.

He gave his full attention to the rest of the ad. Buses were leaving for the shrine tomorrow and would go on to Ocotlan for a late lunch stop before returning to Mexico City. They would leave Mexico City from the Cathedral, which just so happened to be on the route to the language school, and travelers could purchase tickets from the bus drivers. The buses left at

8 a.m., an hour after class started. There had to be a way he could get on one of the buses, which would get him out of the city and give him time to make the connections he needed to get out of the country. Surely there were phones in Ocotlan.

Walt had an old high school buddy in Bozeman, Bonzo Reed, who could get him a phony passport, driver's incense, and even credit cards. Bonzo was a self-taught computer hacker who earned his living breaking into computer systems. He wiped out ridiculously high interest financial service company loans that were made to pay back piles of delinquent accounts people living beyond their incomes accumulate. His fee was a small percent of the loan's pay off figure.

Bonzo made most of his money on phony identifications and on writing programs to protect computer systems from being pirated by people like himself. Walt had never had him busted because he admired the guy. Bonzo had lost both his legs in Viet Nam and refused to collect disability pay from the government, stubbornly wanting to earn his own way. You didn't need legs to operate computers. Bonzo wouldn't help severe criminals, just people who were being knocked around by the system and deserved a second chance. Walt always figured Bonzo would be a help to him some day.

Walt would let himself get dropped off at the language school, leave class, shave his beard and cut his hair in the restroom, strip down to gym shorts and a tee shirt he'd wear under his school clothes, and run to the Cathedral to catch the bus. Hell, he'd even change his hair color, using a bottle of peroxide he had to rinse his mouth with. He'd just dump it on his head in the restroom, and his hair would be lighter by the time he'd dried it running to the bus. The only thing that would foil his plans would be if the assassin he was certain Ben would send got there before morning, and he doubted that would happen because he knew Ben too well. Ben would want to make him think he was still a part of TDP, so he'd wait, probably a day or so to catch him off guard.

• • •

Walt had hoped to have a seat to himself on the bus to the shrine, but it was packed with people when he boarded. He'd sat down next to an old woman, hoping she would not be the conversational type. It turned out he was dead wrong, but that was okay because she was very sweet. Luckily, she was the mother of the man who ran the most popular restaurant in Ocotlan, and there was a phone there he could use. She even invited him to spend the night with her family, noting she intended to stay in Ocotlan a few days before returning to Mexico City on another tour bus.

Her name was Juanita Martinez, and she told Walt all about St. Michael the Archangel, a story he at first forced himself to listen to, and then was strangely attracted to. Michael, she'd told him, was the warrior in heaven in charge of the good angels who fought Lucifer and his legions of bad demons. These spirits of light and darkness were most real, she explained when he laughed at her and said he thought demons were purely mythological.

Walt couldn't avoid noticing how sincere she was, and he began to listen intently to her because somehow what she was saying did connect to his present situation. He'd begun to recall a conversation he'd had months ago with Ben, during one of the rare times Ben had actually spoken seriously to him about TDP's South American operation, before their relationship had become strained. He'd said TDP was partly funded by a very strong, viable Satanic group; he'd said that had made him feel uncomfortable: he'd added that he didn't believe in God or Satan, he just didn't personally like to have any association with any group that was fanatical. And he'd said that the TDP's higher ups did not know that he had any information about the Satanic group. He'd checked into it using his own sources and learned it was based in Chicago and was extremely wealthy.

"Don't kid yourself," he'd told Walt, "there is no idealism here about wiping drugs off the face of the earth. It's all about power and control." Walt had wondered exactly what he'd meant by that, but had learned it was pointless to question Ben in detail about anything.

Now Juanita told him that Satanic organizations were very real, that they did use drugs to control the people who worked for them, and that being close to God and developing oneself spiritually are important actions people should take to counteract the evil in the world.

"Faith in God," she said, "is not just something we old ladies practice to pass the time until we die. There are real spiritual battles being fought in the world. When you attend Mass at the shrine this morning, think about this. The grace you get there could help you."

Walt hadn't been to Mass since he'd married Susan in the Catholic Church, something she'd insisted on not because she was a good Catholic, but because she wanted to please her parents, who were. His parents had also made sure he was baptized Catholic, but the family had rarely gone to church. His mother had often told him that Catholics did weddings, funerals, and baptisms well, but that church people were "clique-y," and she didn't to be involved with them. Walt and Susan had never gone to church, nor had they baptized the kids, even though it was something they had promised the priest they would do when they married in the church.

Walt tried to focus on the Mass at the shrine, but his mind kept wandering. After all, he was on the run and constantly aware that he was looking over his shoulder to see if he was being followed. He'd gone to Communion only so he wouldn't stand out as a non-believer amid all the seemingly sincere people on the tour. Juanita sat next to him at Mass and grabbed his hand and held it throughout the last prayer that everyone recited together.

Most people seemed to have memorized the prayer, but Walt read it off a prayer card Juanita had put in his free hand, and he kept the card. "Michael the Archangel, defend us in battle. Be our protection against the wickedness and snares of the devil. May God rebuke him, we humbly pray, and do thou o Prince of the Heavenly Host, cast into hell Satan and the other evil spirits who prowl the earth seeking the ruin of souls."

After the services, Juanita filled a small plastic bottle with water from the shrine and gave it to him, telling him that the water was holy and had exorcistic powers. He put it in his shorts' pocket, just in case she was right. Walt did not know if Juanita and the other worshipers were crazy, but he did feel that they had an inner peace he'd never felt.

Juanita chatted with a woman across the aisle from them about the Mass and the way her visits to the shrine always strengthened her faith. She turned to Walt and told him, "You know, I have a sense that you were put on this bus for a reason. You are a seeker or in some kind of trouble, and you need St. Michael and the Lord to help you."

Her voice was soft and sweet and her eyes full of love. They were wise eyes, too, and probing. He doubted anyone could lie to her.

"Juanita, you're right. I'm in trouble, but I promise you I have done nothing wrong. For your own protection, I can't tell you what it's all about."

Juanita looked at him for a minute, thinking, never taking her eyes off his.

"I believe you. The Holy Spirit tells me to help you, even though you have done many wrong things, despite what you say. You are a sinner like all of us. But you don't want to be anymore. How can I help you?"

"I need to get to a phone, make a call to a friend in the States who can help me, and then find a place to hide out for a few days, a place where I can receive mail in care of someone else."

Again, Juanita was quiet. This time, her head was bowed and she seemed to be praying. Walt watched her and fear welled up in him. Why had he told her anything? But the fear went away as quickly as it had come. He suddenly realized it was luck, or grace, whichever. She was his ticket out of here.

She raised her head and looked at him. "I will help you," she said with resolve. "My family will help you. God will bless you. Now just don't worry. Look out the window at the beautiful countryside, and let me take a little nap before we get to Ocotlan."

Chapter Thirty Three

An empty tour bus pulled up to the front door of the Old Faithful Inn. Lynx, already about to gag on the smoke-filled air from the nearby North Fork fire, choked on its diesel fumes. "Shit," she thought, turning off her video camera, "I keep forgetting when I cough, this damn thing records me."

She thanked the man she'd been interviewing. His name was Dale, and he was a senior citizen from Iowa who'd been waiting for the bus to carry him and his wife Polly out of the park. It was their first vacation to Yellowstone, and despite the fact that the smoke had been making them sick, they'd stayed in the park as long as possible. Dale told Lynx he was thrilled to be there because he found the fires exciting and hadn't seen this much action since World War II.

All tourists were being evacuated from the Old Faithful area. There was no doubt now that the fire would make a run on the Old Faithful complex, and firefighters were busy getting tourists to leave and mobilizing equipment to wet down as many buildings as possible.

"Polly, wait a sec, give me my camera. Check that out," Dale said excitedly, pointing to the flag on the top of the inn. The flag was flying straight out in the strong, unrelenting wind, pointing east. Lynx turned her camera on and took a shot of it and then of Dale photographing it with his tiny camera, and then of Dale and Polly mounting the bus and waving at her. "Good luck," Dale shouted over the roaring wind. Theirs was the last bus to leave. It was five minutes to noon.

Lynx spent the next three hours taping every image she could find of the inn about to be under siege, taking her time to record every detail of the majestic hand hewn log interior, especially the lobby. She shot an Old Faithful eruption from the inn's lower roof through the smoky air, and zoomed in on the distant tree-covered hills, thinking she was taking some of the last images of the trees before they would burn. She hoped the same was not true for the inn, a place she and people all over the world had many fine memories of.

She interviewed several summer employees who worked in the inn and souvenir shops and were hanging around the area drinking beer, chatting about what they would do the rest of the season, taking bets on whether or not the inn would burn down, and stopping to cheer whenever they saw a large plume of fire jump from the tops of trees west of the area. As the flames got closer, firefighters herded all the employees into the parking lot, told them to stay close to their cars, and suggested they stop drinking and get ready to drive away.

It was nearly 4 p.m., and the fire roared closer, its smoke blocking the sun, its soot turning the air black. Lynx wondered if there was enough light to record, but she quickly popped a new tape in her camera and shot fire crews attempting to spray down some old cabins. The wind was so strong that it blew the water from their high-powered hoses away before it could reach the shingled roofs. Sparks flew on the roofs and ignited them. Lynx glanced at the employees, who were no longer partying. They were frantically jamming their gear into the trunks of their cars and driving away.

A firebrand the size of a beer can hit Lynx's safety helmet and rolled onto the sleeve of her fireproof shirt. She quickly brushed it off, keeping her camera fixed on an old garage that had caught fire. She heard someone scream that an oil truck was inside the garage, and a few seconds later, the truck exploded. Fire flew out of the garage towards some old cabins, and Lynx walked closer to record the cabins burning to the ground, getting on tape the loud explosion of a fire extinguisher that had been hanging on one of the cabins. She rushed back to the inn to record a fire truck pumping water into the inn's rooftop sprinkling system.

A large firebrand blew onto the inn's right wing and a fire truck hit it with water. Lynx heard a firefighter estimate the wind speed at 40 mph, and she gripped her camera with all her strength, hoping the wind wouldn't jiggle it too much and blur the images she was recording. She didn't let herself think about the sound the wind was making on the tape. She hoped the microphone would record her descriptions of the experience, and kept reminding herself not to curse when firebrands fell on and around her.

Sick and weak from breathing the thick smoke, Lynx began to feel faint and checked the camera's recording time. She'd been taping for nearly an hour. Her arms, neck, and back were killing her. She pointed the camera to the hills east of Old Faithful, where firebrands that had blown over the Old Faithful complex were now igniting trees. She walked over to the main power line going into the complex and shot the sprinkler system that was pouring water on the lines. The sprinkler system had been placed there by the same Mormon farmers who had protected West Yellowstone.

After what felt like an eternity, the smoke began to lift. The firestorm had passed. Lynx put another fresh tape in her camera and walked slowly around, recording the damage. Nineteen cabins had burned to the ground; she noted on tape that those cabins were old and had already been earmarked for demolition. She recorded other damage: an employee dormitory, a restroom, vehicles, a water tank, and a TV transmitter station. She recorded comments from exhausted but triumphant firefighters. They'd saved the historic Old Faithful Inn. No one was hurt or killed. One firefighter told her that if the wind had shifted just two or three degrees, the inn would have burned down.

"All of us, including you media folks, are professionals, doing our jobs as we learned them," he told Lynx. "But now that the danger is past, we have to realize that all of us looked death in the face."

Bill, the *Gazette* reporter covering the Old Faithful assault, walked wearily up to her and asked her for a ride back to West Yellowstone. He'd come into the park with a reporter from Billings who had already left to make his deadline. He wanted to take a shower at her house, rest for a while, and then use her computer to file his story. He'd sent his film with the Billings reporter. Reporters from every local and regional newspaper and television station had been there, as well as people from every major national news service. There was no need to be cutthroat about film or stories: everyone would file the same basic story, and not even the best would come close to describing what it was like to be there.

Dozens of vehicles, mostly full of news people, drove slowly through the Firehole Valley. Trees on both sides of the road still burned and smoldered, but the river danced along in its usual way to meet the Gibbon River at Madison Junction and become the Madison River. Near the junction, a herd of tired elk grazed in a fire scorched meadow.

Bill and Lynx didn't talk much. He drove while she turned her camera on now and then to record spots of fire and the elk. All Lynx wanted was to see Merlin and take a shower before watching her videotapes. If this and future tapes were good, and she and Anton could edit them into something the public would like, she could kiss the *Gazette* good-bye and do her own thing.

• • •

Merlin was sitting on the back porch when she returned and smiled at her as if he hadn't seen her for a very long time.

"Mom, I saw some of the fire on the news. That was wicked. I looked for you and I didn't see you and I was worried. Are you okay?"

Lynx saw the concern in his face and remembered how often that summer he'd looked at her that way. What could she do to make up for that? Maybe she could spend more time with him when things got going with CNS. She hugged him, introduced him to Bill, and told him, "You bet it was wicked, but no one was hurt. Wait 'til you see the tapes. I've got more than three hours of stuff, but we can skip over the boring parts, okay?"

None of them saw Anton peeking at them through his curtains, smiling with delight that Lynx was back, holding the videotapes he couldn't wait to get his hands on.

Mystic Warriors of the Yellowstone

Chapter Thirty Four

The red fox had been hunting sage hens in a low mountain meadow when she felt drawn to a power she had never felt before. The power did not feel the same as the instinct-led drives the fox was used to responding to, the drives to hunt and groom herself, to excavate her den, to mate and protect her young.

When she felt this power, she saw in her mind's eye the forms of Humans, forms from which she would normally flee. But now something was drawing her to move up the mountain, where she could smell and hear Human.

She was hungry, however, and the soft light from the setting sun was her signal to hunt, so she ignored the strange desire to seek out the Humans and continued to stalk a sage hen which she could smell and hear breathing not 20 feet away, tucked beneath a large clump of rabbitbrush.

She was an old fox. She'd had five litters there in the Bridger Mountains, where fox were seldom hunted or trapped and had few animal enemies to worry about, once they grew too large to be caught by hawks or eagles.

She was so skilled a hunter that it wasn't necessary that she see the bird. She had an exact sense of where it was, and when she was less than three feet from it, she pounced two feet into the air and came down directly over it, biting its neck with her teeth and killing it instantly. As its body writhed and then stiffened, she held it with her teeth and trotted to the woods at the edge of the meadow where she tore it apart and ate it, continuing to ignore the pull from the Humans somewhere above her.

Soon, the edge was taken off her hunger, and she focused on the strange pull. It reminded her then of something she'd seen long, long ago, in the eyes of her mother, a knowledge about something Other. It was a memory her mother held but had never transmitted directly to her. Her mother had also been drawn to the Humans, but the fox had no idea in what way, in what sense. Now she could see those ancient eyes as if they were alive once more. Impossible. Her mother had been crushed to death years ago by a loud, ugly thing on the hard path the fox had learned never to cross, a path she sometimes went down to look at and which over the years had more and more loud ugly things passing over it. Sometimes the fox had seen other crushed animals on the path, but remembering her mother, she had never given in to the desire to eat those things, even though their smell had tempted her.

Her mother's eyes seemed to be telling her to seek out the Humans, and she began to crisscross through the woods and up the mountain, stopping now and then to smell and listen and adjust her path. As she grew closer, she could hear them more distinctly. She heard singing, and the sound was soothing and friendly. She heard the crackle of a fire and smelled its smoke, a blend of pine and sweetgrass. It made her curious, like she used to feel when she was very small and came upon an animal she'd never seen before. She walked faster and her path grew straighter until she saw the two Humans. She froze.

Arthur Red Fox sat close to Harry Spotted Elk and nudged him when he saw the fox but kept singing. Harry didn't know Arthur's song, but he hummed along with him, easily copying the melody as quickly as Arthur brought it forth. It was an old melody of their People, one he'd heard his mother sing when he was in her womb. Arthur dropped an octave, and Harry stayed with him. The lower tone seemed to awaken the fox. She began to move toward them, keeping her head lower than her back and her tail straight out. Arthur stretched out his arms toward her and opened his hands.

Fear rose in the fox, and she almost fled. But again she saw her mother's eyes and knew she must continue to approach the Humans. Their sounds entered her mind and invited her into their space, a space that she could be safe in, this time. A welcoming, comfortable smell came from the hands that stretched out to her, and she walked slowly toward the Human until her head was between the hands and he touched her.

Arthur continued his song. As Harry hummed along, he watched Arthur bond with the fox, as if the two had become one. Neither man nor animal moved. The fox felt the heat from the fire on her back, and it was almost too much for her, but the man's touch was pleasant. She sat down. Arthur moved his hands and rested them on her head. She shivered with fear, and the fire's heat began to feel unbearable. She looked directly into the man's eyes then, asking him to let her go. In those eyes she saw the same expression she'd seen in her mother's, and she knew then that she couldn't leave until she had given the man something.

Giving. What did that mean to her? The only time she gave was when she fed her young. It was the only time, until now, that she felt the urge to share. It was so strong an urge with her kittens that she would hunt and not even think to eat herself, knowing that her hunting was not for herself but for the survival of her helpless young. The man seemed to know what she was thinking. He took his hands off her and pushed her a little, as if telling her to run. "But come back," his eyes said, "and bring a gift."

Arthur watched the fox run around the fire and back into the woods she'd come from. He stopped singing and threw another log on the fire. "Now we have to wait," he told Harry. "She will be back. All we have to do is keep singing."

It had been a long time since Arthur had sung the "Song of the Fox," a song he learned from his father and grandfather during the month of his vision quest and sang only four times thereafter, during rare meetings of the Red Fox Society. Each time a fox had come, and the aid it had given him had been useful. He had been given creative abilities that made him shine in his career as a filmmaker and videographer. It had inspired him to chronicle the past and present lives of his People and their relationships with the animals and plants they depended on for survival and spiritual renewal. Now his dear friend, Harry, and Harry's family and friends needed help.

As he sang, Arthur thought about the videotapes he'd seen and shuddered. All six tapes were of hunts for large game animals: bighorn sheep, mountain goats, elk, deer, black bear, and grizzly bear. They were not normal hunting tapes, the kind amateur videographers make to instruct hunters on the best way to stalk, kill, and butcher game. The hunters were brutal and uncaring murderers who took some kind of sick pleasure in killing wildlife merely for the sake of killing. Perhaps the videographer was an anti-hunter, trying to show hunters in a bad light to promote his agenda. Or perhaps the person was trying to seek out people who would take pleasure in watching these sick excuses for hunters.

Most frightening was that when Arthur slowed down the tapes on his specialized equipment, he found that they were cut with hundreds of Satanic images: computer generated geometric symbols and cuts of videos of Black Masses and Human sacrifices that appeared to be too real to have been staged. Strangely, these subliminal cuts were placed in sections of the video that were very beautiful, stunning panoramas of the mountains and meadows where the hunters were seeking game or of splendid close-up shots of wildlife.

Arthur hadn't been surprised when Harry told him Anton Devier had made the tapes, although he was surprised that Anton now lived in West Yellowstone. Anton's work on the first image processors was widely known among media experts, as were his skills as an innovative video and sound editor. Arthur thought Anton was working on the West coast somewhere. His work had always identified him as an urban person. It was highly technical, requiring the use of equipment available only in larger cities or universities. And his subject matter had always been urban, mainly colorfully processed images of city life and culture.

Arthur recalled one piece Anton had produced on the day in the life of an assembly worker in a car manufacturing plant. It had cuts from close-ups of the machinery in the plant to the bored faces of the workers. At first the images were in realistic color, and then Anton processed them in neon monochromatic hues, making the cuts shorter and faster to match the crescendo on the tape's soundtrack, the whining sounds of the machinery mixed with high fusion jazz. The video grated on one's nerves, just as the boredom of a day on a noisy assembly line would, and took the viewer from a relaxed state to a nightmare of vibrant, gaudy color and sound. By the end of the tape, you were as fried as you would be if you had worked in the plant all day.

Arthur didn't really know Harry's friend Lynx O'Malley. He'd seen some of her videos and liked her work, although it didn't have the technical perfection of Anton's. And he'd told Harry he'd always enjoyed her articles in the *Gazette*. He'd met her once, when he'd visited the museum and had been so impressed by the Indian exhibits that he'd asked to meet her to learn more about how the museum had acquired its artifacts.

Harry had explained some of what he had perceived as strange behavior on Lynx's part since she'd met Anton and about his headaches and how everyone who knew Lynx was worried about her. Harry and Arthur had pondered at length what Anton was up to, and guessed that he was going to cut these horrible symbols and scenes into Lynx's videos. They would then be seen by millions of people, all innocently wanting to know more about Yellowstone.

Would they do any harm? Arthur heard about subliminal cuts many years ago, when cuts of popcorn and pizza were interjected in short documentary films before feature movies to see if people responded by buying more food at the theater's snack bar. The one book he'd read on subliminal advertising had said that experiments had never proven it worked. After he analyzed the hunting videos, Arthur had visited the only computer expert he knew, Bonzo Reed, who'd told him that a great deal of experimentation was going on all over the world in the use of subliminal cuts in film, video, and computer graphics. Bonzo had told him that these experiments were pretty secretive. Many were funded by governments and large think tanks.

"There can be no doubt," Bonzo had told him, "that there are researchers out there who are trying to find a way to program people subliminally. They're using all types of media, even computer games kids play, and they're working with high frequency sounds, too: photokinesis, all kinds of stuff. Some of it is probably innocent enough, geared to see how the Human minds works and learns and can be influenced. But some of it is warfare, plain and simple."

"Warfare?" Arthur had asked him.

"Sure, if you can control the minds of a group or community, or even of specific leaders who would then influence large numbers of people, you wouldn't need conventional weapons."

Arthur wanted to know how he could find out more about this stuff.

"I doubt if you can. For one, if you started asking questions, they would know about it and try to stop you. Hell, I've even heard they've funded the writing of at least one book that says all this stuff is bogus, just to throw people off track."

"Who the hell is 'They' anyway?" Arthur had asked him.

"They. Governments. Think tanks, I told you."

"Can you be more specific?"

"Yes, I could, but I won't. Let me just say I've stumbled on some of this stuff in my work, and I've learned it's best to look the other way. There's nothing I can do about it. Let them play their games. If you get into thinking the world is full of conspiracies, you'll go nuts. Hell, you'll even get physically ill. Mentally ill. They'll make it look as if your paranoid, schizoid, nutsoid. They'll send viruses into your computer. Don't play around with this stuff, Arthur. Make your pretty films and videos and forget about it."

"What if I know that someone is making videos on Yellowstone and cutting some pretty weird, evil stuff into them?"

"If you know that, you should forget about it. You could try to stop it, but if it's one of the Big Guys doing it, you'll be stopped."

"How?"

"Oh, a number of ways. You won't get tenure. Your won't get funded for a research project. You'll come down with cancer. Your car will blow up."

"I don't know if I can look the other way, not when innocent people are being hurt."

Bonzo had looked at Arthur for a long time, saying nothing, thinking until Arthur could almost see smoke come out of his head.

"Look, dude, if you get into this very deep and want to know more, come to me. Just don't call me or talk with me in any way about this stuff on the phone."

"No problem."

"Who is doing this stuff, anyway?" Bonzo asked.

"A man named Anton Devier. Ever hear of him?"

"The person who worked on the first image processor, the analog one, the precursor of the digital image processor?"

"Unless there are two Anton Deviers into video, he's the one."

Bonzo, usually a non-reactive sort of guy, felt his heart skip a beat. "Then you're in trouble. Devier is working on the other side, lock, stock, and barrel. You better tell me the entire story."

"First you tell me what you mean by the other side."

"There are Satanists and there are Satanists. Kids like to fool around with this stuff. Psychos like to play around with animal sacrifices, rituals, and so on. Then there are the really dedicated Satanists, the ones who are truly in bondage to Satan. Sold their souls to the devil. Devier is one of them. He's a member of the largest Satanic cult in the world."

"How do you know that?"

"I just know. Can't tell you how. You tell me what he's doing in West Yellowstone."

"I don't know how he got there. All I know is that he's hooked a news reporter named Lynx O'Malley."

"I know the name. See her stories in the *Gazette*. Like the way she's covering the fires. Pretty clever writer. Cute, too."

"Have you met her, then?"

"No, I saw a review of a video she did on trumpeter swans, and it had her picture with it. I bought the video, too, because some of the profits from it go to the Swan Fund. It was excellent. I liked the old Indian woman's narrative, too."

"That Indian woman is Nora Spotted Elk. Her son, Harry, is the man who stole the tapes from Anton. Nora and Harry are very close friends of Lynx."

"Then that explains it completely. It's warfare, like I told you." Bonzo suddenly felt very sad.

"Then explain it to me," Arthur urged.

"The Spotted Elks are heavy medicine. Even I know that. They're major players in the secret Sweetgrass Society, which I know a little about. Sweetgrass has been recruiting non-Indian members for quite some time. It's a very spiritual group, dedicated to fighting evil forces throughout the world. If they've recruited Lynx, she has to be a major player, too, have some qualities they see that they want to groom. One of two things is going on here, maybe both. Anton want to use Lynx's expertise on Yellowstone to make videos and/or he wants to infiltrate the Sweetgrass Society through her."

"As long as I've known Harry, I've never known he was in the Sweetgrass Society. In fact, I didn't know it still existed. I've read about it in history books. How would you know about it?"

"I only know about it because I've read it's a target group of several of the Satanic cults I told you about."

"Where did you read that?"

"I can't tell you. Being a hacker has made me a good living, but I've also gotten into places I regret having gotten into. Learning about the Satanic cults had gotten me nowhere but worried all the time."

"So where do you advise I go from here?"

"Exactly how did Lynx connect to Anton?" Bonzo asked.

"She was awarded a grant to make videos for the CNS Foundation. She asked Anton to help her. I don't know how she met him. I think Harry mentioned something about Anton coming to her, asking her if she needed help at the museum and learning she had received the grant, then asking if he could help with her project."

"My advice is to get her away from Anton as soon as possible. But have her cut him off in such a way that he doesn't know the real reason. It may be too late for that, though. If she is Sweetgrass material, she already senses he is evil, and he already knows she senses that. These spiritual warrior types are very psychic."

"You're right about that. Apparently she's been pretty messed up emotionally since she met the guy. Harry stole the videos after he saw how she was acting and suspected Anton had something to do with it, so he searched Anton's studio, which, by the way, is in a trailer parked next to Lynx's house."

"That's not what I wanted to hear. My advice still stands. Tell her to cut him off, but you better be prepared to give her some protection." Bonzo didn't add that he'd also better be prepared for the reality that Lynx may not make it.

Arthur had relayed his conversation with Bonzo to Harry, and they'd gone back and forth numerous times on how to deal with the stolen videotapes. Harry wanted to take a stand, or at least find out more about what the guy was up to. Arthur tended more to taking Bonzo's advice, but Harry had been persistent. He'd verified what Bonzo had said about the importance of the Sweetgrass Society. Arthur had begun to see a bigger picture, one in which Lynx and Nora and Harry and even himself were under attack because the land they lived in and loved so much was under attack. At least, they'd decided finally, they should find out more. But first, Arthur insisted they seek some spiritual protection, and so they'd gone into the mountains and invoked the fox.

Now, driven by the instinct to hunt and the ancient power the Human had sparked in her, the red fox went back to her meadow and found another sage hen. This time, she fought the desire to eat it and ran directly back to the Humans. She slowed down when she saw the fire. Fear nearly overcame her need to bring the bird to them, until she heard them singing. She trotted around the fire, saw Arthur's outstretched arms, and dropped the bird at his feet.

Arthur stopped singing and thanked the fox with his most gentle voice. She walked over to the other side of the fire and sat down while he prepared the bird for roasting. He threw her a tiny bite of fresh meat, and she devoured it zestfully. He coated the rest of the bird with oil, wrapped it in foil, and set it on some coals he'd raked to the side of the fire. He took the bird's tail feathers, bound them together at the bottom with a piece of sinew, and fanned out the feathers.

The fox stayed until they'd eaten the bird, and then walked away, back to her den near the meadow below. Arthur lit his ceremonial pipe, packed with tobacco and sweetgrass, and shared it with Harry.

"Now," he said, holding the new prayer fan he'd made, "we pray for direction. Great Spirit, we thank you for blessing us with the visit from this red fox, whose power as a hunter and stalker is great, who is cunning and wary and full of survival skills. Give us this fox knowledge in our quest for union with you in paradise. Help us to protect our loved ones and discern the evil that may be thrown in their way, perhaps by you, to give them challenges they need to grow closer to you."

Arthur went on, "We sit and listen until first light. If you're tired at any time, go ahead and sleep. It may be that a message will come to you in a dream."

For hours, Harry sat listening to the sounds of the night as he watched the stars and kept the fire going. He tried to empty his mind of all thoughts, worries, and concerns, and asked over and over again that the Great Spirit send him a sign. Suddenly, he felt overwhelmingly tired and, remembering Arthur's advice, he let himself doze off.

His dream took him to a place of great beauty, of meadows replete with wildflowers of every hue rolling into forests of old trees. A singing creek transected the meadow, splashing over round rocks covered with green mosses. A bald eagle sat on a large boulder near the creek watching trout feed on a hatch of mayflies. Deer grazed near the trees, and a Stellar's jay flew out of the woods, buzzed the eagle, and landed near the creek to take a drink of water.

Lynx and Anton walked into the scene, and Lynx pulled a small video camera out of her backpack and began to tape the deer and eagle. Anton walked to the edge of the creek and sat down to watch her. Suddenly a strong wind came up, and the sky filled with dark clouds. Anton stood up, screamed, and turned into a huge bird with a sharp beak and enormous claws. Lynx kept taping, unaware of the change in him. He flew over her head and began to circle over her. Still, she didn't see him. He began to dive straight down, as if he intended to pounce on her. The eagle then flew off its boulder and straight at the Anton monster, digging into its back and lifting it high over the meadow. Lynx looked up, her face in a daze, and watched as the eagle screamed and dropped the beast onto the boulder, breaking its back. It turned back into a limp and broken Anton. Lynx kept taping, as if nothing she saw frightened or surprised her.

Harry heard himself ask Lynx a question, although he did not see his own image in the dream.

"Lynx, why aren't you afraid?"

"Harry, we have nothing to fear. We're spiritual warriors. The evil is given us to overcome. It's the way of the mystic warrior. You know this, my brother."

"How can I help you, Lynx?" Harry asked her.

"Watch and pray, Harry. Watch and pray," she told him. And the dream ended abruptly, as if it were a television show cut off by a power outage.

Harry woke up and saw it was first light. Arthur was fixing coffee. "Some night," he said. "Did you learn anything?"

"Only to watch and pray," Harry said.

"That's about all I've come up with, too. But I assure you, it isn't as simple as it sounds."

"Yeah, well it seems to me," Harry said, his tone agitated, "that after all we went through last night we should have a more concrete plan than that."

"Oh, the plan will evolve. At its root is watch and pray. I take that to mean that we will be challenged into doing the opposite, such as to act irrationally and forget that the Great Spirit is here to help us. In fighting the impulses to act and forget about the spiritual help we have, we'll learn a lot. Watch and see."

Harry raised his eyebrows and took the coffee Arthur handed him.

"Look, Harry, just give it time. You'll see. Have faith. Now let's get going. I've got hours of editing to do."

Chapter Thirty Five

Bonzo Reed finished his last set of biceps curls with 50-pound free weights and wiped the sweat off his face. He looked at himself in the mirror in his workout room and smiled.

Muscle and Fitness magazine covers were taped all around his mirror, and he couldn't see much difference between his body and those on the covers. Most of the photos were of body building contest winners, and he had cut all their legs off with scissors so they would have stumps like his. With his amazing upper body strength, Bonzo could easily do well with his wheelchair in marathon races, basketball games, arm wrestling, and even body building competitions for the disabled, but he chose not to. He trained for maximum upper body strength so he could work 10 to 12 hours a day on his computers without getting fatigued, sore, or flabby. And his strenuous workouts helped him get rid of some of the aggression and frustration he felt most of the time, more so lately than ever before in his life.

Bonzo wheeled himself to his custom-made shower, pulled himself out of his chair into the seat in his shower stall, and turned on the water. He did his best thinking in the shower after a workout. "How can the world be so crazy," he wondered as he lathered his skin and shampooed his wildly curly, nearly waist length hair. His old buddy, Walt, had called him from somewhere in Mexico that morning, begging for help.

Bonzo was relieved that Walt was alive, something he'd suspected all along as he followed the *Gazette*'s coverage of West Yellowstone. But his relief had turned to grave concern when he'd learned the trouble Walt was in. Walt wanted a passport, a driver's license, credit cards, and cash from a bank account he had in Wyoming. Given some time and luck, Bonzo could get Walt these things, but at what cost to himself? And there was the matter of Dave sitting in prison for a murder he didn't commit, and Dave's lawyer, Frank, who not long ago had asked Bonzo to check into an organization called TDP.

Bonzo had never heard of TDP, and that bothered him. He'd even suspected that Frank may be wrong about it. But now that Walt had contacted him and verified that TDP does exist because he was on the run from it, Bonzo was even more confused. He hadn't been able to use one stitch of information Walt had given him about TDP to find a phone number, central computer, or headquarters. Nothing seemed to exist to verify its reality. Most puzzling was that when he'd checked on the activity in Walt's Wyoming bank account, using the name and social security number Walt had given him that he'd gotten from a deceased person, Bonzo had learned that it had been checked on the week Walt had disappeared. Whoever ran the check had covered himself so he couldn't be traced. Bonzo could only assume it was TDP. On top of all that, Arthur Red Fox wanted to know about subliminal cuts in some videotapes he'd ripped off from Anton Devier, whom Bonzo believed was evil incarnate.

After Bonzo looked at the videotapes, he was 99 percent sure he knew what organization was behind their production. Fifteen years ago he'd gotten into one of the main computers at the United Nations Headquarters in New York City, trying to look up information about embassies in the Middle East for someone who was investigating illegal arms sales. He accidentally stumbled into files on an organization called the Arcane Seminary.

Ordinarily, Bonzo would have instantly exited a file he wasn't looking for. That was essential when you were into files you shouldn't be in, searching for other files you shouldn't be searching for. There was always someone at the other side who would learn you were into them. But his fast-reading mind had seen the Arcane Seminary's mission statement, and his blood had gone cold. He was surprised that such an organization would be in the United Nation's files, so he jotted down the codes he'd used to reach the file, returned to his work on embassies, and waited until late that night to re-enter the Arcane Seminary's file. By then, someone had noticed the file had been accessed and changed the code. Based on the original code and how it had been changed, and using his highly developed computer intuition, Bonzo was able to break the new code and enter the file.

The Arcane Seminary, Bonzo learned, is a training center for what it calls People of Goodwill. It teaches basic, intermediate, and advanced occult practices to its students, whom it calls initiates, disciples, and adepts. It is a sub-organization of an ancient group called Lucifer Trust by its innermost circle. Bonzo accessed the trust's file and learned that no one knows exactly when Lucifer Trust was formed or what its original name was, because it came into being not long after the world was created, its structure and knowledge passed down through centuries only by word of mouth and rituals. The first time its name surfaced as Lucifer Trust was 350 AD, in Londinium, "the City," what is now London, England.

Its primary purpose is to establish Satanic cults in the uppermost circles of the Christian Church to promote heresies and keep Christians in the dark about who Jesus really is. LT also works to keep true Christians from gaining economic and political power anywhere in the world. Its leaders work with followers of other religions, such as Buddhism and Hinduism, to create one worldwide belief system.

In the late 18th century, LT continued to remain secret and underground, but established a main branch, Light Trust, that would remain a largely secret organization with some public activities that would grow more public as time went by. Light Trust allows itself to be accessed by very carefully recruited worldwide organizations and individuals. Many of its hierarchy are no longer embodied but remain in contact with humans through dreams, trances, and other methods. LT never lets recruits know its true origins in Satanism until they become adepts, and most never advance that far. Recruits think Light is an organization dedicated to world goodwill.

Light members use occult rituals to achieve the organization's goals. The goals are to establish a worldwide religion with its own universal prayer, The Great Invocation, and to create a world bank and economic system to distribute basic needs to the world's underprivileged and keep all the wealth in the control of a few people.

Light's goals are meant to achieve the primary objective of Lucifer Trust, domination of the planet by Satan.

Bonzo read that Light controls or funds completely or in part countless groups the average person believes serve the basic needs of humanity. He was shocked to see that some of these groups are well-known Christian organizations, even a popular television and radio broadcasting network. Others are internationally respected non-profit foundations which fund research in every imaginable field, including the discovery of new drugs to treat diseases; think tanks feeding ideas into all levels of government, politics, and industry; and even universities that have been thought of for centuries as major centers of knowledge and learning.

Few of these organizations know that some, if not all, of their funding comes from Light. It trickles down through so many organizations that it can rarely be traced with certainty. The Arcane Seminary is directly funded by Light, with nearly all students recruited by Light staff. There is one other way students find their own way to the school, Bonzo read. It is through a small ad the school places in one of its publications, *Laser* magazine, a quarterly distributed to Seminary students and to 50 select libraries in several different countries, including the Unites States.

The ad says: "The Arcane Seminary, a school of esoteric psychology at the United Nations Plaza in New York City, is looking for a few exemplary minds interested in seeking knowledge of a higher order in order to assist World Servers in a great work to save humanity. If interested, contact the Seminary at . . ."

Students must have a minimum IQ of 150, must be at least bilingual, must have a high level of formal education, with at least one degree higher than a bachelor's from a top university, and must be a member of an institutionalized church. They must be experts in one of seven fields: philosophy, psychology, theology, science, economics, education, or social science.

It took Bonzo more than 40 hours to access a file giving the names of present and past Arcane Seminary students, and he printed the file out to study it. It contained 7,000 names and spanned 200 years. He recognized hundreds of names. The list contained some of the world's most well known inventors, scientists, theologians, doctors of medicine and psychology, writers, educators, and national and international leaders. It also contained hundreds of lesser known people, names Bonzo saw in the news from time to time.

When he analyzed the list carefully, Bonzo saw that in the last 30 years, the number of students had risen drastically. The list provided the name and address of the student, phone numbers when applicable, and a few lines under the heading, "Service Project." Bonzo noticed that in the last 10 years, when the number of students seemed to have risen the most sharply, the service projects had become more diverse and less monumental in scope. He concluded that the Seminary is pushing to recruit more students so now allows people to have less complex projects. For example, an entry in 1948 for a scientist working in a well-known federally funded laboratory read, "working on drugs to both cure and induce schizophrenia," while 40 years later a researcher Bonzo had never heard of was listed as "working on a low-cost community recycling project." Bonzo also noticed that in recent years the number of politicians on the list in local government offices had increased. At the same time, the number of world leaders in the Seminary had also risen.

Consistent throughout, he observed, was that some nations have had leaders in the Seminary from the very beginning of their nationhood, including the United States, England, France, India, Japan, China, and Russia. There are fascists, communists, socialists, Marxists, capitalists, Democrats, Republicans, Nazis, and Libertarians.

Bonzo spent another 20 hours searching for more information about current Seminary activities and accessed a file of active students. He saw that each student was assigned an adept in charge of his or her progress. The adept sent the file detailed notes of the student's accomplishments in regularly assigned meditation work and in progress on the service project. Bonzo didn't spend too much time in this new file, because after he'd been in it for less than three minutes, his computer flashed a warning that someone at the Seminary had discovered he was in the file and was searching for him.

Bonzo felt compelled to know more but knew it was too risky to go back into the files and spend much time there. He decided to submit his own application to the Seminary. The Light Trust and Seminary files were the most fascinating he'd ever encountered, and he wanted to know more for himself, and he suspected, future clients. He used his many skills and contacts to create a name, identity, and vitae that fit the requirements of the Arcane Seminary.

In his letter of introduction, Bonzo stated that he had read the Seminary's ad in *Laser* at the library at Yale, which he had visited to do research, after he established by computer that his new name had used the library. He said he was living in a cabin in the mountains near Bozeman, working on a computer project that would create programs to teach children about the present world ecological crisis. He was accepted into the school six weeks later. That told him a great deal. For one, he was more technologically erudite than they, or they would have figured he was a phony.

Initiates, Bonzo learned, are told that their first task is to learn how to tap into the highest powers of the universe. They are told they are part of a very small percentage of humanity. They are gifted with minds, bodies, and spirits given them solely for the purpose of serving all of humanity by helping to unfold a great plan. They are told that whether they were recruited directly by the Seminary or had found the Seminary on their own, their involvement was "meant to be."

Initiates learn they are training to become World Servers. They learn occult basics, like meditation and mind control, to achieve such simple goals as relaxation and the ability to wake themselves up without using an alarm clock. They are told they cannot move to the next stage unless they abstain from alcohol, drugs, unhealthy food, sex except in moderation with a committed partner (homosexual or heterosexual), and low-level entertainment like best selling books and popular movies. They must meditate three times daily and hook up with other initiates at specific times each day and each week for worldwide group meditations. One of these worldwide meditations, taking place at noon every Wednesday, is to visualize all the money in the world as free flowing light that moves into the hands of World Servers.

There is no public Arcane Seminary building, no classrooms or campus. Seminary headquarters are small offices attached to large libraries in New York City, London, Geneva, Tokyo, Peking, and Darjeeling. Students must vow to tell no one they are associated with the Arcane Seminary, and they study in their own home and work environments. Only seminarians can use the library, and it must be the one nearest their headquarters, by mail only. They must file weekly meditation reports with their headquarters detailing what they learned or experienced in their meditation periods and how they are using their new knowledge in their daily lives. They are given specific books to read, tapes to watch and listen to, and specific thoughts and ideas to meditate on.

At the end of the initiate period, the seminarian begins to practice a different meditation form that follows an outline the Seminary provides. This meditation is directed at finding out who the initiate's "master" is. By this time, the Seminary knows a great deal about the person, having carefully read each meditation report. The person is assigned an adept to read the new meditation report.

This adept already knows who the initiate's "master" will be because there are seven masters, each controlling one of the seven fields the initiate belongs to, but the initiate does not have this knowledge. The masters are all "ascended beings." They are the highest members of Satan's army, the first seven former angels of light who swore service to Satan. Each of them took possession of a human being at conception and came into the world to form Lucifer Trust and help fulfill the scripture that says that Satan will rule the world.

At this point along the path, the initiate is told that the Christian Bible and other widely used religious documents deceive people into believing that although Satan does rule the world, if they resist him, they will reach a higher place with God. In fact, initiates learn, there is no higher place where such a God exists, that god is the power within each individual and becomes stronger and more accessible as initiates learn to contact it in themselves and others.

The adept uses mind control and programming techniques to bring the late-stage initiate into what he believes is a personal awareness of who his master is. Then, the initiate becomes a "disciple" of that master. Some masters have several names, depending on what the initiate's religion is. In the case of Christian initiates who are in the religious field, the adept will program the initiate into believing that his master is Jesus Christ. That same master, to a Muslim, will be Allah. The initiate who learns he has Jesus as his master is told Jesus is really the embodied spirit of one of the angels of light who decided to follow Satan, not the Jesus the Bible calls the Son of God.

The disciple is given new meditation formats and told that before he can become an adept, he must attain a leadership role in his field, become the head of an important research project, work on a new publication, and so on. He begins to learn what he is told are ancient secrets available only to his level of intelligence. These secrets deal with using sounds, colors, and crystals to achieve higher states of communication with the master.

As the disciple progresses in his new meditation formats, he begins to attract other disciples but is rarely aware that these are Arcane seminarians because of the secrecy code. It is part of the human condition that like-minded people run into one another and form bonds. At this very high level of practiced self-awareness, the like-minded people who form bonds begin to form power circles and networks, sometimes without ever meeting one another, through the energies they contact and utilize in their meditation.

Bonzo learned the reality of this after he reached the disciple stage and the number of his clients who said they were spiritual seekers increased drastically. Many were involved in projects that were indeed of service to humanity. Bonzo had no way of knowing if these people were seminarians or if their contact with him was coincidental. He also noticed that the New Age movement was becoming more widespread, almost a fad. He wondered if seminarians were making this happen through some kind of mind control. So many New Agers were simple, even stupid, the way they wore crystals around their necks and listened to boring, spacey music, that he doubted they had the clarity of mind to be seminarians. And he also noticed that many video games kids play these days take the player through stages similar to those that seminarians move through on their way to the adept stage.

Eventually, assisted by continued programming from the adept who is carefully tracking the disciple's progress, the disciple is led to direct contact with the master. It begins in dreams. The disciple may have a simple dream about seeing the master. Soon, the master talks to the disciple. The disciple begins to think like the master, write the master's thoughts down on paper, and then has a total awareness that he and the master are one in mind, body, and soul.

When this occurs, the disciple becomes an adept in full service to the master, on one of the seven rays, which is what he learns are the energy forms of the seven fields. He is given his own color: red for philosophy, violet for psychology, white for theology, blue for science, green for economics, orange for education, or yellow for social science, and his own crystal stones. Bonzo was told his service was on the blue ray.

What the Arcane Seminary never seemed to have discovered was that, as Bonzo progressed from one level to another, he learned the true origins and purposes of the Seminary. Most important, he learned how powerful the adepts are at programming minds, because he felt every piece of information they sent him. When he was being programmed, his body and mind felt different. He had more energy. He often felt electrical charges running up and down his spine. He also had intense feelings of anger and rebellion. He was completely convinced that the source of power the Seminary was drawing on was pure evil, that when he'd learned its origins were Satanic, he wasn't dealing with a group that was speaking in symbols. He knew that Light Trust and the Seminary were dangerous. He was convinced he would never accept the belief system they were trying to program him with, but when he felt the intensity of its power, he decided he should create some safeguards.

Bonzo divided his brain into two separate information storage areas he called Drive A, for Arcane Seminary, and Drive B, for Bonzo. He'd power up Drive A only when he dealt with the Seminary. In Drive B, he processed and analyzed the information and interactions in Drive A. In doing this, he kept his true self from discovery by the Seminary, or so he hoped.

The real test, he knew, would be when he met his Master in an awake state. He knew the time had grown near to that meeting when he began to come into contact with even more people who were seeking out people like himself, people with high level computer knowledge and people in research about ecology that could dovetail with the computer program he was writing for his service project.

In his 11th year as an Arcane Seminarian, Bonzo began to feel drawn to a particular spot on the earth that he could not identify. For months, he saw it only in his dreams. He knew it was where he would meet his Master. As the dreams grew more clear, he finally identified the place as being in the Paradise Valley south of Livingston, Montana. That scared him, because he'd expected the place to be far away. If it was close, then perhaps he'd been tricked into being a seminarian. Perhaps all along they'd known he was seeking them only to uncover what they were, perhaps had known this before he knew it, perhaps had led him to them through his computer. He spent days in Drive B analyzing this possibility, reviewing his years of work in Drive A. He concluded that it was simply a pure coincidence that he lived near the place his master hung out. If it wasn't a pure coincidence, then God, his God, the father of Jesus, the God united in the Trinity with Jesus and the Holy Spirit, had led him to the Arcane Seminary for some reason he still did not know about.

Another worry about the fact that it seemed to be that he would meet the master in the Paradise Valley was that recently a Chicago-based church had purchased thousands of acres of land there to establish a spiritual community. The group called itself the Universal New Age Christian Church. UNACC claimed to have several hundred thousand members. It said that its spiritual leader, a woman named Clara Seeker, had been told by God to purchase the Paradise Valley property as a place for members to live in harmony with nature. She planned to build a university emphasizing the study of theology and New Age religions. She warned that the world was nearing a period of vast destruction by nuclear war, and that only those people who were true Christians of the New Age would survive to build a new world. She said that it was essential that every Christian build a shelter in which to survive the upcoming nuclear holocaust. They should plan to spend two years in the shelter, and they should be heavily armed to kill any survivors who tried to invade their shelters. Anyone who did not enter the shelter when she said it was time was not chosen by God to survive and enter into the new age, so killing these people would be God's work.

Bonzo had checked and to see if UNACC was funded by Light Trust, if its hierarchy had been trained by the Arcane Seminary, if there was any connection. He found none. He could only conclude that their connection was incredibly well hidden, or that the place in the Paradise Valley was pure evil that attracted not only Light people but others as well. He knew for certain that Light was the source of evil working its plan on earth, but how many other groups were out there operating on similar levels, with origins obscured by thousands of years of time?

Bonzo continued to follow his adept's instructions, dutifully performing his meditations and filing regular reports on his progress with meditation and his service project. One morning in April of his 12th year as a Seminarian, he woke at 3 a.m., after a few hours of peaceful dreams, and knew it was time to find the exact place in the Paradise Valley. His conscious mind had no idea where he was going. He simply knew when he awoke that morning that he would have to get in his van and drive, and that as he drove along, he'd know where he was going. The fact that he would eventually have to leave his van and use his wheelchair and that the place may not be accessible to him, did not bother him. He knew it would work out.

Bonzo was just 15 miles north of Gardiner, the town at the south end of the Valley and the northwest edge of Yellowstone National Park, when he saw the dirt road he knew he must turn onto. It was a private road on UNACC land. Bonzo followed it, crossing the Yellowstone River over an old wooden bridge. The road ended abruptly. He used his hydraulic lift to exit the van in his wheelchair. It was still dark, so he used his high-powered flashlight to get orientated and saw a steep, narrow trail leading up a forested hill. He wheeled himself to the trail's edge and stopped, trying to think what to do.

Suddenly, he felt a major electric charge run through his body from the base of his spine to his brain, down his arms, and back down his spine. He felt his body leave the wheelchair and fly up the trail. He glanced backwards and saw his van and the empty chair. Was he dreaming? The chair was empty. He could feel tree branches touch his face. A powerful force was indeed sucking him up the hill.

"Remember, Bonzo my man" a calm, steady inner voice told him. "Drive A. Drive B." Yes, he answered. "Drive A is rolling. Save this to Drive B, but don't let them know Drive B exists."

The force slowed down, and Bonzo saw the most beautiful sight he'd ever experienced. A soft blue light emanated from the center of a small meadow up ahead that was encircled with ancient fir trees. In the center of the light was a tall violet flame shooting as high as the trees, 50 or 60 feet into the sky. The power drew Bonzo closer to the center of the meadow and set him down on a large wooden chair.

Bonzo peered into the center of the violet flame and saw a golden heart. Seeing it made him feel more peaceful and relaxed than he'd ever felt. The heart began to pulsate, and Bonzo could hear lovely music playing—stringed instruments, horns, and woodwinds. Then the blue light began to leap in tongues of flames that circled the violet flame and obscured the sharp view he'd had of the golden heart. It swirled around the violet, and the music seemed louder and more intense. Bonzo began to sing with it, and when he did, he heard the voice of what seemed like thousands of other people sing with him. He didn't know what language he was singing in, but it felt ancient, precious, the language of angels. Drive B kicked in and warned him that no angels would be singing here.

"This is the time you do not want to be sucked into this. Remember, there's evil here," Drive B reminded him.

Ah, so sad that evil can appear so beautiful, Bonzo thought, singing as loudly as he dared so the Force wouldn't register his doubts. The blue flames dropped back to their original soft glowing shapes, and the violet flame reappeared. In the center of the golden heart, Bonzo saw a face. It was the kindest, most loving face he'd ever seen, the face of a woman so lovely she could not be called beautiful, or gorgeous, or sexy, or any other word Bonzo could come up with. It was the face filled with pure love and kindness that every wanted and welcomed newborn saw when he first looked at his mother. In a way she resembled Mary, the Mother of God, Bonzo noticed. But no, that couldn't be.

Bonzo was surprised his "master" was a woman. He'd never considered that possibility. He'd reasoned that although the fallen angels of light, the true origins of the face before him, were never human and therefore sex-less, in human form, they would always be male.

"Who are you?" Bonzo asked.

"I am the I Am Presence," she answered. "I am the keeper of the blue ray, the eternal mother, separate yet equal to the father."

"You know, you look like a painting I once saw of the Mother of Jesus."

She smiled at him. "Oh, yes, Mary was a wonderful person. She suffered greatly."

"And who am I?" Bonzo asked, the question coming without his having decided to ask it.

"You, my son, have been my faithful disciple. Without question you have worked with all your heart to know me. Yet I am you, have always been you, and will always be you."

"Are you connected in any way to the people who own this property, the UNACC?"

"Yes and no. They are not seeking me consciously, yet they have an awareness that this place is one of the few on earth where we manifest ourselves."

"We?"

"Yes, we. Put together all you have learned. The I Am Presence is We and I and You. It is All There Is."

"And where do I—I mean we, go now?" Bonzo asked her.

"You have seen this manifestation, experienced its power to draw you who cannot walk on your own. You have been transformed. Your energies vibrate now on a higher plane than few humans have experienced. That is my gift to you. You will take this with you. It is part of you now."

"Somehow I thought there would be more to this than there seems to be."

"Ah, you science types are so pragmatic. You will have to wait and see. Now you must go."

In a split second, she was gone. The golden heart faded from the center of the violet flame, the flame disappeared, and the blue light went out. Bonzo was alone in the middle of the meadow under a brilliant blue morning sky.

He heard birds singing their morning songs and a roaring creek carrying snow melt off the mountain to the river. He looked at the center of the meadow, expecting to see singed grass or some other sign that his vision was real. Nothing. He pulled himself to the center with his powerful arms. A small patch of purple violets peeked out of the new spring grass. He reached into his pants pocket and took out a lucky silver dollar he'd been carrying there for many years. He dug up some of the grass near the violets and buried the coin. Then he picked a violet and put it in his pocket.

Just then a great wind came up. Bonzo felt an explosion of light in his head, closed his eyes because he thought he was being blinded from within, opened his eyes when the light was gone, and found himself in his wheelchair. He lifted himself back into his van and started the engine, but not before he checked his pocket. The flower was still there.

Bonzo decided to not let his adept know about his experience with his so-called master. He assumed the adept would know telepathically it had happened, but he couldn't prove it. He remained most of the time in Drive B, filing the minimum number of reports he could get away with without raising suspicion.

He finished his educational program and sold it under his Arcane Seminary student identity to the first software company he submitted it to. Then he wrote his adept and told him he was leaving the U.S. on six month trip to Europe and would not be doing any student work until he returned. Six months later, he checked the mail in the post office box registered under his Arcane Seminary student name. There was nothing in it. Bonzo hoped the relationship was over.

Three months later, Bonzo took on a client, Ginger Paddington, who said she was running for her life. She told him she'd been a student at a "weird" school, a school whose students had to swear they would tell no one they attended. She said the school required students to undertake a service project, and hers had been to produce a college-level television course on astronomy, her specialty. She had completed the project, and it had been purchased by a large university that had thousands of students living in rural areas all over the state taking television courses.

Somehow, she told Bonzo, the tapes had been cut with subliminal Satanic messages, symbols, and scenes. She wanted to know if Bonzo knew anything about the effectiveness of subliminal cuts, and she wanted to know if Bonzo could find out who had put the cuts in her tape. She'd learned about the cuts by accident, she told Bonzo, and said she was afraid to tell Bonzo how that accident had come about. He guessed someone had tipped her off, a spy for the other side.

Bonzo spoke to her for hours and was convinced, after using mind probing techniques he'd learned as a Seminary student, that she was a seminarian, too, probably at the initiate level. He was also nearly certain that she was not there as a spy from the Seminary to see what he was up to. He had always been sure that the Seminary had never bothered to check him out and truly believed in his phony identity.

He checked with the Seminary's student files and found her name and that her last date of contact with the Seminary had been several weeks before. The file verified that she was working on a television project under the direction of Anton Devier, who was an adept in the Seminary. So Anton Devier was a seminarian, a member of the world's largest Satanic cult! Anton had noted in her file that Ginger was "not Seminary material" and should be cut off after she completed her project. He added a warning: "We should consider tightening up our admissions policies and returning to the old policy that is much stricter."

Bonzo noticed that his own name was still in the active file, with the last date of contact with his adept noted. No note was made that he had had contact with his "master." That was comforting. Perhaps they didn't know. Bonzo began to suspect that the Seminary was so confident it could use its esoteric powers to "know" things that it hadn't bothered to update its technology.

Bonzo had no choice but to confront Ginger about being a Seminary student. She admitted she had been and said she enrolled when she'd read the same ad Bonzo had seen in the *Laser* at a university library. She said she was attracted to the idea of being a person of goodwill, but had had a terrible time with the meditations, and although she didn't realize that the group was evil, she felt it was not something her mind could handle. Bonzo explained the Seminary's true purpose and told her about the note Anton had made in her file.

"How could such a lovely woman have made such a mistake," Bonzo wondered, looking at her as they talked. She was young and beautiful, with totally innocent looking blue eyes and bouncy long blonde hair. He could visualize her teaching little kids about astronomy and imagine them listening to her intently just because she was so cute and they wanted to please her.

Ginger told him she'd never met Anton, but he'd gotten her in touch with the people she'd sent her videos to for editing. She refused to tell Bonzo who the editors were. Bonzo accepted that, but noted that at least one of them had to have been working on the good side because it must have been the person who let her know about the cuts. He told her that somehow this person, or these people, had sensed that she was a good person and had done this to steer her away from the Seminary.

Bonzo produced a new identity for Ginger and helped her get a job as a governess for a wealthy family in a nearby city and a small apartment where she could spend her days off. He then went to work on locating the experts in subliminal messaging, and after months of work, was able to find out that a Light Trust-funded, non-profit foundation had a team of researchers in that field, and they were indeed experimenting with television. Other mind control experiments being done with sub-liminal cuts he learned about were being funded by top-level govern-ments and corporate businesses. Most of the shows they were pro-gramming were videotaped and produced by other people, and some were being programmed live. The researchers actually had "plants" working as technicians broadcasting football games and placing the cuts on the air just before commercials and instant replays. The most cuts they'd ever inserted on live broadcasts had been during the last two Super Bowls. "No wonder," Bonzo thought, "newspapers had re-ported that battered woman's shelters all over America had dealt with a drastic increase in calls on Super Bowl Sunday."

Bonzo met with Ginger and told her what he had found out. She seemed to take the information calmly, but he saw that she was depressed. He didn't hear from her for more than two weeks, so he called her at the family's house. The housekeeper said that the family had hired a new governess because Ginger, whose new name was Carry, had never returned to the house after her last days off three weekends before. The family hadn't even bothered to call her to see if she was all right. The housekeeper said the children were difficult to handle and didn't study too diligently, so they'd assumed "Carry" had become frustrated and quit, as many others before her had.

He called Ginger's apartment manager. He told Bonzo that he'd found her dead in her bed nearly two weeks ago, after he'd smelled something foul coming from her apartment. The coroner concluded she'd had a stroke. Did Bonzo know where her family was? He wanted some kind of compensation for the mess she made. He'd had to replace the bed and have the place fumigated. Bonzo sent him a check to pay for the clean-up.

If Arthur was onto someone who was cutting Satanic messages into public television broadcasts, he'd never survive if he attempted to make his knowledge public. Everyone who worked with information on his level knew all about subliminal cuts, but they also knew that there was no way to tell the public about it and live.

Bonzo was beginning to realize he'd become a person who knows too much, and it made him feel lonely. Most people went about their lives in a complete daze, from day to day thinking only of surviving to their next paycheck, stashing away some savings to live on when they retire, putting in their time for a pension if they were lucky enough to work for a company with a retirement plan.

The world that Bonzo lived in, the world of a first-class computer hacker, was nothing like that. Computers control the universe more than any science fiction prophet had ever envisioned.

Somewhere, there had to be information on a computer about TDP. TDP had to have some computers of its own to communicate with its parent organization, store records, and break into records of organizations it needed to know about. Bonzo was confident that if he put enough time in, he could find TDP. But somewhere in the process, TDP operators would know someone was looking for them. They would increase their security, and Bonzo would have to find a way to break through it.

It was a game he loved to play, a game he'd always won in the past. He and the half dozen other hackers of his caliber had actually been responsible for creating the high level of security that existed in many computer systems. Every time a hacker broke a code and accessed a main computer, that computer's programmers found a way to block the hackers, who in turn found a way to get past the new security, and on and on.

In his electronic meanderings through international, national, and regional computer networks, Bonzo discovered a mind boggling number of covert operations run by established government agencies and organizations. He'd come to believe that the world would be better off if everyone unplugged their modems and stuck to playing mindless computer games. Hell, even the basic computer user plugged into an innocent-appearing computer network like Prodigy or CompuServe was being spied on. Hackers working for big business and the government were always into these networks, getting the names of the users and analyzing what they did on line to see what their interests were. Some of the information simply went to businesses that mailed these people catalogs and other junk mail; some was sent to analysts who use the information to predict what type of candidates political organizations should groom to "represent" these people. And then there was the evil of credit reports.

Just last month a perfect example of how a person could be screwed for life by a bad credit report had walked through his office door. This person was trying to raise money to start what Bonzo thought was a highly creative business dealing with recycling. Four banks had turned down his loan requests, but the man insisted he was clean. Bonzo had broken into the bank's systems and learned they were all accessing the same credit report that said the man had defaulted on three large loans. When he searched further, he found the source of the bad reports. It was from two companies that for political reasons did not want this man to start his business.

Bonzo had accessed the two companies' files and read memos they'd sent to one another by electronic mail that explained the whole thing. Bonzo laid the entire conspiracy out to his client, who at first didn't believe him. Bonzo printed out the memos and other information to prove he was right. The client then took this information to the proper places, righteously believing that he would be loaned the money now that he could prove he had a clean credit record, a good business plan, and his only problem was politically motivated enemies too greedy to give him a chance to fulfill his dreams.

He was still turned down for the loans and threatened with lawsuits for illegally obtaining information from the banks and other parties. Bonzo had covered himself, as always, making sure there was no way it could be proven he'd accessed the information if his client turned him in, although he had trusted the guy to not do so. Bonzo had explained to his client that once the doors are slammed, they're slammed, and he'd better come up with a new, non-threatening idea, and move to a different part of the country to implement it, because he'd be penalized for having found out too much about how things really operate in this world. The guy decided to stay in his dead end job for now. Unfortunately however, his employer was paying off a loan to one of the banks that had turned the man down. Yesterday he'd visited Bonzo to tell him he'd been laid off indefinitely. The reason he was given was that the company was in financial trouble and had to cut costs. But he and Bonzo knew differently. Now this highly educated, highly creative person was jobless and depressed.

Bonzo figured no matter how he worked it, Walt was a dead man if he didn't take his advice, which was to forget about coming back to Montana and trying to clear things up so Dave would be released from prison. TDP would never let that happen. He'd suggested that Walt go to Canada, and

Walt had agreed to consider that. Dave after all is alive, Bonzo had told him, and will get out of prison someday. And perhaps his appeal would succeed. Bonzo had already made up his mind to tell Frank Goodman that he hadn't been able to find any organization named TDP.

Bonzo had seen a lot of death in Viet Nam and faced it himself when he'd nearly died from a severe infection after his legs were amputated. He'd watched the people who knew too much drop like flies, dying in single-car accidents, committing "suicide" (although all these people were highly functional and would never consider suicide, their families always said), and having strokes and heart attacks (although their doctors said they'd been in perfect health the last time they'd seen them). Bonzo wondered how he'd get it, because he knew his time was short if he didn't quit hacking for good.

Bonzo dried off and dressed himself in a fresh pair of sweatpants and T-shirt that said "Shit Keeps Happening" on it in Spanish, a birthday gift from Sandria, his Mexican housekeeper who barely spoke English.

Sandria lived in an apartment over Bonzo's garage. She thought computers were the spawn of the devil but she adored Bonzo because he was kind, paid her well, and made her feel useful, especially when he coached him in Spanish. He smiled, remembering how she always prayed when she had to clean the computer room. Instinct had led her to believe the prayers were necessary protection; experience had drawn Bonzo to the same conclusion.

He had to get to work on Walt's new identity. He called out for a pizza and a six-pack of beer and settled into his work space, thinking that maybe this would be his last job. He'd saved enough money to live on for a good ten years. Maybe it was time to get a place on a beach somewhere and go fishing.

Chapter Thirty Six

As she hoisted her heavy pack onto her back, Lynx was more light-hearted than she'd been in a long, long time. The pack was heavy, but she was unburdened and free.

She and Mullein White Horse were about to climb to the Hilgard Basin, one of her favorite places in all of Yellowstone country. At last, the fires had stopped burning, put out by the same force that had started them: Mother Nature. Snow and rain and cold weather had finally come. Yellowstone's public relations office was working furiously to convince the American public that the park was still a wonderland, despite the fact that more than half its forests had turned to charcoal.

Yellowstone was more interesting now, the PR staff said in its news releases, a "mosaic" of green trees untouched by the fires, singed trees in shades of orange and brown, and charcoal black stumps. Meadows charred by fires were already sporting new grass, and cones from mature trees that had split open in the fires' intense heat had spilled their seeds, which were already sprouting new seedlings. There were some problem areas where burning had been so fierce that the soil was sterilized and devoid of organic material needed to support plant life, and it was predicted that in the spring, there would be mud slides on steep de-vegetated slopes that would temporarily silt up rivers and possibly cause road closures.

Park managers urged the public to re-think its conceptions of what natural beauty really is and look upon Yellowstone's charred landscape as a place where new beginnings could be seen unfolding to benefit the ecosystem. "Visitors to Yellowstone," they said, "now have a magnificent opportunity to see nature working to heal itself."

Lynx had seen the new Yellowstone mosaic in air flights over the park provided by the park service to any news writers interested in follow-up stories. She'd photographed and videoed the mosaic, as well as patches of burned areas she planned to return to on a regular basis to record changes. She'd covered President George Bush's visit to Yellowstone, a real dog-and-pony show. The park service had combed the area close to West Yellowstone where the presidential jet was scheduled to land, trying to find fire rejuvenation, which they called "natural rejen," in full swing. The rejen had to be close to a road a limousine could easily drive to, followed by the typical entourage of politicians, dignitaries, and the Secret Service.

She'd dutifully written stories describing the fire's aftermath, quoting scientists' predictions of the benefits and problems the results of the fires would now bring to the park. And she'd tried to work with her *Gazette* staff replacement, Adam Freedman, a young man straight out of journalism school, on writing an update on Ursus Park, the bear sanctuary Randall P. Duncan had been building all summer.

Ursus Park was scheduled to open in two weeks, and Adam had been assigned an in-depth piece on it. The media, including Lynx, had ignored it all summer while they focused on the fires. The *Gazette* had asked Lynx to help write about it to make Adam's transition a little easier.

Unfortunately, Adam thought that covering West Yellowstone was almost as unattractive as doing a police beat. He saw this first job as a stepping stone to a major paper in a big city somewhere far away from Montana. He wanted to cover issues in Bozeman and Helena, the state capital. He'd managed to convince the *Gazette* to allow him to live in Bozeman and travel to West Yellowstone only once or twice a month. He figured he'd downplay or insult anything that happened in West Yellowstone, which he thought of as a trashy tourist town. He was of the school of reporters who thought it was their job to be as cynical as possible about life. After spending 20 minutes in Ursus Park with Lynx, he'd told her that as far as he was concerned it was a roadside zoo that would scalp tourists and that she could write the story for him—he was heading back to Bozeman. Lynx felt badly about his attitude. She'd hoped the *Gazette* would have cared enough about West Yellowstone, the park, and the other small communities she'd covered to hire a reporter who would do a good job telling their stories. Instead, they were more interested in saving money by hiring a beginner at an entry-level salary.

Lynx had also closed the museum for the winter, turned in her resignation to its directors, and gotten full approval of her project from CNS. She was most excited about the freedom CNS had given her to produce videos on Yellowstone that would be more than postcard panoramas of the park's scenery and wildlife and regurgitations of official information to further the park service's political agendas. She felt that for once some of the bizarre things that were going on in Yellowstone would be brought into the public light.

She'd been thrilled when Mullein strolled into her house Friday not long after she'd filed her last story for the *Gazette*. He found her sprawled out on her couch, listening to a C.D. of old cowboy songs and sipping a beer, reveling in the fact that she no longer had any work to do that she didn't want to do. Gwen was visiting her, and she'd just taken Merlin to the Island Park cabin for the weekend. Lynx planned to stay in town for the weekend and veg out, and then spend a week at the cabin with the kids, coming to town only to drop Merlin off at school and pick him up at the end of the day.

Mullein was in the same position as Lynx, having also resigned his job, and he had a large wad of cash he'd saved all summer. He'd been paid well for his work, earning 30-40 hours of overtime pay each week, and had been able to save it all because he'd had no time to spend it. He had enough money to live on for at least six months without working. Now he wanted to party, but not in town. He wanted to hike somewhere Saturday morning and camp out that night, so they decided to hike to the basin, which was in the Gallatin National Forest in an area untouched by fires. They wanted to be in fresh air, away from the smell of damp, scorched trees that still penetrated the air in Yellowstone Park.

They spent the rest of the afternoon shopping for camping supplies and packing, with Mullein in charge of the tent and bedding and Lynx the food and cookware. In the evening, they drove over to Island Park, ate pizza and watched a stupid action movie with Gwen and Merlin. They stopped at the Sundowner on the way back to West Yellowstone for a few beers and a game of pool.

The bar was empty except for Olive, who was working her last weekend before returning to her winter home in Billings. Olive had the juke box cranked up and blasting her favorite country Western tunes, and she and Lynx took turns dancing with Mullein. Richard Lytle, a recently divorced realtor who looked like a cross between Oliver North and Steve Martin, zigzagged into the bar and ordered a shot of peppermint schnapps. Lynx figured the evening would now take a turn for the worse because Richard was obviously three sheets to the wind and depressed. He'd been on a steady drunk ever since his wife left him because she was tired of hearing that he liked to pick up women in bars.

There was something about Richard that women found attractive. Lynx had always wondered exactly what that was, although she liked Richard as a friend and had tried to listen sympathetically to his lamentations about the divorce. Now she didn't want to hear about it. Richard stumbled over to the jukebox and played a Whitney Houston tune. Mullein looked at Lynx and rolled his eyes. It was time to leave. They weren't Whitney people.

Sitting in the car next to Mullein on the ride back to West Yellowstone, Lynx tried to muster the will power she would need later to tell him she wasn't going to bed with him. He was so attractive, and she remembered how wonderful sex with him had been. But she had to stick to her commitment to be celibate.

"A penny for your thoughts," Mullein said, reaching over and grabbing her hand.

"Oh, Mullein I was thinking about sex," she said, letting him hold her hand on his lap.

"Funny thing—me, too," he answered. "Remember that time on the hill on our hunting trip?"

"Oh, yeah. That was pretty unforgettable."

"You know, I've thought about that all summer," he told her. "It may surprise you to hear that that was the last time I had sex. That was a long time ago, too. I haven't met anyone else I wanted to be with. I think about you often, Lynx. I've looked forward to being with you."

"We don't know each other very well though, Mullein."

"I know that. I've thought about that, too. There is something there, though. Whenever we have spent time together, even on the phone, I've had feelings I've never had before. It has kind of frightened me. Sometimes I've thought about coming to West and seeing you more often, but I always put those thoughts aside. Then I got busy with the fires, and there was no way I could do anything about it. Now I want to."

"The timing may be off, Mullein," Lynx told him.

"How so?"

"Well, since we were together last, I've made up my mind to be celibate."

There was silence. He kept holding her hand, and she could tell he was thinking hard.

"Tell me more about it," he finally said. "But not now. We're almost at your house. Let's go in and make some coffee and talk."

Lynx made coffee while Mullein searched her CD's and loaded her player with three classical albums. They sat on her couch and listened to a few Baroque tunes before he opened the conversation again.

"Okay, let's get back to our talk. You said you're celibate. Tell me why."

"This spring, I had a short affair with someone I really cared about but wasn't in love with. He wanted to spend more time with me, but I could see he was looking for a permanent relationship, and I didn't think that would work out."

She looked at Mullein and saw that he was listening carefully.

"That led me to do some serious soul searching and praying. I suddenly realized I've been much too casual about jumping in bed with people. I've been able to do that without thinking of the consequences. It's strange, because in many other areas of my life, I'm pretty moral. My promiscuity has been a real flaw, but I didn't really see it that way until I made myself take a hard look at my life. And I think praying made me get in touch with my heart. I want to be closer to God, Mullein, and that can't happen to a gal who hops in bed with any guy she decides she likes at the moment."

Mullein put his arm around her and hugged her tightly.

"So you think you should wait to have sex with someone you're in love with, someone you may even want to do the M word with?" He grinned at her.

"M word?" she asked him. "Oh, yeah. Marriage. I get it. You're right." She giggled.

"And I thought you were a Fun Girl. I figured you liked sex so much you would have been seeing other people, and it didn't bother me because we had no commitment, and I like to think of you as giving pleasure to other men. Maybe that makes be a pervert. Although if you were mine, I wouldn't like to think of that. I'm into monogamy once the commitment is made."

"So am I, but now I'm thinking I'm into celibacy until the commitment is made," Lynx told him.

"My body is disappointed," Mullein said, laughing. "But my heart is happy. All the time I've been dreaming about having sex with you again, I've also had thoughts that I really should wait to see if there was potential for a relationship with you. You know, hang out with you and start over. Do a dating thing. We started out ass backwards. But then again, I have to admit that if you'd been ready to jump my bones this weekend, I'd have let you. I've never known any woman like you. I want to get to know you. I would even move here if I thought you felt the same way."

Lynx suddenly felt very frightened. She hadn't thought of having a relationship with Mullein or anyone else.

"Lynx I can see that my train of thought has not been going through your head."

"No, it hasn't. I've been too busy. Sure, sometimes the thought passes briefly through my head that I'd like to get married again someday. But I haven't met anyone around here I feel that deeply connected to. And I really don't know you well. I feel comfortable with you, but that's as far as it goes."

Mullein stood up and paced, his hands in his pockets. Lynx noticed how handsome he was. His body was strong from all the hard work he'd done. His face was weathered and full of character and kindness. His long black hair, tied in a pony tail, was clean and shone like a raven's feathers: she imagined it flying behind him in the wind. There was much more to him than she could see on the surface, she was sure. She wondered what his mind was like, wondered how he'd gotten into firefighting and what he wanted to do for the rest of his life. She realized that one of the main reasons why she'd never thought of a relationship with him was that he was an Indian. She'd assumed that that would be why he wouldn't want to be anything but casual with her, too. Should she mention that?

As if he'd read her mind, he told her, "And the funny thing, for me anyway, is that you are a white woman, and I always thought I should be interested in one of my own people."

"Should be or would be?"

"I was raised by white people who adopted me. I never lived on a reservation, didn't meet my birth parents until I was a teenager, know very few Indians. My adoptive parents are Irish, and they didn't give me their last name when they adopted me because they liked my Indian name and hoped I would some day meet my natural family.

"Did you?"

"Yes. Just my mother, when I was 16. My father was killed in a car accident when I was eight months old, and my mother was pregnant with a second child. She couldn't support me and gave me up for adoption, against her parents' wishes. They wanted to raise me. But she felt the reservation was too full of depression and poverty and wanted me to have a better life."

"That all makes sense."

"The Indian organization at the university I went to confronted me about this. They said the poverty was a worthy trade for the family relationships and rich culture of the reservation. They tried to get me into studying Indian history, but I didn't go for it. They said I should go back to the res to live and get back in touch with my real family. They were confrontational, as if I'd gotten adopted by whites on purpose and it was an evil thing. They even said the tribe should have tried to get me back right after the adoption. Well, I do keep in touch with my birth mother and her family now, but I've never gone back there to live."

Silence again. Lynx felt uncomfortable, but there was something she had to ask him. "I never knew that about you because you're a firefighter, and I thought the Nez Perce firefighters came off the reservation."

"Lynx, stop squirming. You don't have to be uncomfortable with this Indian thing. Yeah, they do come from the reservation. The forest service assigned me to them because they thought I'd do the best job with them. It hasn't been easy because I came in from the outside and to be their boss. I had to deal with a lot of resentment."

"And did you?"

"Yes, Lynx, I earned their respect, but still a few of the younger people on my crew think someone from the res should be in charge."

"How did you get into firefighting then? And how about photography? We met at a photographers' gathering, and for some reason I always thought you would get into photography when you quit firefighting."

"Photography is just a hobby. If I did it for money, it wouldn't be as enjoyable. I went to school to become a physicians' assistant, a P.A. I had a scholarship, but I still had to take out loans. I made more money firefighting than I would have just starting out as a P.A. I've finally paid the loans back, with money to spare, so I can get into my field now, after I take some time off to play."

"That's hard to believe—I mean that you can make more money fighting fires."

"Well, it's true for P.A.'s who live out West in rural areas, which is where I want to be. But now that my loans are paid off, I plan to look for a medical job somewhere around here."

"Won't you have problems because you haven't worked in your field?"

"No, because I've kept current in my field, filled in for P.A.'s who've gone on vacation, and I've done some volunteer work. I'll be fine, although underpaid for awhile."

So he was a hard worker and a person with goals, Lynx thought. And she'd hunted with him, slept with him, and known so little about him. She blushed.

"You're blushing because you've realized you know so little about me, aren't you?" Mullein asked her, laughing.

Lynx laughed, too. "I can't believe myself sometimes. I've made a lot of stupid mistakes. But I'm trying to reform," she said.

"There's time for that. Answer one question, though. Why do you have so many Indian friends? I've wondered about that."

"That goes a long way back," Lynx answered, "to a friendship with a Crow woman introduced to me by my grandmother. I'll tell you about it someday."

"That's what I want to hear," Mullein told her, sitting down close to her again. "That you'll tell me someday. I want to hear it all. The entire story of your life, and I want to tell you mine. I even want to know what that trailer is doing in your back yard. Is there a man in there, someone you're interested in?"

"Yes, there's a man living there, but I told you I'm not interested in anyone. He's someone I'm doing a new project with. That's another long story."

Mullein looked at her, and she felt like jumping into his deep brown eyes.

"We won't run out of things to talk about," he told her. "You still want to camp out this weekend?"

"Oh, yes, I can't wait," she replied.

"Then let's do it. I'll sleep here on the couch, and you set your alarm and get me up. We'll go and not worry about anything else but having fun."

Lynx grinned at him. "Okay, I'll get you blankets. But I hate alarm clocks. I just set my mental clock. What time do you want to get up?"

"At the crack of dawn. That's my favorite time of day. And I hate alarm clocks, too."

Lynx went to her linen closet and grabbed some bedding. She handed it to Mullein, and he leaned over and kissed her. When their lips touched, her stomach flip-flopped, but she ignored the feeling. She would have to practice that, she thought. She was so attracted to him. "Good night, Mullein," she said, trying to keep her voice steady.

"Good night, baby," he told her.

Lynx took a long time getting to sleep. She believed that nothing happens without a reason. Going from there, she figured it was either a good thing or a bad thing that Mullein White Horse had come into her life again. If it was a bad thing, she would feel miserable, and she didn't. And it was definitely a good sign that he was willing to accept that she wanted to be celibate.

She was shocked that he'd been thinking about having a deeper relationship with her while she hadn't been thinking about him at all, except for occasionally wondering if he would show up to visit. Now she could to turn her attention to thinking about whether or not she wanted to be more than Mullein's friend, or she could simply have a fun weekend with him and send him on his way. It bothered her that the entire situation was something that seemed to have been thrown at her without her doing anything to make it happen. But then in a way she had created it because she had spent time with Mullein that included having sex with him. Perhaps this is how relationships started, out of the blue.

She heard Mullein get up and walk around the living room. "He's a pacer," she thought, "like me. What could he be thinking? Oh, well," she concluded. "God knows I'm being celibate. He knows everything. He'll take care of this situation." She focused on taking ten deep breaths and fell asleep in the middle of number five.

• • •

Mullein let Lynx set the pace as they climbed to the basin, and they walked silently to conserve their energy. It was a perfect fall day, with a slight breeze but not a cloud in the sky. The breeze made the dried grasses and willows in the meadows sing like a wooden wind chime. They stopped by a tiny creek that crossed the trail and filled their Sierra cups with water. Gold flakes sparkled and danced in the creek bottom as if they were celebrating the moment with them.

They drank the water and stripped off their top layer of clothing before going on their way again. They walked through a forest of Douglas fir trees and picked up some hiking companions—a trio of Canada jays, whose common name is "camp robbers." The birds flew ahead of them, waited in the trees until they caught up with them, and zipped ahead again all the way through the forest. When they reached another meadow, the birds stayed behind and screamed at them for not leaving a treat.

"Watch," Lynx told Mullein. "They'll catch up to us a in a few minutes. I bet they follow us all the way to camp."

"Oh, yeah," he told her. "They like people. They hung out around our base camps all summer, and we fed them, even though the park rangers told us to quit because you aren't supposed to feed wildlife in the park. That's a stupid rule when it comes to jays, I think. They're symbiotic with campers because people have been feeding them for centuries. I figure we're supposed to feed them because the relationship goes so far back in time."

"I agree. I can't remember a time I camped around these parts without them. I've even named them when I've hung out with the same ones for awhile," Lynx told him.

"Named them what?"

"Oh, obvious names like screecher, squawker, hog, butthead."
Mullein laughed.

"Did you know that some Indian tribes believed that finding a Canada jay nest was a bad sign? It meant you or someone close to you would die soon. They nest in March, one of the earliest times a bird nests, and a time a lot of Indians were struggling with starvation."

"How do you know that?" Mullein asked her.

"I read it in a book by a naturalist named Edwin Way Teale. Then Nora Spotted Elk said she'd heard the same thing. I skied all around the country near West Yellowstone one March looking for a nest and never found one."

"Good. That's why you're still alive," Mullein told her.

"I've wondered about that. But then a few years later, I did find one of their nests when I wasn't looking for it, and I'm still alive!"

"Where did you find it?"

"Down in Island Park. I was shoveling snow off a roof of a cabin that belongs to a friend of mine who winters in Arizona, and I saw it on the roof of the cabin next door. It was a steeply pitched aluminum roof, and it didn't have any snow on it. The nest was snuggled up to the chimney, and a jay was sitting on it while, strangely enough, two other jays were feeding the bird on the nest."

"Cool. What were they feeding her?"

"All kinds of food scraps, it looked like, that they must have been taking out of a cache somewhere nearby: old meat and bread, orange peels, stuff stolen from people."

The jays caught up with them. Mullein pulled a granola bar out of his pocket and crumbled it up. "Okay, little brothers and sisters, here you go," he told them as he spread it on the ground.

They grew silent again, sweating and breathing heavily as the trail grew steeper. Lynx had been on this hike dozens of times, but Mullein had never been there. The trail goes to the top of a ridge that overlooks the basin. When they were nearly at the top, Lynx stopped and told Mullein to go ahead. She knew that the first view of the basin was something a person would never forget, a real scenic climax, and she wanted to watch him experience it. "You're in for a treat," she told him.

He grabbed her hand, and they walked to the top of the ridge.
"Wow!" Mullein exclaimed as he took in the view of the basin. Crystal blue and green lakes sat on rocky terraces like blotches of paint a mystical giant had spilled for the fun of it. A herd of elk grazed near one of them. Part of the other side of the basin was bordered by an enormous talus slope, and a narrow

trail over the talus could barely be detected. It went to the top of the slope to a pass over the mountains. The jagged crests of the Hilgard Peaks, part of the Madison Range, were off to the left, and puffy white clouds were forming over them. Patches of snow from recent storms sparkled in the sun. A red-tail hawk sat on the top of the tallest sub-alpine fir trees in one of the small clumps of trees scattered around the basin. He lifted his wings as if he were going to take off, thought better of it, and settled back down.

Lynx pointed to the lake they would be camping near. "Believe it or not, that lake and a few of the others have fish in them," she told Mullein. The Forest Service stocked them with golden trout over 50 years ago, but the goldens are gone. There're hybrids in them now, rainbow-cutthroat crosses. We can catch one for dinner. I've got a collapsible rod with me."

"God, this is beautiful," Mullein told her. "This is right up there with the best places I've ever been to. Thanks for bringing me here, Lynx. I don't see another human down there."

"It's going to be cold up here very soon. We're over 9,000 feet, and most people think it's too late in the year to be up here. Or maybe they still think the trails are closed because of fire danger. I'm really surprised the elk are still here. There's not much browse for them. They may have been pushed over the pass by hunters on the other side, in the Madison Valley. Let's hope they don't come over. It's great to be the only folks here."

As they descended into the basin, the elk spooked and bolted toward the forest that climbs up the high peaks. Lynx and Mullein spent the next hour setting up their camp. Lynx put her fly rod together, rigging it with a fast sinking line and a large black woolly bugger, since no fish were rising. They sneaked over to the lake's outlet, a tiny trickle of water that flowed to a lake on the terrace below them.

"I've learned," she told Mullein, "that the fish hang near the outlets up here, where food collects. Look at all the dead bugs on the logs that washed over here. There's trout under those logs. If we do this very carefully, we'll catch one by the third cast. If not, we'll have to sit here and wait at least 20 minutes. These are wary fish."

She cast out past the logs, waited for the line to sink, and stripped it in slowly. As she pulled the fly out of the water, they saw a large trout that had looked at it turn over and swim back under a log. She cast again. This time, the trout grabbed the fly and ran toward the middle of the lake with it.

Lynx gave him some line, and he swam fast, bending her rod nearly in half. "This guy weighs five pounds, I bet," she said joyfully. "Here, feel it." She handed the rod to Mullein, keeping the line tight. "Go ahead, bring him in," she told him.

"Far out!" Mullein shouted as he felt the huge fish. "This is heaven!" The trout came to a sudden halt and the line slackened.

"Pull it back," Lynx told him. "He's trying to trick you into giving him some slack so he can get away."

Mullein pulled back the rod, and the fight resumed. The trout leapt out of the water and smashed back down, trying to break loose.

"Feisty fish, for a hybrid," Lynx commented. But it was his final leap. He seemed to have resigned himself to his fate. Mullein hauled him, in and Lynx unhooked him and hit him on the head with a rock. He twitched and died.

"God, you're a heartless killer, aren't you?" Mullein said, laughing at her.

Lynx took a dollar bill out of her back pocket and measured the fish. "Four bills long. He's a big one. Enough meat here for dinner and breakfast, don't you think?"

Mullein was still staring at her, unable to get over the shock of seeing a woman knock out a fish as if she'd done it a million times before. "I thought you were one of those catch and release people," he said.

"Not when I'm hungry. Now think about it. Wouldn't it be stupid to climb all the way up here, catch a fish like this, throw it back, and eat one of those yuppy freeze-dried gourmet meals. I hate those things."

"You mean you don't have a back-up meal in your pack? I thought you said you packed us some food."

"Yeah, butter to fry this monster in, some Spike for seasoning, some potatoes, and a few other things. I knew we'd catch a trout."

Mullein looked at her incredulously. "And what if we'd failed?"

"If you don't think failure is part of the program, it never is, Mullein, " Lynx told him firmly. "Now you gut this fish while I get some side dishes." She walked away, laughing to herself.

Lynx knew where there was a patch of morel mushrooms in a damp and rocky depression in the basin that was in shade most of the day. She didn't expect there to be fresh mushrooms that time of year, but she knew the mushrooms were at their prime at that high altitude in mid-July, and with the season so dry that year, she hoped there would still be some naturally dried mushrooms she could saute in butter and a little water and Spike.

Sure enough, they were there. The basin was the only place she'd ever found naturally dried mushrooms that weren't all broken up or wormy. She'd never heard of anyone else who'd made this discovery there or anywhere else, and she'd never shared her secret with anyone. She gathered enough for two hearty servings and went to a sunny area of the basin where she knew there were dandelions and plantains for a green salad. Then she used her hunting knife to dig some glacier lily bulbs to add to the salad.

Back at camp, Mullein had a good fire going, and while they waited for it to burn into coals, she washed her wild edibles, wrapped half the fish in foil, and boiled water for hot chocolate she spiked with shots of Jack Daniels from her flask.

"Wow, am I impressed," Mullein told her. "This is gourmet living at its best. You're a real find. You hunt, you fish, you gather plants. Very Stone Age. I like it."

"It's so nice to have someone to share this with," she answered. "I think I could live up here a long time."

After dinner they kept their small fire going and watched the stars until it grew very cold and they could see their breaths turn to puffs of smoke. They zipped Lynx's two down sleeping bags together and cuddled inside them. They talked far into the night like people who are falling in love so often do. For Mullein, loving Lynx was a done deal. For Lynx, loving Mullein was a slowly rising star on the horizon.

Chapter Thirty Seven

Merlin watched his mother hustle around the Island Park cabin, making his breakfast and attacking the pile of dirty laundry he and Gwen had generated over the weekend.

He thought that she looked different. She actually seemed happy and rested. She said she hadn't felt this well in a long time. Great, he thought, because Gwen had told him the $300 he'd saved all summer wasn't enough money to take her to Disneyland, even if he just sent her there alone. Learning this had depressed him deeply because he'd looked forward to seeing the look on his mom's face when he handed her the plane tickets to California.

Merlin smiled when he thought of his meeting with Mullein White Horse, when Mullein dropped his mother off at the cabin the night before. He'd liked Mullein instantly. He was into Nintendo, and they played for an hour together, even though Merlin was over his game time allotment for the week. And Mullein took him up to the hill in back of the cabin and taught him how to throw knives.

Gwen told him when she tucked him into bed that she could tell their mother and Mullein were falling in love. Sometimes Gwen was a know-it-all, and that got on Merlin's nerves, like when she laughed at him for thinking $300 would get two people to Disneyland. He was glad his mom was interested in this new guy, because he'd been worrying that she would start dating Anton, and Anton continued to give Merlin the creeps.

Merlin had nightmares about Anton two or three times a week. In his dreams, Anton always turned into a fierce-looking monster who yelled at Lynx in a language Merlin didn't recognize. It told Merlin to stay in his room all day and listen to music that sounded like old creaky machinery.

Lynx went outside to hang her sleeping bags on the clothesline. Gwen came into the kitchen and poured herself some coffee before phoning

Rambon, who hadn't come with her because he'd had to work. Merlin cringed with embarrassment when he heard her tell him about the $300 he'd saved for Disneyland. Then he saw her face light up. "Thanks, hon," she told him. "I'll let Merlin know. He'll be thrilled."

When she got off the phone, she told Merlin Rambon would send him the rest of the money he needed to take Lynx to Disneyland.

"So tell her when she's driving you to school this morning so you can decide on a date and make plans. I'll call a travel agent with you after school, and we'll get it all worked out. Rambon said if our schedules allow it, we may be able to meet you guys there. Wouldn't that be fun?"

Merlin hugged his sister. "Thanks, Gwen. That's great. But I wanted to surprise mom and get the tickets first and then give them to her."

"Okay, we can try doing it that way. I'll book the trip when I know Rambon and I can make it, and we'll hope mom will be able to adjust her schedule. I don't see why she couldn't now that she's basically working for herself. Now, go get ready for school and don't blow our secret."

• • •

Lynx dropped Merlin off at school and turned her car around to go straight back to her cabin. When she was nearly at the end of town, she saw Patsy and Pete just finishing a jog along one of the old logging roads that branched off from the west end of the city. They hailed her to stop and asked her to go to breakfast with them at the Triangle. They hadn't seen each other for a while, so Lynx agreed to go with them and catch up on the news. Lynx called Gwen to tell her she would be late coming back to the cabin.

Gwen hung up the phone after telling Lynx to take her time with Patsy and Pete. She poured herself another cup of coffee and took a mystery novel out to one of the lounge chairs on the cabin's back deck, which faced the foothills of the Henry's Lake Mountains. She watched a herd of mule deer graze at the edge of a meadow near the top of the closest hill before she turned to her book.

She'd just read a few pages when she heard a vehicle turn the corner of their road. She recognized Anton's R.V. and put her book down to greet him. She'd only met him briefly in Lynx's backyard, when he was hauling groceries into his trailer. She'd thought he was incredibly handsome but she had a strange, uncomfortable feeling when she heard his deep voice and watched how intensely he'd looked at her. Now she wished she wasn't home alone.

"My mom's in town having breakfast with some friends," Gwen told him after they said their hellos. She watched a dark look pass across his face, covered up quickly by a wide grin and a shoulder shrug.

"That's disappointing," he told her. "I just finished editing her fire tapes, and I wanted to see what she thought of what I've come up with. She filmed some pretty interesting, ballsy stuff at the Old Faithful siege."

"You can leave the tape here, and my mother and I can watch it to-night," Gwen told him, feeling a great urge to get rid of him. "As soon as she gets back, we're going to climb that hill," she said, pointing to the hill with the deer on it, "and see if we can find some arrowheads. The Indians hunted this area regularly years ago."

"I wanted to be with her when she sees this tape the first time," Anton replied, fully aware that he was making Gwen nervous.

Gwen felt angry and protective of her mother. "Look," she told him, her voice strong and firm, "Lynx is taking this week off because she worked her butt off all summer and needs some time before starting her new project. Time with me and Merlin, time to herself. This tape may be wonderful, but it's work, too. So just leave it, and I'll tell her you stopped by. If she wants to view it with you, she'll give you a call, and you can come back then."

Anton had seen that same protective look on the faces of Lynx's other friends. He'd never considered that she would have had so many friends who seemed to dislike him and want to keep him from being with her. He knew he would have to go along with Gwen in the most gracious way possible to deflect her anger and suspicion.

"The last thing I want to do is keep your mother from getting the rest she deserves," Anton told her. "But I'm heading down to Idaho Falls to buy a few cases of blank tapes, and I'm spending the night there, so it can't be tonight. Just tell her to go ahead and watch it, and I'll catch her next week."

He left the tape and drove away, thinking that Gwen was a strong-willed bitch, her mother's daughter. He put his anger aside and focused on driving. He was running late, and DK didn't like hanging around in air-ports. Picking him up was the top item on his lists of things to do in Idaho Falls. "Something important must be going on for DK to make a second trip to Yellowstone after being here for the Circle of Fire ritual just last month," Anton thought. He pondered what that could be all the way down the road.

Chapter Thirty Eight

Martin and Vicky sat on a hill overlooking a deserted house in a low density subdivision near Horse Butte. The butte is 12 miles north of West Yellowstone, and its winward side rises from the shore of Hebgen Lake. Their spotting scopes were trained on a 500-pound grizzly sow they'd been following for the last week.

She was walking around the house, her nose to the ground, sniffing out a meal. They watched her circle the house four times before giving up and heading into the forest. Martin and Vicky waited until she was out of sight, and then walked to their truck. and drove to their camp, which was a few miles away in a national forest campground at Rainbow Point.

They knew where the bear was headed. She'd taken the same route each day and night since they'd started tracking her, and she was now on her way to bed. Her day bed was in a thick lodgepole pine forest just 200 yards from the house. The house was her first and last stop on her daily food-seeking excursions because the occupant left her a bucket of dog food every morning and evening.

The house's owner had been feeding her regularly, Vicky and Martin figured, all summer. He didn't own any dogs or cats, and they'd observed him watching the bear from his living room's picture window. There could be no doubt that his actions were deliberate, a way to amuse himself at the expense of the bear's wildness. He'd left for his winter in New Mexico very early that day and hadn't put any food out for the bear.

As long as they'd been watching her, Vicky and Martin had seen her scarf down what they estimated to be a five-pound bucket of dog food at around 11 o'clock in the evening. She then traveled slowly through the lodgepole pine forest on old logging roads all the way to West Yellowstone, stopping randomly to stand still in the dark shadows and listen for any danger.

Hitting town around midnight, she visited the same four garbage sites every evening. One of these was a bear-proof dumpster propped open by its owner. Another was an old van that a restaurant threw its garbage in after closing every evening. The back doors of the van were broken. They had to be held shut with bungie cords, and the only time the restaurant's janitor bothered to secure them was just before he made his weekly run to the landfill. The other two sites were large uncovered trailers filled with garbage from another restaurant and a mini-mart. The owners of these businesses hauled the trailers to the landfill every other week. The sides of the trailers were five feet high, and the bear had no difficulty scaling them and jumping into the garbage.

She took her time traveling from one site to the next, stopping often to rest in the town's alleys or to wander a little way into the forest that borders the north end of town. When she had her fill of garbage, she took the same path back to the Horse Butte house, where a fresh bucket of dog food awaited her. Martin had checked with the local police and learned that all the West Yellowstone business owners had been told to lock up their garbage or be fined, but not one had paid any attention to the police. Finally, they'd been told they had 10 days to comply with the bear-proof ordinance or they would be fined. Ten days would have no effect on the situation because the bear was already habituated to the garbage and the dog food. The dog food person had ignored the county sheriff's warning that he would be fined if he didn't stop feeding the bear because he knew he was leaving town for the winter.

Tonight would be the first night the bear would not find garbage at her usual places in West, because the people had finally cleaned up their act. With no more dog food or garbage in town, Martin hoped the bear would go back to eating natural food. It was also time for her to start getting her winter den in order.

Martin had checked with the Interagency Grizzly Bear Study Team to see if they had any data on this bear who was not radio collared or ear tagged. A team biologist came to Horse Butte to observe her and told Martin and Vicky that without a doubt she was Bear Number 88, nick-named "Mystery."

She was an 11-year old who had given birth to a total of seven cubs. She had been radio-collared and tracked for five years, but two years ago, the collar had stopped transmitting. It was later found a few yards from a rarely used backcountry trail in Yellowstone Park's Hayden Valley. It had been cut off her neck, and the team first thought she had been killed by poachers because they never found any sign of her.

Then a year ago they heard that she had been prowling around the Tobacco Root Mountains in an area grizzly bears hadn't frequented for decades. They had no idea how she had gotten to the Tobacco Roots without being spotted. Once there, she'd raided three different camp sites before suddenly disappearing.

As far as the team knew, that was the only time she'd ever sought out human food, and they'd hoped she stop. The biologist decided to do nothing about her West Yellowstone expeditions. He hoped her instinct to den would kick in as soon as her garbage meals were cut off, and she'd go back to the same denning site she'd used for the last several years. It was on the north slope of Mount Hayes in Yellowstone Park, around 12 miles east of West Yellowstone.

Martin's plan was to track Mystery until she began work on her winter den. He was fascinated with the bear, unable to understand why she had apparently given up some of her wildness to eat people's trash. He'd finished all the grizzly bear habitat mapping he had to complete that year, and following Mystery around was a great way to spend time in the outdoors before being cooped up in the city writing his report.

Mystery plopped down in her day bed and listened to the People get in the truck and drive away. There was a time when she would have used all her power to evade the presence of People, but that time, like her life as a wild bear, was ending.

Even the one thrill of her day was gone: there'd been no more crunchy treats by the house. She knew the Man was gone because she now smelled only lingering traces of him and the place was silent. The People who were following her smelled like the man. It was a non-threatening odor, like the odor from the Woman she'd seen at the camp in the Tobacco Roots, the one she'd given the plastic bag filled with food to.

Strange how she'd smelled and heard that exact Woman just a few days ago in town. The Woman lived on one of the alleys Mystery liked to prowl around. When she'd walked by her house, she'd smelled her and remembered that time in the camp, when she and the Woman had locked eyes and seen into one another's souls. It seemed then that the Woman had given her something, a feeling that she was loved and understood. The Woman was not like other People she'd run into, who either tried to capture her or stare at her through clicking and beeping boxes. The Woman had told her to go away and be wild. Mystery had understood her then and given her the food she'd stolen from the campers. She'd leaned against the Woman's house, under a patch of light that beamed into the alley and heard her talking to another person with a deeper voice.

Other People had odors she despised and once ran from: the Men who trapped her and put that thing around her neck; the Men who stuck something sharp into her neck, tied a rope around her and dragged her a long way along a trail to a truck. She was very sleepy after she'd been stuck, and she couldn't resist them. She dozed off and woke with no collar around her neck but with terrible pain in her paws.

The Men had pulled her claws off of her. That's what made her decide to go a long way from her usual haunts. She'd walked slowly and painfully, taking long rests in the daytime, to the mountains that are far away. That's when she'd begun to steal food from People camping in the forest. It was easier to rip off camp food than hunt, with her paws hurting still. When she was healed, she kept stealing food because she enjoyed how easy it was.

Then she met the Woman and had quit stealing food and headed back to Yellowstone. On the way back home, she mated with a boar she'd never seen or smelled before in the Madison Mountains 30 miles west of the park. He was the strongest bear she'd ever been with, and she felt the new life he'd given her grow inside her differently than she had during other pregnancies. It drove her to eat more than she'd ever eaten before. She went into her den last fall in prime shape, having just devoured a bison calf-of-the-year that had been run over by a car. She came out of her den that spring with two new male cubs. They were very aggressive, like their father, and they grew very large on winter-killed elk and bison.

But life began to go bad. The earth was dry and parched, and there weren't nearly as many wildflowers and plants as there usually were. Some of her favorite plants were so scarce that she doubted her cubs had eaten them often enough to have really learned how to seek them out on their own.

And then the fires came. More fire than she'd ever seen, the air choking her and making it difficult to smell where the food was. One afternoon she and the cubs were lounging in a meadow, eating the tops off of coneflowers and taking short naps now and then. The fire seemed a long way off, but the wind grew strong and loud. Suddenly the meadow was surrounded by burning trees, and the grass caught fire. The only way out was to run uphill, and they were doing fine until they reached a large talus slope. They had to slow down and pick their way across the rocks. They looked up and saw that another fire was racing over the crest of the hill. The cubs were uphill of her, and when they saw and smelled the fire at the top, they panicked and started running. That triggered an avalanche of falling rocks that buried both cubs. One was killed instantly, his neck broken by a large boulder. The other broke both his front legs, and he began to whimper in pain. He tried to use his good legs to pull himself out, but it hurt too much. Mystery was able to move the rocks off him, but it was impossible for him to walk. She'd seen this before. A bighorn sheep ram had been caught in a rock avalanche, and she'd found him nearly starved to death.

She'd finished the ram off with one strong swat on his head, and there was so little meat left on him that he was barely worth eating. She killed her cub the same way, but had no heart to eat him.

After the fires passed, there were abundant elk and bison and smaller animals to eat that were weakened by the lack of browse, and she could have stayed in the park and gotten quite fat for the winter. She went to her winter den site and saw immediately that she would have to find a new one. Every tree on the slope was burned to the ground. She decided then to go back to the mountains where she'd met the cubs' father. It wasn't to mate with him again. It wasn't the right time for that. She simply wanted to smell him again, because he smelled like the cubs. It made no sense, but nothing made sense. The fires, the cubs' deaths, her barren denning site, her loneliness.

On the way to the mountains outside the park, Mystery smelled food that reminded her of the food she used to steal from campers. She tracked the odor and saw the Man outside his house cooking. He went inside, and she dashed directly to his barbecue grill, knocked it over, and grabbed the piece of meat off the ground. It was quite tasty. After she gulped it down, she looked up and saw the Man coming out of the house. He made sounds at her, gentle sounds like the Woman had made, so she stared at him for a few seconds and then walked away from him slowly, stopping to look back now and then.

She was still hungry and smelled more human food cooking. She tracked those smells into West Yellowstone and found all kinds of good things to eat. She walked back toward the Man's house and slept off her eating binge in the woods not far from him. In the evening, she smelled more food near his house. That's when she found the crunchy treats, and they'd been there twice a day ever since. The Man always watched her from the window but never spoke to her again.

Mystery figured the man would not come back, but she checked out his house anyway that evening and found nothing to eat. She thought of leaving for the mountains then, but it would be so much easier to walk to town where the pickings were so easy.

In West Yellowstone, Mystery could smell the garbage in all the places she'd eaten before, but she couldn't get at it. She pawed the closed-up garbage dumpsters and vans, and the sound frightened her and reminded her of the men who had ripped her claws off. She grew hungrier by the minute.

She smelled the People who followed her and thought of eating them, but had no knowledge about how to kill people. She ambled over to the Woman's house and listened for her voice. She could smell that the Woman was there, but the house was dark and quiet. She stood near the house and remembered the Woman's eyes again, telling her to be wild.

Suddenly, Mystery knew she must leave. She took a different route out of town, and soon the smell of the People who followed her was distant. She stopped in the darkness and sniffed the air, seeking the odors of wild things that were beneath the greasy smells of human food and People. She heard a coyote howl. It was a long way away, but she knew if she followed it, she would find a more wild place. She headed toward it at full gallop.

At first light, Mystery was sleeping off her frustration and anger in a quickly made day bed in a stand of Douglas fir trees on the east side of Hebgen Mountain. Martin and Vicky were crawling into their camp after prowling around the woods in their truck all night and finding no trace of her.

Chapter Thirty Nine

It was opening day at Ursus. Randall had invited everyone in West Yellowstone to visit without paying admission. Lynx sat on one of the benches in the outdoor viewing area and watched the townspeople mill around, ooh-ing and aah-ing at the large bear on display in the "natural habitat." The 700-pound Alaskan brown bear had been trapped in Denali National Park in Alaska after he had become habituated to human food sources.

She smiled when she saw Mullein in what looked like a deep conversation with the town's P.A., probably trying to learn about jobs. Lynx was now sure she was in love with him. She felt such joy just being around him. He didn't make her feel confused like Anton had, with all his mood swings. She wasn't guilty about having sex with him, as she had been with Jack, because they were sticking to their commitment to be celibate. Lynx didn't even want to think about what their "first time" would be like. She felt sure and even about her feelings for Mullein, and she hoped he found a job and place to live nearby soon.

Jack was there with his new girlfriend, Mona, a woman who worked as a city clerk in a small town in Eastern Montana. He'd met her at a League of Cities and Towns conference and seemed to care deeply for her. They had a lot more in common than he and Lynx had. She was relieved that he'd gotten over her and was dating someone else. When Jack had told her about Mona, he reminded her that they would always be friends, and he would always be there for her, especially if she had any trouble with Anton. He also told her about his meeting in Bozeman with Nora and Dewey and how they'd encouraged him to pray for her. He thanked her for being the catalyst that had gotten him back into prayer.

Lynx winced when she saw Anton, who was taking videos of the bear and the crowd. He'd been unable to hide his jealousy of her relationship with Mullein, and they were barely speaking to one another. Lynx still hadn't reviewed his edit of her fire tapes. She'd had the tape for two weeks now, but had been too busy to watch it.

Gwen, Merlin, and Mullein had convinced her to take a full month off instead of a week before digging into the CNS project. She did need the rest, and she needed to see Mullein as often as she could. Fortunately, CNS had been very supportive of her taking a longer rest between jobs.

Lynx looked over at Merlin, who was there with several of his friends, devouring snacks off the refreshment table. He'd been so sweet when he'd handed her the tickets to Disneyland. She still couldn't figure how he'd gotten the money to pay for it, although she guessed Gwen and Rambon had something to do with it. Mullein had immediately gone and bought tickets for himself so he could go with them. She was proud that at least some of the money Merlin saved came from sacrificing his video games. She'd always taught her children that making some sacrifices for people you love was good for their character.

Pete and Patsy strolled by and waved. They walked hand in hand and looked more in love than ever. Lynx missed seeing her best gal friend regularly, but she figured that once each of them was settled into their new relationships, they would spend more time together.

Vicky and Martin walked out of the door of the Discovery Center, which housed exhibits on bear biology, bear habitat, and how people should behave in bear country. They were talking intently with the Ursus veterinarian, probably about their experience with Mystery, Lynx guessed. They seemed to be obsessed with that bear.

So was Lynx, in a different way. She was certain, after looking at photos they'd taken of her, that Mystery and her vision bear were one and the same. She didn't tell anyone her suspicion, however. She honored the tradition to not discuss your vision with anyone, except in very general terms with your vision guides. It concerned Lynx that Mystery was sure to meet some terrible fate if she returned to town or anywhere else to seek human food. Lynx was happy that Martin and Vicky had broken away somewhat from their Earth First! crowd to work on bear issues with the Ursus staff and other bear experts.

Martin would never go back to working within the system, but at least his independent research project was funded by a group that bear experts in local and federal agencies respected. Earth First! made some good points, but Lynx had never seen the group change anyone's mind. She wasn't an advocate of eco-terrorism because she didn't think violence solved anything.

Frank Goodman sauntered by with Maria, and they stopped to tell Lynx they'd seen Dave in prison recently, and he was doing fine. Maria whispered that she and Dave had decided to get married. They planned a more or less secret wedding in his prison cell, after which they could have conjugal visits. Lynx, however, was invited, along with two very close friends of Dave's, two members of Maria's family, and of course, Frank. Lynx agreed to go and keep the union a secret.

Nora, Dewey, Harry, and Arthur were chatting together as they watched the bear, who seemed unaware he was the center of attention. They were there to have a special meeting with Lynx after they visited Ursus. Lynx figured it had something to do with their continued concern about her working with Anton. Lynx also invited Yurt and Mullein to the meeting. Yurt recently told her he had learned an amazing amount of information about Satanic cults on his hunting trip with his New Age expert friend, and she wanted everyone to hear his information.

Lynx looked around at the crowd again, realizing she knew nearly everyone there by name and had written stories about many of them. There was Ned, the councilman, one of the few city officials who had supported Randall's project without worrying that it would rob tourist dollars from other businesses in town. There was Susan with her young boyfriend; Lynx wondered if she missed Walt. Even Tami was there, looking quite glamorous, on the arm of her personal trainer. She'd moved to Bozeman but paraded through West Yellowstone every so often with a different hunk on her arm. Lynx and, from their raised eyebrows, a few other people, were surprised to see her at such a public event. As months had gone by, many people had forgotten about Dave's alleged murder of Walt, but others had not. Many who remembered still believed Walt was alive somewhere and were somewhat repulsed by Tami, who seemed to be rejoicing in her new independence.

Adam sat down next to Lynx and immediately began complaining about Ursus, saying he was going to make sure his story portrayed it in the worst light possible as a real side show tourist trap.

"If you've already made up your mind about this place, why don't you get the hell back to Bozeman and file your story then?" Lynx asked him. "The fact that the *Gazette* hired you and you don't even like this community is making me sick," she added.

"Well, aren't we touchy?" he shot back. "I think you got too attached to this place to be objective. And I'm sticking around only because Earth First!ers tipped me off that they plan to stage an event here this afternoon—any time now, in fact. That's good copy."

"Oh, you're right about that," Lynx replied. "Earth First! is good copy. I've always thought that. In this situation, however, I've hoped they would support Ursus rather than try to trash it. It is raising funds to buy more bear habitat, and it is keeping wild bears alive who would have been put to death. I happen to think it has good motives, not just the desire to rip off tourists."

Mullein came over and asked Adam to scoot over so he could sit next to Lynx.

"Just take the whole bench," he told Mullein sneeringly. "Ms. Rosy Color Glasses and I don't get along." He stood up and looked toward the entrance to the outdoor exhibit area, grinning when he saw that Earth First! had indeed arrived. There were ten of them. Half were dressed in bear costumes, the rest in Grim Reaper outfits. They began to pass out leaflets.

Mullein put his arm around Lynx and asked her if she wanted him to punch Adam in the face.

"Nah, he's right about me. I am more positive than negative most of the time. We move in different realities. Let him go; he's harmless. No one here will pay much attention to him, and he'll be on his way to a bigger paper soon enough. Maybe then they'll get a more community-minded person to take his place. I can't worry about it."

"Check that out," Mullein said, changing the subject and nodding toward Anton. A couple who looked totally out of place in the casually dressed crowd had just walked up to him. The man was wearing a three piece silk suit, the woman a tight black dress, mink stole, and spike heels. Diamond earrings dropped from her ear lobes almost to her shoulders. Her blonde hair was cut very short and straight on one side, curled onto her face on the other.

"Wow," Lynx remarked. "Real glamour has come to town. She makes Tami look dowdy. I wonder who they are."

She watched them intently, and after they'd chatted with Anton for a few seconds, they both looked over at her and Mullein.

"He must have told them we're over here," Mullein said. "Go ahead, smile at them." He waved, and DK and Goldie nodded to them and walked over to their bench with Anton.

Anton introduced them as Mr. and Mrs. Carter from Chicago, old friends of his visiting Yellowstone on their way to L.A. Lynx noticed they weren't wearing wedding rings. Goldie appeared to be spaced out on tranquilizers. She wouldn't make eye contact with anyone because she could barely take her eyes off her "husband," whom Lynx thought had the most plastic look of anyone she'd ever seen.

Strangely, when she shook his hand she felt the same electric shivers in her spine she'd felt when she'd first touched Anton. Looking over his shoulder, Lynx could see that many people were staring at them, probably wondering who the hell they were. Her head began to pound, and suddenly all the joy she'd felt that day seeing her friends and neighbors seemed to have disappeared. Mr. Carter was asking her something, and she hadn't heard him. She noticed that Mullein, Anton, and Mr. and Mrs. Carter were staring at her, waiting for her answer.

"Oh, sorry," she said quickly. "I was looking for my son and didn't hear you. What did you say?"

"I said," Mr. Carter replied, looking at her coldly, "that I wondered if you would join us for dinner. I'm most interested in your CNS project. Anton has spoken to me about it only in the most general terms."

Lynx suddenly felt sick to her stomach. Yurt was standing just slightly behind Mr. Carter, staring at him with his mouth open. She tried not to let Mr. Carter see that she was trying to read Yurt's lips. He was pointing to Mr. Carter and mouthing the words "purple robe," she was certain. So Mr. Carter had been with Anton at the ritual in the Centennials!

"I think that's a little premature," she said, looking squarely into his eyes and forcing herself to think of nothing else but the words she was saying. "I'm on vacation and won't be working on the project for a couple more weeks. Maybe some other time."

Mr. Carter gave her an Anton look. She glanced at Goldie and saw raw fear all over her face. "You controlling son of a bitch, you're scaring her," Lynx thought. She returned his look, thinking with all her power, "get the hell away from me." She stood up and he took three steps back, staring at her. "Have a nice vacation," she told him. "Maybe we'll get to talk another time."

"You can be certain of that," he quipped.

Lynx looked at Goldie again. Her eyes were still glued on DK. "Mrs. Carter," she said, holding out her hand. Goldie had no choice but to turn toward Lynx. Lynx saw the face of a totally battered, defeated woman, and her heart ached for her.

Goldie gave Lynx her hand and looked at her for a second, but a second was all it took to see that Lynx's look was concerned and caring. It reminded Goldie of her mother, whom she'd stopped thinking about years ago. Her mother died of cancer when Goldie was very young, and Goldie could not think about her without wanting to cry.

Lynx shook her hand and told her, "Nice meeting you. I love your mink. Hope to see you again."

Goldie shuddered when she felt Lynx's warmth and muttered, "Likewise," and took her hand back, fumbling nervously with her purse.

Lynx took Mullein's hand and they walked around, gathering up their friends for their meeting at her house.

Goldie watched them out of the corner of her eye and saw that there was something very special in the way Mullein and Lynx were together. Was it that Mullein cared deeply for Lynx? She knew that she and DK never looked that way when they were together. Sure, people stared at them, but she knew that was only because of the way she dressed, the way DK forced her to dress, so she would look like a whore and no one would respect her or want to talk with her.

Chapter Forty

Goldie lay on the motel bed, her arms and legs spread out, her body naked and cold, waiting for DK to tie her up with the four gold chains and padlocks he held in his hands.

He was her man, and he needed to do this. She could not protest, could never tell him how much she hated being bound this way, hated waiting for him in the dark for hours after he'd finished with her to return and free her. She tried not to think of how much his physical presence frightened her.

DK was a huge man, six feet six inches tall with a well-built body. His face was ageless, unlined, smooth skinned, with high cheekbones and large lips. His eyes were dark and penetrating. His hair was as white and silky as ripe cotton, thick and wavy and short. It wasn't the white or gray hair of an older person, or the colorless hair of an albino. It was impossible to guess his age or nationality. It was as if he were a composite of all races, all ages. He didn't look like anyone else, yet he looked like everyone. At first glance, he appeared to be so handsome that he was difficult to look at. At second glance, he seemed unbelievably ugly.

"Turn over," DK commanded, "I want you on your stomach. I'm sick of looking at your face."

Goldie obeyed. She hoped he wouldn't ask her to turn over. She hated it that way. He chained her to the bed, first securing her ankles, then her wrists, pulling the chains tight so that if she moved, she would feel pain. He placed a pillow under her middle to raise her butt into the air, and she heard him unzip his pants. He walked to the bedside table and opened a drawer where she had placed the lubricant she knew he would use some time on their trip, and she saw his enormous erection. He noticed her looking at him, and asked her, "You would much rather have this in your mouth, wouldn't you, darling?"

"Oh, yes," she said, hoping he would change his mind and let her give him a blow job. "Just turn me over, and I'll satisfy you. You love it that way."

"Not so, not now. There's only one way I want you now, and you know that. I want you to hurt. Hurt for me and like it."

DK smeared his penis with the lubricant and mounted Goldie from behind, holding the tip of his penis at the opening of her anus. He held it there for a second and then plunged into her. Goldie screamed.

DK reached for her mouth and covered it. "What do you say?" he asked her. "Do I allow you to scream when I do this? I don't think so."

Goldie reached past the incredible pain she felt as he pumped harder and harder into her and told him what he had trained her to say, "Yes, I love it, give me more, harder and harder."

DK accommodated her. "Keep telling me how much you like it. I know you love it. You love the pain."

"Oh, yes, I love it. Hurt me, hurt me more."

DK forced himself to last 20 minutes, watching the digital alarm clock on the bed stand and thinking of nothing but his desire to hurt Goldie, loving the pain he knew was wracking through her body. Then he let himself go, deep inside her, until he felt her pass out in agony. He got off her and looked at her limp body. "You bitch," he told her. He dressed and left for his meeting with Anton.

Goldie came to an hour after DK left, cold, full of pain, needing to go to the bathroom. She thought of Lynx, felt her warm handshake again, remembered her mother, and tried to push both Lynx and her mother out of her mind. But this time she couldn't. She began to cry, and as she cried she remembered her mother holding her, reading story books to her, hugging her and smiling at her.

"Why don't men love like women do," she wondered, sobbing and spilling tears all over her pillow. She tried to hold back the tears, knowing they were smearing her make-up, knowing that DK would beat her if he found out she'd cried. He would demand to know why, and even if she didn't tell him about thinking about her mother and Lynx, he would probe her mind and find out exactly what she thought.

Why weren't Lynx and her friend afraid of DK? Goldie had never seen anyone handle him as Lynx had, looking at him with open hatred. Anyone else she'd seen with bowed to his power. DK took great care of her, or so she had convinced herself, giving her everything she needed materially, although his taste in clothing was not like hers. She worked hard in his office, but the work was challenging. She didn't even have a high school diploma, and he'd hired her a tutor so she could get one, and then computer and office skills specialists to teach her how to run his office efficiently.

She knew she wasn't stupid. She'd dropped out of high school to get away from her father, who'd become a drunk after her mother died and had begun to verbally and physically abuse her. She lived on the street for awhile, working in a toy manufacturing plant and sleeping at a homeless girls shelter, until she met Lyland, her pimp. He convinced her that she could make a lot more money turning tricks, even after he took his cut, than packing toys.

Goldie was on her way to having a story exactly like those of thousands of other young girls like her when she met DK. Lyland told her DK was a regular customer and liked bondage, something she didn't even know existed. Lyland told her it was all in fun, although it may hurt a little bit. All she had to do, DK told her their first night together, was lay in front of him naked and let him say whatever he wanted her to, answer his questions the way he wanted them answered, let him tie her to the bed, and let him whip her. He used a whip made of braided silk, and it stung but never really hurt.

DK had assured her then that he had no interest in having sex with her. She got used to his visits and was willing to allow him to insult her, to beg him to insult her and whip her, rather than have to have sex with him. She hated the tricks she had to pretend to enjoy sex with, even though most of them came fast and were in and out of her room in less than a half hour. And DK always tipped her, putting the money in a place he knew Lyland would never look. But then DK asked Lyland to sell her to him because he needed a secretary. Lyland said he would let her go only if she consented. She told Lyland she didn't know how to type and couldn't read a newspaper without finding words she didn't understand. Lyland explained that DK had bought other "secretaries" before who were just as stupid as she was. Lyland explained that what DK wanted was to have her around for his sexual pleasure more than as office help. Lyland didn't know if DK would continue his sexual encounters with Goldie at the same level as he did on his visits, and he didn't know what had happened to the other girls. He told Goldie he really didn't care, once broads left him, what happened to them. There were always dozens more ready to take their place.

So Goldie went with DK, even though something deep inside herself warned her not to. During her training as a secretary, DK never came near her. She figured he'd gone back to Lyland's place for a different woman, and she didn't worry about it. But once she was able to work in the office without any help, he'd told her she was his full-time slave, and part of being a slave was that she serve his every need, business and pleasure. Then he'd resumed the bondage thing in a very serious way, beating her with whips that stung and left marks on her and raping her in every orifice, whenever he wanted to.

DK had told her time and again that his love for her was ultimate, and she'd better appreciate it and understand that a real woman wants nothing more than to be a slave to a man. Most women would give anything to trade places with her. Did she really believe him? Her mother had been a slave to her father. She'd seen her work herself to death, literally, to support the family while her husband drank and watched sports on television all day and all night long. She'd died of cancer because she was too busy working to find the time to go to a doctor. Her father hadn't grieved too much, Goldie remembered. He collected her life insurance money as soon as he could. He seemed relieved that he could now drink whenever he wanted, with no wife around to beg him to tone it down. And he'd made Goldie his slave in a way, forcing her to clean the house, do all his laundry, and work a part-time job after school to pay for the food.

If a different kind of love existed, a love like Lynx and her friend seemed to have, Goldie knew she could never have it. DK would know she wanted to leave, and he would keep her from leaving. It was best to stop thinking, stop wondering, stop dreaming, and go to sleep until he returned.

• • •

Anton and DK drove Anton's van to a wooded area within 100 yards of Lynx's Island Park cabin, turned off the head lights, and got to work setting up Anton's listening devices.

DK had become obsessed with Lynx and her continued refusal to bend to his and Anton's constant programming. He wanted to know why she was so independent, so fearless. He also suspected that she and her friends knew something about what Anton was up to. He rarely made field visits, other than to participate in special rituals, but he was compelled to check Lynx out first hand.

Whatever he learned on this trip could be applied in any number of situations he had to deal with. Violating Yellowstone had always been a dream of his, and he'd thought that Lynx would be one of the easiest pawns in his game. Now that it seemed that she would be resistant, he wanted to personally experience her power. He'd seen it at the Ursus opening. She'd hated him immediately, and she had also known instantly that Goldie was someone she should sympathize with, not dismiss as a stupid whore like most people did.

Arthur Red Fox watched Anton's van pull up and laughed quietly to himself. He'd expected such. He'd agreed to watch and wait outside Lynx's cabin throughout the meeting and warn them if anyone showed up. He did what Harry had told him to do if he saw Anton or anyone else who seemed to want to prowl around Lynx's: he thought of something not at all related to the present situation. He thought of swimming in the Firehole River in Yellowstone Park. He kept the image of the water and the sun and the sky overhead strong within his mind as he crept through the shadows to Lynx's cabin. He knocked gently three times and waited for someone to open the door.

It was Lynx. He held his hand to his mouth and motioned her and everyone else who was watching them to be silent. They immediately began talking about the events of the day, commenting on their impressions of Ursus. Lynx put a Mozart CD on, and everyone keep chatting while they gathered around the table and watched Arthur write on a note pad: "Anton and 'Mr. Carter' are in Anton's van, parked down the road a bit."

"I guess it's time to start the movie," Lynx said. She walked over to her VCR and put in a John Wayne movie. Everyone sat around the T.V., as they'd agreed to do if Anton showed up, each person focused entirely on the movie, pushing aside all thoughts about what they'd been discussing until then.

When the movie was nearly over, Lynx got up and moved around the house, making beds for everyone to sleep in that night.

In the van, Anton and DK listened and concentrated with all their skills on picking up any thoughts coming from any of the people inside. All they could get was that each person was involved in the movie's plot.

"This is ridiculous," DK finally said. "No group like that could possibly care a hoot about a John Wayne movie, at least not enough to concentrate on it. Everyone must have already seen it, or one like it. The plot wouldn't challenge a mole."

"You're right," Anton replied. "They know we're here, and they're messing with us."

"How do they know that?"

"Look, DK, I have no idea. Somehow, however, they know something about us. I suspect it isn't much, but all it would take would be for that Nora Spotted Elk medicine woman to suspect I'm on a side opposite hers. She is one powerful woman, and so is her son, Harry. They have a great deal of influence on Lynx. We may as well leave, pull out of this entire scene for now, and come back another way."

"I refuse to admit defeat," DK hissed angrily. "We are more powerful than they. You know that. Has the Indian woman said anything specific to you that would make you think she knows something?"

"Yes. She told me to stay away from any romantic involvement with Lynx."

"Why would she say that?"

Anton had to be very cautious. He didn't want DK to know about the stolen videotapes. He didn't want DK to know that somehow Nora and Harry had sensed from the very beginning that he was on the opposite side from them.

"She is just very protective of Lynx."

"It has to be more than that, and you know it."

"Look, DK," Anton said. "Be realistic. As groups like ours increase in power and activity, you have to know that groups like theirs would become aware of us. After all, it's spiritual warfare that we are involved in here."

DK pondered a moment. "You're right. I miscalculated. I didn't count on their ability to put blocks on us, to know that we are able to contact their thoughts."

"Yes, I know you may have miscalculated. The fact is, though, that these are very sensitive people who would certainly feel our probing sooner and with more intensity than an average person. If they're on to us, all we can do is back off for now. If we stick around, they'll get us to come out, expose us somehow. Sure, we can stop them, and blood will be shed, but why call attention to ourselves at this crucial time?"

DK and Anton grew silent. Inside her cabin, Lynx shuddered. She was fully aware that Anton and DK were aware of their deliberate plan to divert them. She knew she could go inside their minds now and see what they were doing, but she didn't. It was too risky.

Nora kept praying. She was surrounding Lynx's cabin and all of the souls within it with the Go Away Spirit.

"I have a plan," DK said at last. "I have people in Colorado who could use you to edit some of their tapes. Never mind now what they're about. They need to learn some higher level video skills. You go down there and work with them. I'll find a way to get Lynx's material to you to edit before it goes to CNS for broadcasting. I cannot lose Yellowstone."

"What do I tell Lynx?"

"Tell her you've fallen in love with her and can't stand to see her with another man. That's half true anyway, isn't it?" DK looked darkly at Anton.

"Yes, I guess it is. I didn't mean for that to happen. Perhaps I can recommend one of your other people to help her."

"She's too smart for that. She would never trust anyone you sent her. I doubt if she'll hire any assistant now, unless it's someone she's known all her life. She's too stubborn. She'll learn all the technical things she needs to know and do it all herself. To win this battle, we must withdraw, re-group, and return when they least expect us, in a form they do not recognize. Now let's get going. To hell with them."

"Okay, then I'll be on my way to Colorado as soon as I pack."

"As soon as you pack. I'll take the car I rented here in town to the airport and fly out of here tomorrow. I'll call you when I return with exact instructions."

Anton started his van. Arthur Red Fox heard the engine start and nodded to the others. Nora smiled at him. It had worked. What would happen next, they didn't know. The lines were drawn. Each group knew the other knew. Fighting any thoughts of the battle at hand, all of Lynx's friends went quietly to bed.

Lynx went out on her front deck and watched the stars twinkle over the lake, praying silently that Anton would leave and she would have the peace she so longed for.

• • •

When DK returned to the motel, he sensed that Goldie was awake but pretending to sleep. He quietly unlocked her padlocks and set her free. She sat up, pretended to yawn as if nothing had happened, and walked to the bathroom. He was waiting for her outside the door with one of the chains in his hands. He threw it around her neck and pulled it taut, laughing as her body writhed and struggled for air, sneering coldly into her bulging, terror-filled eyes.

He stuffed her body into his suit carrier and hauled her down the back staircase. He threw her in the trunk of the car and drove to Anton's. Then he tossed her into Anton's R.V. Anton would be surprised, but he would know the best place to dump a body. At least all that time he'd spent getting to know this wild country wouldn't be wasted.

Chapter Forty One

Lynx got up from the chair on her deck and went inside the cabin. All was peaceful. She knew not everyone was asleep because it was too quiet. She went to the bottom of the stairway and listened. Nora and Harry were whispering to one another upstairs. Merlin was snoring in the room next to them, so he was okay. He'd fallen asleep not long after dinner, and she was pretty sure he had no idea what they'd talked about. She could see Yurt on the couch, his back to her, breathing deeply as if he were concentrating on relaxing. Arthur was on a cot near the back door, staring at the ceiling. Mullein was somewhere outside, taking the first watch. The men had agreed to take three-hour turns sitting outside throughout the night.

Dewey was in the downstairs guest room next to Lynx's bedroom. Lynx tiptoed over and opened her door a crack. She was sitting on the edge of the bed, her head bowed, praying. She looked up at Lynx and smiled, beckoning her to come in.

"Not now, Dewey," Lynx whispered. "I'm checking on everyone, waiting for Mullein's watch to be over." Dewey nodded to her and bent her head again.

Lynx grabbed a sleeping bag and pillow out of her closet, took her .38 Special out of her purse, and went back to the front deck. She listened to the sounds of the night: two horned owls were conversing. She remembered a neighbor had said they spent the entire winter there. She heard a truck change gears far off in the distance and the aspen trees near the cabin rustle in the soft wind.

Anton and DK could have driven all the way back to West, or could be nearby, parked in a driveway. Most of her neighbors had left the area for the winter. The closest occupied cabin was over a half mile away. Lynx called Anton and Mr. Carter's faces to mind in the most vivid detail she could muster. "Two can play this game," she thought. She saw Carter's eyes vibrant with hate, a sick, ugly smile on his face, and suddenly his wife's face leapt into her mind. It was swollen, blue, dead. Lynx began to shiver. Was this real? She focused on her again, seeing the same face. Then Anton's face came into her vision, looking tired and angry, sitting at the table in his trailer. Lynx felt they were both back in town, and that Carter had hurt, maybe even murdered, his so-called wife.

They'd all promised to cease any conversation or thoughts about the events that had led them to their meeting that night, if it turned out that Anton and Carter showed up there. Well, they came, just as Harry and Nora had said they would. The plan was that if this happened, the group would think as little as possible about them until they met again the following weekend. They would gather at a campground in south-central Montana, at a lower elevation than Yellowstone, warmer and snow-free.

Lynx felt the chilly air and made a mental note to arrange for her winter wood supply. Winter was imminent in West Yellowstone and Island Park. Any day now, the first serious snowstorm was expected, closing the park until snowmobile season, closing the backcountry trails all around the area until spring.

Feeling a little guilty that she had "cheated" by thinking about Anton and Carter, Lynx resolved to turn her thoughts to other things. She thought of her trip to Disneyland, scheduled soon after they returned from the camping trip. She thought of what it would be like to make love to Mullein again and fell into a deep sleep, a smile on her face.

Mullein went inside the cabin and woke up Arthur. He told him he'd walked all around the cabin and up and down the road and had seen nothing. Arthur went outside, and Mullein went out to the front deck to awaken Lynx and take her to bed. She seemed so exhausted that he didn't make her undress. He took off her shoes, helped her crawl under the covers, laid down next to her, and waited until she was in a deep sleep again before falling asleep himself.

· · ·

Revitalized from the power he'd felt choking Goldie to death, DK scurried around the motel room, packing all his and Goldie's things. Sure, they would retreat for now, and he would learn from his mistakes. It was better to work from afar. Close personal contact with people he was trying to use was not a good idea, apparently.

DK drew a bath and put three drops of his favorite essential oil, an extract from the sex glands of a musk ox, into the hot water. The raw animal smell swirled around him. He closed his eyes and brought before him the image of Merlin as he had seen him that day at Ursus. "Such an innocent, loving little boy," he thought. "How heartbreaking it would be for Lynx if he were to turn into a little monster."

He called to mind the children Merlin was hanging out with, focusing in particular on a dark-haired boy who was a year or two older than Merlin. He'd picked up immediately that that boy was vulnerable, highly programmable, and already interested in Satan's power, which he was learning about through listening to heavy metal music. He brought this boy into his mind so clearly that he was able to know his name—Roger.

"Roger, Roger," DK hissed over and over again, keeping the image of the boy before him, his eyes wide open.

DK left his own body soaking in the tub and was instantly inside Roger's mind and body. The boy was sleeping peacefully in his small bedroom just four blocks from DK's motel room.

DK searched Roger's mind and saw that Roger was having trouble with his parents. He pushed further and saw the essence of that trouble. Roger's father was a Presbyterian minister, his mother a computer specialist. The father wanted the mother to stay home and take care of the children; the mother wanted to pursue her career. They fought all the time. Roger was the eldest, and he hated the fighting. His brothers and sisters demanded that he make the parents stop, and he couldn't. If only his father would lighten up, quit being a minister, and get a job that pays a lot more money. It was embarrassing having a father for a minister, especially when you weren't even sure there was a God. Roger wanted to run away and become a heavy metal guitar player. But his parents said heavy metal is evil. He wasn't allowed to play it, let alone listen to it. Roger had a stash of forbidden music under his bed. He played along with it when his parents weren't home, and had made his siblings promise not to tell his parents about it. Roger was in the throes of becoming an adolescent, feeling persecuted by his parents and wanting nothing more than to be left alone.

DK pushed his way into the very center of Roger's soul and told him he need only give his soul to Satan, his father's major enemy, to become the most outstanding heavy metal guitarist that ever lived.

"Try it tomorrow when they leave, you will see. You will know. It will be easy for you," DK whispered, making himself look like the most evil, twisted, ugly devil he could.

Roger's nightmare began. The Devil appeared to him, holding an electric guitar in each hand. "Take this, Roger, and play with me," the Devil said. He handed a guitar over and began to play the most intense music Roger had ever heard. "Come," the Devil said, "play with me." And Roger did. He played as well as the Devil, as long and as loud and as crazy.

The music was so loud that Roger wanted to stop it. "Quiet down, it's too loud, it hurts my ears," he told the Devil.

The Devil played louder. Roger began to scream. He woke himself up, covered with sweat, shaking, afraid yet exhilarated. He reviewed the dream. It was scary, but what if he could play like that?

"Roger, are you all right?" he heard his mother whisper. She was standing in his doorway.

"Yes, Mom, I'm fine. I had a bad dream," he told her.

"Okay, honey, just go back to sleep then. Say a prayer first," she said, wondering why his voice sounded so deep and calm. He was growing up, she guessed.

Roger heard the change in the sound of his voice, too. He felt strong and powerful. He couldn't wait until after school the next day, when he would have two hours alone in the house to play the music the Devil had taught him. He thought of Merlin, who'd told him yesterday he wanted to start playing the guitar, too, and was thinking about taking lessons from his dad. Maybe he would have Merlin over. He could teach him more than his father could. That folksy stuff Lou played was for pussies.

DK was back in his body, laughing. "Unless ye be like little children," he chanted, "ye shall not enter the kingdom of heaven."

He lathered his hard body with musk-scented soap. "Ah, yes," he said, "like little children. I guess that leaves you boys out, Merlin and Roger." And he laughed so deeply that his body made waves in the water, and the tub overflowed onto the floor.

Chapter Forty Two

It was perfect fall weather on the plains of Montana. The air was pure and crisp, the sky brimming with stars. The cottonwood trees were golden even in the moonlight. The world was so quiet that the tiny creek near the camp could be heard for miles babbling its way to the Little Bighorn River, which seemed to be roaring to it to "hurry up, let's go."

Lynx and Mullein crawled out of their teepee hours before sunrise and drove the short distance to the Little Bighorn Battlefield National Monument. Mullein was a Sioux Wars enthusiast, and the battlefield where Custer made his famous "last stand" was a sacred place to him. He wanted to be there when the sun came up that morning. The night before, one of the rangers had given Mullein, a regular visitor he knew well, a key to the gate. They opened it quietly and walked to the top of a hill that overlooks the entire battlefield. They spread out on wool blankets and watched the stars.

"Look, Orion," Lynx said, pointing to the constellation shaped like an ancient hunter.

Mullein located the constellation right away. "Funny you should point that one out. I just finished reading a book about it. Well, it wasn't on Orion per se, it was on a star system that is supposed to exist somewhere in his belt." Mullein pointed to Orion's belt.

"I don't see it," Lynx joked.

"The book is written by a woman who says she spent a few years talking with a man who said he came from there. Supposedly he and a group of 12 arrived on Earth in a spaceship some 20 years ago and took human forms to observe what's going on here."

"What do they look like when they aren't in human bodies?" Lynx asked, giggling.

"Balls of light. I think the book was a little offbeat. It's not the kind of stuff I usually read, by it was given me by someone I respect, and it made an interesting point."

"That being?"

"The Orionids, as they call themselves, were appalled by the astounding number of conflicts that exist on earth. They were shocked that so many families are broken up, the divorce rate is so high, that there are so many religions on Earth yet so much immorality."

"Apparently their society is peaceful and harmonious."

"Oh, yes, and they say it's been that way since the beginning, that it is the nature of Orionids to be peaceful."

"So how are they doing here on Earth with all our problems?"

"They say they're on a mission to spread peace and goodwill but that they are failing at it because they say Earth people basically thrive on conflict. They say there are too many people on Earth who are dedicated to evil and too few to stop them. It's pretty pessimistic, but you know if you think about it, it seems that there are a great many people who seek out conflict, who enjoy it more than they do joy and harmony."

"What are the Orionids going to do about it?"

"They are starting to speak out in books like the one I read. The main Orionid in this book says Earthlings should look at the systems they have created that, if followed, would end all the evil and conflict. Christianity, and so on. It wasn't saying anything new, it's just that it comes from outer space."

"Do you think there are really Orionids?" Lynx asked.

"I like to believe there are other beings out there, doing a better job than we, but I don't know. I've never met one, that I know of anyway."

"That you know of . . . well, I don't know if there are or not, but I don't think that any other species but our own is going to save us. I think its pipedreaming to fantasize that we'll be saved by anything other than what we've been promised we'll be saved by."

"Which is?" Mullein reached over and tool Lynx's hand.

"By God. He sent his only Son to us, who died for us and saved us. That was the promise, and Jesus continues to forgive us if we ask for forgiveness and have some kind of commitment to do better each time we mess up."

"And how about all those people who don't believe in Jesus?"

"Oh, He saved them, too. If they lead good lives within the context of their belief systems, they'll be okay."

"What if they believe they should worship Orionids?" Mullein squeezed her hand and laughed.

"If Orionids are good, then anyone who worships them will be saved, as long as they didn't reject God to serve Orionids."

"What is good, Lynx?"

"Oh, Mullein, you sound like Merlin! Good is good. It's simple, the natural instinct or drive to love one another, to do onto others as we want done to us. It's not difficult."

"What if someone believes it's good to kill another person, or steal from the rich, or rob banks?"

"No one in his right mind would justify those things as good. They go against the natural order. Look what happens to societies when these things are the norm, go unpunished, are rampant, and so on. You've got to be kidding me, right?"

"Yeah, I'm jokin' you. You're fun to pseudo argue with. But take a look at this battleground—burial ground, I should say. The Cavalry thought it was doing good, trying to wipe out the Indians."

"Yes, and look what happened to them. The Indians wiped them out."

"So were the Indians right?"

"Yes. It was a just action, I think. And you know the Indian people lost, lost their land, the sacred Black Hills, much of their culture; their very lives were turned inside out. Custer had it coming; that bumper sticker at the gift shop is correct."

"Well, only God knows that."

"Mullein, that is true. I shouldn't have said that, but I feel that God agrees with me!"

Mullein laughed. "Anyway. I've been thinking a lot about the Orionids in relation to our present situation."

"How so?"

"It's like these people, whoever Anton and his buddy Mr. Carter are, are trying to mess up the entire world, and we are Orionids, trying to make peace."

"I know what you're saying. It's almost supernatural, the way all of us have been more or less thrown together. We've become spiritual warriors, in a sense. We know that Satanism is real, and it's not just some adolescent fad. So many other people are living as if nothing is happening, acting as if the world isn't getting more and more filled with evil. They have no idea."

"Lynx, along that train of thought I ask you, who would believe us if we told them what was going on?"

"I don't know, Mullein, and that scares me. I don't think many people would. Yet I wonder what damage Anton and his people are doing in the world, if perhaps they are the cause of more evil, more unhappiness, than even we can imagine."

"The book I've been telling you about speaks of the end times for the earth, says that in 2,000 AD, the earth as we know it will be demolished by the forces we created with our own evil."

"Oh, Mullein, I have a problem with all that end time stuff."

"Why do you think it's being discussed so much now then?"

"Because it's the end of the millennium, because some people interpret Biblical and other prophets as having said the world will end 2,000 years after the birth of Christ, or thereabouts."

"I see that argument, but I also see the signs of the end times. An increase in evil, immorality, abortion, famine, pestilence, like AIDS, destructive earth events like the fires, earthquakes, hurricanes, the ozone layer disappearing, and on and on."

"Perhaps we're creating our own reality, reading books that say the world is ending, so making it happen. I don't know. All I know is that I want to end my relationship with Anton and go on with my business."

"Lynx, I'm stalling you, in a sense. You see, there's something I want to tell you, plain and simple but painful."

Lynx took a deep breath. "I'm ready, spit it out."

"I knew the moment I met you that you were special, different, a major leaguer. You're under attack, Lynx. It was no coincidence that all this has happened. You'll get rid of Anton, but you won't get rid of the evil. It will challenge you, provoke you, try to destroy you, and all your wonderful friends."

"You included?"

"Yes, me included. That's why we're here, to stick together, all of us. We're mystic warriors, darling. We have to focus on strengthening our bonds with one another, attracting more people like us, and just being who we are. That should be enough."

"Mullein, I love you."

"Lynx, I love you so much." He leaned over and kissed her.

The sun was coming up, lighting up the gravestones spread over the battleground. A feisty meadowlark sang a greeting to the new day.

"We have to get going, Mullein," Lynx said. "The others will be up and waiting for us." She stood up and reached out for his arms. He looked up at her and grinned. The sun made a golden halo around her hair, which was a mess with dew and grass in it. She was beautiful. He let her try to pull him up, and then tugged at her once, so she fell into his arms.

He held her very close. "Lynx, I want to marry you, soon. I want to be with you forever. You need me, and I need you. This world is too crazy for either of us to navigate alone. Let's do it, please."

"God, Mullein, I want to marry you, too. I know it's the right thing to do." She ran her hands through his hair, smoothing out his tangles.

"Well then, when?" he asked her.

"And how?"

"In the Church, with a priest. We need a spiritually-based marriage, blessed in a public ceremony. It's what we both want, and you can do it. Your marriage to Lou was civil, right, so the church doesn't even recognize it?"

"No, the Church doesn't recognize civil unions. I can marry you in the Church."

"Well, then when we get back, we'll go to a priest and see how to go about it. Okay?"

Lynx took a deep breath. Her heart was pounding. Was it fear or excitement, or both? She was sure about Mullein, she knew that. And he was right, she needed him. Life would be too hard without him.

"And what about Merlin?" she asked.

"What about Merlin?" he answered. "I love the kid. He digs me. We'll get along. I promise."

Lynx knew Merlin wouldn't object to her marrying Mullein. She wondered how he was doing back in West Yellowstone, spending the weekend at his good buddy Roger's. Suddenly a chill ran down her spine, and she felt he wasn't safe. She dismissed the feeling as motherly over-protectiveness, but decided to call him as soon as she was near a phone.

She took another breath. "Okay, we'll see a priest. We'll do it. Now kiss me!"

He kissed her, and they left the battlefield, where the dead lay in peace, to another battleground where the living were in complete combat mode.

Chapter Forty Three

Camp was hopping when Lynx and Mullein arrived. Nora and Dewey had coffee brewing on a portable gas stove, but no food was being prepared. They'd all fasted to prepare for the sweat.

Lynx and Mullein helped Harry and Yurt pile firewood near the sweatlodge, and Arthur placed the sweatlodge rocks on a pile of hot coals. Patsy explained the role of lodge protector to Pete. They had asked if they could come along when Lynx told them they were having a last camp before winter.

When the group met at Lynx's Island Park cabin after the Ursus opening, people had little time to discuss Anton in detail before they discovered that Anton and DK were nearby.

Arthur reported to them what he'd learned from Bonzo. Yurt confirmed that his New Age expert friend had said there were all kinds of Satanic cults operating in the world, performing rituals like Yurt had seen in the Centennials. He said the groups had varying degrees and levels of power and influence.

The main points they'd touched on were that Light and the Arcane Seminary were the oldest and most powerful groups that investigators had so far discovered, and its workers possessed highly developed abilities to probe anyone's minds they wanted to know about. In addition to probing minds, they could program individuals and groups to direct their activities to serve their evil purposes and could even surround individuals and groups with numbness to the existence of Satanism. People who have fluctuating moral values and no consistent sense of right or wrong who are most influenced by programming.

According to Yurt's source, strong-minded people are attacked because they are in positions of spiritual, economic, and social power the Satanists want to corrupt or destroy. The programmers rarely make these people go against their highly developed moral standards, but they may make them physically ill or put weaker people they love or serve in crisis. This makes it more difficult for the stronger people to stay focused.

Yurt said his source told him that Satanists are behind most of the world's most powerful illegal drug trafficking operations. The abuse of drugs has negative impacts on every level of society. It destroys children, rips families apart, and costs society billions of dollars.

Once everyone let these facts sink in, the group realized that they were being attacked because they were strong-minded people trying to lead lives with purpose and positive goals. They focused on how to repel probing from Anton and his group. They agreed that for now it would be best to discuss the situation only when they were together in a safe place, and that Lynx's home was not safe. They figured that Anton and Mr. Carter were aware that they were there together and may even come to Lynx's house. They decided that until they could do more research on the reality of probing, they would clear their minds of any thoughts of the current problem whenever they figured Anton or one of his people was about.

Then they made the camping plans. They would travel there in pairs: Nora and Harry, Dewey and Yurt, Pete and Patsy, and Mullein and Lynx, and watch out for any indication that they were being followed.

Then something splendid happened during the week before camp. Anton told Lynx he was leaving West Yellowstone.

Nora opened the sweat council with a prayer for help and of thanksgiving, and asked that all pray silently before they began their discussion.

Lynx wandered off to her last conversation with Anton in her living room just four days ago. He'd brought her his copies of the edits of her fire tapes. She and Dewey were sitting on the floor, folding laundry together.

"Lynx, I regret we never watched these together. I did a lot of work on them. I think they'll turn into a good piece."

"Well," Lynx said, working to push aside all thoughts of the meeting at her cabin, "I have my own copies, remember?" She forced herself to sound amiable. "We could watch them tonight, I guess. Dewey here may want to join us." She looked at Dewey, who was watching Anton intently.

"By all means," Dewey told him. "I never went into the park the entire time it was burning. I may enjoy the tapes."

Anton looked at Dewey. "You can watch them with Lynx, of course. But I won't be here. I'm giving her these copies because I won't be working with them again. Would you mind if Lynx and I left you alone for a few minutes? I have something to say to her in private."

Dewey was great, Lynx recalled. She didn't miss a beat, although later she told Lynx she'd felt very scared to leave them alone together.

"Go ahead and talk," Dewey said. "I'll get this done in no time, Lynx."

They went downstairs to Lynx's basement, which had a large wood furnace surrounded by old furniture. In cold weather, she and her friends often hung out there, stoking up the stove and chatting while it reached a high enough temperature to heat the house. He sat on the couch and motioned her to sit next to him. She ignored his gesture and plopped down on a chair across from him.

"Lynx, I'm leaving town. I won't be coming back, so I won't be helping you with your project."

Lynx felt the dark cloud that had been hanging over her entire being lift. But this was too good to be true. There had to be a catch. She put a concerned look on her face and asked him, "Is it because you're upset that I haven't watched your edit yet, Anton? I just really needed a rest."

"No, I understand your need to take a break. A more lucrative opportunity has come up for me, one in which I'll be my own boss."

"Want to tell me about it?"

"It's not important. It's just another video project."

"Anton, you don't sound too excited about it."

"Lynx. I'm not. I wanted to work with you. But you see I had to look for something else," he lied, "because I discovered it would be impossible for us to work together."

"Why is that?" Lynx asked, thrilled he felt that way but curious about why.

"I've fallen in love with you, and you love another man."

Lynx shuddered impulsively.

Anton saw how repulsed she was and wanted to hit her. "It just wouldn't work out for us to work together now. I never meant to fall in love with you, but I find it impossible to work with you given the attraction I feel for you and your unavailability."

That was that. Lynx wasn't sure whether to believe him, but at least he was leaving. And to think she'd almost felt attracted to him. It must have been that he was programming her to want him, knowing her weakness is sexual areas. She kept an understanding smile on her face and told him, "Anton, I'm sorry. I do love Mullein deeply. I knew him long before I met you, and I reckon someday we'll decide to get married." She regretted saying that as soon as it came out of her mouth.

"Marriage?" Anton asked, an angry look passing over his face. "I didn't think you were the marrying kind anymore."

"I guess we all change," Lynx said. She stood up and started for the stairs.

Anton followed her, and she walked him to the door and shook his hand. "Thanks for all your help," she forced herself to say.

"Perhaps we'll meet again. In any case, I look forward to seeing your work on television." He hugged her and kissed her cheek. She felt like vomiting.

Anton left the next day. The day after that, a moving company came to town and hauled his trailer away.

• • •

Lynx began to pray, thanking God for removing Anton from her life, asking him for guidance when the council began.

Outside, Pete walked slowly around the lodge, praying for protection as he smudged the lodge with burning sweetgrass. He sat down near the doorway and stoked the fire. Suddenly, his mind filled with a very clear picture of Merlin. Merlin had a horribly frightened look on his face, one Pete had never seen. Pete wondered if he should go inside and tell Lynx that Merlin may be in trouble. But he didn't trust his first instinct. He had never had a vision like that before. He put it out of his mind and got up and walked around the lodge again.

Nora opened the discussion. "Anton has left West Yellowstone, and we have to consider the possibility that he has been defeated for now. We also have to be aware that he may be back in some form or another. At this point, I think we should think about why we were selected by Anton and his group and what it means to our own development, individually and as a group."

Harry spoke next. "In our last regional Sweetgrass council, we heard story after story from all the medicine people that they were having difficulty in their work. I think that it is a reality we have to face. We aren't just people dedicated to healing the earth and its people—we're mystic warriors; we have enemies of a spiritual nature."

Arthur responded. "And we have to face the fact that we have been thrown together to protect one another, to give one another encouragement whenever possible."

"We have to really listen to what Yurt's friend said," Lynx added. "Satanism is a real force in the world. Satanists attack people like us, and they attack the weaker, undeveloped souls in our lives." She suddenly thought of Merlin.

Dewey picked up on Lynx's thought. "Yes," she said softly. "The weaker souls, including our children. We have to give a great deal of attention to making Merlin and the other children we are in charge of strong and at peace."

"What can we do that we aren't doing?" Mullein wondered.

"For one, Lynx needs as much support as we can give her in her new work," Arthur said.

"I'd like to help you with that," Yurt told Lynx. "I've been thinking for awhile that I'd like to get out of guiding and into some kind of media work. I can help you, if you're willing to teach me. I know a lot about Yellowstone, and I know how to use a camera. I'm sort of creative."

"And you're strong," Lynx said, laughing. "You would come in handy toting equipment around, and I could teach you how to edit."

"So could I," Arthur noted. "We three can get together back in West Yellowstone and figure out how to go about this."

"Nora and Harry and I can help a great deal with our prayers," Dewey said. "In fact, we all need to pray together, if not physically, then in spirit."

"I'm wondering if we should expand this group, and if we could tell other people what we're going through," Mullein offered.

"I think that groups such as ours expand on their own. As we grow stronger, we'll attract people to us. I think it's best to not discuss the crisis we are in with anyone unless it's with someone who comes to us that we feel is a seeker like us," Nora said.

"I agree," Lynx replied. "Look how we formed."

"Lynx, I've been thinking about that a great deal lately. You realize that you've been the pivot, the center of this group." Dewey said. "You met me and Nora through your grandmother, then introduced us to one another." Dewey reached over and took Nora's hand. "Nora has become one of the most precious people in my life. Through Nora we have Harry and all their relatives, and through you we have Mullein, Yurt, Pete, and Patsy."

"And your work is actively seeking to teach people about the beauty of creation manifested in Yellowstone," Nora added.

"You're making me squirm, folks," Lynx said. "I don't think of myself as a pivot. And if that's true, look at the trouble I've brought upon us, through Anton and who knows who else."

"Think of it not as trouble but as a challenge, a way we can grow, as in Hebrews, 'Encourage each other while it is still today,'" Nora said.

"Lynx," Patsy said, "I think you have to accept that you're a pivot. You certainly have been in my life and in Pete's. I used to think there wasn't a God, think that life had no purpose. Now, so many wonderful things have happened to me because you've shown me how richer life is when a person has a spiritual focus."

Lynx looked at all her friends and smiled gratefully. "I appreciate and value all your love," she told them. "I'm thinking about a few things we need to focus on now. First, I accept all your help and feel very energized by it. I'm ready to begin my new work. Second, I'd like to think about how to strengthen the children in our group, and third, I'd like to talk a little more about the concept of being mystical warriors simply by being stronger spiritually."

The group decided to hold a get together soon with all the children and to pray at set times for protection and strength. They also discussed the use of weapons. Nearly everyone in the group owned at least one handgun and a rifle because they all either hunted or used to hunt. They knew that Anton possessed an arsenal and assumed he would use his weapons against people if he thought it was necessary. The Mystic Warriors agreed they preferred to use prayer to battle the evil Anton represented, but they also agreed that they would defend themselves against anyone who used weapons against them. They concurred, however, that they would not discuss the use of weapons in front of the children.

When their council was over, it seemed to everyone that the world was bright again. They spent the rest of the day and all of the next hunting and fishing in the Big Horn Mountains in Wyoming. By Sunday evening, Mullein and Harry had each bagged a deer, and all had caught at least one trout in the Tongue River.

They broke camp and caravaned to the Big Horn Medicine Wheel to pray and leave offerings of thanksgiving to the Great Spirit. The Medicine Wheel sits on top of a ridge that overviews miles and miles of mountains and plains. As long as Indians remember, it has been a sacred place of prayer, but archaeologists aren't certain when it was built.

The wheel is surrounded by an iron fence, and barbed wire is installed over the fence to keep people from climbing over it. Only Indians holding ceremonies are allowed inside. Indians and people of all races and nationalities visit the Medicine Wheel and hang offerings on the fence and barbed wire: colorful clap clothes, herb bundles, feathers, flowers, photographs of people who need help, even crosses and rosary beads.

The Mystic Warriors were surprised to see a group of people sitting in a circle near the Medicine Wheel's center cairn. Nora signaled that they should draw back and stop for a moment. Everyone surrounded her.

"As far as I know," she told them, "there isn't any special ceremony scheduled here now. We should be careful when we approach the Medicine Wheel. Perhaps those people aren't supposed to be here."

"You mean they may have broken in?" Harry asked.

"Let's see," his mother replied. Just then someone in the circle stood up, opened the gate, and walked over to them.

As the person came closer, Nora grinned from ear to ear. "Why, Father Victor, how are you? We're surprised to see you here."

Father Victor was a short, stocky, bald Italian Catholic priest from northern Montana. He was 84 years old and, like Nora, his vitality made him appear much younger than his age.

He was a Marianist, a person who is committed to devotions to Mary, Jesus' mother. He traveled all over the Rocky Mountains to talk to small communities about Mary and the favorite prayer of Marianists, the rosary.

Father Victor visited places all over the world where Mary is believed to be appearing either to individual mystics or entire groups of people. He then relayed Mary's messages to the communities he visited.

Nora once accompanied him to a church in Scottsdale, Arizona, where a woman claimed to be having weekly visitations from Our Lady. The messages she gave that woman were the same given at the other apparition sites. Mary told people to pray, fast, and reform their lives. She warned that a time of great chastisement is near in which natural disasters will wipe out large numbers of people. The faithful who devote their lives to her Son will be spared, Mary promised. Mary also urged people to pray the rosary and meditate on each of the 15 mysteries of the life of Christ that the rosary honors. The rosary, she promised, was a way to soften hearts hardened by sin and corruption.

Father Victor hugged Nora and shook everyone's hand as she introduced him to them. "What a blessing to see you," he told them all.

"Good to see you as well. What are you doing here, Father?" Nora asked.

"I'm here praying with a young woman from Hardin, Montana. Her name is Salinda Pretty Weasel. Some of her close friends are also here with us. Salinda comes here often to pray and usually comes alone. Most people her age don't bother to pray, as you know."

"Yes, we know," Nora said sadly.

"Last week when Salinda was here, she says she had a vision of the Blessed Mother. She said she was praying over there, by those rocks, looking into the center of the wheel. And Mary suddenly appeared right there in the middle." Father Victor pointed to both spots.

"When we came up here today, the gate was open, so we went inside and formed a circle around the spot. I feel it's right for us to be there, and since most of the people we are with are Native Americans, we aren't violating any rule, strictly speaking."

"Do you think she really saw Mary?" Lynx asked.

"Salinda is a very devout, very stable woman," Father Victor replied. "She is a Marianist, but not the kind that thinks a person has to have an actual vision of Mary or anyone or anything else to have faith. Her faith is strong without proof. I think she did have a vision, and I think it was given her by God."

Lynx looked thoughtful. "I can accept that."

"Why are you here, my child?" he asked her.

Dewey answered. "We've been camping together to get a sense of who we are as a group and what we have to do. We have all been under intense spiritual attack. Lynx here more than the rest of us."

Father Victor raised his eyebrows.

Mullein explained. "A Satanic cult has sent at least one person we know of to West Yellowstone to do damage to people who come to Yellowstone to enjoy nature and renew themselves. It's a long, long story, Father."

The priest laughed. "And one I hear more and more these days."

Patsy touched his arm. "Are you serious?"

"Most serious. These groups are getting stronger, and they are giving us all quite a run for our money, aren't they?" Father Victor's voice was sad.

"And so we felt we should get stronger and closer as a group so we can deal with this better, Father," Dewey said.

"Yes, and now we're on our way home and stopped here to pray a bit before we separate. We're not all going the same way, and it may be a while before we meet together alone. The next time we get together, we'll have children with us," Yurt told him.

"My children, it is no coincidence that we all ran into one another here, I think," Father Victor told the group. "Come, join us in the Medicine Wheel."

Father led them into the center of the wheel and introduced them to Salinda and her four friends, all women in their late 30's. They all appeared to be very down to earth. Salinda was tall and thin with short, black hair. She said she was a nurse at the hospital in Hardin. She had four children and a husband who worked on the state road crew. One of her friends owned a small cafe, the other managed a gift shop, and the third was a full-time housewife with six children. They attended the same church and met every morning to say the rosary together. Salinda explained that she often comes alone to the Medicine Wheel to pray before hiking in the mountains, to renew herself.

Her job, she said, could sometimes be rather stressful. She pointed to where she'd been sitting, just to the left of the gate, when she saw Mary in the center of the wheel.

"I was spellbound. I blinked. I closed my eyes. I opened them again. Next thing I knew, I was on my knees, overwhelmed with a feeling of peace and joy like I never felt before, not even when my children were born. It was supernatural. Mary was dressed like she is in most of the pictures you see, in a long white dress, blue shawl, long reddish hair, glowing but not transparent like a ghost. She looked more like a marble statue lit from within. And she didn't leave. She spoke to me."

Lynx listened intently to Salinda and knew in her heart that Salinda had experienced exactly what she said she had. "What did she say to you?" she asked her.

"First understand I didn't hear a voice like I hear you. I didn't see her mouth move, either. I heard the words in my head."

"Everyone nodded that they understood. "You had a locution, then," Nora said.

"That's what Father called it," Salinda replied.

Mary didn't tell me much of anything different than she's been telling the others she is appearing to, as far as I can see," Salinda said.

"And what would that be?" Mullein asked her.

"She said the time is short. She said her son is allowing her to manifest herself all over the world to say that the time is short. That people must turn back to God, that there will be great chastisements all over the earth and many people will suffer. The most personal message she gave me was related to my work."

"What was that?" Pete asked.

"She said abortion must stop. She said nurses and other health care workers must refuse to help doctors who perform abortions of every type because it is murder. She said the killing of the unborn has made the United States a center of evil, and our country will suffer greatly because of it."

"Tell that to the politicians," Mullein said.

Salinda nodded. "I know, or to the feminists and the pro-choicers! Actually, I do know people I can talk with about this, believe me. There are doctors around performing abortions."

Nora nodded sympathetically. "This must be a great burden to you."

"Yes, because I feel hopeless about giving this message to the people who seem to need it the most. They won't listen."

"We need to pray more, especially for faith," Father Victor interjected. "Tell them the rest of the message, child."

"Mary said the time is nearing when her son will return to the earth, and He wants as many people as possible to know Him. But people don't have relationships with Him as they should. For example, she said people who believe in abortion go to church and receive Holy Communion, yet abortion is a mortal sin. She said Jesus is ready to forgive all sinners, but first people have to know they've sinned and ask for forgiveness. Mary said the chastisements are needed to give people the opportunity to turn to God in their suffering. They will be so great that the only thing left for some people will be to turn to Jesus. And she said not everyone will do this. Those people will never know God."

"Did she say anything specific about why she was with you?" Lynx wanted to know.

"Yes. She said that I must pray more than I do for the Indian people to have the strength to unite and pray more. And she said that the Evil One is everywhere, even in the most beautiful places the Creator has given us."

Lynx looked at Mullein and nodded.

Salinda went on. "And she told me to stay as close to my children as possible and to help all my friends with children to do this as well, as children are under great attack. She said to do all I can to get the children to pray."

"Wow. It's quite interesting how we have been having very similar experiences," Harry told her.

"Yes, we have," Nora added. "And we've been trying to avoid dealing with this in the context of what I call Millennium Madness. That is, although we may feel it is getting near the end of the world as we know it, we shouldn't be ruled by an obsession with knowing exactly when that will happen. That is not for us to know."

"Right," Dewey added, "we are concentrating on being strong warriors when needed."

"That's part of what Mary is saying, too, and I think you people should keep in touch," Father Victor said, smiling. "Now, let's pray. Let's say a rosary together in thanksgiving for the blessings given us and in petition for strength and increased faith."

The group formed a new circle, each person sitting cross-legged on blankets they placed on the ground. Halfway through the rosary, Salinda suddenly knelt down and stared unblinking at the center of the circle. Her face appeared to be lit by an intense source of light, but no one in the group could see that source. Father Victor, who had witnessed other people having apparitions of Mary, angels, and saints, whispered, "She is seeing Mary. I'm sure of it. Continue to pray."

Each person in the circle felt a wide range of emotions, from fear to awe to peace and gratitude. There was no doubt as they continued reciting the prayers of the rosary that Salinda was in a state of intense ecstasy. She continued to gaze at the vision in the center of the circle without blinking or moving until the rosary was over. Then she fell to the ground. Father Victor put his hands on her head and said a silent prayer for her.

In a few minutes, she was able to sit up and talk to the group. "It was Mary again," she told them.

"We know," Father Victor said. "No one else saw her, but I think we all believe you." Everyone nodded.

"I don't know why she has chosen to appear to me," Salinda said. "And I am grateful but very, very scared. She said the same things she said before, but she said she is pleased that there are more people here, and she encouraged us to form a prayer group. She said that anyone here with grave concerns about their children should have faith, because those children are being given special blessings. I must tell you all, however, that Mary emphasized that her appearances to me are private. She said they are not something she wants us to share with the entire world."

"We've been greatly blessed," Father Victor said. "This is truly a holy day for all of us. I hope you all spend some time thanking God for this and seeing what you can do about what Mary said. But most important, just go on with your lives. Don't get too immersed in this experience. It is not meant to make you confused or even awed. It is meant to make you live most fully in the present. Enjoy yourselves." He looked at his watch. "We must go now. These gals have families to return to."

Outside the wheel, everyone, still a bit dazed from the experience, exchanged hugs, phone numbers, and addresses, and went to their vehicles for the long winding drive down the mountain.

At the foothills, Nora, Harry, Dewey, Yurt, and Arthur left the group and headed north toward Billings, where they planned to spend the night before going their separate ways. Lynx and Mullein and Pete and Patsy caravaned east to Cody, where they planned to meet at a good restaurant, eat, and then dance the night away at a county Western bar. They would spend the night in a motel there and head through Yellowstone Park to West Yellowstone.

• • •

Lynx always told herself that if she ever settled down with one man, he would have to love to dance. It was something she joked about, but the fact that Mullein was a great dancer was something she really appreciated, a real bonus. What delighted her and surprised her even more was that he could sing.

When they reached the dancing bar, Mullein grinned from ear to ear when he saw the band. It was the Lone Rangers, a country Western band from Boise, and he knew all the players. The lead guitarist and the fiddler-mandolinist had been his friends since childhood, and they were delighted to see him. When they asked him to sing a song during the next set, he agreed.

"I didn't know you could sing," Lynx told him, laughing. I thought you were talented, but this is beyond belief. What else can you do?"

"I can sing harmony with beautiful women," he answered. "Let's do one together. I know you sing well—I heard you at deer camp, remember?"

Lynx suddenly felt scared. She'd only sung in public with Lou. It was the only thing they'd been able to do easily together, the only memory of their relationship, other than the birth of Merlin, that she treasured. She swallowed hard and asked him what song he thought they could do together.

"How about an old cowboy song, one I know you know because it's on your Bob Wills C.D. The name is "My Life's Been a Pleasure."

"Oh, yes," Lynx said, "the Jesse Ashlock number."

"That's the one. The words kind of apply to us, and I hope they always will. Do we have to practice it?"

"Nah," Lynx told him. "Let's wing it. This crowd seems to be pretty tolerant, and they're all half loaded, anyway. Just ask the fiddler if I can borrow his mandolin. I like to play when I sing."

"Okay then, you sing the melody, and I'll harmonize."

When Lynx and Mullein started singing, the people stopped dancing to watch them. They were a striking couple. Lynx was wearing a straight denim skirt, slit deeply up the back for freedom in dancing, black leather cowboy boots, and a red silk Western shirt with fringe that cascaded off her breasts. Her long hair was curled softly and tied back with a silver barrette. Mullein was dressed in well fitting jeans, a white cowboy shirt, and a black leather vest. His straight black hair was tied back, too, and almost as long as Lynx's. Her Irish skin was white and soft; his Indian skin was tanned brown and hardened by work and the sun. She was tall and straight, taller than nearly everyone in the room, but he was even taller, by a good six inches. Their physical beauty and strength was complimented by their obvious love and respect for one another. Even if they were ugly and oddly matched physically, they would have stopped the hearts of those who saw them with the energy that flowed and vibrated between them.

Both had sung enough in public to deal with being stared at, but Lynx still felt a little queasy. This was the first time singing with Mullein. It would mean that she had gotten over her block of singing with anyone but Lou, a block she had wanted to overcome for a long time. It was stupid and unproductive, and it kept her tied to someone she no longer wanted to have any ties with, other than those associated with having to parent Merlin.

"I still love you as I did in yesterday,
Many years have gone by tho' it seems just like a day,
It's no wonder that I love you, you've been so kind and true,
There'll never be another—it will always be just you.
We've come a long way together, and you've proved your love is true,
My life's been a pleasure, and it's all because of you.
And to me you'll always be just as sweet as flowers in May,
And I'll still love you as I did in yesterday."

The people cheered and asked for another tune.
"Only if you dance this time," Mullein told them.
"Then make it a slow one," an old cowboy holding tightly to his sweet little wife hollered.
Lynx laughed. "Okay, we'll do a slow one. What do you want to hear?"
The cowboy looked at his wife. She whispered into his ear. "Will we ever be that old together?" Lynx wondered.
"The little woman wants to hear "Please Don't Leave Me," the cowboy said.
Lynx nodded. "We can do that," Mullein answered. The fiddler started the introduction, and the band played on as the dancers swung one another around the room.
When the song was over, Lynx and Mullein sat down and drank a cold one.
"Wouldn't it be great if life was always this easy?" Mullein asked her.
"Oh, yes, I'd like that," she told him. "But if it can't be, thank goodness we can have times like these. That was fun, singing together. I wasn't even that scared once we got going."
Pete and Patsy sat down with them, and Patsy leaned over and whis-

pered to Lynx. "You guys are great. Remember to call Merlin. You told me to remind you to call him and see how he's doing. Pete said he had a vision about Merlin outside our sweat yesterday. Ask him about it."

Lynx looked at Pete. "What vision did you have of Merlin?" she asked, starting to worry and wishing the peace she'd just felt with Mullein would linger a while longer.

"It was weird. I saw his face as clear as a bell, with a strangely terrified expression on it. That was all. I'm sure it doesn't mean a thing."

"Probably not," Lynx said. "But I'd better call him. In fact I had made a note to call him as soon as I found a phone, and then forgot to. I'm feeling really guilty about that, especially after all the commitments we've been making to be more aware of children. And I don't usually leave him with other people this long when I'm so far away from town."

Mullein looked concerned. "How could we be so stupid? We made a decision to be more thoughtful about kids, and then we forgot the kid."

Lynx felt sick to her stomach. She stood up to find a pay phone, and Mullein followed her.

Chapter Forty Four

Merlin was miserable. He wished his mother would call him. He wanted to go home. He hated being at Roger's house, although at first he'd had fun practicing guitar with him. He didn't like the heavy metal music Roger was into that much, but it was okay and easy to play along with. He much preferred softer rock and the stuff his parents played. Roger told him finger picking and country music was stupid, but Merlin liked it. The times he'd heard his parents play together were special, and now he liked to hear them separately, too.

Roger played music that made him feel sick, by bands he'd never heard of. He'd especially hated Deicide, a band Roger told him was dedicated to Satan. It even had a fan club Roger had joined, and membership required that you dedicate your soul to Satan. Their music was loud and discordant, and the songs had words Merlin knew would freak his mother out. There were songs like "Don't Tell Your Parents, But You're Sexual," "Let's Nail Jesus Everyday," and "Dedicated to the Devil."

Roger told him his father had thrown away his first Deicide CD, but he'd bought another one and hid it with the others under his bed. He said the woman who ran the music store in town would special order Deicide and any of the other heavy metal Satanic favorites and not tell parents about it. She was against the group that was trying to rate CD's and cassettes so kids under a certain age couldn't buy them. She was cool, Roger had told him, and had even told him who in town would deal pot to kids.

Merlin was having enough trouble dealing with Roger's music. The fact that Roger smoked pot and told him a lot of other kids their age did, too, really frightened him. He turned Roger down when he'd offered him a puff of his joint. Roger had mocked him for not smoking, and Merlin had become totally depressed.

To make matters worse, Roger had spent all of Sunday morning painting weird pictures of demons and monsters he said he was inspired to paint by the music. That started after he had a fight with his parents that had embarrassed Merlin. His parents had told him to get ready for church, and he had refused. They ended up in a shouting match, with Roger's father yelling at him that he had to obey him, and Roger yelling back that he was too old to be forced to go to church. Then Roger's mother had come in his room and begged him to go for her sake. He'd refused, and she'd cried. His father came back and said that if he chose to stay home, he would have to spend the rest of the day in his room.

"That was stupid," Merlin thought. "It's just what he wants." And so they'd listened to the music again as Roger painted and Merlin pretended to read one of his schoolbooks.

Roger's family, Merlin had discovered, was not the happy, well rounded family everyone in town assumed they were, with a minister at its head and a sweet, demure woman by his side. Merlin wanted his mom, or even his dad. They may be divorced and a little offbeat, but they were nice—and safe.

Then Roger threatened to beat the hell out of Merlin if he told about the music, the paintings, and the pot. He'd promised not to mention it to anyone, including his parents.

Merlin had made up his mind he would have to make it through the night and get up and go to school with Roger, no matter how badly he felt. He wasn't going to call Lou and have him come to his rescue. He would never live that down in front of Roger, it would upset Roger's parents, and his mother would worry about him too much. But if only she would call . . .

The phone rang, and Merlin heard Roger's mom talk to Lynx and then walk toward Roger's room to call him to the phone. God, she looked awful, Merlin thought, so tired and worn out. He wondered if he ever worried his mom that much.

"Hi, Mom," Merlin told Lynx cheerfully.

"Are you having fun; are you okay?" Lynx asked him.

"Yeah, it's okay here, but I miss you, Mom."

"I miss you, too, honey. We'll be home tomorrow by the time you're out of school though."

"Did you have a good weekend?"

"Oh, yes, and Mullein bagged a deer. He's giving it to us to eat this winter. Nice, huh?"

"He bagged a deer? Wow! Didn't you get one?"

"No, honey, I didn't want to spend the money on out-of-state tags. I just hunted with him. It was fun. We're dancing now, and we'll be going back to the motel in a half hour so we can get up early and get home."

"Okay, Mom, because you have to get us packed for Disneyland."

"No kidding. Just imagine. In less than a week, we'll be in California, where it will be hot and sunny and lots of fun."

"Yeah, I can't wait. See ya soon then, Mom. I love you."

"I love you, too." Lynx hung up. She felt strange. Merlin's voice was different. He wasn't feeling as joyful as he'd made himself sound. He was worrying about something. Oh, well, there wasn't a lot she could do about it now. She thought of calling Lou and having him run over and check on Merlin, but then Lou would tell her she shouldn't be away with another man so long, and they'd argue. It wasn't worth it. What could happen to Merlin between now and when they got back home? He was safe, with a good family. She was just a worrier. She looked at Mullein. He was watching her curiously, wondering why she was standing there with the phone hung up, deep in thought, looking at the floor.

"Are you in there?" he asked her.

"Oh, yes, I just worry about him too much."

"You're a mommy. He's fine. Remember what Mary said—our kids have been given a special blessing. Now let's dance the next set and get going to bed."

Lynx couldn't forget about him, though. She trusted her intuition, and there had to be something to what Pete felt. Lynx knew Merlin well enough to know he was worrying about something and had decided not to bother her with it. She said a prayer for his safety.

Keeping their commitment to stay celibate until they decided if they were going to remain committed to one another had been very difficult for both Mullein and Lynx. Now, after they'd agreed to marry, had a lovely weekend together, and were in the same motel room together, it was harder than ever. They took separate showers and climbed into separate beds. Still worrying about Merlin, Lynx wanted nothing but to crawl into bed with Mullein and ask him to hold her in his arms until she fell asleep. That would have to wait, though. They said their good nights and fell asleep, dreaming of what was to come.

Back in West Yellowstone Merlin slept fitfully. Roger was in the bunk bed over him, heavy metal blasting on his Walkman, turned up so loud Merlin could hear it all night.

Chapter Forty Five

Walt was restless. Bonzo said it would be a week, a week and a half, before he got back to him. It was over the time now, the 14th day since he'd called his Bozeman friend. He was enjoying himself with Juanita's family, but he wanted to get going. He was sure by now TDP hadn't been able to track him, but he was still looking over his shoulder nervously.

Juanita's family was religious but tough. Her son, Miguel, had six brothers, all married with at least three children. Everyone worked in the restaurant in some capacity or other. It was a busy place, visited every day by tour buses running back and forth from Mexico City to the shrines.

All the men had loaded guns, ready to defend Walt or anyone in the family against any threat, if necessary. He'd been earning his keep with them by cooking a few shifts in the restaurant, freeing the regular cook to spend time hunting and fishing with his sons. And he'd been teaching English to the little kids, who learned eagerly and helped him with his already excellent Spanish. He and Miguel and various members of the rest of the family began each day with Mass at the tiny church not far from the restaurant. Walt prayed his heart out for the help he needed to get back to the States.

The family had agreed to tell a white lie if anyone asked about Walt—he was a relative from up north, visiting for awhile. They explained his blonde hair by saying he was the son of one of their American cousins who was married to a Swede. The family was the most loving, hard working group of people he'd ever met. They'd asked him to consider staying with them, but there was no way it would be safe for him to apply for a visa let alone citizenship. He had to get going, had to get back to the states and see that Dave was free.

Bonzo had warned Walt not to call him, even if for some reason he was late getting back to him, but Walt began to consider contacting him anyway. He decided to wait three more days and then give him a call. Bonzo would be ticked off at him for being impatient, but Walt had to know that his friend was okay, that TDP hadn't discovered he was trying to help him.

On the morning of his 16th day in Octolan, Walt got up early as usual to walk to the church with Miguel. That day was one of the children's birthdays, and all the kids in the family and their mothers and some of their fathers met them at various places along the way to the church. The family named their children after the saint whose feast day was on or closest to the day the child was born. They always began the child's birthday celebration with Mass.

Walt felt at peace, despite his restlessness about Bonzo. The children were all polished and shining in their best clothes, their mothers smiling proudly at them, their fathers looking macho for having produced such lovely sons and daughters. This was the kind of family everyone wants, Walt thought, a family he would never have. That thought didn't make him bitter. At least he had the chance to experience it some time in his life, at least such a group had found it in their hearts to reach out to him.

Miguel wrenched him from his daydreams by grabbing his arm and pulling him behind a tall clump of shrubbery that edged a park not far from the church.

"Look, over there. An American is getting out of that car. Do you know him?"

In front of the church, Walt saw Ben and two TDP goons pile out of a rented car. He froze.

"Yes, I know them. They're the people I'm running from. How did they know I'm here?'

"Perhaps they don't know," Miguel said. Perhaps they only have a hunch you came here on the tour bus. It would be logical for them to ask the priest if he's seen you. The tour stopped at the church before lunch, remember?"

"What will the priest say?"

"We told Father Andre that you are hiding from people who want to kill you. He promised to say nothing, and he won't. He is a most trustworthy person. Now, we must go back home and put you somewhere where you won't be found. We'll take the alleys."

Ben and his agents walked into the church and wandered around, looking for the priest. The manager of the resort they were staying in told them the priest would know if an American had been with one of the tours.

An old woman nudged him when he walked by her. She was kneeling in one of the pews, holding a rosary. "Are you looking for father?" she asked in Spanish.

"Yes," Ben said, his accent making her smile.

"Father is in the Confessional. He hears confessions until Mass begins. He will not talk with anyone until Mass is over. He is a very spiritual man, our priest," she told him.

"Great," Ben thought, he would have to sit through Mass. But if the priest would tip him off as to Walt's whereabouts, it would be worth it.

"Thanks," he told the woman.

"God bless you," she replied.

"And your little dog, too," Ben muttered in English.

Ben sent the agents outside to watch for Walt, in case for some strange reason Walt had got religion at the shrine and would be coming to Mass. He found a pew in the back of the church and sat down, trying to stay calm. He watched Juanita's large family file in and sit in the front. The sight of all those clean, smiling children made him want to puke. He fidgeted.

Church. What a place. Why did his superiors insist that he find the bastard anyway? Walt didn't know enough about TDP to do any damage. Sure, he may return to Montana and try to free his buddy, but so what? TDP had enough power to shut up any local authorities who wanted to know more. The press would never know. It had to be an ego thing. No agent had ever bolted and lived. It was just the way they did things. Meanwhile, his entire operation in South America was on hold, and the big boys in Chicago were threatening to take away their backing. What a bunch of shit. When he found Walt, the first bullet was his. Right in the nuts. Make him suffer before he blew his head off.

Father Andre left the Confessional and glanced at the congregation. Ah, yes, the Martinez family, here to celebrate little Theresa's eighth birthday. And the usual steady customers, the old women of the village fingering their rosaries. He looked in the very back of the church and saw the American. What would he be doing here, dressed in a suit and looking most un-Catholic? Certainly not a stranger from yesterday's tour who had decided to spend the night.

Father Andre remembered his conversation with Miguel about Walt, the American he'd been bringing to church every day. Perhaps this rough looking man was looking for him. Well, he'd promised to give Walt sanctuary, and he would keep his word. He would do anything for the Martinez family. In his ups and downs as a small parish priest, they were often his one shining light. And he'd looked into Walt's soul. There a was a kind, loving, if misguided person there. He'd heard his confession, heard his list of sins: adultery, anger, violence. It wasn't too different from many other confessions he'd heard in his life. The point was that Walt had decided to confess his sins and start a new life, even though he knew he would most likely be killed attempting to leave the old one behind.

Father Andre dressed for Mass hurriedly, assisted by one of the Martinez boys, and began the ritual by blessing the congregation, being sure to look directly at the man in the back. He would pray for this man as much as for any of the others.

"Son of a bitch, get going." Ben cursed the priest when he saw him look at him.

Walt and Miguel hurriedly packed all of Walt's meager belongings and hid them in the restaurant's walk-in cooler. Miguel sent him upstairs to the attic with a thermos of coffee and a chicken dinner he grabbed from the steam table. Then he took one of his handguns out of its hiding place, loaded it, and ran back to the church. Mass had just started. He slipped in and sat in the pew across the aisle from Ben.

Walt could see the steeple of the church from the attic window, but not the street out front. So old Ben was tracking him. He'd have been free and clear back in the States if only Bonzo had come through. Now he had to move, Bonzo or not. TDP may be tracking all long distance calls out of Octolan, so he couldn't call Bonzo from here. He checked the rifle Miguel had left him— a Ruger Mini-14 semiautomatic with a 20-round shot box magazine. Miguel would surely be armed and let his brothers know they'd caught up to Walt. With luck, there would be no violence. Father Andre would cover for him, and Ben would be on his way. He may check the restaurant, since he surely knew the tour bus stopped here, but he was covered here, too. All he could do was stay calm and sit it out.

An hour later, Miguel climbed the stairs and told Walt that Father Andre had told Ben he knew nothing about an American staying anywhere in town. Miguel assured Walt that two of his brothers were tailing Ben with their bicycles and would report back soon. Miguel said as soon as the coast was clear, he would help Walt get to Vera Cruz, as long as they were sure Ben didn't head in that direction. Walt could stay with Miguel's cousins there, call Bonzo from there, and hopefully be on his way.

Miguel went back to the kitchen to prepare for the lunch rush. A half hour later Miguel's brother, Fredrico, came up and told Walt that Ben and his agents had checked into a resort three blocks down the street.

Walt was confused. Did Ben disbelieve the priest, or was he resting a day, trying to decide which way to go now? After the lunch rush was over, he talked with Miguel and Fredrico about what to do. Fredrico advised him to move rather than stick around, and Walt agreed. He did not want to bring any violence down on the Martinez family. Fredrico said he could get Walt all the way to Vera Cruz in one of their brothers' refrigerated vegetable trucks. The truck would leave just after sundown that evening. In case the restaurant was being watched, they would pack Walt into a fruit crate and carry him to the truck.

Ben paced back and forth in his motel room, wondering whether or not to trust his instinct that the priest knew something. But priests don't lie, he thought. Or do they? Did he word his response in such a way that it wasn't a lie? Ben tried to remember the exact words the priest had used, but he couldn't. His Spanish was terrible, and the priest couldn't speak English. His agents had asked numerous people around town if they'd seen an American fitting Walt's description, and no one had. The bastard was probably disguised.

The only other lead he may find would be at the restaurant, where the tour bus always stopped. He was probably on a wild goose chase, anyway. The only reason he'd come there was that he'd found a newspaper in Walt's room in Mexico City, opened to the ad for the pilgrimage bus tour. His intuition had told him that perhaps Walt had taken the bus out of town. But no one he'd spoken with who had taken the bus had seen Walt. He'd covered every possible other trail Walt would have taken out of the city and come up cold.

He decided to trust his first instinct, that Walt left on the bus. Still, he didn't pursue it until he followed up another lead he'd been given by his superiors. They went over Walt's past again with their best computer hackers and learned that Walt knew one of the best hackers in the nation, a Viet Nam vet named Bonzo Reed, with whom he went to high school. What a resource, surely one he would contact for help getting out of Mexico, they figured. But TDP reported that Walt had not contacted Reed as far as they could tell, although they were watching him closely.

Ben was beginning to believe his legendary ability to have hunches that ended up in successful investigations was waning. It was that Walt son-of-a-bitch. Almost from the start, the asshole had given him nothing but trouble. He rounded up his agents and told them they would meet at the restaurant in 15 minutes. They were all to take separate routes, in case Walt was really around and they could catch him by surprise.

It was 7:45 p.m. when they reached the restaurant. The Martinez family was ready to serve them, giving them triple the usual amount of hospitality and saying all the beer they wanted to drink was on the house. No, they hadn't seen an American that looked like Walt's picture. Americans rarely stuck around their part of town. The only ones they saw were very religious types on the pilgrimage bus.

"Fuck it, then," Ben told his men. "Let's just get drunk and maybe we can get lucky with one of these lovely senoritas." The Martinez women were flirting with the Americans, as their men had encouraged them to do, trying to stretch out their dinner past the time Walt would be pulling out.

It worked. Ben and the boys were totally distracted by the good food and hospitality. Walt slipped down the back stairs and out the back door without even having to hide in a crate, as Ben and his men were beginning their final course. Fredrico had decided to drive the truck that night, and he was steaming at the thought of those ugly Americans flirting with his wife, Leone, and the other women in the family. He stopped by the resort and quick as lightning slashed all four of Ben's rented car's tires, four places on each tire, with his well-honed hunting knife.

Things were getting wild in the restaurant, and Miguel kept pouring free shots of his brandy, hoping Ben and his men would pass out. These Americans, he learned, could hold their booze. The women were getting tired of flirting with them and began giving them less open looks. That made Ben angry. He grabbed Leone, Fredrico's wife, and pulled her onto his lap. Miguel was on him in a flash, hitting him squarely on the head with an empty brandy bottle. Ben passed out cold. This amused his men, who decided to let him wake up in the broken glass in his own time. They'd had enough of the senoritas, who were obviously not interested in Americans. They left for the resort and stumbled into their cabin, not even noticing the four flat tires on the car. Ben woke up four hours later groggy and with a splitting headache. The restaurant was dark. Everyone had gone home to bed but Miguel, who was sitting across the room from him, waiting for him to wake up.

"You may look but you may never touch a Martinez woman," he told Ben. "Now get out of here and never come back, or I will call the U.S. embassy and report you."

Ben's head pounded too intensely to argue. God, he hated Mexicans. He would be outta this shit hole first thing in the morning. He left without a word. Miguel grabbed a broom and cleaned up the mess, laughing to himself, and praying that Walt would have a safe trip home.

Chapter Forty Six

Walt called Bonzo the next afternoon from a public phone in Vera Cruz. He told him TDP had found his hiding place and that he'd moved.

"Get me out of here, Bonzo, please. What's delaying you? You've always worked more quickly than this."

Bonzo hurriedly took down Walt's number and promised to call him back in a half hour. He didn't want to talk on his home phone.

Bonzo had had Walt's papers ready for several days. He'd used all the resources at his disposal to generate a new identity for Walt, including a passport with a very decent photo, credit cards, and everything else Walt would need to get out of the country. Getting the picture had been the most difficult. He'd had to engage the help of "X-Ray," who occasionally worked for him in exchange for hacker lessons, to go down to West Yellowstone and rip off the photo albums Walt had told him were stored in his garage. He could trust X-Ray, not because he was sure of his character so much as he had too much on him. He could turn X-Ray in for all kinds of illegal activities, and X-Ray knew he would if he messed with him.

Bonzo spent hours in his darkroom creating a regulation passport photo out of three different photos X-Ray had stolen, all of Walt at different ages, with different backgrounds, lighting, and clothing. Walt had made it more difficult by lightening his hair, but it was best he kept it that way, so Bonzo lived with it. Then he'd sent X-Ray to Minneapolis to deliver all of Walt's papers to his most trusted hacker friend's house, a 16-year old prodigy, "Zipper," he'd met on line four years ago. Zipper was waiting to mail the package to Walt. All they had left to do was purchase Walt a plane ticket.

Bonzo was absolutely certain his work on Walt's papers could not be traced, but now he had a hunch he was being watched. His computers were completely shut down, all modems disconnected, because every time he'd gone on line for nearly a week, someone had tried to access him. And when he wasn't on line, his alarm had sounded letting him know someone was trying to get into his files.

His first guess as to who was pressing him was that it was the Seminary. But since he still didn't know a thing about TDP, he figured they had to be pretty sophisticated, and they may have looked into Walt's background enough to know that Walt happened to be personal friends with him. Bonzo had delayed calling Walt because he was still trying to decide if he should turn his computers back on and do battle with whoever was trying to access him, just to find out who it was. If he did that, he would satisfy his curiosity but may also put Walt in jeopardy. Walt's call had forced him to make a decision. He would get Walt out of Mexico, and then he'd put some time in locating the computer that was spying on him.

Luckily, he had a wild card he was certain no one knew he had. It was an LSD, or "line sucker device." It was a fine piece of technology he'd built himself from untraceable materials. It had taken him three years to put it together from plans he'd swiped out of a Defense Department file. It was a remote-controlled box that allowed him to make a call from any phone he'd programmed to receive the LSD's signals. He could program the LSD so the call was registered to the phone it was made from, to another number, or, best of all, to no number at all. And the LSD could wipe out the record of a call having been received at the other end. Bonzo rarely used the LSD because there was always a remote chance that while the call was underway it could be detected, especially if it was made from or going into a phone system in a major city where criminals were being spied on. Bozeman was not one of the places he would worry about, nor was Vera Cruz.

Bonzo put the LSD in one of his fly boxes, loaded it into his fishing vest, and headed out of town to one of his favorite wheelchair-accessible fishing holes on the Gallatin River, five miles from a pay phone he'd programmed. If anyone were watching him, it would look if he were taking some time to enjoy his favorite sport. In a sense, he was.

Bonzo pushed the tiny buttons on the LSD. It looked as if he were searching for a match to the hatch as he muttered into his fly box. Walt's voice was as clear as if he were standing in front of Bonzo, who was sitting in his wheelchair by the river, his line in the water.

"Let's get this call over as quickly as possible," Bonzo told his friend. "I have all the stuff you need. I just need a name and address to send it to. Fortunately, the fact that you're in Vera Cruz is a real advantage. I can get a plane ticket out of there for you. You'll have everything you need in four days. Just tell me what city you want to fly in to. I suggest Salt Lake. I know someone who will pick you up there and hide you out for as long as you need. His name will be in the papers I'm sending you."

"You're telling me everything I want to hear. Salt Lake is fine. Thanks. What's my new name?"

"You'll know in four days. It's a name that suits you."

"You sure you can get it to me without a problem?"

"Yes. It's coming from another state. But someone is watching me. They didn't catch up to me until after I had your papers together. Worrying about that is why I haven't called yet."

"Okay. I owe you forever."

"Pay me back by doing one thing, that's all I ask." Bonzo said.

"As you wish. What?"

"Stay away from me. I'm hot."

"How can I pay for this then?"

"It's on me, bro. And I'll miss you." Bonzo felt very sad and alone. He held back tears. "Now, good-bye and good luck."

He cut off the call, not wanting to hear Walt's voice. It would have to be as if Walt were dead to him. He pulled his line in and cast it upstream, trying to see his fly through his tears. He thought he'd better look as if he were doing some serious fishing, in case some asshole was watching him.

Walt hung up the phone, sadly thinking that his freedom would be achieved at the cost of a friendship he'd always treasured. Bonzo had always been good to him, despite what a fuck up he'd been. And now he may never see the guy again, share a brew with him, wet a line with him. Bonzo had put his own life on the line for him. He had to think of that, had to think of getting Dave free, of turning this nightmare into something good for someone.

• • •

Ben stormed into Miguel's restaurant and demanded to know if anyone there knew anything about his tires being slashed. Miguel cursed Fredrico under his breath. Fredrico had called him from Vera Cruz to say they'd made it there safely and he was on his way home. He wanted to know if the women were okay and mentioned that he'd slashed the tires. "Damn him," Miguel thought, although he also admired his brother's spunk and secretly wished he'd done the same thing himself.

Miguel assured Ben he knew nothing about the incident and offered to call the police so he could report the crime.

"No, no, no," Ben yelled. "I don't need any cops. I need tires. They tell me at the garage that it will take at least three days to get some here. That's got to be bullshit. If I call the rental company, they'll make me report it to the police so they can collect the insurance."

"Can't they be repaired?"

"No, they're shredded too much for that. Don't you have any tires that would fit or a vehicle I could borrow? I'll pay you well."

"The best I could suggest," Miguel said, "is that you go back on the pilgrimage bus. You can call Mexico City and reserve three seats. You'll have to pay for a round trip is all. Now I must ask you to leave. As I told you last night, you aren't welcome here."

Ben didn't remember much about last night, but he had no energy to argue with Miguel. He tried to decide if he should go back on the bus. They couldn't conceal their guns and ammo on a tour bus, and he didn't want to leave them where they would be stolen. He supposed they could find a place somewhere around town to stash them.

"Okay, I'll leave. Just let me use your phone first."

Miguel hesitated but decided he could listen to the conversation and maybe learn where Ben was headed next, in case he would have to warn Walt. He told him to go ahead and use the phone and went to the kitchen. He turned off the exhaust fan over the grill so he could hear and put his ear to the wall. Ben's Spanish was terrible, but his voice was loud.

Ben called the tour bus company. Their buses were booked for the next two days. He wasn't going to hang around that long; the place was making him sick. He did what he most dreaded, called his superiors in Mexico City for help. They agreed to send him a car and driver early the next morning. They were curious as to why he still hadn't found Walt and why his car had been vandalized. Ben told them he would give them a full report when he got back. Without a good-bye or thank you, he ran out of the restaurant.

On his way back to the motel, Ben saw Leone hanging a fresh batch of laundry on the clothesline next to her house, a half block from the restaurant. He remembered how friendly and then cold she'd been to him last night and decided to mess with her head. He had nothing better to do. He sneaked up behind her and put his arms around her waist. Assuming he was Fredrico returned from Vera Cruz, Leone relaxed and turned around, ready and willing to return the embrace. She screamed when she saw it was the ugly American. Ben held her tightly and put his mouth to her ear.

"Wouldn't you prefer to fool around with me than do this hard work?" he asked her in Spanish.

Leone struggled to break free and slapped Ben across the face. "Go away," she yelled. She twisted out of his arms and ran to the back door of her house. He followed her, putting his considerable weight in the doorway before she could slam the door on him.

He pushed her into the kitchen and grabbed her again, holding her tightly and running his hand up and down her thighs. She spit on him.

"Feisty senorita," he whispered, continuing to touch her. He twisted her arm behind her back and kissed her mouth hard. Leone kicked him, aiming for his nuts and missing.

"You like to wrestle, little whore?" he laughed, and kicked her legs, making her fall to the floor. He lowered himself over her and lifted up her skirt, putting his hand between her legs.

"Stop," she screamed. He put his free hand over her mouth and continued touching her.

Leone struggled but could not overpower this determined man who outweighed her by at least 100 pounds. She tightened every muscle in her body and kicked with all her strength as he continued to touch her and cover her face with wet kisses. A truck pulled up to the back door and cut its engine.

"Fredrico," Leone tried to scream. Ben tightened his hand over her mouth and told her to shut up. He climbed off her and hurried through the house and out the front door.

Fredrico found his wife sitting on the floor, crying with rage and pain from being touched so roughly. She calmed down and told him what happened. Fredrico was so outraged he kicked the kitchen wall and slammed his fist on the table.

"Goddamn those Americans," he said angrily. "First they threaten to mess up our good friend, Walt, and now this. I can't let them get away with it."

Leone was silent. Rarely had she seen her husband so angry. When he got this way, it was best to be silent until he calmed down.

"You stay here. I'm going to get your sister to stay with you. I'll tell Miguel you won't be at work tonight. We'll take care of that son of a bitch. I'll lock the doors now, and don't let anyone in but your sister. He held her gently for a few minutes and let her cry a bit. But he was just too angry to stick around and comfort her. That was woman's work. He had his own way of dealing with what happened. He left her sitting at the table and went to her sister's, then to see Miguel.

Miguel was nearly as angry as Fredrico once he heard the story of Ben assaulting Leone. It was the last straw. Ben would have to pay.

"Let him think he's gotten away with this for a while," he advised his brother. "When we close the restaurant tonight, we'll pay him a visit. We'll see what shape he leaves town in tomorrow in the car they're sending down here."

That night, Miguel put on his most colorful poncho and hid his mini 14, still loaded from when Walt had it, underneath it. Fredrico stuck his .44 mag. down his pants. They walked to the resort and knocked on Ben's door. Ben was inside with his agents, eating junk food they'd bought at a grocery store.

"My wife says you attacked her, tried to rape her," Fredrico told him, his eyes dark and angry as he kept his voice steady.

"That was your wife? A cute little thing. She wasn't acting like your wife last night," Ben told him. "She wanted me bad. I thought she was one of the town's whores."

"You thought wrong," Miguel said, pulling his rifle from under his poncho and aiming it at Ben. "Now don't move."

The agents stood up. Fredrico took his pistol out of his pants and pointed it at them. "Don't move," he commanded.

Miguel glanced around the cabin and saw three had handguns holstered and sitting on the bed and two shotguns leaning against the wall near the bathroom door. Ben looked at his weapon and Miguel took a step closer to him. "Don't think of trying to get that."

"Fuck you," Ben told him, and he dove for his gun. Both agents moved toward theirs as well.

Without hesitating, Miguel unloaded his rifle, back and forth among all three men, aiming for the centers of their chests. He didn't stop until all rounds were fired. Ben fell over on his face. Fredrico kicked his body over and put his pistol directly between the dead man's eyes. He fired it twice, splattering half his head all over the floor and onto the bed and walls.

"Fuck you," he said.

Miguel put his rifle down and opened the cabin's door a crack, looking to see if anyone had heard the gun shots. The street was deserted. There were no guests in the other cabins, and the owner was gone that night, playing in a band at one of the bars.

Miguel told Fredrico to stay with the bodies. He hurried back to the restaurant, where he gathered up a pile of old potato sacks, then he drove the vegetable truck back to the cabin. Fredrico and Miguel loaded the bodies into the sacks, putting a sack over the heads and another one over the feet, and hauled them to the truck. They drove 20 miles out of town to a secluded area where lovers hang out, play guitars and sing songs, and drink beer around bonfires. No one was there and wouldn't be until after the bars closed. They dumped the bodies in some thick brush, removed the potato sacks, and covered them and the brush with gasoline before piling on the bodies and igniting the gas with a match.

Neither man looked back at the fire. It was seen for miles around by people who smiled and wondered who was in love now, why they had started partying so early in the night, and were they making love in the light of the fire or just thinking about it as they sipped their beers and sang their songs.

When TDP's driver found the blood-covered cabin the next morning, he cursed his bad luck. TDP's policy was to never work with local police, especially in Mexico. It could blow their cover and tie up their work for months. Also, in many parts of Mexico and South America, the police were owned by the drug dealers TDP was trying to bust. He had to assume that Ben and his men were all dead. At least one person was, by the amount of brain tissue he saw in the cabin. Apparently no one knew yet that something had happened here, he thought, and it was best he not be discovered there. He quickly packed the guns and everything else he could find that belonged to Ben and his men, got in the car, and headed back to Mexico City.

Meanwhile Miguel and Fredrico were kneeling in church, waiting to go to confession. Each told Father Andre the same story. They'd murdered three men to defend the honor of one of their women. Father Andre advised them to turn themselves in to the police. Each told the priest that they would not do this but would not lie if the police questioned them. Father Andre figured they would have to have good reason for not turning themselves in, and perhaps the Americans would bring all kinds of trouble to the village. He gave them penance. Each man had to say three rosaries and attend Mass every day for a month. Then he absolved their sins, in Jesus' name.

Chapter Forty Seven

Walt escaped from Mexico without a hitch. Bonzo's Salt Lake City friend, Kelly Jordan, was willing to keep him for as long as he wanted to stay and put him to work caretaking his ranch, 30 miles out of town. It was an easy job. All he had to do was make sure the sheep were watered and grained and the fences were in repair. Other than that, he had two truck engines to work on and piles of firewood to split and stack.

Kelly, a banker in town, stopped by two or three times a week to bring him groceries and other supplies. As luck would have it, Kelly owned a cabin near Mack's Inn in Island Park and knew quite a few people in Island Park and West Yellowstone, mostly business owners and Boys Club regulars to whom his bank had loaned money. Walt was able to find out what was going on in West whenever Kelly went there for a brief getaway.

Walt never told Kelly his real name or his story. He told him only that he'd been involved in an undercover operation and that the government had paid Bonzo as a private contractor to get him out of Mexico, get him a new identity, and arrange for him to hide out for awhile. Kelly had helped Bonzo before and knew it was best not to ask questions. He did wonder, however, why Walt was so interested in West Yellowstone events. He didn't completely buy Walt's explanation that he had an old girlfriend there years ago and had fond memories of partying with her.

One Saturday when he was staying up in Island Park, Kelly went to the Triangle and had coffee with the Boys Club. On Saturday mornings, the gossip flowed more thickly than usual after some of the Boys made their early morning rounds to see who had slept with whom the night before. He'd returned with some good news for Walt, although Walt was careful to not let him know he was happy to hear it. He explained the story of Dave's arrest for murdering the Triangle's owner, Walt. Dave's appeal would be heard in court just after the first of the year, some nine weeks away. Kelly said that he'd never met Walt any of the times he'd been to the Triangle and had asked if anyone there had a photo of him. No one had. In fact, one of the Boys Club regulars had told Kelly that photos of Walt had been strangely unavailable when they were searching for him.

Walt was relieved to hear that. He decided then to wait until Dave's appeal was over. If Dave was successful, Walt would not have to come out of hiding and risk being killed by TDP.

Walt had by then phoned the Martinez family and learned all about the murders of Ben and his agents. He'd driven to Provo to deliver some sheep to another rancher and called the restaurant from a phone booth. Miguel had told him that the local police had found the charred bodies and sent them up to Mexico City to be stored in a morgue as John Does. So far, no one had come to town to investigate the murders. Walt figured that TDP thought the affair was too hot to touch, but he couldn't discount the possibility that TDP suspected he committed the crime and was looking for him harder than ever.

Kelly had filled Walt in about some of the other hot news in West. The Boys had been joking about Susan and her young boyfriend. Some of them had even mentioned that they believed Walt was still alive and, given her behavior, better off without her. Others had said it was rather odd that she'd never bothered to look for her husband. He told her that Lynx, one of the people the Boys Club liked to yak about, was in love with an Indian from Boise and no longer a *Gazette* reporter because she was doing television specials. And he told Walt that Ursus was a hot topic. The grizzly sanctuary had opened and was clearly taking income away from some of the town's more established businesses. He said they'd discussed a rumor that Dave had re-married. Supposedly a woman from Island Park had married him secretly, but another prisoner related to someone in West had learned about it and spilled the beans in a letter home.

"Good," Walt thought, "at least Dave may be finding some happiness while he's locked up."

Slowly Walt was becoming a man with a conscience. Now it seemed to him that joining TDP had been a grave mistake. He attributed the beginning of his change of heart to the time he'd spent with Juanita and her family. Lately, he'd been having qualms about having deserted the kids and having hurt Ursula. Someday he hoped he could find a way to see the children again, but he knew he would have to be very careful. He had no intention of taking things up with Ursula again, but he wanted to know she was at peace. He also dreamed of seeing Lynx again, just to tell her he was sorry for having burdened him with his secret. Even though he didn't see

Kelly too often, the time he spent with him was also helping him. Kelly was like Bonzo and the Martinez family, a good friend who could be trusted. Walt was beginning to see that although he had messed up his life time after time, he'd always been sent good people to help him without judging him too harshly. He began to see that he had been selfish taking so much from these people without giving too much back. He looked forward to the day he could tell Kelly the whole truth.

Walt concentrated on altering his appearance in the event he had to stay underground for a considerable length of time. He kept his hair tinted blonde and his face clean-shaven. He worked out two to three hours a day and bulked out so much that his waist size increased from 34 to 36. All his other measurements increased as well, from medium size to large. His muscular body and lighter hair color made him look several years younger than he was. He changed the frames of his eyeglasses from silver wire rims to black plastic and mail ordered non-prescription contact lenses that changed his eye color from blue to hazel. He even worked on his voice, something that was actually fun to do. Kelly was originally from the north woods of Minnesota, and had a thick mid-Western twang that Walt, with his skill in learning languages, could easily imitate.

Walt was terribly lonely, especially as he began to miss his children and realize that he may never see Bonzo or any of his other friends again. He filled his days with a tight schedule of work on the ranch, weight training, reading, and watching television, but he longed for a time when he could be a social being again. When he felt this may never happen, he would fight the wish that the TDP would catch up to him and put a bullet through his head.

Chapter Forty Eight

Merlin was miserable and trying hard to keep Lynx, Gwen, and Rambon from finding out how he felt. His mother had "surprised" him minutes before they left West Yellowstone for Disneyland. She'd bought Roger a ticket so he could go along with them and keep Merlin company. It had actually been Gwen's idea to invite Roger. She told her mother that when she was a girl, she liked it when Lynx let her take a friend along on vacations and other excursions.

Lynx had been so touched by Merlin's gift of the Disneyland trip that she wanted to do all she could to see that he had a great time. And he seemed so depressed lately, less talkative and energetic as he usually was. Gwen said it was because he was beginning to go through puberty. She advised Lynx to let him be and give him every opportunity to spend as much time as possible with other boys his age.

Lynx and Gwen had been dead wrong. "Sure," Merlin thought, I like hanging around with kids my own age, but not Roger and not some of the other kids Roger has sucked into his circle of Satan worshippers."

Roger, dressed in camouflage shirt, slacks, baseball cap, and sneakers, told Merlin on the drive to the airport that he thought the very idea of Disneyland was bogus. It was a playground for little kids, and he was going only because his parents made him. "They want me to be a little kid forever, but fuck them," he told Merlin. "They forced me to come with you, and I only went along with them to get away from them."

Once again Merlin followed his parents' advice, which he'd heard all his life, that when things are unpleasant and you can't do anything about them, make the best of it. That's what he was trying to do now, and sometimes it worked. He blocked Roger out and listened to his mother and Gwen chat about the clothes they'd packed, what restaurants they wanted to eat in, and all kinds of other boring girl stuff. Then he got into a deep conversation with Rambon about science fiction books he'd read. Luckily Rambon was a sci-fi nut who read good books, like the *Dune* series. Roger didn't seem to mind being left alone. He put his Walkman on and spaced out on heavy metal.

At the West Yellowstone Airport, the metal detector went wild when Roger walked through it. Roger had never flown before and had assumed that only major airports had metal detectors. He was asked to empty his pockets. He pretended to do so completely, handing over a key ring and some change. The detector still beeped. He had no choice but to pull out his pistol—a .25 caliber Sterling Model 300 Auto, loaded with six rounds.

The airport security officer was shocked. "What are you doing with this? Don't you know it's illegal to have this weapon? Don't you know it is illegal to carry an handgun on an airplane?" He looked at Lynx. "Is this your kid?"

"No, he's a friend of our family. He's traveling with us. Please, can I talk with you in private?" She gave Roger and Merlin a stern look and walked to the office with the security cop. Rambon remained with the boys while Gwen followed Lynx.

"Look, I had no idea, obviously, that this kid had a gun. He's the son of a minister in town, for chrissake. We're going to Disneyland on a vacation I need more than anything you could imagine. Please just take the gun and let us go. I'll talk to the kid all the way to California about it if I have to."

"Hey—I know you. You're Lynx O'Malley, the news reporter aren't you? I saw your picture in the *Gazette*."

"The former reporter. I'm in between jobs. I'll be doing television specials soon when this vacation, if you let me take it, is over. This is my daughter, Gwen. This is our first family trip in a long time."

"Shit," he said. "I'm supposed to call the feds on this. They're supposed to call the kid's parents. If I let you go and my coworkers rat on me, I'm in trouble."

"Well," Lynx said, "perhaps you'd better do your duty then."

He looked at Lynx. "Yeah, but I know you're okay. I wouldn't want my trip ruined. Disneyland is an okay place. Took the wife and kids there just last year. Had a good time. Go ahead and go. Half the reason I'm being soft on you is that I'm a fly fishing nut and I like the way you write about that stuff. Not too many women fish, let alone write about it like you do. Now, get going before I chicken out."

Lynx hugged him. "Thanks so much. What's you name, anyway?"

"Charlie. Charlie Newman. Charlie the Fool, I guess. Now catch your plane."

"Well, Charlie, thanks again," she told him, giving him her brightest smile. She hurried over to her traveling companions and motioned them to get going to their gate.

"Wow, mom," Gwen said. "I guess it helps to have connections."

"No, honey," Lynx said, laughing. "It helps to know how to fly fish and write about it."

Lynx sat on the plane between Roger and Merlin, with Gwen and Merlin across the aisle from them. She waited until they were in the air and snacking on stale nuts and soft drinks before she asked Roger about the gun.

"What were you doing with a gun, Roger?"

"Going to California. All the kids there are in gangs and they all have guns. I have a right to defend myself. I don't think anyone should go to California unarmed."

Lynx thought he may be partly correct. If they'd been driving, she would be armed for sure. She didn't share her thoughts with Roger, however. "Do your parents know you have it?"

"No." He started to put his earphones on his head to listen to his music and tune her out. She grabbed them away from him gently.

"No music until I have an explanation."

"Look, I told you. A person is nuts to go to California unarmed."

"That's ridiculous. We're going to Disneyland."

Roger was silent. He stared into her eyes, and the look he gave her made her shiver. He looked like Anton had sometimes, when he was angry but trying to control his feelings.

"Roger, I want to know where you got that gun."

Roger didn't answer. He kept staring at her. Her head began to ache, and she felt angry. "The little shit," she thought. "He's trying to make me exhausted so I stop talking to him."

"Look, Roger, I could have turned you over to the police, who would have called your parents. They would have come and gotten you and you wouldn't be on this plane right now. We all went through a lot of trouble to get you kids out of school for this."

"Look, Mrs. O'Malley," Roger said, imitating her voice so that she cringed and wanted to slap him, "I never wanted to go on this trip in the first place. Disneyland is for sissies. Merlin and I aren't even friends."

"Is this true?" Lynx turned to Merlin and asked. "You kids grew up together. You hang out together. What's going on here?"

Merlin looked at his mom and wanted to die. That asshole Roger was ruining their trip. "I guess we're friends, Mom. He's just being ornery. Right, Roger?" Merlin shot Roger a look that told him he'd better cool it or else.

"We're friends, sort of," Roger conceded halfheartedly.

"Roger, tell me where you got that gun," Lynx demanded with power in her voice that made Roger and Merlin sit up straight in their seats.

"Off a kid from out of town. He said he was in a gang in Twin Falls, down in Idaho. He was selling it."

"Where did you meet this kid?"

"He was hanging around the Geyser. He was in West on vacation last summer."

"How much did it cost?"

"A hundred bucks. It ain't the best gun on earth, so why don't you lay off me?" Roger said defiantly.

"Look, kid, you'd better watch the way you speak to me. You have a problem. It may be a cheap piece, but it's still lethal and illegal for you to own. Get that through your rebellious little skull." Lynx was having trouble controlling her anger. "What would your parents say if they knew about it?"

"What do you think they would say? Probably the same thing you would say to Merlin if you found his gun." Roger still sounded like a brat.

"What gun?" Merlin squealed. "Mom, he's lying! I don't have a gun. I use your guns when we go hunting. I don't touch them otherwise, you know that."

"Roger, why are you implying that Merlin has a gun? He says he doesn't have one. Explain yourself," Lynx demanded.

Roger stared at Lynx. "I was just kidding."

"I don't appreciate your jokes," Lynx said, glaring at him. She had no idea what else to say. Clearly she'd made a mistake asking Roger along, but she would have to live with it. She suddenly remembered the council at camp last week, and the group's decision to focus on children. Had Anton somehow scattered his poison into the minds of the kids in West Yellowstone? Was he hurting Roger to get to Merlin?

Roger had always seemed to be one of the sweetest, most practical, cherubic kids in town, and he had wonderful parents. It was just the kind of family Anton would like to mess up. She would have to watch him closely.

"Okay, we'll drop this for now. You made a mistake, Roger. Let me repeat that it's wrong, not to mention illegal, to carry guns on airplanes. We're not going to encounter any gangs. You won't get the gun back. Perhaps you and Merlin aren't as close as you once were, but you can be civil to one another. I just want you to do one thing for all of us."

Roger would do anything she said, he decided, just to shut her up so he could listen to his music again. "What, Mrs. O'Malley?"

"Come to Disneyland with us the first day. If you don't enjoy it and still think it's for sissies, I'll let you stay in the motel."

"Alone?"

"Yes, alone. You're old enough to stay alone, aren't you?"

"I like to."

"Okay, then it's a deal. All you have to do is go the first day, just in case it really is something you would like. I'd hate to see you come all this way and not give it a chance."

"Can I listen to my music now?"

"Sure, just don't turn up the earphones too much. It hurts your ears, and other people can hear it. Do you want me to get your bag so you can get your Walkman, too, Merlin?"

"Nah, Mom. I want to look out the window. Thanks," Merlin answered. "But first, let's trade seats. Gwen and Rambon can come over here, and you and I can sit with Mullein."

"Poor Merlin," Lynx thought, hoping he would forgive her for asking Roger along. They moved around, and Roger didn't seem to notice. His eyes were closed, and he was tuned into his music. Lynx settled in the aisle seat across from him. She reached over and took the case of the CD he was listening to off his lap.

"Look, Mullein, he's listening to a group called Deicide. Ever hear of them?"

Mullein took the CD notes out of the case and read them. "Lynx, look at this. Deicide means "to kill God." Look at the words to these songs." There were songs invoking Satan's power, dedicating your soul to Satan, words to chants in the Black Mass, and songs praising the power a person can get from doing drugs, having sex, and offering Satan human sacrifices.

"Can you imagine what his father would do if he saw this?" Mullein asked.

"I can't imagine what any parent would do." She looked at Merlin, who was watching them and reading some of the words to the songs. "Merlin, do you have CD's like this?" she asked.

"No. I don't like heavy metal. It's all Roger and his group listen to."

"So, Merlin, you aren't in Roger's group then? I thought you were."

"Not since the beginning of the summer. They don't hang out at the Geyser too much any more. They go to one another's houses and play music."

"This kind of music?"

Merlin didn't want to rat on other kids, but he knew his mother was very upset and would make him talk. "Yeah, they play this stuff. They think Satan is cool."

"What do you think?" Lynx tried to stay calm.

"I told you I hate the music. I see how they think Satan is cool. Satan has a lot of power. They ask him for it, and they get all the money they need to buy tapes and guns and stuff."

"How?"

"They say they get it out of their parents. They pray to Satan for big allowances and get it. I tried it, but you didn't give me a raise. Remember?"

"I remember turning you down for a raise because I bought the cabin, changed jobs, and am watching the money for awhile. You didn't tell me you prayed to Satan, or I would have thrown a fit. You know that."

"This Satan stuff isn't real, Mom," Merlin said.

"Oh, yes it is, Merlin. It's very real. And I am very upset."

"Your mother is right," Mullein joined in. "Satanists are drawing kids into their power circles, getting them into this music, and drugs, and all kinds of unacceptable behavior. It isn't something you should play around with."

Lynx, Mullein, and Merlin spent the rest of the trip discussing Satan. They gave him a summary of what they'd gone through with Anton. They explained how Satan came to be and how God dealt with him and would deal with him. They debated how to deal with Roger and decided that Lynx would tell Roger's parents what was going on. For now, however, they would be as nice to Roger as possible and hope that he would respond to their love, and they would pray for him, too.

"I know Merlin that you are disappointed that Roger is with us, and I'm sorry for having been so insensitive to you. But perhaps Roger's coming with us was something God wanted. Perhaps we can help him."

"I knew you would say something like that, Mom," Merlin told her. "Make the best of it, right?" He smiled at her.

"Right. It's either that or be miserable. I want to have fun, don't you?"

"Yeah, I do," Merlin said. "I hope our motel has a cool pool."

The motel had three cool pools, and they swam in all of them after dinner that night. Even Roger took his earphones off and enjoyed the water. Lynx was impressed by his talent at diving and told him so. He accepted the compliment and even had a conversation with her about how he had taken numerous swimming and diving lessons at the swim center in Bozeman. But when she told him he was lucky he had parents who took the time to make sure he learned as much as possible about something he had talent in, he suddenly turned surly and uncommunicative. He seemed determined to have conflicts with his parents, and Lynx saw that he was so hardhearted about it that it would do her no good to continue talking to him then. That night, she and Mullein sat quietly together for an hour before going to bed, praying silently for Roger and all the kids in West Yellowstone.

The next morning, however, Roger seemed almost cheerful as they took a shuttle bus to Disneyland. The group went on three rides, and Lynx watched him closely. He was having fun despite himself. At Merlin's urging, they decided to find a snack bar and buy some hot dogs, even though it wasn't lunch time yet. Merlin had heard from a friend back home that Disneyland hot dogs were the best in the world. He bet Mullein five bucks he could eat three of them, loaded with onions, relish, and mustard, and not barf on the next ride.

They wove their way through the crowds and found a snack bar. As they stood in line, Mickey Mouse stopped by and said hello to Merlin, Lynx, and Mullein. Gwen and Rambon were talking to Roger about the rides and didn't notice Mickey. Lynx laughed at his squeaky little voice, wondering if a man or woman was inside his costume. A group of very young children gathered around him, in total awe that they were meeting one of their cartoon heroes face to face.

Suddenly, Lynx saw Roger glance over at Mickey Mouse. Her blood ran cold. Roger glared at Mickey as if he were the ugliest, most hateful thing he'd ever seen. She looked at Gwen, who hadn't noticed Roger's look yet. Gwen was asking Roger something, and he turned back to look at her for a second. Lynx moved closer to them to hear what Gwen was saying.

"Roger, I'm happy you're having fun. I knew you would. I bet you would like to come back here during spring break with your family. Your sisters and brothers would love it here, don't you think?"

"Oh, God, Lynx thought," Gwen shouldn't have mentioned his family.

Roger looked at Gwen with the most chilling look Lynx had ever seen on a human being. Suddenly, he moved as fast as lightning and stood right in front of Mickey Mouse.

Mickey nodded hello to Roger and reached out to shake his hand.

"Fuck you!" Roger shouted. Lynx froze. All around her, she saw people stop dead in their tracks to stare at Roger and Mickey.

Roger glared back at the staring faces and grinned. "Fuck you, Mickey Mouse!" he yelled so loudly his voice cracked.

And then he kicked Mickey squarely in the groin with all his strength. Mickey doubled over, groaning in pain. Two security guards rushed to the scene. One grabbed Roger, who kicked him over and over again until Mullein stepped in, threw the kid on the ground and sat on him.

"Please, I need air," a female voice inside Mickey begged. The other guard lifted Mickey's giant head off and halfway unzipped the costume. Mickey Mouse was a young woman, Lynx saw, shocked and sick to her stomach. The woman was five or six months pregnant, sobbing in pain and saying over and over again, "What if that kid hurt my baby?"

Medics appeared with a stretcher and an electric car and carried the frightened Mickey woman away. Roger was sitting up now. Mullein was holding his arms tightly behind his back, but he wasn't resisting him anymore. He was having too much fun watching Mickey.

As the cart drove away, he screamed, "Mickey's a fat pregnant bitch."

That was the last straw. Lynx snapped and walked over to Roger, wanting nothing more than to slap his face. But the second guard stepped in front of her. "Are you this person's mother?"

"No, of course not." Lynx wanted to tell him she'd never seen the kid before. "He's with me, though. So is the man holding him, and them." Lynx pointed to each person in her party.

"Where are you all from?" he asked.

"We're from Montana."

"You, and you," he said, pointing to her and Mullein, "get this kid up and come with us."

Lynx turned to Gwen, Rambon, and Merlin and told them to go on with their plans, and the rest of them would meet them back at the motel at 5 p.m. "Forget this happened, if you can," she told them. "Enjoy yourselves. We'll work this out. Now go." She watched Gwen take Merlin's hand and lead him away.

Lynx and Mullein spent the next few hours in Disneyland's main offices, with Roger locked in a room by himself. A juvenile counselor from the local police force was brought in to advise them. She said she would make no recommendations until she heard a report from the hospital about Mickey's condition.

Meanwhile, Lynx and Mullein told her about Roger's moodiness, negativity, involvement with Satanism, and the gun they'd discovered at the airport. She wasn't surprised. She told them that over half of the young offenders she saw had at least dabbled in Satanism. The world, she told them, was getting uglier and uglier, and criminals younger and younger. She said she had little hope that kids like Roger would ever turn out okay. She said many of the kids she dealt with were from caring, loving families. She said that once a kid gives himself over to hate, the love his family extends him falls on deaf, defiant, angry ears. Mullein and Lynx felt hopeless.

The only good news they heard was that Mickey would be fine. She could return to work the next day if she wanted, but Disneyland agreed to give her two days off with pay to rest and put the experience behind her.

The counselor decided to call Roger's parents and recommend that he be flown home immediately. She arranged for airline escorts to accompany him during plane changes and stay with him until his parents picked him up. She recommended he receive regular counseling. The police agreed to let him go but said they would ask his parents' permission to hold him until it was time to leave California. They said they would take him to the airport. But first, they talked with him and told him that if he were an adult, he would be in jail, charged with assault. They also told him that Disneyland authorities had taken his name and banned him from Disneyland for life. Disneyland treasured their cartoon character actors, he said. Never in its history had any of them exposed their identities to the public so that the little children visiting the park could see they were really human.

It was a very sad day for the theme park. Roger showed no reaction. He stared at the wall without moving a muscle anywhere.

Roger's parents were on the phone with the counselor for nearly an hour. Lynx and Mullein listened to their end of the conversation, holding hands and wanting the entire incident to be over. They could tell Roger's parents were overcome with shock and grief. Lynx felt badly for them and so grateful Mullein was there to help her.

Finally, it was time to say good-bye. Lynx and Mullein went into the room where Roger was being held, hoping they would see a contrite young man. Surely he must feel badly about hurting a pregnant woman. But not so. Roger was grinning that same sick grin he'd directed at Mickey.

"I told you Disneyland was for sissies," he said. "Even Mickey Mouse is a girl."

Lynx stared at him, not knowing what to say. Mullein put his arm around her and looked at Roger. "You have a long way to go, man," he told him, "before you can even call yourself a human being. Lynx, let's get away from him before we get sick." They left, drained and depressed, for the bar at the motel. Three gin and tonics later, they were relaxed enough to face Merlin, Gwen, and Rambon.

Everyone was happy that Roger had left, and Lynx put on her most optimistic face, hoping to put the experience behind them so they could enjoy the rest of the trip. Secretly she wondered how much more damage Roger would do, and how Merlin would be affected by it.

Chapter Forty Nine

Mystery rested in her winter den on a bed she'd made of dried leaves, pine boughs, and old man's beard. It was an old grizzly den. She'd found it quite by accident, when she was hunting pikas on a talus slope near Hebgen Mountain.

The pikas were busy stockpiling bales of raspberry plants between the rocks to eat later that fall and winter. Mystery scarfed down two of them and was tracking a third when she caught the faint smell of grizzly and followed it to the den. It was a small cave on the side of Red Rock Canyon. The floor at its opening jutted out enough to collect snow, and it faced north. Once the snow piled at the opening, she would be safely plugged inside. She made the cave larger by scraping away some of its dirt floor, and her sweat and the smell of fresh dirt erased the old bear odor.

Now she was waiting for winter sleep to overtake her, denning up a few more hours each day and taking short excursions close to the den to catch a quick meal. Her ravenous summer appetite had waned. Her winter coat was thick over the best layer of fat she'd ever had. It would keep her well this winter, since there were no embryos to sustain. She often visualized what she would eat when she emerged from the den next spring. There would be fresh flowers, pikas, of course, and maybe a winter-weakened elk from the herd that was now up the canyon. This was still good bear habitat, and she would work her way through the mountains to the place she'd mated with her last litter's father, and mate with him again.

Even during the deepest sleep of her rest periods, she smelled people coming up the canyon. Not many days ago, she was sure she smelled the man and woman who followed her all those days. She recognized their voices, too. They'd walked along the trail by the creek, some 50 yards below her. They were moving very slowly, it seemed, like they had when they followed her. A few hours later, she heard them again coming back down the trail. And nearly every morning, men and horses went by. Sometimes she heard a rifle shot, but this was the first time she'd smelled fresh meat not long after she heard a shot. It was the smell of a male elk, blood and musk mixed together. It came from a mile, maybe two miles, up the canyon.

At first, Mystery had no desire to follow the elk smell. But as the hours passed, it was mixed with other smells that roused her curiosity. It was the smell of men, their sweat, their campfire, and the food they were cooking. It reminded her of her nights carousing around West Yellowstone, tasting so many new foods that she became unable to stay away from what she knew was a dangerous place, so full of people as it was.

It began to snow lightly. Mystery waddled to the door and looked out. Her bones told her this gentle snow flurry would develop into a major storm. She stretched, and before she knew it, she was walking a few yards parallel to the trail, up the canyon, drawn by the camp smell. It would be the last time that smell would come from that spot, she knew. The snows would drive the people away for the winter.

By the time Mystery reached the camp, the snow had stopped but thick snow clouds covered the sky, promising the storm her bones had predicted. Three men were in the throes of a party they believed they'd earned. They'd been up and down the mountains all around Hebgen Lake for nearly two weeks, looking for a trophy bull, and now they had one. It was an 8 by 7 monarch whose colossal antlers glistened in the fire's light.

It was late in the season, and the hunters were tired and ready to party. They hadn't seen any fresh bear sign that day, so they took a chance they thought was worth taking. They didn't hang the elk in a tree at a safe distance from their camp. They hadn't gotten around to hanging him at all. He was sprawled out eight feet from the campfire. Tomorrow they would quarter him and haul him to the truck, and then to the wild meat butcher in Ennis. The man who shot the elk planned to give his buddies all the meat. He only wanted the head for his den's wall. They didn't bother to hang their food either, like campers are required to do in grizzly country. The last thing they expected to see was a bear, black or grizzly. They were eating beef steaks covered with sauteed onions, mushrooms, and green peppers, beans loaded with salt pork, and pan-fried biscuits.

The first person to see Mystery's dark bulk in the camp thought she was one of the horses that had gotten loose. The second man thought she was a moose. The third, who by then had stood up and walked toward the critter, saw Mystery's humped profile silhouetted by the fire and hollered, "Griz. It's a goddamn grizzly bear!"

Mystery ignored him and stood up, sniffing all the wonderful smells and taking her time deciding which to go for: the elk, which she'd eaten many times before, or the human food, which she'd just recently developed a fondness for. She went for the food. She strolled right over to the campfire and stuck her face in the pot of beans. She sucked it up and moved over to a plate with a half eaten steak on it. It disappeared.

By then, each man had a loaded rifle in his hand, a round chambered, barrel pointed at the intruder. The man who had killed the elk was a seasoned hunter. He knew they'd been wrong to keep such a messy camp, and he wanted to give the griz every chance possible to just trash the place and leave. He knew if they stayed calm she would probably not hurt them. He told the others to hold their fire and step back to give her room.

He spoke to Mystery in his lowest, gentlest voice. "Okay, girl, have your fun and then go now, please. Let's go, honey. Come on now. We don't mean to harm you."

One of the men put his gun down and slipped into the tent to grab a camera. He returned, walked as close to Mystery as he dared, and snapped three shots of her.

Mystery ignored the camera's flash as she sniffed the ground and moved toward the elk. The man kept talking, and she remembered the Woman long ago who had talked to her that way. The Woman had wanted her to leave her camp, Mystery remembered.

That made her stop in her tracks and lose interest in the elk. She wasn't really hungry anyway. Better get back. The snow was starting to fall harder. She walked away, leaving the men in shock and feeling guilty about having attracted her there to begin with.

• • •

Two days later, Martin and Vicky got the call they'd been hoping for, under circumstances they dreaded. A grizzly bear had invaded a hunting camp. A hunter had taken its picture and had it developed right away. He'd given it to the game warden when he filed a report of the encounter, and the warden compared it to pictures he had of Mystery. There was no mistake that it was she.

Martin wasn't surprised Mystery was up Red Rock Canyon, although they'd searched there for her numerous times and seen no signs. He'd had a strong hunch she was there, and his hunches were usually right.

It had been storming since the evening Mystery was spotted, and now the only way they could get there was to ski. It was more important than ever that he know where she was so he could track her next spring. Mystery fascinated him, a bear who had been so wild for so long gone bad. He wanted more time with her before the inevitable happened.

By now, the Interagency Grizzly Bear Study Team knew she'd grown accustomed to human food sources. Although everyone hoped she'd quit, she hadn't. They prayed the storm had driven her to den for the winter. It would be a miracle, but still within the realm of possibility, that she may forget about human food and regain her wild behavior next spring. If not, the next time she got into human food, she would be trapped and killed.

Vicky and Martin packed their winter camping gear and waxed their backcountry skis. They set up their base camp less than a quarter mile from the sleeping bear and skied several hours a day for three snowy days searching for her. They never found the den. Mystery had slipped into her winter sleep, the door to her cave covered with fresh snow.

Chapter Fifty

It was Christmas Eve in Yellowstone National Park, and Lynx stood at the edge of the Grand Canyon of the Yellowstone and leaned against her ski poles. No Christmas decorations or lights could have made the canyon more beautiful or festive. The late afternoon sun sparkled on fresh, powdery snow piled on flat places on the canyon's yellow, russet, and orange walls. The Lower Falls of the majestic Yellowstone River ripped and roared to the canyon bottom. The falls were partially frozen, locked in opaque green-blue ice, a giant lime popsicle.

Back in the cities, people were pushing through crowds in shopping malls doing their last minute shopping, living through traffic jams, money worries, and all the other stresses of commercial Christmases. West Yellowstone teemed with snowmobiling tourists. Every motel room was full, and the din of snowmobiles on the groomed trails in Yellowstone and the national forest could be heard for miles. The blue-black smoke from their clamorous engines made the town look and smell like L.A. without skyscrapers.

Only nature spoke here, in the dancing water, the wind brushing through the pine trees, and the cry of a bald eagle diving toward the river, searching for a trout.

Lynx heard the swish, swish, swish of another pair of skis. That would be Mullein. He'd given her a head start, knowing she treasured minutes like these when she was completely alone, and knowing, too that she would be happy to greet him and take him into her alone-ness.

He stopped next to her and reached out for her hand. At times like this, they didn't need to talk, they could just be. They watched the canyon for several minutes before Lynx broke the silence with a question. She wanted to know if the rest of their friends had arrived at the Yurt's Canyon Camp. That evening, she and Mullein would be married in the community yurt in which Yurt had built a small altar for the ceremony.

The guest list was small: their parents, Merlin, Gwen and Rambon, Dewey, Nora, Harry and his wife, Yurt and his four helpers, Jack and Mona, Pete and Patsy, Frank Goodman, Maria, Vicky and Martin, Arthur, and three close friends of Mullein's with their wives. Mullein's friends were guitarists and singers and would provide the music. And there was Father Peter, a priest from Bozeman who had gone through Catholic marriage preparation with them the entire month of November.

The wedding guests were supposed to arrive that afternoon in three oversnow vans. Lynx was relieved to hear everyone had arrived safely and all were delighted with the camp. Yurt made sure all the propane heaters in the cabins and three outhouses were cranked up, fires were burning in the yurts' woodstoves, and there were enough skis, boots, and poles to fit everyone. Bison steaks, the main course of the wedding dinner, were marinating in a special sauce of Yurt's. The meat was from a bison farm in northern Montana.

"It's getting cold, just standing here. We should ski a bit to get warm. And anyway, we'd better get back to camp and greet everyone," Lynx said.

Mullein looked at his watch. "Wow, it's getting late. The Mass is three hours from now. I shouldn't even be talking to you."

"Yeah, I know," Lynx laughed. "The groom isn't supposed to see the bride until the ceremony starts."

"Would that be because he might change his mind?" Mullein joked.

"Could be. Mullein, seriously, have you had any doubts?" Lynx stopped skiing and waited for his answer.

"Not a one. I promise."

"Me either," she told him.

"Look there, a bison. Right in our tracks" Mullein whispered.

A bull bison had just walked out of the forest and onto the ski trail. He faced the couple, lowered his head, and snorted. His icy breath surrounded his snow covered head with white steam.

"Hello," Lynx told him.

"This is a good sign," Mullein told Lynx. "My Indian great grandparents had bison at their wedding. My adopted parents told me the story over and over when I was a little kid because they were making sure I knew about my Indian heritage."

"What happened?" Lynx asked.

"They got married in Eastern Montana, on my great grandfather's ranch outside of Browning. People came from miles around because he was a heavy medicine man. One of his nephews was walking around near the ranch boundary when he saw six bison cows. He used his magic to lead them to the wedding. After the ceremony, they shot one and gave the meat to the bride and groom. My Indian mother has the hide.

"Have you seen it?"

"Oh, yes. It was the first thing I noticed in her house when I finally met her. I was 16 years old, as I told you before, and my adopted parents took me there for Christmas."

"Wow, and it's Christmas now, and we're having bison for dinner! I bet your ancestors sent us this bison."

"I don't doubt that. Too bad we can't shoot him," Mullein said wistfully.

"Yeah, they won't let us shoot the wild bison, even though they're overpopulating the park, so we have to buy meat from domestic ones. Do you think he smells the meat?"

"He may, but how would he know it was bison?" Mullein wondered.

"Mullein, how did your relative bring the bison to the wedding?"

"The Indian way. He coaxed them. They followed him."

"Why don't you try it?"

Mullein looked thoughtful and then smiled. "Okay, but I have to be alone with him. You ski around him that way, through the woods, and I'll wait here 'til I think you're back in camp. Then I'll bring him along."

"Good luck, "Lynx laughed. "I'll see you at the wedding. Don't be late." She skied away.

Mullein watched the bison turn his head to see what Lynx was doing, then turn back to stare at him. He waited, reviewing the story of his ancestors, trying to remember anything specific about how the bison had been led.

"He led them with his spirit, the part of it that was a wild as they." Those were the words of the story that had struck him the deepest. He'd always recalled those words when he hunted, just before he killed the animal. He felt this meant the animal let him take its life.

Mullein thought of his deep love for Lynx, of the absolute certainty that marrying her was right. He thought of her wildness, the wildness he touched when they hunted and fished together and the time they'd made love. He would have that again very soon. It had been worth the discipline to wait for her, to make love to her for the first time after they marry in this wonderful place. She was back at camp now, washing in a basin of hot water heated on the cabin stove, dressing in her elkskin dress. His deerskin leggings and beaded wedding shirt were laid out on his cot, waiting for him. It would be the last time he dressed alone. Their first marriage bed would be a queen-sized mattress Yurt had hauled in a few days ago and placed on the floor of Mullein's cabin. Mullein had lovingly made it up with white flannel sheets and a red woolen blanket, and placed his wedding gift to Lynx on top. It was a grizzly bear hide from an animal he shot a few years back. She would love it. He thought of her naked body lying on the fur and smiled.

Mullein began to sing to the bison, a song in his Indian language he learned from his birth mother. It was a song of praise to the Great Spirit at the end of a day of good hunting and feasting. The bison took a step toward him. He kept singing and began to ski toward camp. The bison stopped and waited until Mullein was off the main trail, in Lynx's tracks, and began to follow him again. Mullein finished the old song and began to hum a tune his spirit composed as he went along.

The camp was still when Mullein reached it. The guests were in their cabins, resting and getting ready for the ceremony. Mullein walked to his cabin, took off his skis, and opened the door.

"Stay here," he told the bison, who was still close behind him. The bison stopped and snorted. He walked to the center of the camp, around which the three yurts stood, and began pushing his head through the snow, looking for grass he could smell with his powerful nose.

Mullein laughed softly, closed his door quietly, sat on his cot, and began to pray. He asked God to bless everyone in camp and bless the bison, too.

• • •

Patsy, Nora, and Dewey fussed over Lynx as if she were a little girl going to her first party. Nora insisted she lace Lynx's white deerskin leggings herself so they would be snug and wrinkle free. She spent many hours making the wedding moccasins from a deerskin she brain-tanned more than 40 years ago. She had stored it carefully all those years, waiting for the right time to make something beautiful with it. She beaded the tops with tiny white and blue glass beads and beaded the tops of the matching moccasins with blue and white star designs. Dewey fixed Lynx's hair in one braid that went nearly to her waist, tied with a narrow, hand-woven, blue-wool ribbon.

Patsy made Lynx a bouquet of dried wildflowers and herbs held together with some of Dewey's wool ribbon. Lynx's dress was handmade by Sally Afraid of Bear from Lynx's own elk skins. Its long sleeves, back yolk, and hem were fringed with narrow strips of elkskin. The dress was straight, tapering at the waist, and buttoned from top to bottom with small elk antler fasteners. Lynx wore a blue beaded choker and small silver hoop earrings, borrowed from Patsy, with three blue topaz beads on them.

Sally also made Mullein's wedding clothes and his moccasins from a traditional pattern, using Mullein's own elkskins tanned by his birth mother. The couple dressed in Indian clothing to show respect for Mullein's heritage and for Lynx's membership in the Sweetgrass Society. The Mass would be traditional Catholic. Mullein and Lynx hadn't changed a word of the traditional ceremony except that at the beginning, the priest would face the Four Directions. He would smudge the guests with burning sweetgrass as he asked God to bless the people there to witness the union.

Patsy was Lynx's bridesmaid, and Mullein's best friend, Spencer Jordan, a pediatrician who worked in Boise, was Mullein's best man. Merlin was the ring bearer. Their wedding rings were gold bands set with black star sapphires, made by a West Yellowstone jeweler Lynx had known for years. The stones were Mullein's idea. To him they symbolized the belief that light of great beauty can be found even in the darkness when there is love.

The altar was in the center of the yurt, in front of the woodstove. The guests gathered around it and faced the wide open doorway that looked out on the circle of cabins and the bison Mullein had brought to camp. The musicians played an instrumental medley of Hank Williams and Bob Wills songs as Lynx walked on a carpet of fresh pine boughs with Merlin and Gwen, as lovely as a bride should be. They took their places at the altar and turned to wait for Mullein, who was at his cabin waiting for Spencer to tell him it was time. They watched Mullein's door open and saw him call the buffalo, who followed him and Spencer without hesitation, making everyone laugh and clap their hands.

Mullein and Spencer entered the yurt, and the bison stayed close to the door, looking in, as if he'd been to weddings before. The musicians played the opening hymn, "O Holy Night," and the priest began the blessing. Lynx and Mullein focused on every word of this Mass that began their new life as one, living in a marriage covenant with God. When the prayers blessing their union were over, they kissed one another ardently and placed their rings on one another's fingers. They gave each another Communion— blessed whole wheat hosts made by Patsy and blessed sacramental wine brought by Father Pete, the body and blood of Christ. They then gave Communion to everyone else.

The Mass ended with Father Pete telling them to "go in peace to love and serve God and one another." The musicians asked everyone to sing the closing song, "As I Did in Yesterday."

When they were nearly finished singing and Lynx and Mullein were ready to walk to Mullein's cabin, the yurt began to shake. The bison was outside, rubbing himself on one of its supporting log poles. Before anyone could decide whether to laugh or scream, the shaking stopped. They heard the buffalo snort, and then there was silence.

Mullein took Lynx's hand and led her out of the yurt as everyone clapped and Yurt reminded them to be back in two hours for dinner.

The bison was gone, but he'd left a gift, a fat ball of his fur clung to the pole. Mullein peeled it off and handed it to his wife.

"Put this in your medicine bag," he told her, and he picked her up and carried her all the way to bed.

Chapter Fifty One

Mullein rolled his office chair over to the picture window that over-looked Henry's Lake and watched a family of trumpeter swans circle over a patch of open water near the fish hatchery. It landed with hardly a splash. Aerators were running there 24 hours a day to keep some of the lake open so the fish could have enough oxygen to survive the winter. Swans, geese, ducks, and bald eagles were wintering there, enjoying the easy access to food the open water provided.

He and Lynx had sold their homes in Boise and West Yellowstone and built an annex on the Island Park cabin. The annex contained his new medical "clinic," a small waiting area, an examining room, and an office. It also had Lynx's office and editing studio and an outdoor Jacuzzi built into a new redwood deck.

Using a physician from Idaho Falls as his supervisor, Mullein was seeing patients from Island Park with basic medical care needs. Most of his patients needed check ups for high blood pressure, minor heart conditions, colds and flu, and minor injuries. In the two months he'd been open, he'd seen an average of five people a day. It beat working in a city hospital or in a large office and gave him plenty of extra time to fish, hunt, ski, read, and accompany Lynx when she was taping. The community had welcomed him there. Most of their neighbors were older people who felt more secure knowing they had close-by medical care if they needed it.

But at that moment, he wished he'd never opened the office. He held in his hands a potentially miserable piece of information, a positive test result for the HIV virus. The patient was Belinda, a 43-year-old married heterosexual female who lived in West Yellowstone.

Belinda told Mullein her marriage was miserable. Her husband was an alcoholic, and when she learned he'd had an affair with one of her close friends, she left him for a time to heal from the hurt. She stayed in Big

Sky, house-sitting a vacation home for some people who lived in California. There, more out of revenge than passion or love, she had a brief affair with a bisexual 46-year-old man. She broke off the relationship when she learned he was an extremely active bisexual, even when he was with her. She returned to her husband, and they decided to work on improving their marriage. He stopped drinking and running around, and their sex life had become exciting and romantic. Then he was laid off his job, and he started drinking and fooling around with other women again.

Belinda divorced him and got into a very self-destructive lifestyle for a short time that included drug and alcohol abuse and promiscuity. She slept with 15 men in less than three months before she took a look at her life and decided to quit drugs, booze, and sex and get on a more productive track. That was eight months ago. A month after that, Belinda received a phone call from the bisexual who told her he just learned he was not only HIV positive, but had full blown AIDS. He planned to move to San Francisco and live with the man who had most likely given him HIV. That man was seriously ill and being treated at San Francisco General Hospital's AIDS clinic and would get Belinda's ex-lover into the treatment program.

Mullein and Belinda talked about her test results and how she would deal with being HIV positive. And they ran through all the people who would have to be contacted because either she or her ex-husband had sex with them. Then they talked about the people who may have had sex with the people Belinda and her ex-husband had sex with.

Mullein made Belinda an appointment with an AIDS counselor who was also an epidemiologist and would see that all the people were contacted and urged to get tested. Mullein did all he could do on a professional level, but he was heartsick. AIDS had come to Yellowstone. Just with this one case, there would surely be HIV positive people in West Yellowstone, Island Park, Big Sky, Bozeman, and even Ennis.

And he wasn't sure about Lynx. Perhaps she'd had sex with someone who'd messed around with someone who'd messed around with Belinda's ex. He would have to tell her what was going on and encourage her to be tested, just in case. He planned to wait and discuss this with her tomorrow. Tonight was going to be special. Lynx's first television special was airing, and they planned to watch it together with Merlin, Pete, and Patsy.

• • •

It was a beautiful winter morning at Old Faithful. With no wind to interfere, the grand old geyser shot its water straight into the still blue sky. A herd of bison rested on the bare earth nearby, enjoying the warm soil heated by underground hot springs. The geyser basin played its symphony in surround sound: bubbling mud, gurgling geysers, the Firehole River tumbling over rocks. Ravens and magpies joined in, announcing their joy in having plenty to eat. There was a delicious rotten bison carcass at the edge of the basin.

For a full 30 seconds, Lynx let the viewer enjoy the sounds of Yellowstone's winter. Then all hell broke loose. In full stereo sound, a line of snowmobiles could be heard churning their way to the geyser basin. The birds stopped chatting. The geysers seemed to die, the mud pots no longer bubbled. The screaming snowmobiles turned nature's symphony into discord.

Cut. A snowmobile flashes into view and runs right up to a bison, forcing the animal to escape into deep snow. Cut. A snowmobile takes off across a meadow where elk are resting. They pull themselves up slowly, cold and shocked, using precious energy stored in their winter fat, and head for the trees. Cut. A snowmobile races over a tiny stream, just for the fun of it. Cut. A trio of snowmobilers are resting near the Madison River, drinking beer and tossing the empty cans into the river. Cut. A snowmobiler throws a ball of snow at a swan feeding on aquatic plants in the Madison River, and the swan trumpets and takes off, wasting all the energy it stored eating that morning, and more. Cut. Another peaceful scene by the Grand Prismatic Pool. It's so quiet you can hear the water wash out of the pool and ripple over tiny colored pebbles of sand on its way downhill to the Firehole River.

Close-up. An icicle drips playfully off the bough of a pine tree and pings onto a rock. A very pretty sound. Let's hear it again. Ping. Lovely. And then the snowmobiles come, and the music stops.

Yes, people, this is the real Yellowstone. It's a noisy place, and it smells like exhaust, and the air is polluted with fumes, and the animals are harassed. No one tells you this when they send you a brochure telling you to come to winter wonderland. At the end of a day touring the park on your wonderful snowmobile, all your bones will seem broken, the muscles in your back, arms, and hands sprained and strained, and your eardrums will never be the same. They will feel as if you have been at a Jimi Hendrix concert and stood in front of his loudest amplifier, only worse.

Your head will ache from breathing the fumes of the hundreds of snow-mobiles in front of you. Yes, hundreds, sometimes thousands, ride in the park every day. It's not uncommon to see a person who's waited in line at the gate for 20 minutes pull over to the side of the road and puke, sick from breathing the exhaust. It's nauseating, literally.

Cut. Interview: typical West Yellowstone business owner. "Snowmobiling is the greatest thing that ever happened to the town. Brings in millions of dollars a year. We prosper. We can stay here year round; our kids have everything they need. We build on to the business every spring with the income."

Interview: Yellowstone Park biologist. "Snowmobiles don't hurt animals."

"Not even when they drive up to them and force them to move?"

"Not really—it happens with cars in the summer. It can't be helped."

Interview: independent researcher. "Snowmobiling has many negative impacts on wildlife and plants."

"Tell us some."

"Noise and proximity of machines raises metabolic rates of animals who are conserving as much energy as possible, living off stored fat. Heart rates increase. Observers may not see it, but the animal is using more calories than it should. Wild animals use groomed roads to exit park, get into trouble outside park, bison are killed, elk graze on private land and destroy landscaping. Grizzly bears haven't as much winter-kill to feed on when they emerge from dens because the animals left park."

"Then should snowmobiling be eliminated from Yellowstone?"

"Oh, yes, if not eliminated, then seriously limited."

"Why isn't it?"

"Greed, money, fear of lawsuits."

Interview: senior citizen. "Allowing snowmobilers to take over a national park is discriminatory. The national parks should be accessible to everyone. If open in winter, roads should be plowed so everyone can go in. It's unfair and illegal to cater to such an exclusive group of people, especially since they pollute the air and harass the wildlife."

Back to Park Service. "How about all the fatalities in recent years from snowmobilers speeding in park, crashing into trees, bison, one another?"

"We try to monitor them. We enforce speeding laws whenever possible."

"How about the noise level? Is it legal?"

"No, actually, most older sleds exceed minimum noise standards. We turn them away when we can."

"How about the air pollution?"

"We're looking into it."

Lynx watched the others view her "Sounds of Yellowstone" production on the public television station, saw that no one was fidgeting, and smiled. These were her friends, and of course they would give her work all their attention, but she could tell they were more than just interested. It was even holding Merlin's attention.

But as she watched, something bothered her, nagged at the back of her mind. The color was off. It didn't look like her master tape, and she'd seen it on the same monitor. The color was super saturated, and she also noticed something was a little off on some of the cuts. All the sound cuts were okay, but the visuals weren't. God, she knew every second of this tape so thoroughly. She'd edited 23 hours into this 58-minute show. At least 10 visuals seemed to have been cut by a split second. It wasn't enough to make the editing appear abrupt. Only the person who made the tape would ever see it. When the show ended, she checked the VCR she was using to tape a copy. It had timed it at 47 minutes 55 seconds. Five seconds were missing then, or the VCR was slightly off. She doubted that, though. It was one of the best professional decks you could buy. Someone had cut her tape and not told her about it, and messed with the color, too.

Lynx tried to stay focused on the discussion that was going on. They were commenting on the show, telling her it was outstanding and would surely raise public awareness of problems in Yellowstone. They couldn't wait to see next week's show on the fires. All she wanted to do was take the tape and check out its color and light signals and slow down the sections with the cuts. Maybe she was being paranoid. Maybe things were just too joyful for her, now that she and Mullein were together in peace. Maybe her suspicion that Anton had somehow gotten to her tape and messed with it was pure fantasy.

. . .

Soon after their guests left and Merlin was in bed, Lynx and Mullein sank into the hot water of their Jacuzzi. They let the water relax them as they sipped champagne and leaned back, looking at the winter sky. Lynx had calmed down about her videotape and decided to take a close look at it tomorrow, when Mullein was working and Merlin was in school.

Mullein watched Lynx's breasts move in the swirling water and smiled. It was sexy, she was sexy. He thought of making love to her later, and how awesome it would be. Each time was better than the last. She was most giving and willing. It was heaven not having to repress his sexual desires.

They often made love in the middle of the day after his last patient left and she wanted a break from editing. They would unplug the phones, pull the shades, lock the doors, and run around the house naked, making love wherever they felt like it. It was the easiest thing in the world to do. He was a lucky man. But he did have to get this HIV issue out in the open. If there was any chance she had sex with anyone who may be HIV positive, they would have to use condoms until both of them had clear tests. That would hamper the spontaneity they were enjoying, but he would have to live with it.

He moved to her side of the Jacuzzi and told her about Belinda, reminding her that he was breaking a rule about confidentiality, but explaining that he felt it was necessary to do so. Lynx was quiet for several minutes. She knew Belinda well. She had lived in West Yellowstone many years, and although she always seemed to be a troubled person, she'd always been friendly to Lynx and Merlin.

Lynx thought back, wondering if she'd had sex with anyone that might have had sex with Belinda or with a boyfriend of Belinda's ex-husband's girlfriends. She didn't think so. That is, she didn't think so if everyone she'd been with had told her the truth. But in West Yellowstone, you never know. People lied about their sexual experiences, either implying they had more sex than they did, or less, depending on the situation.

Thinking of all the people involved made her head spin. Jack had told her the truth, she was sure, that she was his first sexual encounter after his divorce. But how about Vicky? Had she cheated on Jack? She hung out in the same bars Belinda's ex frequented, and Lynx had seen her dance with him a few times. Lynx shuddered, thinking about how not that long ago she'd justified her sexual behavior, thought she may as well enjoy herself, believed she would never find the right man to marry, so why not? And here he was, and their life seemed almost perfect.

Mullein patiently waited for her to talk.

"Man, this is a real pain. Just when we're rolling along so nicely, too," she told him, thinking not just of the HIV problem but of her videotape. "I can tell you, though, that I don't think I had sex with anyone affected by this, but I'm not 100 percent sure because people lie. I can't be sure that I knew everything about the sexual history of everyone I ever went to bed with. I believed then I was with people who wouldn't lie, but now I am not so sure. I was wrong, careless, a little too frivolous, and now I have to face up to it. You'd better draw my blood.'"

"And I have to be tested, too."

Lynx stared at Mullein, letting the reality sink in. How could she live if she'd hurt him like that?

"You're not going to like this next one at all," Mullein told her, putting his arm around her. "We should really use condoms until we know for sure."

"Wow. I hate those things. Do we even have any?"

"I've some samples a company sent me a while back."

"For how long do we use them?"

"Through two tests. We'll get the first done tomorrow, and then we should wait six months for another."

"Six whole months? We'll use up a forest of rubber trees!"

"Well, say you are HIV positive and you transmitted it to me yesterday. My body wouldn't have started reacting to it yet. It takes about six months for the stuff to be read in a test. To be really safe, you have to get tested twice, and take precautions between tests."

Lynx frowned. "Mullein do you realize that when this information gets to everyone involved there will be an awful lot of worried, unhappy people around?"

"Yes, I realize that. I've thought a lot about it. At least a few people are going to test positive."

"The druggist will make a fortune in condom sales," Lynx laughed.

Mullein laughed, too, but grew very serious. "These small communities around here are going to see an increase in suicides, in deaths from pneumonia, cancer, all kinds of diseases that shouldn't hit this age group. People with positive tests, especially when they get AIDS, will slip quietly out of town. It will be very subtle, not many eyebrows will be raised. People move in and out of resort areas pretty often anyway."

Lynx poured them another glass of champagne. "I know how lucky I am to have you," she told Mullein. "This makes me feel even luckier. I don't think we are HIV positive. I somehow just know we're okay. But this is making me think about myself, my past, what could have happened, and how safe I am now with you."

Mullein kissed her. "Don't look back too much and be too hard on yourself. Be here now. Let's go in and try out those samples," he said. "We'll find a way to make it fun."

Chapter Fifty Two

For the third time, Daren Bush read the Hemlock Association's directions for self-euthanasia. Which of the three recommended methods would he use: a mixture of easily obtainable over-the-counter drugs, prescription sleeping pills with anti-nausea medication to hold them down, or asphyxiation in his automobile? Should he shoot himself with his hunting rifle, drive his car off a cliff, or overdose on street drugs?

The world was too horrible a place for Daren now. Lynx, that sweet woman from West Yellowstone he had such high hopes for, had shown him what Anton Devier had done to her first television production. She and her husband had flown all the way to Washington with the tape. Daren was shocked when he saw the cuts. He'd always detested Devier without knowing exactly why. Now he did. Lynx made it clear that she would stop production until CNS prosecuted Devier and guaranteed her that her work would no longer be messed with. That seemed a simple enough thing to do, he told them. He would discuss the matter with his most trusted friend on the CNS Board.

Daren held his head in his hands. He'd met with the Board member for four hours, and his head was still spinning with what he'd found out. Subliminal editing wasn't something Devier was fooling around with on his own. He was part of a larger organization that was part of a larger group of organizations that were doing subliminal editing experiments, as well as other experiments utilizing all forms of media to control people's lives. Who would have thought the major players in the broadcasting industry were aware of the subliminal editing and allowing it to be used all over the globe? The fact that some of it was Satanic wasn't their concern, he'd told Daren. If the Satanists wanted to spend their money on the experiments, fine. Other messages more important than telling people to give their souls to the Devil were being programmed into the minds of innocent people.

Daren was assured there was nothing he could do about it. The conspiracy was growing more powerful. A new group had just been formed called Network Nighthawk. It was a coalition of all the government and private sector agencies that were funding subliminal research, photokenetic programming, and mind control projects. Nighthawk had been given the power to decide which experiments would be used on media accessed by the public, such as television, films, video arcade games, computer games, and computer information services.

Nighthawk's first decision was to withdraw all experiments on network and cable television that were utilizing subliminal cuts, except the use of newly developed laser cuts during live broadcasts and on a limited number of educational shows. The educational shows were all funded by CNS, the foundation Nighthawk could trust the most. The new edits couldn't be recorded by even the most sophisticated videotape decks. They were light signals created by lasers that stimulated the brain to register the images without the person having to see them first. Subliminal edits like those Anton was putting in television productions were outdated and too easily detectable.

Daren paced his office and took a copy of *Four Arguments for the Elimination of Television* off his bookshelf. Its author, Jerry Mander, wrote ten years ago that television can not be reformed. Daren saw much truth in Mander's contention that television numbed the human spirit. At the time, starting his own career in the media, he believed that Mander had been too pessimistic, that there could be good television. That's why he'd come to work for CNS to scout creative people who would produce television that would educate and enlighten.

Now he'd discovered there is a very well funded, powerful conspiracy to use television to spiritually, psychically, and even physically program people into performing all kinds of irrational acts, and/or allowing them to take place without protesting. Daren worked to see that CNS funded hundreds of productions that had seemed so valuable. He now knew the productions had been used to destroy independent, intelligent, and spiritual thinking, even in very young children. He was warned. Talk, Bush, and you die. You'll die after we convince the public that you are a paranoid schizophrenic. Just look as what's happened to so many of the other people who tracked down some of the conspiracies that are going on.

Daren had asked his Board member buddy why CNS was involved, and the man had given him a look that implied surprise that Daren was so naive.

"Get real, Bush," he'd said. "We're funded by some of the groups doing the research. We have to go along with their programs or there would be no more CNS."

Lynx's fire video was stunningly beautiful, a testimony to the power of nature, to how nature triumphs even when politics try to manipulate it. That and her snowmobiling piece portrayed exactly the type of messages Daren believed are most important. They asked people to examine how necessary it is that they keep in close contact with nature, not exploit it. It didn't simply portray a "television Yellowstone" that would play into people's misconceptions that Yellowstone is a quiet, untouched place of beauty. It said, "Wake up! That park you think the government is preserving as a pristine wilderness is noisy and polluted, its wild animals harassed by consumers who don't care about wilderness. They want to go fast on expensive, loud, polluting machines. And the people who live close to the park aren't the nature lovers you imagine them to be, expect them to be. They're there to make money on Yellowstone any way they can."

And the fire tape was exceptional, packed with great video of burning trees, animals in peril, firefighters working to put the flames out, and interviews discussing what had gone wrong and what was right about the situation.

CNS and the stations that aired the show had been deluged with praise for the productions. CNS had received donations to fund more shows like them. Daren had personally seen that Lynx's original fire tape was used and been warned by his Board contact that if he ever interfered with what tapes were broadcast again, his end would come much sooner than he'd expected. And he may not have a wife or children anymore, either.

Daren's wife Zoe was his best friend, his lover for over 20 years. His kids were the pride and joy of his life. His work had always been important to him not only because he believed in what he was doing, but also because it supported his family well, gave them all of life's necessities, good schooling, great vacations, and more.

Daren thought of his conversation with Lynx and Mullein. They told him about their circle of friends who were praying about the situation, about what they went through with Anton. They told him about "Mr. and Mrs. Carter," and about their suspicion that Anton's rituals had been directed at the young teenagers in West Yellowstone. Daren advised them to forget about trying to uncover and expose the conspiracy. He told them about Loretta Yarndo and Elizabeth Carter's deaths and the deaths of a few other people he now suspected were caused by their trying to bring the truth to light.

He wasn't sure if they listened, but they gave him their word that if he turned up dead, they would not ask questions. He had to believe they would keep their word. They'd promised only because he told them that if his death were investigated, his family would be at risk. Lynx understood that. He hoped she also saw what would happen to her children and friends if she talked.

Daren had to kill himself and make sure his death was seen as a suicide. He had to do this not only for his family but for all the other people who may be thinking about making the truth known. He had to do it to get Lynx to quit making tapes, because there would be no one there to guarantee they wouldn't be cut if he wasn't around.

Above all, escaping life by his own hand was a logical choice for Daren because his life's work had been to serve humanity, not God. He had no idea that in his desperate situation, he had one final choice, and that choice was not suicide. It was to put his life, and the lives of all he was intertwined with, in God's hands. It was a mistake he made throughout his life. He simply never accepted that only God gives life and only God can take it away.

The rifle would make a mess. The over-the-counter drugs, if reported as the cause of death, may make it easy for other suicidal people to take the step rather than get help. The prescription drugs were too iffy. He may go into a coma and be revived. He would drive his car into the garage, plug up any holes that let fresh air in, run a hose from the exhaust pipe to the inside of the car, and go to sleep forever. But first, he would get his papers in order and write his family a letter. He would tell Zoe he was too depressed to go on. He loved them too much to put them through having to deal with a mentally ill husband and father.

Would Zoe believe him? He had been depressed lately and uncommunicative. She'd observed this and tried to get him to talk, but he couldn't tell her what was going on. She may believe him. She may not. She wouldn't become suicidal herself, he was sure. She was too strong for that and would force herself to go on to take care of the children. She would perhaps hate him for hurting them. She would blame herself, feel that she could have done something. He would tell her in the letter not to blame herself in any way, and she would read that letter many times, trying to find a reason, trying to find strength.

Zoe was leaving town for the weekend, taking the kids to her parents' house. He already told her he wouldn't be going because he had to work. He would invite Manny Simpson, one of his colleagues and a close friend, over for dinner Saturday night. He was pretty sure Manny had no idea that

CNS was involved with subliminal programming. Manny was a script writer and editor. He had nothing directly to do with video or film editing. Manny would find his body, sparing Zoe the sight.

Was it right to do this to someone he cared about? He felt he had no choice. Manny was solid and strong, the kind of person who would see it as a duty to perform. And it wasn't necessary to tell Manny about CNS. Manny had recently notified CNS he was retiring in two months. Let him leave his job thinking everything was fine.

Daren hated to think of the suffering he was causing, but he had to look at the bigger picture, at how much more suffering going on living would cause. He made the call. Manny said he would be delighted to come for dinner. Good, now it was time to start work on the letter, get files in order, leave as many clues as he could that he was a depressed man, contemplating his own death in a most methodical, organized manner. Time to focus only on that and stop thinking about the hearts that would be broken forever.

As Daren began sorting through his library, looking for books to donate to the public library, books to earmark to each of his children's collections, books to put in a special pile for Zoe, he thought of making love to his wife. It had been a while. He'd been so distracted by the pain of his discovery that he hadn't felt sexual, and she'd understood and held him in her arms each night until she thought he'd fallen to sleep. Funny, he wondered, in the past when he'd had worries about his work, she seduced him through it, brought him out of his troubles and gotten him horny. This time, she hadn't. Was he right to assume that she was just being sensitive, or had she stopped wanting to make love to him?

Daren stopped packing and sat at his desk, trying to remember exactly when they'd made love last. It was two months ago, after going out to dinner and the symphony. The kids were at friends' houses. Zoe was wearing a sexy, low cut dress and she smelled wonderful. He remembered looking down her dress at the concert and then at dinner, and wanting her. He'd practically ripped her clothes off as soon as they'd walked in the house. She'd seemed a little standoffish, and he'd wondered about that. That was unusual for her. Daren stood up and paced his office, thinking when they'd made love before that. He couldn't be sure. He realized that somehow the regular sex he'd enjoyed for 20 years, lovemaking at least three times a week after the first year or two of daily rolls in the hay, had stopped several months ago.

As he thought about this, he realized it had been Zoe who had been responsible for them tapering off. He recalled several times when he'd started to make love to her, and she'd said she was too tired or didn't feel well. Had she been playing the old headache trick, had she lost interest in him? Was she having an affair? He ran through the possibilities of that. Zoe was an honest person. He'd always believed she was where she said she was. She ran her own company out of their home, a computer consulting business that advised senior citizens what computers to buy, helped with the purchases, and then went to their homes to train them. She was out of the house 20 or 30 hours a week, mostly during the day when he was at CNS, but sometimes in the evenings. Had she met someone, an older man, perhaps, who had purchased his first computer and needed her help learning it?

Daren would never know. There was no use looking into it now. Zoe was too good a person to cheat on her husband. He would have to believe that, wanted to die believing it. And if for some reason she had been sleeping with someone else, perhaps it was partially his fault. Perhaps he'd given her less attention than she deserved as his work had consumed his time and energy. If that were true, it would make his death easier for her. She would have someone to take his place. But he also wanted to die remembering the last lovemaking they'd had together, and he wanted that to be one of the last things he did. He called her and asked her to dinner that night at their favorite restaurant. That would get her in the mood.

• • •

Zoe looked at herself in the full-length mirror in her dressing room. She was wearing a new dress, a red satin shift, short with a low-cut, heart-shaped bodice. It wasn't the favorite black dress Daren had asked her to wear. She liked it better; it showed off her firm pecs, lightly muscled arms, and hard thighs. Her weekly six hours at the gym were worth it. If only she'd been doing it for Daren.

She felt a twinge of guilt that it was for her lover that she spent time making herself look good. At least Manny noticed. Manny, who was always there for her, whom Daren sent to take his place when she needed an escort and he had to be out of town scouting CNS grantees. Manny, who was attentive and caring and passionate, who made her reach ecstasy when her husband seldom gave her orgasms and rarely noticed the fact. Daren liked to joke about his sexual mediocrity, blaming it on being 46 years old. She'd let him joke, understanding that it would be useless to let him know he simply didn't satisfy her. He was a good man and a good provider and intelligent enough to fulfill her need for intellectual stimulation. She could have spent the rest of her life with him, comfortable yet sexually unfulfilled. But Manny had interfered with that.

For the 15 years they'd known one another, they resisted the raw animal attraction they felt whenever they were in the same room. Neither mentioned the feeling to the other. Both assumed the other didn't feel it. Each controlled it all those times Manny came to fill Daren's place because he couldn't make it home for a concert or a football game or a CNS party.

Then Zoe's company landed a large contract with a computer firm that wanted to purchase her services for 100 people who had just bought their product. It would mean that Zoe would have to hire more people. That was okay because she would make a great deal of money on the deal. The money didn't mean much to her, except that she secretly delighted in the fact that now she would be making more than her husband, and by a substantial amount. Most interesting was that all the customers were severally disabled. Their new computers would give them all kinds of opportunities to overcome their disabilities, communicate with other people, and earn good livings.

Zoe had assumed Daren would share her joy in this new opportunity, as she had stood by him all through his career. He promised her he would be back in time for the party celebrating her new contract. He was on a trip to Montana to scout a new television producer at a film and video festival. His plane was to have arrived five hours before the party, in plenty of time for him to contact the office on his return, rest, and dress.

He didn't even get on the plane. He'd decided to stay an extra day because he was enjoying the films and videotapes he was seeing at the festival. Once again, he assumed his work was more important than hers and she would understand. And as usual, he relayed the messages about his delay to her through Manny. He didn't bother to call her himself.

Manny showed up two hours before the party, looking exceptionally handsome in his suit and tie with a bottle of good red wine and apologies from Daren.

Zoe lost it. She sat down, took a huge swallow of the wine, and cried. She told Manny all the frustration she felt, the neglect, the resentment. Manny sympathized with her. He often wondered how she handled it. He told her that he divorced his wife just before he came to work for CNS because she'd been too involved in her work to have any time for him, and she'd been lukewarm sexually, at her best. He said he would rather live alone than in a void with another person.

For the first time, Zoe thought of herself divorced from Daren, alone or with someone who was more interested in her. The thought didn't scare her. It excited her. She shared that thought with Manny, and he told her he'd been head over heels in love with her for years. He held her and kissed her and next thing she knew, they were making love in the guest room. Passionate, crazy, wild love that drove her to ecstasy and beyond. Every muscle in her body let go of years of tension, and her mind exploded, emptying all thoughts and awareness of anything around her. They'd been a few minutes late for the party. She smiled when she remembered how she glowed like a schoolgirl with a first crush when they walked into the room.

She giggled as she brushed her hair. Manny certainly shot Daren's myth that older men have no sexual energy. He had more than Daren had when he was humping her two and three times a day at the beginning of their marriage, the methodical, hormone-driven, sexual release young men are prone to confuse with lovemaking. Sexual power had nothing to do with age. It was that you actually liked the person you were with, cherished them and honored them. Daren treated her sexually as he did in every other way. He thought he could use her for what he needed, and she should go along with it because she was Zoe, his cute little wife who had nothing great to do in the world. Daren thought he was a good husband because he screwed her two or three times a week. He didn't even seem to notice she started playing the old headache trick after she began making love to Manny.

It was the same as or better than the first time every time she and Manny made love, she thought as she put on her diamond earrings and choker. They were gifts to herself, Daren never shopped for her. He thought he was a good husband, allowing her to buy whatever she wanted with his credit cards and then letting him know later what he'd "given" her. He simply didn't know he made Al Bundy and Homer Simpson look sensitive. The tragic thing was that he trusted her and Manny so much that he would never suspect they were lovers. Sometimes that made them feel guilty. But more often than not, it made her realize just how much he took her for granted, just how arrogant he was to constantly put her in the arms of a handsome, sexy man just so he wouldn't have to bother with her.

She slipped on her high heels and took her full-length mink, another "gift," out of the closet, wondering why Daren suddenly wanted to take her to dinner. Perhaps he'd finally gotten horny. Well, she would do her wifely duty. It would be a while before she told him she was moving with Manny to another state when Manny retired.

• • •

Lynx and Mullein were just beginning to make love when the phone rang. Lynx was relieved that she'd forgotten to take it off the hook. Safe sex was a drag: condoms were hurting their sex life. She hated the way they felt, and she hated the destruction of the spontaneity they'd enjoyed.

She disliked seeing the changes it put Mullein through when he sometimes lost his erection hassling with them. A man despised having to worry about such things, even if he had an obvious, practical reason. They'd even gotten to the point where it seemed as if they were forcing themselves to have sex just to prove they could do it with those damn things.

"Thousands of other people dealing with HIV positive tests must be going through the same thing," she thought. "Too bad this wasn't discussed a little more in the AIDS prevention commercials. Maybe it would be another deterrent to thoughtless sex." Mullein had even joked that he would rather die with her of AIDS and have a good time doing it.

Lynx picked up the phone. Zoe Bush's voice was strangely even and mechanical.

"Lynx, I'm Daren Bush's wife, Zoe. We had dinner with you and your husband last month, remember?"

"Oh, yes, and it was such fun," Lynx told her. She meant it. Zoe had made them all relaxed and comfortable, and the dinner she prepared in her lovely home was four star. Lynx had forgotten the tapes for a time, discussing all kinds of interesting topics with her. She was brilliant and very loving.

"Lynx, Daren killed himself last night. In the garage. Carbon monoxide poisoning. A friend found him. I was out of town with the children."

Lynx stopped breathing and looked at Mullein. He was staring at her, wondering why she was as white as a ghost. She grabbed a sheet of paper and wrote, "Daren killed himself." Mullein read it and gasped. He put his arm around her.

"Zoe, I don't know what to say."

"He left a long letter, said he was depressed, said there wasn't anything we could have done. He said he'd worked so hard all his life for nothing and didn't have the strength to find something outside of television to do."

"Then please believe him. How are the kids?"

"They're devastated. We've all taken valium. I always thought it was stupid to take sedatives. But I can't function now without them."

"Go ahead and take them. You need to absorb this slowly."

"Lynx, do you think Daren was murdered?"

"Why do you say that, Zoe?"

"Because I feel it in my heart. I don't see how he would have chosen to hurt us like this."

"Did you tell the police your suspicion?"

"Yes, of course. They spent hours looking for clues. They say they don't see anything that indicates anyone else was involved. They say it's the opposite. Daren got his affairs in order the same way a lot of suicides do. They say the letter is his handwriting, which I of course already knew, and it is a typical suicide note, if there is such a thing. But something very controversial was going on at CNS."

"How do you know that?"

"Daren always talked with me about his work. It would sometimes irritate me because I sometimes pretended to be interested, and he never asked about my job."

"That can be a man thing," Lynx said.

"Right, I know that. But during the last few weeks, including the time you and Mullein were here, he clammed up. He was distracted and upset, but he wouldn't let it out, no matter how forcefully I encouraged him."

"So that leads you to think that he found something out that he shouldn't have, and he was murdered, and the murderer or murderers made it look like a suicide? That sounds like the plot to a "Murder She Wrote" episode."

"Right, or he found something out that was so hard to live with that he went against a deep personal belief about suicide. That would mean it was a terrible thing. Terrible." She sighed.

Lynx thought. Zoe was right on the money. "Zoe, think this through. If you are right, then you don't want to stick your nose in this. It would only bring you and the kids a lot of grief."

"Lynx, am I in danger? Do you really know nothing about this?"

"Zoe, I advise you to assume you would be in danger if you try to find out what was troubling Daren. It isn't worth the risk."

Zoe coughed, holding back tears. "Lynx, just a few days ago my life was peaceful. Now it's a mess."

"Zoe, it will be peaceful again. You may simply be focusing on thinking Daren was murdered to avoid feeling the grief. That's a natural thing to do. Are you with some friends?"

"Yes, I have many friends. They're saying the same thing you are."

"Will you think about listening to us?"

"You're right. For now. I have the funeral and the kids, so much to deal with. But I won't let this rest until I talk to the people he worked with and see what they think, too."

"Okay, do what you have to do. Just take it slowly."

"I'll try. If you hear anything, please let me know."

"We shall," Lynx told her.

"Then good-bye, and thank you." Zoe hung up the phone, not waiting for a final word from Lynx. How could she explain to someone she barely knew that the grief confused her, that she'd been planning to leave Daren to be with his best friend, her lover? How could she say that seeing Lynx had made him not come home that time Manny had first made love to her, and she'd been grateful for that?

Manny had called her at her parents' as soon as he found Daren. She rushed home, and the car had already been removed. Manny stored it somewhere. Daren was in a body bag in the living room. She didn't want to see him, and Manny told her that was probably a good idea. Later, after she had calmed down and gotten the children settled with friends to talk with, she asked Manny if he thought Daren knew about their affair.

Manny said he doubted that. She thought back to their last dinner, to their lovemaking. Daren had been more passionate than ever before. Would he have been so if he knew she was having sex with another man? If he was one type of man, he might do that to win her back. But Daren was too arrogant for that, or was it just that she saw him that way? None of the people he worked with had ever referred to him as arrogant. They said he was dedicated, hard working, a real genius, and humble about it. But they weren't his wife. And as passionate as he'd been that last time, he still didn't satisfy her as Manny did. No, she guessed that his lovemaking was another one of the items he'd taken care of before his death.

Manny mentioned that he, too, had noticed that Daren had been distracted and upset at work. He assumed it had something to do with Lynx O'Malley's television production, although it had been praised highly. Manny even asked him about Lynx. Daren told him only that he was becoming dissatisfied with CNS, but his reasons were personal. Still a red flag went up in Manny's head. He had a sense that Daren knew something dark and unsettling but wouldn't tell his friend to protect him. He knew Manny was retiring soon.

Years ago, Manny would have made an effort to look into the situation. But now all he wanted was to make it to retirement and take Zoe away. She was his happiness. He would put all his energy into helping her through this.

• • •

Lynx and Mullein didn't take up where they'd left off in their lovemaking. They got dressed and went to the kitchen to make coffee and think. Mullein agreed with Lynx that Daren's death was probably not a suicide in the classic sense. He'd sacrificed himself for his family and for Lynx, too. Lynx decided she had no choice but to turn the balance of her grant money back and find something else to do.

She went to her office and wrote CNS a brief letter saying she was halting her project for "highly personal reasons." She mailed the letter, found Mullein, and took him to bed.

"No use worrying about what to do next," she told him. "Something will come up. It always does. If anything, I feel a great weight off my shoulders."

This time, the condom slipped on easily, and the closeness they felt overcame the numbing effect of high tech latex.

Chapter Fifty Three

DK was furious, and he took it out on his new sex slave and office manager, Heidi, another whore he rescued from the street. He chained her to the four-poster mahogany bed in the bedroom of his office suite and beat her with a horse hair whip until she was covered with red marks. He made her take care of his erection with a blow job, nearly choking her to death when he came. He left her tied up on the bed, uncovered and shivering with cold and fear.

Abusing Heidi didn't make him feel better. Anton had messed up by stealing Lynx's tapes and editing them just at the time Nighthawk had organized and decided to use the new, undetectable technology. He was sure Anton did it out of revenge for being rejected by Lynx, but part of it was his own fault for not briefing Anton on Nighthawk.

And Lynx had quit CNS. Bad timing. If Anton hadn't blown it, they could be trying the new technology on her tapes. The Yellowstone opportunity was trashed.

Then there was the matter of TDP. They'd failed in South America. They lost that Walt asshole from West Yellowstone. He disappeared, helped by a goody-goody computer hacker, Bonzo Reed, who's been snooping around the Seminary files for years, even posed as a seminarian for a long time. They let him live only because their hackers learned a great deal from him. His gig would soon be up, though. DK decided to take care of Bonzo himself. And then TDP lost some of its best people, murdered by who knows whom. It was probably Walt, but they didn't know. DK hated not knowing. It infuriated him.

TDP wasted so much time, money, and effort looking for Walt that the drug dealers they planned to bust had time to reorganize and go underground so deeply that it would take months to figure out what they were doing.

DK and the other investors met with TDP and decided to reorganize, too. Rather than bust drug operations, they would become partners in one. They settled on Rengakyo, a growing drug operation in Japan. Rengakyo manufactured new designer drugs they were smuggling into the U.S. in the most simple way possible, the luggage of so-called tourists. The drugs were easy to handle, tiny odorless, tasteless pills that got a person more blasted than heroin or cocaine. Any surplus could readily be traded for pot and cocaine.

The Japs were very clever—DK had to give them that. Rengakyo had connections with another organization, Seeking a New Japan, or SNJ. It included a team of economic experts sent a few years ago to Montana, Texas, and Connecticut. Their mission was to scout out ways to exploit these states' resources and provide jobs to Japanese willing to leave their country for a new life in America.

SNJ had numerous ways to colonize America. They proposed buying huge tracts of land in Montana and Texas on which to build high tech factories and communities of Japanese workers. Another proposal was to develop resorts with theme parks, gambling casinos, museums, and zoos. These resorts would be developed in limited partnerships with American corporations and would employ a mixture of American and Japanese workers. Still another proposal was to develop cowboy "resorts."

This third idea was in full swing, with several resorts in operation. SNJ's investors acquired thousands of acres of ranch land in Montana they were managing as working cattle ranches. Their top executives actually thought it was a great stress reliever to dress up like cowboys and spend two or three weeks on the range rounding up cows, branding them, and playing around with horses. These were many of Japan's most honored businessmen and government leaders.

Their suitcases were lined with Rengakyo's dope. Many didn't have any idea they were exporting one of their nation's most valuable products, but some did. TDP guaranteed Rengakyo they would not bust its operation and would help if they were given some of the dope and a whole lot of cash.

And now the Japs were negotiating to purchase property in West Yellowstone, of all places. Why was it that that Lynx bitch always seemed to be in the middle of things? Ursus's developer, Randall Duncan, had solid connections with Montana's Foreign Trade Commission, which helped SNJ scout business opportunities in their state. SNJ proposed teaming up with Duncan to build a theme park next to the bear sanctuary that would feature a museum on Yellowstone's natural history, complete with high tech multimedia educational exhibits. Rengakyo contacted DK about smuggling drugs into the new resort in West Yellowstone, since it was near an airport and would be visited by hundreds of thousands of Japanese tourists, making it easy for smugglers to go unnoticed.

The Seminary informed DK that, like TDP, it had undergone a strict period of self-examination and discovered that it had to go back to its old way of recruiting Seminarians. There were too many half-hearted students in its ranks. It needed more money to upgrade its computer technology and to spend the time scouting potentially good students. It had to get rid of hundreds of students it should never have accepted and wouldn't have accepted if its computers had been powerful enough to do proper surveillance. There were too many inane service projects underway all over the world, being conducted by people who had no intention of disciplining themselves to reach higher levels. And something had to be done to battle with Sweetgrass and all the other societies that were getting more and more skilled at counteracting the Seminary's work.

It was time to work harder, to invoke more power, to weed out all the people who weren't playing hard ball. It was time to use the Circle of Fire for some serious battle. He must go into the wilderness and fast to prepare for the work to come. But first, he would have a little fun with Bonzo Reed and the people in West Yellowstone.

DK unchained Heidi, ordered her to get dressed, and told her to make plane reservations for him to fly alone, first class, to Bozeman. He told her to phone Anton and tell him to take the next flight to Bozeman, too, and meet him at the GreenTree Inn.

Chapter Fifty Four

Bonzo awoke in the middle of the night with a splitting headache, his body covered with sweat, his forehead burning with fever. His mind raced with the vivid dream images that had made him restless all night.

In his dream he was working on his computer, and the woman in his "master" vision visited him and ordered him to come back to her. He told her she wasn't his master, that he'd been playing at being a Seminary student to find out about what the Seminary was up to. She told him that that had been a terrible mistake. He told her to go away, and she said that was impossible as she would always be a part of him. He picked up the 12-gauge, double-barreled shotgun he kept under his desk and fired it at her. Her head blew apart, but she didn't leave.

She changed into a very tall man with weird-looking white hair and deep-set dark eyes. The man told Bonzo that he was "disappointed" in him for invading the Seminary like he had and that the Seminary could not allow him to exist anymore. A double-edged sword appeared in the man's hand, and he lunged at Bonzo, aiming for his heart. Bonzo tried to recall what happened after that, but he couldn't.

Bonzo pulled himself into his wheelchair, noticing that his arms felt incredibly weak. He wheeled to his bathroom and took a shower to cool himself down. The shower refreshed, him and the fever subsided. He felt hungry and went to his kitchen to make a sandwich. That gave him a little more energy, but still he felt listless and the nightmare lingered. He knew it was best to not dwell on the images that were still running through his mind, to not think about who the white-haired man was, to not wonder if it was simply a bad dream or if the Seminary was trying to contact him.

He thought of Daren Bush's alleged suicide. Arthur told him all about it when he stopped by to see him yesterday. Arthur was delighted to learn Lynx decided to can her CNS project, and so, too, was Bonzo. He hoped he could meet Lynx and her husband someday. And he thought of Walt, still hanging out in Utah, wishing he could just talk with him on the phone. No wonder he was having nightmares, he conceded. He was so damned alone. Had any of his work been worthwhile? Sure, Lynx was probably safe, and with luck Walt would be able to stop living in hiding, but where did that leave him now? He was totally alone and beginning to detest his emptiness. There was nothing to do but go back to bed and force himself to vacate his mind until the anxiety dissipated. In 15 minutes, he was in a deep sleep.

It was nearly noon when he woke up, far past the time he usually slept. He got up and showered again. His arms still felt weak. He wondered if he was getting the flu. He buzzed Sandria and asked her to comb and braid his long, thick hair, explaining that he felt lousy and too weak to do it himself.

"My God, you look a bit sick," she told him. "You must be in bad shape if you want me to fix your hair, but I'll be happy to do it. It's such a nice head of hair." She started a pot of coffee and went to work.

Bonzo felt better just feeling her touch. Except for rare women clients, Sandria was the only female presence in his life, and he loved her. He loved watching her strong, curvy body move around his house, caring for his things as if they were her own. Bonzo's disability had made him impotent, and he had faced that fact and accepted it long ago. Women hit on him whenever he went out in public because he was a handsome, sexy man, but he never responded. Who would really want a man who couldn't make love to them completely?

He once confided that thought to Sandria. She was safe and easy to talk to, a good 30 years older than he. She'd been married for many years and said many times she stopped being interested in men after her husband died of Lou Gehrig's disease. She told Bonzo that there were women out there who would be honored to love Bonzo and accept the ways he could satisfy them. "She's probably right," Bonzo thought for the millionth time as Sandria tied his braid with a rubber band. Perhaps it was just that he didn't think he could find a woman that would understand his work.

Sandria cooked him a big breakfast, and they ate together in comfortable silence. Then he went to his computer to check his electronic mail. He was reading the day's top news stories when his doorbell rang. He switched on the video monitor connected to the camera that watched his door and felt his heart skip a beat. A white-haired man who looked exactly like the man in his nightmare had spotted the camera built into the side of the house near the doorway and was smiling into it, waving.

Bonzo took a deep breath. He pushed the button on his intercom and said, "Yes?"

"Bonzo Reed?" said the man, still looking into the camera.

"Yes. What can I do for you?"

"I'd like to discuss some business with you. May I please come in?" His voice had a liquid, high-pitched hiss at its very edge, like Tolkien's gollem, Bonzo thought.

"I don't know you. You didn't call first, you know. Please state your name," Bonzo answered.

"My name is DK. I've come from Chicago more or less on the spur of the moment, and I apologize for not calling first. I've heard you are an expert at something I need."

Bonzo thought quickly, staring at DK's image on his 15-inch color monitor as he checked to see that the tape was turned on. He rarely taped the brief interactions at his door. He usually knew who was visiting him, and the camera only made it easier for him to greet people and explain to those he didn't know that he was in a wheelchair and they would have to let themselves in and follow the hallway to his office, or weight room, the two places he spent the most time in. By his closeness to the camera, Bonzo guessed DK was at least six feet six. Most people had to look up to see the lens; DK was practically face to face with it. His eyes were ugly, Bonzo thought, full of evil, like in the dream.

DK had never seen Bonzo and didn't know he was in a wheelchair. He tried to probe inside the house to get a mental image of what Bonzo looked like. Bonzo didn't give him time.

"Come in when you hear the door unlock and follow the hallway straight back to my office." Bonzo released the remote-controlled door latch and checked to see if his shotgun was in its usual place and loaded. It was.

Bonzo listened to DK's footsteps as he walked over the hallway's smooth tile floor, custom built to help him move around faster in his chair. A medium weight, he thought, very aggressive and single-minded. He leaned back in his chair, ready for what he sensed would be some kind of confrontation. How he'd foretold this meeting in his dream puzzled him, but he chose not to let it freak him out.

DK hid his surprise at Bonzo's appearance. No wonder he had never gotten a clear picture of this man; he'd mistakenly started out with a stereotyped image of a computer hacker as a wimpy, skinny, myopic geek with thick glasses and a pencil stuck behind one ear. Bonzo glowed with health and masculinity. His office was spotless and organized, not piled high with floppy discs, notebooks, and rotting, empty, take-out food cartons. Bonzo exuded personal power. The look coming from his clear green eyes said, "Don't fuck with me."

Bonzo resisted the natural instinct to flex his huge arm muscles as he let DK look him over, laughing silently that DK hadn't noticed yet that he was sitting in a wheelchair. From behind his desk, it must appear to be a high tech office chair.

"Have a seat," Bonzo told his visitor. He buzzed Sandria and asked her to bring them coffee.

"Quite a set up you have here," DK said, nodding to Bonzo's computers, printers, videotape decks, monitors, and shelves packed with books.

"I am quite comfortable in this work environment," Bonzo replied coolly. "Now, who are you, and why are you here?"

"Bonzo, I am of the Seminary."

"Of the Seminary? Not with or from, but of? Prepositionally speaking you can shove the Seminary UP your ass," Bonzo said, keeping his voice friendly and even. Sandria walked in with a tray carrying coffee and sweet rolls. She looked at DK and froze, hating him instantly. DK saw her reaction and smiled sweetly at her. She glared back, muttering the first words of a Hail Mary in Spanish.

"Just set it there," Bonzo told her. "And you can go now. Thanks for all your help." He winked at her.

Sandria walked out of the room with no intention of going back to her apartment. That man was mean and ugly. She had felt the presence of his sort of evil before. He may want to hurt her Bonzo. She went to Bonzo's bedroom, took the revolver out of his bed stand drawer, and slipped it in the pocket of her sweater. Bonzo taught her how to shoot, and they went to the mountains outside town many times for target practice. He also taught her the history and special features of every weapon he owned. She knew how to assemble them, clean them, and load them. This revolver was one of his favorites, a Smith and Wesson Model 38, hand ejector, double-action military and police first model built in 1899. She checked to see that all six rounds were loaded and walked quietly back to the hall. She planted herself outside his office and breathed deeply until she was calmer.

DK had watched Sandria intently when she served Bonzo. There was something familiar about her, as if he'd met her before. He would think of it later. Or perhaps it was that she looked very much like one of the Mexicans he'd enslaved not long ago, two or three whores before Goldie. She could be the girl's grandmother.

"Is she a live-in housekeeper?" DK asked. Bonzo nodded.

"I'm surprised a handsome man like you isn't married. Wives are always better at such things than maids," he lied, thinking of his long line of sex slaves.

Still realizing that DK hadn't seen his wheelchair, Bonzo didn't bother to explain Sandria, whom he sensed was near the door. If he moved to wave her away, DK would see that he had no legs, and he wasn't sure that was a good idea.

"Bonzo," DK returned to the conversation, "I am fully aware of the number of years you wasted the Seminary's time by posing as a serious student. You fooled us. You even reached the point of vision with your master, although you saw her as a woman. We can speak freely of this. You can't hide anything from me now."

Bonzo knew that DK was there to confront him. Why not seek some answers to questions he had for so long? "What do you mean I saw her as a woman? She was female, I assure you."

"The ascended masters appear to us as we wish to see them. Somewhere in your deepest soul you long for a spiritual union with a woman. You saw a woman."

Bonzo pondered this, accepting that there was truth in it. He'd seen the eternal mother, the mother he'd never had and also the purely loving mother of children he'd never spawned.

"Then tell me how this master thing works. I admit I was surprised. I did enough research into the Seminary to discover its connection to Lucifer Trust. I figured the masters would be one of the seven servants of Satan."

"Oh, yes, they are. But they are disguised. You will see them in their truest forms only when you have truly given yourself to Master Satan. Otherwise, he will deceive you in the way you deceive yourself. You see Bonzo, you erroneously seek love, the love of a woman, the love of the people you help. That's your mistake."

"Wow, I never knew it was a mistake to want love in your life."

"You will learn that fact soon enough. It was love, you must remember, that made you seek knowledge of the Seminary. Your love of righteousness. That was a mistake. You thought you could expose us to others like you, show the world that we are here, that our power is growing, and that we are evil. To you, evil is wrong, ugly, unacceptable. You try to do good, to help people."

"DK, I don't know how I would have gone on without you. I've been a fuck up all my life, it seems, loving my fellow man and trying to lift people out of their misery. What a fool am I," Bonzo said, his voice dripping with sarcasm.

"And you didn't know that you have helped us immensely in our work to manifest Satan's power throughout the planet."

"How so?" Bonzo looked squarely into DK's eyes and already knew the answer.

"Your genius is almost supernatural. You've an intuition that is finely developed. It's a natural talent, but then you trained yourself to enhance it, and then you used our meditation and mind control techniques to further develop yourself. We watched you and learned a great deal."

"Like what?"

"Oh, many things. Most important may be that we learned that we were not impenetrable and that we have to utilize the new technology to protect ourselves from spies like you."

"I'm glad I could be of use."

"I'm sure you aren't glad. Not at all. You see, we admit we messed up when we grew lax about certain things. But we don't let people get away with taking our knowledge if they aren't going to stay with us. Ask Ginger Paddington about that."

Bonzo did not give DK the reaction he wanted. He used his Seminary-learned skills to shut out any picture of lovely Ginger. She was at peace. They'd given her that.

In the hall Sandria prayed Hail Marys, asking the Holy Mother to help her understand what Bonzo and that awful man were saying. Mary answered. Sandria was able to understand nearly everything. Mary was giving her the grace to overcome the fear she always had that she couldn't understand a different language well. All that English she'd blocked out as impossible to deal with was becoming as clear to her as her own language. When she heard Ginger's name and deduced that DK was responsible for her death, she prayed harder for the grace to not storm in there and shoot the bastard. Sandria had noticed how caring Bonzo had been to Ginger and dreamed that maybe they would have a relationship. If that son of a bitch—"Excuse me Mary," she prayed—had ruined Bonzo's chance to have love in his life, he should go straight to hell.

"So who the hell are you, anyway?" Bonzo demanded.

"I am a manifestation of the One."

"Of the one, huh?" Bonzo mocked him. "What does DK stand for?"

"Few people know the meaning of my initials. They stand for a name I once used, a name I am most proud of."

"What was that, Degenerate Kook?"

"Ah, you mock me. Laugh at me. DK stands for Duwar Kahul. It is that name I took when I did a most fine piece of work. I became a Buddhist monk, a member of a sect of men whose prayer life, mediation, and examination of Christian theology led them to believe that Jesus Christ is indeed the Son of God and that Buddhism must evolve into Christianity."

"Never heard of it."

"No, you wouldn't have, because I destroyed every one of them and nearly every record of their thinking. What records of their existence survive are in the hands of my affiliates."

"When was this?" Bonzo asked. Somehow, he believed this man was telling him the truth.

"Hundreds of years ago now. It was a close call. What do you think the world would be like now if all those people had become Christians?" He shuddered.

"I must still ask the question, as you haven't answered me," Bonzo told him, beginning to wonder if perhaps he should simply blow this idiot's head off.

"It would be better if I show you who I am so you have no doubts."

DK stood up and walked to the center of the room. He closed his eyes and lifted his arms, his palms facing the ceiling. Every one of Bonzo's computers screamed, sounding the alarm that the power had gone off. The battery back-ups kicked in, and they began to hum again. DK opened his eyes, looked at the center of Bonzo's forehead, and the back-ups quit. The room grew silent and dark. DK began to hum, and Bonzo felt the hum send pain through the center of his head as if he were being hit with a sharp dart.

Sandria froze in the dark and looked down the hall at the thin ray of light beaming onto the floor from under the door. It stopped at her feet. She listened and heard the humming, not sure if it was human or coming from one of the computers. But if there was no electricity, she thought, it must be from something else. The Devil himself. She took her shoes off without a sound and tiptoed toward the kitchen pantry, where the breaker boxes were. She grabbed a flashlight off a nearby shelf and turned it on. Its light seemed awfully dim, but it was enough to see that every switch was blown.

Then it wasn't at power outage, it was the house. Something terrible must be happening. Bonzo told her once he had the "cleanest" electricity in town. He explained that he had a constantly even amount of "juice" going into the house. He spent thousands of dollars on his wiring to make sure there were no power surges or dims to hurt his equipment. And if there was a power outage, he had a back-up gasoline-powered generator he taught Sandria how to start. Sandria flipped the breakers, but they wouldn't stay in the "on" position. She would have to fire up the generator after all.

She knew she had plenty of time to go to the backyard and get it going because Bonzo's equipment had battery back-ups, so she decided to go back and check on Bonzo first. Surely it would be okay if she knocked on his office door to ask about starting the generator.

She shone the flashlight on the shelf she'd taken it off of and found a pack of fresh batteries. She replaced the older ones, and the light was stronger. She walked toward the office and heard the humming. It seemed much louder and higher pitched than at first. She flashed her light straight ahead and spotted the bronze door handle to the office, set lower on the door than an average one so Bonzo could reach it from his wheelchair. The door handle was red, as if it was being heated by an invisible blow torch. Sandria looked at her flashlight, thinking it was lighting up the knob. The light was out. How could new batteries have run down so fast?

The humming intensified. Sandria walked faster, put the flashlight down on the chair by the door, and touched the knob. It burned her instantly, and she held back a scream. She willed herself to suppress the instinct to run to the bathroom and plunge her hand into cold water.

"Mother Mary, help me," Sandria whispered as she took off her sweater, rolled it up with the revolver still in the pocket, and used it to open the door. She felt and smelled the hot metal singe the wool.

DK turned to Sandria when she walked in the door, putting the smoking sweater back on. How did she get through his shield? Now he knew for certain he'd seen her before. He strained to think where.

Sandria looked at DK and realized that she had seen him in the past. The existence of the Devil was an accepted fact in Mexican Catholic theology. In the backward village where she grew up, mentally ill people weren't sent to sanitariums for rest and medication. They were exorcised, and nearly always healed. She'd seen DK at the exorcism of a young man who went crazy just before he was to have received the sacrament of Confirmation. Since he was a very little boy, he told the villagers he would be a priest someday. When he went berserk and tried to choke his little sister to death, the village priest was called in. He pronounced the boy under oppression form the Devil who was doing all he could to prevent God's child from becoming a priest.

The priest asked the bishop for help. Even in those days it was the bishop who did exorcisms. Sandria had been chosen with a handful of other devout Catholics to pray during the exorcism ritual. It took many hours of prayer to overpower the evil. When the spirit left the young man, Sandria saw what she was seeing before her now. Pure, unadulterated evil. It was just beneath the surface of this man's skin. He couldn't hide it from her.

She began to pray in Latin the words used at the exorcism, starting with the sign of the cross, "In nomine patris, et filius, et spiritus. Pray with me, Bonzo. Any prayer you wish."

DK had heard those Latin words many times before, and he registered the level of power that stood behind him. It was way up there, he thought, on the level of a Mary worshipper. Of course, the bitch was Mexican. They really believed in Mary. And then he remembered. He'd seen her at the exorcism of a young would-be priest, and he, DK, had watched for a while before stepping in. He'd assigned a lesser demon to the boy, one of his most promising apprentices, incarnated in one of the boy's friends. The apprentice had done well programming his friend to get into pornography and fucking a whore in the next village. But just when the good little Catholic was going to visit the whore for the first time, pumped up by giving in to the apprentice and looking at some relatively soft porn, he'd gone nuts trying to overcome his temptations. Then they'd brought the goddamn bishop in. The apprentice couldn't get near the ritual, but he'd stood outside the house, calling on DK to help him.

DK had responded and entered the room, something much easier to do when he wasn't burdened with embodiment, like now. DK sent his power into the young man, who foamed at the mouth and defecated on himself. The would-be priest had absolutely no resolve left, but he did still have a tiny bit of faith.

At the same moment DK began to etch away at that faith, Sandria started to pray loudly and clearly, right from her heart. She drowned out the bishop's low, even chanting. DK felt a great desire to kill her on the spot, give her a stroke or heart attack, anything. She looked into the young man's eyes with total, complete love, the love that DK had seen nearly 2,000 years before in the eyes of Jesus. Jesus forced him to return to the darkness then and did so again in Mexico, through Sandria.

Only when the words of exorcism are spoken with full and total faith and authority will an evil spirit of DK's power respond and depart. Some weaker evil spirits dwelling in humans may be afraid of the old cross and garlic tricks and half-hearted prayers. DK had been assaulted by these weak rituals and words thousands of times. But he had the first exorcism to compare it too, when God Himself was the exorcist. Jesus of Nazareth had cast him out in an instant, thrown him and his fellow demons into some pigs.

When DK flashed on his memory of Sandria and the Mexican exorcism, he knew he had to work harder than ever. He transformed himself into Mother Mary. He made himself the most beautiful, most glowing

Blessed Mother he could conjure. He filled the room with the fragrance of roses. That always fooled them. It played into all those Mary freak's dreams to have an apparition, complete with rose-oiled air.

Sandria gasped and looked at Mary's eyes. She saw they were DK's, where love had never shone.

She fell to her knees and began the litany that is part of every exorcism. "Michael the Archangel, pray for us. Mother of God, pray for us"

Bonzo remembered litanies from Catholic rituals he'd attended as a boy, and he joined in, saying "pray for us" each time Sandria called on a saint or angel and Jesus and Mary for help.

DK transformed into the most frightening monster he could create. Should scare the shit out of her. This is the big leagues, far more frightening than a young man writhing on the floor.

"And where is your bishop now?" he hissed. "And your priest? You can't do this without them."

A grain of doubt entered Sandria's mind. Her mind focused on DK's words rather than the prayers that were in her heart. "Yes, he's right," she thought. "I'm just a humble Catholic. I can't do this alone." She looked at Bonzo, who was staring at her, wondering why she stopped praying, racing into her mind to read her thoughts. He saw her doubt and suddenly words he'd read long ago in the New Testament came into his mind.

He shouted, "No, Sandria, we can do this. 'Wherever two are more are gathered,' remember?"

Sandria hesitated again, thinking of what that meant. "Oh, yes, they could do this. It was promised."

But she was too late. Her mental doubts had left her wide open. DK returned to his human form and took a deep breath, concentrating all the electrical energy he'd stolen into a compact ball at the base of his spine. He inhaled the energy up his spine, into his arms and inhaled it again, pushing it through his hands, out into the room in jagged rays of red light and straight into Sandria's heart. The hate he hurled at her overcame her. She dropped to the floor, crying in despair, as the revolver slid out of her pocket and across the floor.

"Father," she whispered, "save us, in Jesus's name." She lost consciousness.

Bonzo saw how DK had used the same breathing techniques he'd been taught by the Seminary, with an important step left out, perhaps one he would have learned later on. He hadn't learned to deliberately draw electricity from his surroundings. Now the only electricity in the room was somewhere within DK. Bonzo ordered his mind to take it, asked to draw it from DK in the name of Jesus. Something within him said he must have faith to make it work, must ask with his heart as well as his mind.

He asked again, with faith, willing himself to believe he could do it. He felt his body heat up and pushed the energy into the base of his spine with a deep breath. Something told him to make the light he was preparing to draw forth white. He pictured white light, stretched out his hands, and zapped it at DK as he prayed the words he'd finally remembered, "In the name of Jesus, get thee behind me Satan." He said them again, with faith in their power. And again. Suddenly he felt the presence of other souls helping them. He felt one of them was Lynx, and another Arthur, and Sandria and Ginger and others he couldn't name.

Just before Bonzo's white light reached DK, DK shot forth his blue rays. They merged with Bonzo's light and pierced Bonzo's heart.

"Nice try, asshole. But in this world I have the power! Remember, I trained you. Your pride, not your beliefs, not faith in your beliefs, not even your love powered you."

What was he saying, Bonzo wondered, losing his resolve in his confusion. Wasn't doing the best he could enough?

Suddenly the lights came on and the computers started humming. Sandria moaned but her eyes didn't open. Bonzo fiddled with his wheelchair. The battery was still dead. He switched it into manual and started toward Sandria.

"So you are disabled?" DK laughed at Bonzo, noticing the wheelchair. "I see why you longed for a woman and did nothing about it. You poor thing. And look how well you turned your suffering into good." He spit the word "good" out of his mouth.

Bonzo ignored him and wheeled toward Sandria.

"Go to her. That will make it easier for me," DK said, pulling a small handgun out of his pants pocket. It was a Heckler and Koch Model P7M13(9mm with a 13-shot magazine). He pointed it at Bonzo.

"It's a lot more fun killing you people spiritually," he told Bonzo. "And there isn't quite the mess or investigations by authorities as the death I am about to deal you. You're good, very good. Too bad you won't live long enough to learn more. Say your prayers. That will make you even more disappointed when you find in a few seconds that there is no Jesus waiting for you."

Bonzo looked at DK and saw him begin to squeeze the trigger. He heard the shot. Sandria twitched at his feet. She never even woke up.

"Now bow your head," DK screamed, "and pray."

Bonzo spun around and made for the revolver that Sandria had dropped. It was not to be. DK's accurate shot hit him between the eyes and splattered his brains across the room, all over Sandria and the wall behind her.

DK laughed. He phoned Anton and told him he had bodies to get rid of. He told him to walk the five miles from the motel to Bonzo's house, load the bodies into Bonzo's van, and dump them wherever he thought best. DK said he was going to West Yellowstone and then to the wilderness and would contact Anton in a month or so. He walked out the front door and headed for West Yellowstone.

• • •

Anton hung up the phone and thought. So DK had killed Bonzo and someone else. Good. Bonzo had become a hassle. DK sounded drained, as if someone had sapped all his energy. Perhaps whomever he'd murdered had fought back and hurt him. He certainly hadn't made sense, expecting him to drive a stolen van, a handicapped vehicle no less that would protrude anywhere. And where was he supposed to dump bodies in the winter? He would have to think of another plan. He left the motel for Bonzo's house.

Bonzo's soul hovered over his body, tormented with the loss of Sandria, not knowing yet that it had to leave those human feelings aside in order to go on. His soul registered DK's instructions to Anton. He knew that although DK would get even more powerful, the Bonzo personality the soul had departed from could still fight a little longer as a human. He saw DK leave, and then Bonzo filled the room with light that penetrated every microchip in the house, even the little computer in the microwave, even the computer that controlled Bonzo's custom van's remote-control door lock and engine functions. Any microchips that had survived DK's power drains were now wiped out completely.

"Come now, Bonzo," he heard Sandria call. Out of her body, her voice was a song. He was drawn to her light, the light of a soul that had led a life full of love and service. He was compelled to move toward it.

That's when Bonzo discovered the truth and the lie. The truth was that DK had been right. He, Bonzo, had at times been powered by pride, not always by the best motives, not always by love. The lie was that DK said there is no Jesus. Jesus was there, and Jesus forgave him.

Chapter Fifty Five

Lynx kissed Mullein good-bye and watched him drive down the road. She snapped her silver and blue boots into her skating skis, turned her Walkman on, adjusted the earphones, picked up her ski poles, and launched.

Mullein had dropped her off on his way to town to pick up Merlin, at the spot where Targhee Creek runs under the road that goes around Henry's Lake. She was nearly two miles from the lake, all slightly downhill. She would skate-ski over meadows covered with sun and wind packed snow that was as hard as ice. The meadows were owned by Californians who never winter in Island Park. They had no idea the absolute thrill it was to be at Henry's Lake in the winter and fly nearly frictionless over the land they saw only when covered with sagebrush and tall grass. Not even Mullein, as outdoorsy as he was, had any idea what a high it was to skate-ski in these perfect conditions.

Lynx settled into rhythm with the rock n' roll tunes of Jimmy Dale Gilmore, double poling herself into the highest speed possible, the wind at her back. At this rate, she would skate the two miles in less than 11 minutes. She kept her speed up but zigzagged in a wide pattern, extending the amount of ground she covered and hence the time heading downhill.

It was a glorious, cloudless day, 23 degrees F. She was wearing a sleeveless one piece neon blue lycra suit, keeping her body hot with the powerful stride and poling technique of someone who'd skied for 30 years. She crossed coyote tracks, and then the deep holes made by a big old moose. She whizzed by him a moment later; he was as a statue in the willows off to her right. Swish. Swish. Swish. She got closer to the lake and spotted three bald eagles sitting on some fence posts. She reached the lake and kept going, slowing down a bit to look for slushy areas. It was not a safe place to ski because there were many warm springs in the shallow lake bottom, so some areas never froze over. She finally stopped in the middle of the lake and turned around slowly, taking in the view of the mountains, their icy peaks shimmering in the sunlight.

The frigid air dissipated the warmth her body furnace had generated when she was moving and told her to get going. She turned the tape off, wanting to listen to the sounds of nature on the return trip. She skied slowly to the shore and stood there a few minutes, breathing the pure air and listening. Willow branches near the mouth of the creek chimed in the wind, and a snowmobile somewhere across the lake screamed. It was stuck. Good. The driver gave up and cut his engine. Lynx giggled, imagining him plodding through the snow, sweating like a pig inside his thick suit. Such naughty thoughts.

She launched again. With not much additional effort, she skied uphill as fast as she had flown down. In no time she was back at the road and flying over the packed snow that paralleled it. She skied a bit slower now, concentrating on her technique and the scenery, stopping to watch a herd of elk cross the road and head to hay piles on a ranch that kept cattle all winter. The ranch hands hated the wild animals that raided their hay, but the neighbors all around loved seeing the wildlife. Lynx covered the five minutes along the road to her house in half an hour.

She went inside, took a hot shower, and turned on the Jacuzzi. She would have it ready for Mullein and Merlin when they came home. Merlin had been at Lou's house that weekend, and the hot water would mellow him out, she hoped. She opened a bottle of wine for her and Mullein and a juice for Merlin and sat down on the couch that overlooked the road waiting for them to come home.

Strange, she thought, how different the house felt when she was home alone. Empty, even melancholy. She liked having her favorite men around her. Suddenly, she felt overwhelmed with unhappiness. How could such feelings descend upon her after a ski like that? She closed her eyes and focused. The intensity of the emotional pain she felt had to be real. Something terrible must be happening to someone she knew. She reached out for Mullein and Merlin. They seemed to be okay. She sensed they were on the road home. And Nora? She saw Nora bowing her head in prayer, and then heard Nora's voice as plain as day in her head saying, "Lynx, join me."

The second Lynx hooked up to Nora, she saw Mr. Carter's face, full frame in her mind, sneering and ugly. He was threatening someone on their side, someone she didn't really know. Lynx visualized all of the Mystic warriors: Nora, Dewey, Harry and Sally, Pete and Patsy, Arthur, Yurt, Salinda, even Jack and Vicky and Martin. She pictured her vision bear, Mystery, and asked her friends to send the powerful protection a bear had for her cubs to whoever needed it.

Lynx heard the car pull into the driveway and composed herself, hoping her prayers had helped. She wouldn't mention the incident to Mullein until later, she decided, when Merlin was asleep. When they opened the door and walked into the house, she greeted them with hugs and kisses.

• • •

It was Arthur Red Fox who had called the Mystic Warriors to prayer. He was editing a videotape on bald eagles wintering at Canyon Ferry near Helena when the vision of someone needing help hit him. He stopped work and called the others to help him.

As soon as he felt their prayers flow, he tried to focus on the source of his vision and saw that Bonzo was in some kind of trouble. He called Bonzo's house and no one answered the phone. He thought it strange that the answering machine wasn't on, but remembered that Bonzo told him once he turned it off when he was doing something that needed all his concentration. He went back to his prayers but suddenly knew he had to do more than pray. He had to go to Bonzo's house.

Chapter Fifty Six

Arthur tried every door of Bonzo's house. They were all locked, but Arthur knew something was wrong not only through his intuition, but because the van was in the garage. He could see it through the window, and the lights were on in his office. Bonzo had to be inside, but he just wasn't answering the door. Arthur held a flashlight up to the video camera and moved it back and forth. The camera was not running because he saw that the auto focus lens did not move.

Arthur walked around the house, looking in every window. All the shades were pulled, and he didn't hear any noises. Sandria's apartment was dark, and no one answered her door. He went to the back of the house again and used an iron lawn chair to bust open the pantry window.

Arthur resisted the urge to vomit when he found the bodies. There was very little left of Bonzo's head. Sandria's face looked peaceful, as if she'd seen something beautiful beyond the barrel of the gun that had murdered her. Arthur wished he could wipe Bonzo's blood and brains off her face. Who did this to these two wonderful people? He remembered the video camera. Perhaps Bonzo had a tape running when the murderer came in. He searched the office for the videocassette recorder hooked up to the camera, found the tape, and played it through the monitor.

He ran the tape three times. So that Mr. Carter they'd seen at the Ursus opening was a man named DK from Chicago. He was either the last person to see Bonzo alive, or the murderer. Why had he left the tape? He was looking right into the camera so he had to know there was a record of his visit, unless he was stupid and thought there was no tape, or he'd simply forgotten it.

· · ·

DK was just south of Big Sky on the road to West Yellowstone when he remembered the video camera at Bonzo's house and cursed his own carelessness. What if the camera was hooked up to a recorder and had recorded him? He increased his speed as much as he dared on the snow-packed road. He would have to hope for some luck.

He would phone Bonzo's house as soon as he reached West Yellowstone and hope Anton was still there. He would ask him to check for a tape. It would be too risky to head back to Bozeman now, and he was very tired. Bonzo had sucked the energy right out of him, and the only way he would get it back would be to eat a good meal, sleep, and focus on the next steps in his plan.

DK tried to send Anton a message, "Look for a tape, look for a tape." He was so tired that he couldn't picture Anton's face clearly. He wished he'd grabbed some coffee back at the mini-mart at the Big Sky road. Now he was entering Yellowstone National Park, a most desolate place in winter.

A semi truck passed him and threw snow all over his little front wheel drive rental car, reducing his visibility to zero. He braked and skidded from one side of the road to another, swearing at the truck. He corrected his steering and stabilized the car. He was overwrought with his near-accident and his inability to focus on Anton. He was so distracted, he didn't see the hundreds of red eyes staring at him from all over the road. It was the elk herd that winters in that section of the park, where the snowpack along the Gallatin River is relatively light and there is plenty of browse to eat.

Five hundred animals were crossing the road on their way to the river. The semi had plowed unharmed through the herd and splattered a half dozen cows all over the road. The rest of the herd was in a state of panic, running back and forth across the road, their fright increased by DK's weaving lights. DK braked and skidded, smacking into the side of a huge bull. The impact sent his little car over the ice into another elk, and then another, and then another. The mangled car stopped. The leader of the herd, a 7 by 7 bull who had lived many years in Yellowstone's wilderness, snorted angrily and bugled at the top of his lungs. This commotion was too much for him. The instinct to protect his harem had dimmed somewhat in the weeks since the rut had ended, but it kicked in full force now. He would kill this thing that was threatening his cows, all pregnant by his hard work. He scraped his front hooves on the ice and lowered his head. He raced toward the thing. He could see the man's face through the driver's side window and he aimed for it.

DK saw the elk coming and tried to squirm out of the passenger side door, but the door was smashed in and locked shut. It wouldn't budge. The elk kept coming and slammed right through the car window, his sharp antlers plunging into DK's ass. Using all his strength to free himself of DK's weight, the elk skewered him deeper, crushing DK's head against the door and breaking his neck. DK's last experience of life in his most recent embodiment was the pain of an antler shoved as far up his ass as it could go.

The unharmed bulls and cows and calves of the year scattered to the safety of the trees near the river and heard the next insane sound of the night. A semi truck was beeping its horn, trying to get the thing he saw in the middle of the road to move.

"What the fuck?" the driver yelled when he got close enough to see the twisted car with elk feet sticking out of the window, kicking. If he braked, he would roll the truck. There was no room to pass it on either side. He braced himself and hit DK's wreck. It spun across the road into a ditch. The trucker down-shifted and came to a stop a quarter mile down the road. He called 911 on his CB and reached the dispatcher in West Yellowstone, who promised to send a wrecker and an ambulance. Then he took his handgun, a Llama large frame .45 auto-IXA, meant to defend himself against gangs in the city, and a flashlight and walked back to the wreck. He knew it was his duty to see if anyone was alive.

The trucker saw that the elk was still breathing and the man was dead, his head at a right angle to his neck and his face black and blue and swollen. He found a jack in the trunk of the car and used the handle to pry open the passenger door. The man's arm poked stiffly out of the car, and the elk sensed he had more room to move. He tried to scoot out the door, but he was still stuck. The trucker carefully pulled open the driver's side door as he used all his weight to push the elk's legs into the car, keeping his head as far away from the hooves as he could. The elk flinched in pain from the broken glass that was stuck in his legs and pushed himself out of the car. He rolled on his side, the dead man still stuck to his antlers.

"Jesus Christ," the trucker said. "You've impaled that poor son of a bitch."

The elk tried to stand up but his hooves kept slipping on the ice. DK's blood trickled out of his body and froze on the ice. The trucker saw that the elk was ripping this guy apart every time it moved. He drew his gun and waited until the elk stopped to rest between struggles and shot it in the head.

In his 12 years as a trucker, he'd seen a lot of accidents, but this one took the cake, he thought, reaching into his back pocket for his flask of Yukon Jack. Fuck it, he was having a nip.

"Here's to you, you poor unlucky son of a bitch," he told DK. DK's bulging, empty eyes stared back at him.

• • •

Arthur paused the VCR on a frame of DK's face and walked to the phone to call the police. Just as he was picking up the receiver, he heard someone fiddle with the door. "Great, he thought, I bet it's DK coming back for the tape. He looked around the room quickly and found the revolver Sandria had dropped. He picked it up and saw that it was loaded. He cranked a round into the chamber, walked to the door, and opened it.

"Ah, Anton," he said, the weapon in clear sight. "Here to see the slaughter? Do come in."

Anton followed him into the office and coldly surveyed the blood bath. He looked at DK's face, frozen on the VCR.

"What's that doing here?" he asked, ignoring the gun pointed at him.

"That's your buddy. Seems as if he posed for the surveillance camera but didn't know he was being taped. Poor asshole. Better than fingerprints, don't you think?"

"So you've shot your friends and you're going to blame him?" Anton nodded at DK.

"Nice try, asshole," Arthur quipped as he walked backwards to the phone, keeping his gun pointed at Anton.

"Ah, yes," wheezed the spirit of DK as it hovered over his wasted body. "So much better to be free of a body. They're so cumbersome, so limiting. And so ugly in death."

He zapped himself to Bonzo Reed's house and registered everything that was happening there in a split second. He would have to materialize for a time and take care of the unfinished business. It would be fun.

"Anton, it seems you're having a little difficulty carrying out my orders?"

Arthur and Anton were equally startled by the sound of DK's voice, deep and evil and hissing like a mad rattlesnake. They looked at the monitor. DK's lips were moving. The sound was coming from the speakers attached to the monitor's amplifier, but the VCR was still on pause.

"Then you're gone, master," Anton said, looking at the monitor.

"Yes. You'll read all about that in the papers tomorrow, I'm sure."

Arthur picked up the phone.

"Not so fast," DK hissed, and the headset flew out of Arthur's hand as the phone crashed to the floor and the cord flew out of the jack.

"And now the gun," DK commanded. Arthur felt strong hands grab his wrist and try to make him drop the gun. He used all his strength to break free of the grip, aimed the gun at the monitor, and shot four rounds into it.

"That was really stupid," the voice spittled.

The force grabbed Arthur's wrist again and squeezed so hard Arthur felt his bones snap. The gun fell to the floor. Anton had it in an instant, aimed it at Arthur's chest, and fired. Arthur collapsed the floor.

"Carry on the work, Anton," DK told him. And he was gone.

Anton looked at his watch. The news would be on in half an hour. Perhaps it would carry the story of DK's death. He went outside and found Arthur's car and parked it in the garage and went to the kitchen to fix himself a snack. He powered up all the computers and was surprised to find that there wasn't one file in any of them. They were blank. He stared at the bodies as he ate, and then wandered around the house looking for a television. He found one in Bonzo's bedroom and turned it on, half watching the end of a sitcom.

The news announcer promised a story a little later on the program of a recent accident involving a fatality and an elk herd on U.S. 20 in Yellowstone Park, north of West Yellowstone. Anton sat up and waited.

"A man was killed tonight in a single-car accident," the announcer droned. "Apparently his car ran into the elk herd that winters near the Gallatin River. The man was killed instantly. The accident is under investigation, and the man's name will not be released until his relatives are notified."

"What relatives?" Anton sneered. So DK was dead, and he was supposed to carry on the work.

He thought of Lynx. His mind went to her more often than he wanted to admit. In truth, she was all he wanted. He was tired of the battle, tired of living in service to the Great Plan that seemed unreachable and impersonal. Without DK, he would not be able to find any purpose. The plan would evolve without him.

Obviously, the power that Lynx and her people had was greater than DK had ever wanted to admit. Anton knew now that the people who believe in love are willing to die for love. He saw that they believe that only in death would they experience love in its true form.

Those who believe something on faith walk a different path than those who know something for certain, Anton had discovered. Lynx and her friends believe in Jesus Christ on faith. Anton knew for certain that Satan is real and what his power can do. He was rewarded here and now, not in a fantasy somewhere down the road that would never become fact.

Daren Bush was somewhere in between. He believed in the power of his work and that he alone was in charge of his life. He led his wife into believing he was in charge of her life, too, and when he didn't satisfy her, she figured another man would.

Bonzo was somewhere in between. He had isolated himself from people who may have led him to either side. He believed in himself more than in God or Satan because he was convinced that he had overcome his handicap through his own hard work.

Anton knew that DK would return in some other form. It may be after he spent years and years out of embodiment, sending his evil to countless people who wanted its power.

Anton knew he was supposed to stay here and do what DK had planned, go into the wilderness and invoke the Circle of Power to garner the strength to revamp and revitalize the forces. He just didn't think he could do it. It had stopped pleasuring him to fight the Lynxes of the world.

Anton clicked off the television and wandered around the house and garage, gathering the things he needed. He found two 20-gallon cans of gasoline. He discovered that the furnace, hot water heater, and kitchen stove were fueled by propane. He blew out all the pilot lights and let the gas leak out. He doused the bodies in the studio with gas and scurried around the house, dumping gas on anything that looked like it would burn quickly. He saved a half gallon for himself, threw a match onto Bonzo, and waited until he saw that the fire was burning strongly. He stuck Arthur's gun in his mouth and fired it just as the gas fumes from the leaking propane exploded.

He met DK somewhere in the dark cosmos where love and light never manifest themselves. DK didn't bother to go over all the mistakes Anton had made, including the greatest one of all, letting himself think he could love Lynx. He wasted no time banishing Anton to another task on earth. He cast him into the soul of Roger, asleep in his West Yellowstone bed, his earphones lacing his dreams with heavy metal, music DK knew Anton despised. Roger could do a lot of damage as he grew up in West Yellowstone, and DK would return then and have more to work with. Meanwhile, he was heading to Yugoslavia's Bosnia and Herzegovina province. He hadn't been in Europe for quite some time, and there were many opportunities to manifest pure, raw, evil there.

Anton's spirit spent the rest of the night prowling through Roger's body and mind, learning that his new embodiment was in a very confused teenager who was once a close friend of Merlin's. DK had punished him in more ways than one, making him live where he would surely see Lynx . . . and Lynx him.

Anton was so angry with his new state that he made Roger oversleep and miss school. His parents were so disgusted and confused by his behavior that they didn't even bother to wake him up. Ever since the Disneyland episode, it has become too painful to argue with him any more.

Chapter Fifty Seven

Walt savored his last bite of pan-fried steak, chewing it slowly and finally washing it down with a slug of Jack Daniels. Spring in Yellowstone country was glorious, and how he'd missed it. If things went well for him, he would have many more, and he would never leave this place again. He threw some more wood on his campfire and drew his blanket closer around him.

Images of West Yellowstone floated through his mind. It had changed so much while he was gone, with the new Ursus development and the high tech Japanese museum under construction. Dave had lost his appeal, which had been postponed several times until just last week while Walt waited patiently in Utah. The wait had been good, though. He'd had time to at least begin to heal over Bonzo's death, for which he still felt somehow responsible. He thought back to the news of that horrible night, a man impaled by an elk, Bonzo's house burned to the ground, with Bonzo, Arthur, and his housekeeper inside, all murdered, the murders still unsolved.

Walt told Kelly that he no longer needed to be in hiding, but had still not told him what he had been hiding from. Kelly hadn't pushed the issue, but had suggested that Walt use the snowmobile, truck, and trailer he kept at his Island Park cabin and go spring camping to celebrate his new freedom. Walt had accepted, reasoning that a few more days in the Deer Lodge prison wouldn't bother Dave.

Kelly had visited West all winter, whenever he went up to Island Park for a few days of rest, and kept Walt abreast of events there. Lynx would be in charge of the theater at the museum, which had given her a grant to make videos on Yellowstone issues. Until the theater was finished, she was showing her work at Ursus's smaller theater. Kelly had seen her first piece and tried to buy a copy from her to bring home to Walt. She said she hadn't planned to make or distribute any copies of her tapes; they would be shown in West Yellowstone only. Kelly told Walt he argued with her about that, telling her she would reach more people if she mass-produced her work, but she wouldn't be swayed. Kelly told Walt the video exposed a strange operation in Yellowstone. Park rangers were skiing and snowmobiling through the park, looking for winter-killed elk. There were literally hundreds of them that spring, Kelly said, because so many animals had starved to death since the fires had destroyed their food sources. The rangers were cutting the antlers off the elks' heads. They told Lynx in on-camera interviews that they were doing this so that horn hunters wouldn't come into the park and take them, since horn hunting is illegal in Yellowstone. They were also yanking the elks' two ivory teeth out of their heads, also so that they wouldn't be taken by poachers. Lynx had investigated the rangers further and found that some of them were not hiding the antlers and teeth in the park, as the park service officials said they were doing. They were selling them to dealers in Ennis and Bozeman who were in turn supplying jewelry and antler crafts makers with the stuff. Some rangers had sold several thousand dollars worth of teeth and antlers to the dealers, always pocketing the money. The park service had denied knowledge of this until Lynx's video showed interviews with dealers who insisted they had bought the stuff from rangers.

Walt laughed, thinking of Lynx out there confronting people with all this stuff. "Good for her," he thought. "She's still working at what she loves despite all the hard times."

He'd parked the truck in a designated parking area off the main highway into West Yellowstone and snowmobiled over slushy snow to the forest service campground at Rainbow Point. He wasn't worried about leaving the truck. If a cop checked on it, he would see it was registered to Kelly and assume Kelly was snowmobiling somewhere nearby.

Walt walked down to Hebgen Lake and watched a flock of pelicans land on a patch of open water not far from shore. Next month he would have his old boat out there, trolling for rainbows, if the pelicans hadn't eaten them all. He could hardly wait. He walked back to his tent and sat by his fire until it grew dark. He crawled into his sleeping bag and fell asleep. Tomorrow he would get up before dawn and head to Deer Lodge.

• • •

Mystery emerged from her Cabin Creek den in great shape, still planning to head north to find her former mate. But there was still too much snow in the higher mountains, so she stuck close to the den and fed on a winter-killed elk.

She could smell the spawning trout in Hebgen Lake pooling near the mouth of Grayling Creek and the pelicans, ducks, and geese that were returning to the area every day. She decided to stroll down to the lake. There was too much traffic on the north side near Highway 287, so she crossed the road and headed south, toward the road to Rainbow Point. She paralleled the road, staying in the trees, and began to smell Walt's campfire and steak. A camper! She hadn't smelled such wonderful things in a while, and she picked up her pace.

She saw the Man crawl into his tent and sat down in the trees not 50 yards away, listening and sniffing. Wow. A new smell. It wasn't anything she'd ever tasted before, but she recalled that some bear had tasted such a thing. Last year she'd smelled it in the scat of another sow and her cubs, somewhere near West Yellowstone, she thought. Or was it in the park, near Old Faithful?

Mystery trudged toward the new smell. It was just under the fake leopard skin vinyl of the Man's machine, one of those noisy things she'd seen roaring over the snow. Yum. She tore into the vinyl and bit off a chunk of the foam rubber. Delicious. She took another bite.

The ripping sound of the vinyl being torn off the snowmobile woke Walt up. What could it be? He listened. It was nothing he'd ever heard before. He dressed quietly and crawled outside just as Mystery was pulling her third chunk of foam rubber off the seat.

A grizzly bear! He remembered reading Lynx's story in the *Gazette* last year about the bear that had vandalized the snowmobiles in West. What did they see in that stuff?

Mystery knew the Man was standing behind her, but she didn't care. The new treat was too distracting.

Walt came to his senses. It wasn't his snowmachine, and the last thing he needed was to have to hassle with a broken sled if the bear damaged something that would keep him from starting it. He leaned down and picked up a wad of snow, rolled it into a hard ball, and hit Mystery's butt with it as hard as he could.

Mystery felt the snowball and ignored it. Walt hurled another at her, and another and shouted, "Go away now, go on."

Anger flowed through Mystery's veins. This man was trying to drive her away from her enjoyment. She would make him stop. She stood up and charged him with all her strength. Walt had nowhere to hide. He would never make it past her to the snowmobile, the tent was not safe, and there were no climbable trees close by. Play dead, he remembered: that's what the bear experts say to do when a griz is charging you and you can't get to a tree. You lie very still and don't panic. She'll toss you around a bit and get bored and leave. He dropped to the ground

Mystery halted her charge and looked at the Man. Why was he so still? She sniffed his hair. Not bad. She ripped a chunk out with her teeth. Walt suppressed the urge to scream. It hurt like hell. She bit a chunk of skin off his scalp, exposing his skull and licking it. Yum. She sniffed harder and smelled the steak still undigested in his belly. With a half-hearted slap, she turned him over and pounced at the center of his body, ripping easily through his flannel shirt and the skin of his belly, looking for the steak just as she searched loose soil for a tasty treat of ants.

Walt screamed then, unable to control himself, knowing he was seriously injured. Mystery continued, searching through his intestines, licking up little chunks of food and bile. Walt passed out. Mystery ate her way through his body to his spine, and began working on his meaty thighs and arms. She thought of all the times she'd been so close to Men and never considered eating them. Dumb, since there were more men around than anything else. She would have an endless supply of food.

When Mystery was finished with Walt, she had 75 pounds of human flesh, bones, and innards in her belly, not to mention a huge chunk of foam rubber, and she felt great. She paddled back to her den, registering the experience in her brain as one she would repeat the next chance she got.

• • •

A honeymoon couple from Minnesota found Walt. They were cross country skiing from a nearby condominium resort to Rainbow Point and had stopped to kiss one another for the hundredth time that day, like newlyweds do. The bride spotted Walt's tent, and they skied over to it to say hello to this most interesting person who was camping in the snow. There were no hellos. Both of them fell to their hands and knees, vomiting.

The county sheriff given the chore of investigating the death scene also vomited. He'd never seen anything like it, not even in Viet Nam. It even beat the man with the elk antler shoved up his ass, although he'd only seen photos of that one. What were the animals up to these days, anyway? The whole world was going nuts.

He called for help and he and two other officers donned masks and rubber gloves before they scraped Walt off the snow and placed him in plastic bags. They impounded all his gear and tent. The sheriff was haunted by Walt's eyes. The fear and despair he must have felt in his last moments was frozen in them, but behind that there was something the sheriff had seen before. He'd seen those eyes, talked to this man when he was living. Who was he? He didn't recognize the name on his driver's license. Funny, he had no family, according to his buddy, that Utah banker Kelly who vacationed up here quite often.

Too bad about the guy's snowmobile, but he could afford a new one. The sheriff had agreed to release the man's remains to Kelly, who said he would scatter his ashes on his ranch in Utah. All the papers were in order, and he'd gone ahead and released the remains, but something didn't seem right. Nothing he could put his finger on, nothing that would give him a good reason to hold the remains and justify a further investigation. No, it was not enough that the man had dyed hair and tinted contact lenses. Apparently lots of guys dyed their hair these days and played around with different color eyes. Maybe he was a fag. It just seemed fishy somehow. But it wasn't anything he wanted to dwell on, either, the memory of Walt's torn up scalp and the dark roots of his real hair color plain as day mixed with his blood and brains and flesh.

. . .

Walt's body never made it to Utah, however. Walt's final minutes on this earth may have been horrifying with the attack of Mystery, but those last minutes would have been worse if TDP finally found him. Less than a day after Kelly made arrangements to have Walt cremated, TDP agents showed up at his home and demanded he turn Walt over. They refused to explain who Walt was, but Kelly had no trouble telling them where Walt was. Why not, he figured. What harm would it do? He signed papers giving TDP permission to pick up Walt's remains.

With all the changes underway at TDP, the agents wanted to get rid of Walt as soon as possible while closing the case in such a way that no holes were left in it. They went to Deer Lodge and made a deal with Dave, revealing only sketchy information about themselves and what Walt had done for them. They would bury Walt on property Dave used to own, and Dave would confess to the murder in two years, after the body was severely decomposed.

The confession would make it easier for him to bargain for early release, and the money they would pay him for his deed would allow him to live in luxury for the rest of his life. Did Dave have another choice? Sure, his neck could be broken by an unknown prison mate. Dave made the deal, and Walt was laid to rest.

• • •

Vicky watched Mystery paw restlessly at the dead tree in the middle of Ursus's outdoor bear habitat and thought of the times she'd followed the bear in the wild.

Vicky wanted to cry. She'd actually prayed that Mystery would stay away from humans and return to her wild behavior. She was such a special bear. Now she would live out her life being gawked at by tourists. Maybe seeing her locked up at Ursus would make people keep cleaner camps. Martin said Mystery might have made it if she hadn't gotten into trouble in the hunting camp just before she denned up for the winter.

Mystery's mauling had made front page news in papers all over the world. A coalition of grizzly bear support groups had said they would start a campaign to raise money to fund a study of what Yellowstone bears were attracted to in snowmobile upholstery. They said they would demand that a new material be used if necessary.

No matter how much good came out of Mystery's being locked up, Vicky knew it would never make up for the tragedy of losing her to the wild. Vicky looked at Lynx sitting on the bench closest to the habitat, staring at Mystery. Lynx had tearfully told her that Mystery was her vision bear. She hadn't shared the details of the vision, but she had told Vicky that Mystery's incarceration was a personal tragedy to her because it meant she'd failed. Lynx had devoted herself to grizzly bears and a lot of other wild creatures that lived in Yellowstone. She took it personally when any animal was killed needlessly or locked up. Vicky walked up to the bench and stood behind Lynx and rubbed her head.

"Let's go now, Lynx. It just hurts too much to see her here," she told her softly.

Lynx nodded and stood up. Mystery saw the Woman she was connected to get ready to leave. It was her fifth visit, and Mystery did what she'd done every time Lynx left her. She walked as close to the edge of the habitat as she could, looked at Lynx, nodded her head up and down, and growled. Lynx growled back.

"See ya, girl," she told her bear sister. She walked away and didn't look back. Mystery plopped down on the grass and closed her eyes, not moving until she couldn't smell the Woman any more.

Chapter Fifty Eight

Adam Freedman was just walking into Ursus as Lynx and Vicky were leaving. Lynx resisted the urge to turn around and hide; she detested him more than ever. He was still devoted to reporting as much negative news as he could scrape up.

"You're just the person I'm looking for," he told Lynx.

"Whatever for?" she asked, shooting him a dirty look.

"You still work at the museum, right?"

"Last I knew. And I'm going over there now to finish my work for today, so don't bug me."

"I'll walk you over. Did you hear about the bust?"

"Bust?" Lynx did know about it but wanted to pretend she didn't to avoid talking with him. Randall had discussed it with her yesterday, told her it was coming down that morning. He'd discovered some of his business partners were smuggling dope into the airport, and he'd turned them in. There was a possibility that the feds would freeze all the Japanese money invested in the new museum and it would have to close, unless Randall found some other money fast. Lynx wasn't worried about losing her job. She'd stopped worrying about anything, after what she'd been through that year.

"Yeah, a few hours ago, at the airport. The Japs you're catering to over here are smuggling dope into West. Sending it all over the country. Your boss is about ready to give a press conference denouncing any involvement."

"Why would he be involved?"

"Oh, come on, Lynx, he set up the deal to use the museum and the rest of this trashy development with the same people who are smuggling the dope."

"Can you prove he did?"

"I aim to."

"Good luck," she told him. "You hate Japanese people, you hate all developers, you hate West Yellowstone. But there's a problem with this one. You're dead wrong."

"Well, I wasn't wrong about your old buddy Anton."

"No, you did okay on that one."

Adam had investigated the murders at Bonzo's house and helped the police conclude that Anton had been responsible for all of them. Lynx figured differently. She figured DK had killed Bonzo and Sandria and Arthur and that Anton had killed himself and burned the house down to cover for DK. But she didn't care if the truth ever came out. It wouldn't make any difference anyway because the entire world was going to hell as far as she was concerned. One evil was replaced by another. That was a given. All she wanted to do was live her life out in peace.

"Since you're dummying up on the bust, I guess you don't know one of your employees was arrested, too, along with the Japs."

That Lynx didn't know. Randall had told her only the Japanese people who were running the airplane tours to West Yellowstone were being popped.

"Who?" she asked.

"Roger, the minister's kid. He works for you, doesn't he?"

"In a manner of speaking. The judge sentenced him to us, and he's doing community service here for the non-profit foundation, passing out brochures asking for donations to buy more bear habitat."

"Well, he got busted for running some of the dope up to Billings."

Lynx wasn't surprised. Roger was committed to being on a losing streak. He'd been busted four times that summer for vandalism and drug possession and told he would be treated as an adult the next time he got into trouble. Now he was looking at some serious prison time, she assumed. She'd tried to work with him, but he made her uncomfortable. He was beginning to look and sound more like Anton every day, and she despised even thinking of that man. She kept Roger and Merlin apart as much as possible, and Merlin was grateful for that. The most obvious result of the Mystic Warriors' prayers was that Merlin was happy, strong, and creative, an all around good kid.

"Do you have a comment for my story? Something to say about Roger? The museum? Come on, Lynx, cooperate."

"The only comment I have for you is off the record. Go to hell. Now let me go. Come on Vicky," Lynx said. "Let's get going." They broke into a jog. Adam couldn't follow them. He was too loaded down with camera equipment.

Vicky and Lynx slowed down when they knew they were clear of Adam and laughed.

"I don't know why I'm laughing," Lynx told her. "My world may be about to end."

"Come on now, keep your chin up." Vicky was with Lynx for moral support. Before Lynx returned to work, she had to stop at the clinic for the results of her and Mullein's last HIV test. Lynx looked at her watch. They were late. Mullein would already be there.

They made sure Adam wasn't tailing them and walked to the clinic.

Lynx knew everything was fine as soon as she saw her husband. He was grinning from ear to ear, holding a box of Trojans and a match.

"We're clear," he told her, hugging her tightly.

"All right. Yes!" Lynx shouted.

"Should we?" He held up the Trojans.

"Oh, yes," she said. They walked around to the back of the clinic and set the box on fire. "Never again," he told her, "will I ever touch one of those things."

Lynx kissed him. He was the best thing in her life.

"Go on now, he told her. Get your work done and meet me at home. We have things to do." He smiled seductively.

Vicky walked her back to the museum, and they said good-bye. She had to meet Martin and Yurt and go into the park with them. They were going to check on some bear sightings near Old Faithful. Yurt was going to tape anything interesting for Lynx.

Lynx finished her business at the museum and headed home. She knew she should feel like hurrying, but she didn't. She wanted to stop at Black Sands spring and say a prayer of thanksgiving for the test results. She needed time to collect herself before she made love to Mullein.

She turned of the highway onto the dirt road to the spring and saw a car behind her. She slowed down to check it out. It was Mullein. He must have stopped at a store before he left town and gotten behind her. Good. She should have thought to ask him to come along anyway. She reached her hand out of her window and waved to him.

They sat close together at the edge of the spring, but neither talked. That was a special thing about their relationship, Lynx thought. They knew each other so well they didn't have to explain things.

Lynx though of Dewey and Nora and wished they were there, too. They were traveling around the country together with Harry and Sally and their children, attending Sweetgrass meetings and trying to raise people's interest in prayer. She wouldn't see them again until September when the

Montana and Idaho Sweetgrass societies were scheduled to hold a council. By then, Patsy and Salinda would be members.

Lynx watched the water bubble out of the earth and flow downstream. She pictured every stretch of the stream. She saw where it met the South Fork and flowed into Hebgen Lake, then where it flowed out of Hebgen Dam and became the river again. She watched it dance through the Beartrap Canyon and meet the Gallatin and Jefferson Rivers at Three Forks to form the Missouri River.

"The river is like our life," she thought, squeezing Mullein's hand. "We flow over bumps and under snags and are stopped now and then by dams and drought. Yet we always find the freedom to flow to something greater and mysterious. Mullein and I," she thought, "mingled together as one, better together than each is alone."

They were one as well with the Mystic Warriors. How they'd suffered this past year and a half! It wasn't clear if any battles were won. It was certain there would be more to fight. Their faith would have to be like the river, flowing and picking up more strength, never forgetting where it started, always remembering that love was its source.

Lynx kissed Mullein's hand.

"Come on baby," he told her. He pulled her up and led her around the spring, across a tiny brook that branched off on its own for awhile before flowing back to the stream, and into a meadow of tall grass surrounded by willow trees. They couldn't be seen by anyone coming from the road. They didn't care what the bald eagle flying overhead thought. They undressed and tumbled to the ground. There was no need for foreplay. That had already happened at the spring, when he had entered her heart and become one with her. The eagle flew over them in quiet circles and then screamed. They screamed back, their orgasms simultaneous and strong, their love as powerful as the wings taking the eagle away to the mountain tops.

The End